The Dark Side of Civil

A Novel

Cynthia, My Friend and
fellow sufferer ☺. Love
you bunches.
Carla Ramsey Weeks
December, 2017
Merry Christmas!

CARLA RAMSEY WEEKS

ISBN: 099912840X
ISBN 13: 9780999128404
Library of Congress Control Number: 2017912554
Carla Ramsey Weeks, Author, Sherwood, ARKANSAS

For my family, here and elsewhere.

Contents

Characters

Mammy (Daisy)—slave of Frederick Barret. Came to him along with her three children when he married his first wife, Luella. Mother of Lew, Minda, and Dovie. Oversees household.

Lewis—slave of Frederick Barret. Acts as butler and groundskeeper. Son of Mammy. Husband of Cressa. Father of Deke and Lizzy.

Minda—slave of Frederick Barret. Cook. Mother of Frederick's children Daisy, Jude, and Ishmael. Daughter of Mammy.

Dovie—slave of Frederick Barret. House servant and children's nurse. Daughter of Mammy.

Daisy—slave of Frederick Barret and his daughter by Minda. House girl to Mattie Barret.

Jude—slave of Frederick Barret and his son by Minda.

Ishmael (Ish)—slave of Frederick Barret and his son by Minda.

Cressa—slave of Frederick Barret. Wife of Lewis. Mother of Deke and Lizzy. Nurse to Ella and Maxie.

Deke and Lizzy—slaves of Frederick Barret. Children of Lew and Cressa.

Ben—slave of Frederick Barret. Son of Dovie.

Frederick Barret—Immigrant from Saint Domingue. Married first Luella Middleton, then her younger sister Abigail (Abby) after Luella's death. Father of Mattie, Robart, Fredie, Ella, and Maxie. Father of slaves Daisy, Jude, and Ish. Prosperous Savannah businessman and slave owner.

Mattie Barret—oldest child and only daughter of Frederick and Luella.

Robart Barret—oldest son of Frederick and Luella.

Fredie Barret—youngest son of Frederick and Luella.

Ella Barret—oldest daughter of Frederick and Abigail.

Maxie Barret—youngest daughter of Frederick and Abigail.

Jessalyn (Jessie) Devereux (Tucker)—immigrant from Saint Domingue. Free person of color and Frederick's aunt. Widow of Moses Tucker. Adoptive Mother of Diana.

Diana Devereux—biological daughter of Rube and Lavinie. Niece of Moses Tucker. Adopted daughter of Moses and Jessie. Free person of color.

Sophia Middleton Howe—sister of Frederick's wives, Luella and Abigail. Aunt to Barret children. Wife of James. Mother of Gail and Cedric.

Gail Howe—daughter of Sophia Howe. Cousin to Barret girls. Friend of Diana.

Bette Stiles—friend of Abigail Barret. Wife to Clarence Stiles. Mother of Thomas, Reggie, and Eliza.

Clarence Stiles—husband of Bette. Father of Thomas, Reggie, and Eliza. Savannah businessman.

Pearl—servant of Bette. Free person of color. Bette's biological half-sister.

Cook—servant of Bette. Cook. Free person of color.

Quentin Rylee—free man of color. Owner of a wood-working shop in Baltimore.

Nance and Elb—Jessie's slaves and benefactors in Saint Domingue.

Susan—Emile's nursemaid.

Call Me a Crow

Call me a crow
An let me be
Free as a bird
In da live oak tree.

If I be a crow
Like you say I be,
I make my nest
In da live oak tree.
I fly up high,
As far as I can
Out of reach
Of da Massah man.

If I be a crow
In da live oak tree
I fine me a place
Where I be free.
An I take my chicks
An my life-long mate
Far from da jail bird
An da life I hate.

Call me a crow
But best you know,
Birds doan chop
An birds doan hoe.
An far above
From da live oak tree
A crow doan foget
Da things he see.

If I be a crow,
I be crafty and kind
With my big bird brain
An my sharp crow mind.
A crow can love,
He know spite too,
An he woan fogive,
Like a lesser bird do.

So call me a crow,
An I break free,
From da fetter on my claw
To da live oak tree.
An I live right dare
On da branch next ta you
In a nest of my own,
Like da white dove do.

Carla Ramsey Weeks

Whereas Some doubts have arrisen whether children got by any Englishman upon a Negro woman should be slave or free, Be it therefore enacted and declared by this present grand assembly, that all children borne in this country shalbe held bond or free only according to the condition of the mother...

Act XII
Law Library of Congress
1661

Chapter 1
The Master's Boy

Savannah, Georgia—1844

Jude walks head down, hands fisted into the pockets of his overalls, a sandy back path from Yamacraw to the mansion on Madison Square. Though the sun has not yet completely banished night, he has no trouble finding his way. He has traveled this same, narrow trail since he could walk, so long he isn't aware when the ramshackle huts and small dwellings transition into larger homes, then to mansions of which his destination is one. The Barret house sits amidst one and a half prime lots on the corner of Bull and Harris. It is fronted by Madison square, yet it is still one of few houses.

Not much distracts him from his thoughts because he has managed to get out of the house before his mama and Ish. If he were in a better mood, he would relish this hour of freedom. He would acknowledge his luck. He doesn't live directly under Master Barret's nose, and with Miss Abby gone, he has no mistress unless you count Mattie, Ella, or Maxie. Of the three, Mattie is the only one who garners his respect. She is old enough to give him orders, but she doesn't, maybe because she's too nice for her own good or maybe because she is too caught up in the affairs of being a young lady. Though her world is as foreign to the boy as the far shores of Africa from which his great, great grandmother came, Jude wouldn't mind having his sister Daisy's job. She is lucky to have the sole duty of tending to Miss Mattie's needs. The one downside is his older sister has to sleep on a pallet at the foot of her mistress's bed instead of at home with Mama, Ish, and him. Daisy has an easy life, as far as slave lives go, but his poor Aunt Cressa's role as nurse to the younger two is probably the hardest on the place. He is between the two of them in age,

1

so Jude has had years to learn each girl's quirks. Maxie can be decent enough when she wants to be, but Ella—Cressa calls her a handful, and the whole family thinks her moods are as changing as low-country tides.

Jude stops at a trail leading east. He considers making his way to the river but thinks better of the idea. He hasn't enough of a head start to make it there and back before he and Deke are expected to have the water drawn for the kitchen and Frederick's morning wash-up. His pace slows when his mind turns to the master. Thinking about the man is like having a toothache—a constant dull pain forgotten until he's reminded by biting down. Once the pain makes itself known, there is no ignoring it. If only God would yank Master Barret out of his life as easily as Uncle Clell had pulled his bad tooth a few months back. Ridding himself of the master wouldn't hurt at all. In fact, everybody's life would be better. Then again, the young Master Rob would probably be giving the orders, and that possibility is one Jude refuses to waste what little time he has considering.

Jude's obsession with Frederick is nothing new. His mother has scolded him at least once a week for as long as he can remember for asking questions and speculating on the actions of the man they both call master. She tells him nothing good can come from him thinking so much on the man—that he is old enough to accept what is and quit wishing for things to be otherwise. She reminds him often of the many people with much worse lots in life—advises him to concentrate on his blessings instead of looking for things to complain about. Jude thinks he has much to gripe about, but he has to admit he cannot dwell on the man and be at peace. He tries to think about him in the same way his Uncle Lewis and Cousin Deke do, as the master of the house and the man who decides where they live, what they are allowed to do, even what they eat with a few exceptions. Uncle Lewis has told him they are lucky to have a master who treats them well and has kept the family together when they can name many who have not been as lucky. Jude has to admit, in this, Lewis is right. He can name few other slaves he goes to church with or runs across in his duties about town who live with as large an extended family. Mammy tells him it is common on the plantations like the one in Virginia she, Mama, Dovie, and Lew came from when the first mistress married Mr. Barret. Daisy has actually gone to Hickory Grove with Mattie for the summer, and Cressa and Dovie have taken their children along when they went to see to the missies. Jude and Ish have always stayed behind because their mama has to remain to serve Master Barret, something she has being doing for years before the second mistress died, and in more ways than Miss Abby could have imagined back then. Consequently, Jude has never seen a plantation, but he claims he would prefer just about any job anywhere that would keep him out from underfoot of Master Barret, and more importantly, keep his mother as far from the man as possible.

Though Jude is only twelve, he has understood for years why they have their own house in Yamacraw. It's because Frederick uses Mama as a wife since Miss Abby jumped out of the upstairs window of the mansion. Minda thinks he doesn't remember, but he knows Mr. Barret used his mother as a wife even before the missus died. Jude knows even more. He has heard Minda and Dovie talking about the reason he, Daisy, and Ish have skin the color of milked coffee while that of their cousins is like the beverage brewed strong and left to sit. Jude knows these things, but none of them are the reason he hates the master.

If Jude had not spent his whole life in the midst of his extended family, he might not have realized some fathers care about their children. Even though he has always known he came to be because of Mr. Barret's late night grunting and moaning, he probably would not have thought much about the caring way Frederick treats his own children—the ones he claims. They are white and Jude, Daisy, and Ish are colored. What gnaws at him is knowing Master Barret's visits have kept him from having a father like Uncle Lewis or Clell—one who actually looks his children in the eyes and speaks kindly to them. One who likes his offspring. He would much rather receive a slap on the side of his head like Lewis and Clell give their kids when they step out of line than the cold, indifference Frederick directs his way. All his life, Jude has had to leave the room when he comes to Yamacraw or lie awake and listen to sounds he's never heard anywhere else. Now the master has made him his own body servant, a chore that insures contact of the most personal kind every day.

Jude is immune to the beauty of the Savannah sky as the sun rises to heat the sand that will eventually penetrate even the thickest contact-hardened soles of bare feet. He is oblivious to his surroundings and remembers little of the trek before he sets himself down on the back steps at the mansion across from the out building where his cousins Deke, Lizzy, and Ben still sleep. Ben's situation isn't a whole lot better than Jude's. He doesn't live with his papa either. Clell lives over on Price Street when he is in Savannah which isn't often. Right now he is out repairing tracks for the railroad like he is most of the time. Minda told Dovie it was just as well she hadn't married him as he's rarely around. Dovie told Minda at least she could be seen in public with her man. His mama had laughed and assured her she had no desire to be seen in public with Master Barret, and he wasn't her man. It did Jude's heart good to hear her words.

No one is up and about unless you count Mammy's pet crow she calls Missy. The bird is perched on the ledge of the attic window, and it caws out a greeting. He thinks of trying to lure her to see if she will converse with him like Mammy claims she does with her. All the children have failed in drawing Missy in, so he decides not to make the effort. Though she doesn't fly down, the bird chatters from above, cocking her head to the side to listen. Jude stills and tries to capture what she hears, but he is rewarded with only the twittering of non-crows. He wonders if she is disappointed with silence from friends or does she receive responses beyond his human range.

Little time passes before Jude spies Minda through the wrought iron fence. She enters the double gates that are rarely closed, her rigid backbone holding her slender frame strong and unbending against whatever the day holds hidden from them. In one hand she carries an empty flour sack; by the other she has the hand of Ishmael. Jude's heart softens at the sight of Ish. His little brother's face still retains the peace of sleep and the dry dullness produced by lye soap and well water. He has the urge to go to him, to take in his unique scent, to pick his matted hair into soft curls with his own fingers. His mother seems to read his mind. She sets her bag on the ground, turns her youngest to her, and pulls and tugs at his hair until it halos his head in a dark auburn cap. She slaps him on the bottom, and Ish turns toward the big house garden where he will sit on his butt and pull weeds until Mammy gives him another task. Jude watches him walk away, his left foot making a hermit crab trail behind him in the sand like it is trying to beat a path back home.

Jude was present for his little brother's birth. He had not been allowed to be in the room as Mammy delivered the child, but he had hurried in when he heard a noise somewhat like a loud, mewling cat. Mammy was holding a slick, squirming creature no bigger than the creature it sounded like. He had moved in for a better view, but Mammy had covered what he knew must be a baby so completely, all he could see was a pale oval framed in linen. Jude had touched the miniature face with a finger. Its mouth had closed, and the little being seemed determined to doze. Mammy had allowed Jude a moment to gaze at the bundle before she had proclaimed, "Da chile a boy," and turned to place him in Minda's arms. Jude's mother had pulled the linen wrap back to reveal tiny arms and legs. The little man who was to be Ish had waved both arms in the air to protest the chill upon his still wet skin, and Jude had wished he could offer his finger as his mother was doing for him to fist around.

"Oh no, Mama!" Minda had cried, and Jude's hand had flown to the center of his narrow chest to calm the fear his mother's tone had elicited. He had looked to the center of his brother and had seen the long, snake-like braid that rested curled and bloody on the boy's stomach. He thought the ugly rope was the cause of his mother's distress, but Minda had continued to cry even after Mammy had cut the rope away and thrown it in a slop jar already containing mysterious, unsavory matter. Jude had thought maybe she should have cut it closer. He had experienced an instant sympathy for the little guy who Jude assumed would have to go through life with two tails on his front side instead of the one Jude himself had between his legs. He was relieved when Mammy hid the wound by wrapping two wide strips of sun- bleached linen around the baby's center and tying them in a flat knot. The action didn't soothe his mother, however, for she continued to cry quiet tears of grief.

"Doan cry, Mama. Nobidy see dat extry tail he keeps a shirt on aw da time. Nobidy eben haftah know."

Minda and Mammy had looked at each other, then both had laughed—Minda barely—but Jude had been glad his words had stopped his mother's crying.

"Dat no tail, Boy," his grandmother had told him. "Dat his nabel, an da res ub dat mess fall off in a few days, den dis chile's be jus like da one you hab."

"Den wy Mama cryin like dat?"

"Her cryin cause da chile come easy, an her glad to be hyur ta raise him, dat wy."

Mammy had given his mama a mean look before rewrapping the baby so tightly Jude was afraid he wouldn't be able to breathe. Minda had then held him to her breast like he had seen countless church women do. Jude had been fascinated by the hungry Ish latching onto his mama's teat. He later learned Mammy had lied to him. His mother was not crying tears of happiness but was upset about the twisted foot at the bottom of his brother's leg. They called it a club foot, and his mother feared she had done something to cause it. Mammy had scolded her and said her thoughts were nonsense, and she didn't want to hear any more foolishness. Though Mammy claimed there was nothing to worry about, the tiny twisted foot was cause for much concern among the grownups. Any time Minda held Ish, she massaged the foot, gently turning it toward its mate. He had spent time each night in the bed the two boys share mimicking their mother's actions. So often had he done it, Ish still immediately offers up his foot as soon as the candle is snuffed if he is awake when put to bed. But all their efforts have done nothing to right the wrong Ish was born with, and the owner of the malformation appears to be more unbothered than anyone. Judging by the smile on his face today, he is cheerful as usual. Jude's face, however, must reveal his general dissatisfaction with life.

"Why da sour face, Young'un? You step in somethin foul on da way ovahhyur?"

Minda asks Jude. "Ish," she calls to his brother who is almost to the garden, "go rouse Unc Lew an da res uh dose sleepy haid."

"Nuthin wrong wid me, Mama. I jus cain wait ta git up dare ta hep da massah wursh his nassy backside."

"Jude, I tole you I doan wannah lissen ta dat mess no mo, an you sho bettah naw let nobidy else hyur dat sassy mouf uh yose. Now go on an git dat watah in hyur sose I kin git somethin ta eat on da table. You thinkin on eatin aftah you git a good look at da massah's rump, ain you?"

Minda reaches out and cups her son's head as he walks past her. "An less see a smile on dat hansome face fo yo Mama."

Jude rises, goes to the sideyard, takes two wooden buckets from their nails and drops the first one over the rim of the wooden well wall. The rope coils out behind it. He allows a minute or two to pass after the bucket hits the water in order for the weight at the lip on one side to do its job. He can tell by the tension the bucket has filled. He leans forward and hand over hand draws it to the surface. The physical exertion, his mama's teasing, and the thought of breakfast lift his spirits. He transfers the contents of the bucket into the carrying pail. He hauls it, then two more like it, along the wide brick-floored hallway that separates the bottom of the house, and into the kitchen used to prepare the upstairs family's meals. He pours the contents of one into the pans and pitchers on his mother's counter. He takes the other across the hall and fills the one his own family drinks from. He puts the gourd dipper lying in its usual place into the water and dips himself a cold drink before returning to the well. He finds his cousin Deke waiting. The younger boy will draw a couple of buckets for Jude to set outside the girls' doors while Jude is delivering water to the master's bedroom and helping him with his toilet.

"Mawnin," Jude greets Deke.

There is little resemblance between the two. Deke is almost as tall as Jude, a source of dismay for the older boy. Deke is stocky where Jude is thin. He is as dark as a moonless midnight, and his round face is still puffed from sleep.

"Howdy," Deke responds. "Papa say mabe we goes fishin bout dawk we gits da choes done by den."

Jude smiles. His chores will take much more time to complete than those of nine year-old Deke.

"Sho nuff? You gits yose done, mabe you kin fine us some bait fo I gits done wid mine—gib us mo time ta fish."

"Whar you thinks I fine some crickets?"

"Try da woodpile, but it migh be a lil late in da day fo dem now."

Deke jumps down from the base of the well and heads for the woodpile.

"Hole dem hosses, Deke. You still hab some watah ta draw."

Deke returns to the well and waits as Jude transfers the water into the pail he will carry up to Frederick's room. Deke makes no comment as Jude clears his throat with all his might to produce as much phlegm as possible. He then bends over, spits the effluence into the pail, stirs the water with his hand, picks the bucket up, and heads to the house. He holds his left hand out to the side to balance the weight of the bucket, but the cold water still sloshes down his leg and between his toes. He has learned to walk to the side of the second story stairs just off the carpet runner, and today he does what he has done many times before. He sets the container down two steps up, turns his back to the riser, sits down in the puddle, and wiggles his bottom back and forth until the water is absorbed. He doesn't worry about what the master will say because he'd had to explain his wet pants long ago when Master asked him if he had pissed himself. His reenactment had elicited one of the few smiles the man has ever turned his way.

Jude taps lightly on the door before turning the knob and entering the bedroom.

Frederick is exactly where Jude expects him to be, sitting on the necessary chair reading from the stack of material he keeps on the table nearby. Jude should be used to the odor, but he still has to fight the urge to wrinkle his nose. He walks across the room and fills both the pitcher and the basin with cold water. Though Jude's back is to Frederick when he fills his drinking glass, he makes sure his face does not reflect the pleasure his previous act of sabotage brings him.

By the time Jude finishes filling the vessels, Frederick is off the pot and crossing to the stand where he begins his daily ablutions. Jude has to stretch to reach the pegs from which the man's clothes hang, but the task has become much easier for him from a month ago. When Jude first became the master's personal boy, he had to drag the bed steps to the wall to retrieve the clothes. Two years have given him an equal number of inches, and he longs for the growth spurt his family keeps assuring him will come. Jude lays the master's clothes on the bed (why he doesn't fetch them from the pegs himself, he has never understood), buffs the dress boots sitting in their usual place with the container that holds a shoe rag and polish, returns the boots to their customary place, and asks the same question he asks every day.

"You be needin enthin else, Massah?"

"Nothing more," comes the man's usual response, and Jude is left to face his least favorite chore, the removal and cleaning of the chamber pot. He picks the pot up by the handle, glad Frederick has put the lid on it, then turns as he does each morning with his hand on the door. Today is what Jude calls one of his *spit on da massah* days. Mr. Barret makes a comical figure standing in his underclothes with his black sock garters already in place, but the sight that brings Jude the most pleasure is that of his master tipping his glass to down the water Jude has prepared for him. After closing the door, the boy allows a toothy grin to spread across his face as he runs to share his victory with Deke.

Chapter 2

Devereux's

Baltimore, Maryland—1844

In a neat two-story row house on a street in Baltimore, the shop *Devereux's* is nestled among the other buildings. Unlike the residences flanking each side, on this one, two delicate chains support an unpretentious placard to the frame above a solid wooden door painted an eye-catching azure reminiscent of the sea bathing the shore not far away. If the sign itself is not enough to denote the building a place of business, the large plate glass windows on each side of the door display samples of the craft within. In one window is a cream-colored silk ball gown trimmed in cloth covered buttons and ribbon of the same blue, purposely matched to the door. The dress has been suspended from the ceiling to reveal its full length. The neck of the dress ends at the top of the window. A passerby might imagine a woman actually standing inside, her hands tucked artfully in the connected long sleeves in front of the crinoline full skirt of the gown. A diminutive blue beaded purse is tucked in the bent elbow of the right sleeve. The overall effect is one of a finely dressed lady ready to step from the frame at any minute to make her way to some festive gala among the genteel. In the other window, five hats of different designs rest upon wire racks at varying heights. The samples are in colors that complement the dress, the door, and even the sign above the entry. Someone of artistic talent has gone to great lengths to reveal the skill of the merchant within. One might imagine the inhabitants socializing with the women who retain their services, but nothing could be farther from the truth. A small boutique, a bakery, and an apothecary shop neighbor the building, but unlike Devereux, their proprietors are men. Maryland is home to the greatest number of freed slaves of any state in the Union, but few businesses are owned by blacks or by women. Though Baltimore has become a booming, modern seaport, women rarely own businesses, and Jessalyn Devereux is the lone one of color to be found in so affluent a neighborhood. Jessalyn's taste and talents may equal any of those for whom she sews, but she and her daughter live the lives of servants. Within these walls they work; they eat; they sleep. They find happiness in each other and in simple pleasures costing little but effort and will.

For Jessie and Diana, today is much like many that have come before over the course of the seven and a half years they have made their home and their livelihood at 208 Pratt Street.

"How's the dress coming, my little black-eyed Susan?" Jessie asks her daughter.

"That's a new nickname, Mama. Why are you calling me that?" comes a voice from the voluminous mound of yellow silk draped around the rocking chair in the corner of the room.

"Because you look like one with your sweet face surrounded by all that yellow. A beautiful, oversized, black-eyed Susan."

Diana laughs but doesn't take her eyes off her work. She is hemming a ball gown.

"It wouldn't hurt you to take an occasional break, Sweetheart. Mrs. Howe isn't expected until late afternoon."

"Honestly, Mama, I am not thinking about what I am doing. My mind goes elsewhere while I'm hemming. I like the task because I can daydream all I want while I work. My fingers have a mind of their own."

"A flower with fingers!" Jessie jokes.

"You are being silly, Mama!"

Looking at Diana's smiling face, Jessie thinks again how mature she acts for her twelve years. It's hard for her to remember Diana ever behaving like a child. Only her small stature and vulnerability are child-like. Moses thinks she has inherited his sister's calm, rather serious demeanor. Fortunately for her, Jessie thinks, she favors her father Rube more than Lavinie who looked too much like her big, manly brother to be considered pretty.

"It wouldn't hurt you to be a little sillier, My Dear. You have years ahead of you to be all grown up."

The girl catches the wistfulness in Jessie's tone. She lowers the material to her lap and stills her hands.

"You worry too much. I am happy—why wouldn't I be? I have a Mama who loves me and buys me books to read. I work as little as I want, and I have all the good food I can eat. Of all the colored children we know, can you think of one who has a better life?"

"We know few colored children, Diana, and the fact you are thinking about those things is proof you are old beyond your years. I must admit, I don't know what I would have done had you not been mature for your age. I would have had a hard time making a go of this store without your help. The work load would have been impossible for me to manage alone."

Diana basks in the praise. She loves to consider herself her mother's partner in their dress and millinery shop. She has been at her elbow since they arrived in Baltimore not long after Moses died in Savannah. She had sensed her mother's deep grief, and though she was too young to understand, she has tried to somehow make things better and easier for Jessie. Too, their constant proximity has had to ease her own loss of Moses, the giant of a man she had loved. He had been with her one day and gone the next; it would be natural for her to subconsciously fear the same thing happening to her second mother.

"We make a good team, Mama, don't we?"

"Indeed we do, Miss Devereux!"

Upon their move to Baltimore, the two of them had reverted to Jessie's true maiden name *Devereux* for the shop and themselves in the belief its French origins might lend an elegance to the establishment, one that would act as a draw to Baltimore's wealthiest clientele.

Jessie puts the hat she is working on down to cross the room, take her daughter's heart-shaped face in her hands, and plant a kiss on her forehead. "I love you, my black-eyed Susan partner! Ooh, what do I hear! An actual chuckle? For that, I will fix you some dinner."

Jessie leaves Diana to her work and goes to the kitchen behind their store. The room is not half the size of the one she presided over at the Barret mansion, but Jessie loves this one more because it is hers and Diana's, and it carries no sad memories. She goes to the fireplace and ladles gumbo from the pot simmering over coals and collects the loaf of bread still warm in the recess built into the brick above.

The parlor they use for their business was once two smaller rooms. The renovation fronts a roomy kitchen that spans the width of the shop. Two rooms upstairs serve as private living space and a bedroom each for her and Diana. The money she received from the sale of her cabin and Moses's boardinghouse was enough to buy the building, make repairs, furnish both home and store, and purchase the supplies they needed to set up business. Jessie situation is unusual, but she refuses to dwell on what life would have been like for the two of them had she not had the means to buy the property. Frederick Barret has caused her heartbreak, but without his letter of support to the previous owner, she and Diana would not have a roof over their head or a means to make a living. For his assistance, she is grateful.

Jessie places the noon meal on the table and returns to the front where Diana has finished hemming the gown and is preparing to take the iron from the fireplace to press it. She convinces the girl the ironing can wait until after dinner, and knowing the bell attached to the front door will alert them to customers, the two go to the kitchen and sit opposite each other at the long table Jessie uses for both preparation and dining. Diana shudders, but the occurrence is common, so Jessie makes no mention of it. She, too, often feels a cold draft she associates with Moses. Though Jessie cannot see her former husband, she tells herself she can sense his presence, He has told her in her dreams he is rarely where she is not. She smiles as she stokes the fire.

The noon meal and the time she spends after work each evening in her room with her daughter are the most pleasant times of day for them. Jessie always hopes they will not be interrupted by the ringing of the bell.

"What were you daydreaming about while you were working?" Jessie asks.

"I don't know if you would call it daydreaming. I was thinking how exciting it would be if my father showed up one day. Not Papa Moses, of course. I know he died. My father Rube, the one I don't remember. I wonder where he is and if he might find us someday."

Jessie's smile fades.

"Oh Sweetheart, you know we've discussed this before—how unlikely it is we will see Rube again. What has made you think of him now?"

"I don't know." Diana lowers her eyes and concentrates on taking a bite of her soup. "But you cannot know for sure we will never hear from him. He could have found out we left Savannah and be searching for us."

Jessie reaches out to take Diana's hand but stops, afraid Diana will construe the gesture as babying.

"Rube left long ago, and he was a runaway. He would be foolish to return to Savannah without papers. How would he know we came to Baltimore—and if he did come here, how would he find us?"

"He could ask around and someone would tell him about us, a mother and daughter who are the ages of the people he is looking for."

"You have been giving considerable thought to this, haven't you, Child?"

"I would like to have more family. Wouldn't you? I would love to meet my father, and I am sure he would want to know what happened to me and how I turned out."

"Of course Rube would like to be with you. He and Lavinie loved you very much. His desire to be with you both is what led to him fleeing. He got caught one too many times sneaking away after dark."

She purposely does not mention Lavinie's drowning when the boat taking her to visit her husband capsized. Though she has told Diana her mother died, she has spared her the details of the accident and the subsequent bloody beating her grief-stricken father had received when he had been caught sneaking away to see his child afterward.

"He took grave risks to see you one last time before he was smuggled away. I hope you can take solace in the knowledge you were loved. I assure you Rube would choose to be a part of your life, but I would be doing you a disservice to let you dream of what I feel to be extremely unlikely if not impossible."

Jessie wants to say something to remove the disappointment from Diana's face.

"I agree it would be nice to have more family." Jessie thinks of her great nieces and nephews in Savannah, the ones she will never be able to claim. "We, as free people, can be a family—you and I. I know you don't know many slaves and probably cannot remember the ones you used to know, but even if they are aware of who their parents, brothers, and sisters are, they are often separated from them, even sold away from each other."

"But you said the Barret slaves were all family, and they live together," Diana speaks to her plate. "I kind of remember Mammy and Dovie and Lewis. Maybe I just remember you talking about them, but it seems like I remember. They all lived together."

"You are right; they did—they still do. But their circumstances are more uncommon than not. You are certainly not the only one who doesn't know her father or has lost her mother. I hate this is something you dwell on because I fear you are hoping for something that isn't going to happen. Your father would be hunting for Jessie and Diana Davis, and he would be unsafe searching for us at all. He probably doesn't even know what happened to Moses. Harboring runaways is illegal, even here in Maryland. Few people will take such a risk. If Rube is alive, he would be foolish to call attention to himself. Many things can happen to a slave on the run, and it has been many years since he fled. Can you pray he is safe and happy somewhere and not long for things that will probably never happen?"

"Yes, Mama." Diana still doesn't look up from her meal. "I know I am being unrealistic. I will try to count my blessings and be content." Finally, she lifts her eyes. "We do well for two women alone."

Diana is serious, but Jessie laughs anyway.

"I wish you would quit trying to grow up so fast. Can't you just pretend you're still my little girl for another couple of years? I would love to go back and let my dear mother look after me."

Diana's face brightens. "Remember when you promised to tell me about your parents and your family on the Island when I got older. I am older now. I want to know about your life before you came to America. Tell me about when you were young and your mama and papa took care of you."

"I am not sure you are old enough for my story yet, and my dear father was gone long before I was your age."

Diana opens her mouth to protest, but the bell jingles informing them a customer has entered the shop. For once, Jessie is glad to have her midday meal with Diana interrupted. That customer is followed by two more, one who drops off a hat to be reworked, one who has brought her two daughters to be fitted for under linens and day dresses, along with a son in need of longer britches and a set of church clothes. Regardless, by the time the bell rings a little after four o'clock, Diana has managed to find time to dampen a fine linen cloth with which she presses the yellow silk ball gown Sophia Howe has arrived to pick up.

Sophia and Jessie did not know each other well before Abby's death, yet Jessie is drawn to her. Sophia has Abby's dark hair and eyes, but unlike her sister, she appears stronger, both physically and temperamentally. Too, Sophia gives no indication she thinks herself superior to Jessie, though she must, considering the difference in their stations in life. The young woman seems to sincerely like both Jessie and Diana, perhaps because Sophia was privy to Abby's fondness for Jessie and her attachment to the Barret children. Sophia is always courteous beyond the norm and has done all she can for *Devereux's* by recommending the service to friends and acquaintances. Jessie owes much of her success to Sophia and to customers she previously catered to while she worked for the Maxwells before she moved to Savannah to cook for the Barrets. Those connections were the reason Jessie had stopped off in Baltimore instead of migrating farther north. She knew she was going to have a hard time supporting herself and Diana, and she decided any advantage she could garner from previous contacts in Baltimore outweighed the benefits of putting more distance between them and the South. Jessie has not regretted her decision. Sophia has also provided a connection to the Barret family she left behind.

Today, Sophia has eleven-year-old Gail in tow. Both Jessie and Diana are relieved she has not brought young Cedric. The last time he came to the store with his mother, he was into everything. Diana spent her time following him around re-rolling ribbon, taking scissors away from him, picking up buttons he had scattered on the floor. His mother apologized for Cedric's behavior, but she seemed at a loss to keep up with him. Sophia often appears distracted in a way she did not when she was younger. Jessie attributes the child's lack of discipline to the fact he was born soon after the Howe's tragic loss of their son Jimmy the last summer they were together in Virginia at the Middleton plantation. Neither Jessie nor Sophia will ever forget the night Jimmy drowned and Frederick and Abby's last child was born still and cold. All the tragedy that came afterward seemed to be set in motion by that last visit, a time all concerned would like to forget. Jessie has never referred to the tragedies, nor has Sophia. The visit had resulted in horrible loss to both the Barret and Howe families.

"I have news!" Sophia exclaims. "Mattie is coming back to Baltimore for an extended stay!"

"I thought Miss Barret is all but set to wed. When you said you had news, I expected the announcement of her engagement."

"We've all been expecting the same, especially her father and Clarence Stiles. I am beginning to suspect Mattie is not quite as enamored with the young Thomas Stiles as he with her. Her father was loath to have her wed young; he may now wish he had pushed the union sooner. With Mattie's education and time away from home, she has developed an independence one would expect from Ella, not her. The two fathers have no choice but to force an immediate resolution or give the girl time to come to her senses. Frederick must have chosen the latter."

It has become customary for Jessie and Mrs. Howe to talk openly about the Barret children, so Jessie is comfortable asking, "Is Mrs. Stiles distraught Mattie has not made a commitment to the union?"

"I think not. Mattie says Bette has assured her she has never formally accepted Thomas's proposal, and if she needs more time to come to a decision, she should have it. In fact, Bette paid Frederick a visit to tell him the same thing, and her opinion is the reason Mattie is being allowed to return to Baltimore. I am glad my niece is coming, but she does need to tell the young man one way or the other if he can count on her."

Jessie is delighted Mattie is coming back to Baltimore. She had read no signs of passion in Mattie when she had visited the year before, and she now wonders if she may be achieving some distance from both Thomas and her father before she rejects him as a suitor. Jessie's good opinion of the sensible Bette she remembers as Abby's one real friend increases. Many mothers would be thinking solely of what was best for their own children, but Bette is giving Mattie an opportunity to clear her head without pressure from her father. She must know all too well the strength of Frederick's will.

"Please tell Miss Barret I hope she can come by while she is in town. I enjoyed her visits during her last stay so much."

"You can be assured you will see her often, for she tells me one of her objectives while here is to persuade you to update her wardrobe which she assures me is abysmal!"

They laugh for they both know Mattie's love for clothes, one that pales in comparison to her younger sister Ella's. Ella is thirteen-years-old and barely beyond playing with dolls, yet she goes nowhere without spending hours on her appearance.

After Sophia has caught Jessie up on the news in the Barret household, they turn to the needs of young Gail. Gail was named after her aunt Abigail, but she has inherited her father James's fair looks. Diana holds several fabrics up against her pale skin, and they finally decide on two—a soft rose shade that hopefully flatters her light complexion as opposed to overpowering it and a deep blue that brings some definition to her pale eyes. In spite of their efforts, Jessie fears she may compare unfavorably with her more vivacious cousins. Jessie makes a point to place a hand directly on the girl's forearm. So porcelain-like is her skin, Jessie is surprised at its warmth. She is pleased to find a strong life current, one that defies her placid exterior. Apparently, there is no cause for worry about the girl's health. Still waters run deep in Miss Gail, Jessie concludes.

Jessie and Diana have had a full day, and they are relieved to lock their doors after the departing Howes. They close the shop, hurriedly fix themselves a light meal, and climb the stairs to Jessie's room. The two of them had originally shared the bigger bedroom and used the extra for a small family parlor, but when Diana turned ten, Jessie had moved their second-hand sofa to her bedroom to be used for their time together, and Diana had inherited their one chair in which she often curls up to read. Now, Jessie takes with her a cup of tea and a piece of needlework that will eventually adorn the neckline of a linen nightdress. She has settled into the sofa when Diana joins her.

"Don't want to sketch tonight?"

Diana is in the habit of using the time before retiring to her room to draw something from one of her collections or produce a creative, if somewhat amateurish, dress design.

"No, Mama, I want you to tell me the story of your family on the Island. I am plenty old enough to understand. I've had bad things happen in my life; surely I won't be too dismayed by a story of long ago and far away. Tell me, Mama. You promised."

"I don't recall promising any such thing, and you are too young to remember most of the bad things in your life, but you are old enough to learn from our history, and our stories should not be forgotten. You are the only one left to carry them into the future."

Jessie puts her sewing aside, wraps an arm around her daughter, and pulls her close. The girl tucks her feet up under her dress and lays her head on Jessie's shoulder. Maybe the comfort of having Diana snuggled to her side is worth the pain of digging up the past. Besides, the sooner she satisfies Diana's curiosity, the sooner she can go to bed where Moses waits for her.

Chapter 3
Cooking School

Savannah, Georgia—1844

Many miles and states to the south, another woman drags herself around the kitchen in which Jessie once cooked elaborate meals to be carried upstairs to some of the city's wealthiest and most influential inhabitants. Minda, however, is not the cook Jessie was, and she cares not one bit. She takes none of the pleasure in cooking Jessie did, and she would love to be done with the tasks before her so she can head to Yamacraw for a few hours with her boys. Even the thought of time with them can bring no real pleasure, for their time in the cabin may not be their own. It bodes well Frederick has not dismissed her early as he does when he wants time alone with her. It's not that she dreads what he will do to her any more than any of the other tasks that fill her day. She had learned long ago how to let her mind escape to more pleasant thoughts. At least she will be off her feet, she reflects. Lying with him will be one more chore before she has a minute to call her own. When she hears someone coming down the stairs leading from the family floors, she hopes Daisy is sneaking away while she can, but she is not surprised to see Frederick instead. She sighs heavily. She is quick to tell her children to count their blessings, but Minda sometimes has a hard time practicing what she preaches.

Frederick wastes no time getting to the point, but the message is not the one she expects.

"Mrs. Stiles has graciously offered to let you spend some time with her cook in order to improve your skills. Since she serves the largest meal at midday, you will go over after breakfast and observe...help... learn something."

Frederick turns on his heel without reference to leaving early and caught up in the relief the omission brings, it takes a minute for his message to register with Minda.

"Who goan cook fo you an da young'uns?" she manages to ask before he is gone.

"Mammy will go back to cooking, and she, Dovie, and Cressa will have to divide her other duties until you are ready to prepare a decent meal. Mammy cooked before Jessie came, and as I recall, her offerings were better than what we have been eating."

Frederick's tone is matter of fact. Minda doesn't take offense because she doesn't particularly care if any of them like her cooking. After all, where was she supposed to learn? Mammy had tried to teach her a few things in her spare time, but when Abby died, Mammy lost a lot of the pride she had once taken in the running of the big house. She still oversees the cleaning, which means she does a lot of the work herself to cover for Dovie, but she spends a lot of her time tending the house garden as well as her own and doing laundry.

Minda lowers herself onto the one stool in the room and tries to decide how she feels about this unexpected development. The news is too fresh and sudden for her to determine. She wonders how her mother and sister will react. She doesn't have to wonder long because she can hear the two of them arguing as they come into the house from the back yard. They are half a huge house away, but neither sounds particularly pleased.

"Cressa jus hab ta do mo dan care fo does two guls dat be perfeckly capeble uh takin care uh theysef," Dovie is asserting.

"Cressa ain hab ta do no sech thing," Mamie argues. "Youse da one dat hab ta do yo share fo a change. Ise too ole ta be cuvrun yo lazy backside!"

By the time they cross the breezeway, Minda has taken off her apron and poured them each a glass of lemonade though it is not meant for the help. It is unlikely the master will be back, and the rest of the Barret family rarely steps foot below the family floors unless it is Mattie, and she left shortly after the midday meal to go to the river with Thomas Stiles. As she often does when she thinks she won't be caught, she serves the women in her family out of the glasses for the Barrets. She smiles at her small act of defiance, one that would be a terrible affront to some of the gentle folk above stairs if they suspected. Minda has never understood how the master can become all worked up about using the same dishes but thinks nothing of being inside her as much as possible.

"Youse pushin yo luck agin, Minda," Mammy says as she sits at the table and takes a gulp of lemonade. "I membah a time we aw eat wid da missus, an nobidy says a thing bout it. Bu dat aw come ta a en wen Mizz Abby die."

Dovie rolls her eyes. Neither wants to listen to their mother go on and on about Abby's virtues. Mammy has elevated her to Virgin Mary status since her death. Both young women shudder at the same time.

"Haint wawk cross yo grave?" Mammy asks.

"Jus a draff, dat all," Dovie says.

"Sho it be," Mammy says. "It hot nuff ta fry bacon on da flo in dis kitchen. I tole you her still hyur, bu da two uh youse too smawt ta lissen."

Neither bothers to comment because nothing they have said in the past has convinced their mother her tragically departed Abigail is gone forever.

"So I ta undahstan neitha uh youse too happy I be goin cross town ta cookin school?"

"I doan know wy youse da one dat git way from hyur fo mos da day. Youse awready git ta spen da night in yo own house lack reglar wite foke!"

"Youse thinkin we doan knows youse trapsin aw ovah town wen youse spose ta be cleanin but Mama doin it fo you? An doan think I doan knows whar you spen mos yo nights wen dat man ub yose be enwhar close. You spen mo time ouddah dis house dan enbidy hyur, cep Massah Rob, mabe!"

Mammy and Minda laugh, and Dovie smiles as she sits down to enjoy her drink.

"Mizz Mattie a good missy, bu she naw upta runnin dis househole. Good thing she hab me ta look aftah da place wen da massah naw hyur. Ise happy fo you, Minda. Youse bettah off ouddah dis house an ouddah da way uh da massah."

"Naw gonna make no diffrence, Mama. Him know whar ta fine me, same as awways."

"Mabe da change take Jude mine off da way things be some," Mammy says.

"Gonna take mo dan dat fo Jude ta stop thinkin on how much he wannah be rid uh da massah," Dovie adds.

"I doan knows whut I gonna do bout dat boy," Minda worries. "He eat up wid hate an dat ain gonna huht nobidy bu hissef. Mattahs ain goan be changin roun hyur ta please him."

"Wese cain do nuthin bout da massah," Mammy says, "bu wid you goan fo mos uh da day, wese gonna hab ta makes some change roun hyur. An mos uh dat gonna hab ta come from you, Dovie."

"Ise a lil full up wid da two uh you sayin Ise lazy!" Dovie glares at them as she slams her glass on the wooden table.

Both Mammy and Minda laugh again, but Minda warns her, "You bettah naw be breakin dat glass or theys be hell ta pay."

"Dovie, you been gittin ouddah choes sin da day you ole nuff ta work. You work hawdah ta git ouddah work dan ta jus do da work in da furse place! Po Cressa be sleepin on da flo wid da missies wen her could be wid Lew in da quattah cep you cain be trust ta stay wid em! Now dat Minda goan be ovah da Stiles, youse gonna do da cleanin youse spose ta, an youse gonna hep wid da wursh, an yo gonna stay in dis house aw day sted uh runnin wharevah you takes a mine ta!"

Dovie's face shows she is none too pleased with either of them, but she knows better than to argue with Mammy.

"I goan be a prisnah roun hyur stawtin tamorrah, Ise goan git Ben an sees we cain fine Clell."

"You knows Clell on da tracks," Mammy scolds, "sose you jus check on Ben an da res uh da chilren, an den you git on back hyur an hep me mens some cloes dat pilin up in da laundry."

Dovie disappears and Minda suspects she won't be back when she finds Ish playing in the dirt with Lew and Cressa's youngest Lizzy outside the quarter. Ben is not with them, so wherever Dovie has gone, she has taken her son with her. Minda looks for Lew before she goes, but he is not around either. She heads home with Ish.

"You see Daisy, Mama?"

Ish is a sensitive boy, and he has observed his mother is always a little sad if she doesn't say goodbye to her daughter each day before they leave. Minda hasn't seen her today except for the short time she took to eat her breakfast and midday meal. Daisy is in the habit of taking something with her for later. Today she had wrapped a piece of bread and a slice of leftover fatback in a scrap of flour sack.

Upon arriving at their small house in Yamacraw, Minda heats water to bathe Ish. He is dirty as usual from playing in the dirt, and the water in the pan turns brown before she has gotten to his feet. He chatters about the events of the day with his cousins and pays little attention to Minda as she takes the cloth from him. He immediately sits on the floor and extends his feet to his mother. She washes both, the right one first, then gently twists the left one against the turn it naturally takes. She cannot tell her efforts have made any difference at all. Because she has performed the ritual every night of his life, Jude automatically submits.

Minda warns him to stay away from the fire and walks to the well three streets down to draw two buckets of water, one for her and one for Jude. After Jude bathes, he will go back for two more so they will have one for morning and one for Ish in the afternoon—so is their routine. Jude has two to three hours each evening before he returns to the big house to attend the master's toilet. Afterward, he comes home, does a quick wash up if Minda is awake to make him, then falls into bed to sleep a few hours before he rises early to head back to the mansion.

Ish wants to wait up for his brother, but after nodding off lying on the floor, Minda picks him up and carries him to the room he shares with Jude now Daisy is living at the mansion. Minda sits idly by the fire waiting for Jude. She remembers he had planned to go fishing with Deke and Lew. Two hours pass insuring the boy will not be home until after he has attended to Mr. Barret's needs.

Minda lies on the bed in the living room, the one she sleeps in alone unless Frederick comes. She falls asleep, something she tries not to do until Jude is home. She is awakened when the front door opens. He crosses quietly by her bed but stops when she addresses him.

"Son, you needs ta wursh dat grime off fo you goes ta bed."

"Sho, Mama," he says and crosses to the table. Water splashes into the pan. Not enough time passes for him to wash his face, let alone the rest of his body, before he opens the door and throws the water out the front. Minda doesn't remind him he is to throw it to the side of the house, nor does she make him go for the water he was supposed to draw from the well earlier.

She feels as if she has hardly closed her eyes before she opens them to light creeping through the one window in the room. She wakes the boys and sends Jude for the water he didn't get the night before. Minda is excited and tries to discern why. She isn't overly interested in becoming a better cook, but anything that breaks the monotony of her day-to-day routine is something to look forward to. The slave community has ways of communicating their owners know nothing about. The grapevine says Mrs. Stiles is a good person, as white people go.

"Jude," Minda tells her son, "I be at da Stiles' place mos uh da day, sose you need ta behave yosef wile I ouddah da house. Enthin go wrong, you fines Mammy, Lew, or Cressa. Ebben Dovie if you cain fine one uh da othahs. You hyur me?"

"Sho, Mamma. Bu whut you thinks I git upta wile you gone?"

"You doan hab ta do nothin, Son. Jus try an stays ouddah da way uh Massah Rob an da massah, too. An keep an eye on Ish."

23

Jude takes off before she and Ish are ready. They walk along hand-in-hand, but this morning, the conversation is one-sided. Ish tugs his hand from hers and steps in front of her on the path.

"Somethin da maddah, Mama? Youse quite as a flea."

"Sorry Son. Ise jus thinkin on whut da day bring. I wanse you ta stay ouddah da way today at da big house bess you kin. An like I tells Jude, you needs somethin, you go fine Lew or Mammy or Dovie."

"I do dat, Mama, I needs ta. You be back ta wawk home wid me?"

"Uh course I be back ta wawk you home. I be ovah dare jus pawt uh da day. Long nough ta larn me somethin, I magine. An I naw leavin til aftah breakfess, sose I sees you an Jude an Daisy den jus lack I awways do."

Minda leaves Ish at the quarters and heads for the kitchen. Every day she prepares Frederick's breakfast before she feeds the servants. Today she poaches him two eggs, both of which are less done than he will like, then flips them onto bread she has sliced and toasted over the fire. She places those with another piece of toasted and buttered bread, a rasher of flaccid bacon, a small bowl of peach jam, two pats of butter, a cup of hot coffee, and some freshly squeezed orange juice on a tray for Lew to take upstairs to serve in the family dining room. Lew lifts an eyebrow when he notices the condition of the eggs and bacon, but all he says is, "Gul, you jus tryin yosef, ain you?"

After Mr. Barret leaves for work, she begins the second breakfast for the servants—her own children and the rest of the family from the quarter consisting of Lew, Cressa, their Deke and Lizzy, Dovie and her Ben, and Mammy. She is provided with provisions for the slaves, and she understands she may supplement their meals with leftovers the family upstairs won't use and food the slaves come by on their own. The extras come from the fishing Lew and the boys do when they have a chance, from the little square of garden behind the privy designated as theirs that Mammy works after she is finished with the house garden, or from trade with other slaves and free blacks. This morning, Jude and Deke proudly produce the fish they caught the evening before, and Mammy helps Minda roll them in cornmeal, salt them, and drop them in sizzling lard. The fish come out golden with a fine-as-sand coating. They snap cleanly when bitten, and the tender white meat practically melts in their mouths. The catch along with the hash Minda makes from leftovers from the day before provide a better meal than those to which they are accustomed. The atmosphere is somewhat festive, even though they must eat quickly because each has to be elsewhere soon.

Minda asks Dovie what happened to her effort to find Clell on her last day to roam, but Dovie refuses to rise to the bait and ignores her.

Minda is enjoying the meal and the togetherness until Daisy finally spills the news she has been dying to tell since last night.

"Mama, Mizz Mattie say her goan go stay wid Mizz Sophie. Ise goin wid her, an her doan knows wen we comin back!"

This is the moment Minda has prayed would never come. She had actually braved Frederick's displeasure a couple of years back and asked him to please keep Daisy close—told him separation from her would grieve her something fierce. At the time Frederick said he had no intention of sending her away, and with Daisy remaining in Savannah when Miss Mattie went off to school, and with the rumor that Mattie was marrying Mr. Stiles, Minda had made the mistake of lowering her guard. Now one of her worst fears is being realized.

"Wy da massah lettin her go off agin aftah her jus comes home no time back?" Mammy asks what they all want to know.

"Cuz her wanse ta go an her ain let up on her Papa fo day on ens. Da massah say her beddah git dis ouddah her mine fo good, cause it be high time her set down wid Massah Tom."

Minda releases her breath. "So youse ain gonna be goan long? Dis jus a shawt stay?"

"Naw if her hab her way," Daisy confides. "Yo acks me, Mizz Mattie doan wanse Massah Tom, an dat da reason her goin."

Daisy goes on and on about the adventure to come, while the rest of the family listens, each of them from Ish on up sobered. Jude and Ish may be losing a sister, Mammy a granddaughter, Lew, Cressa, and Dovie their niece, and worst of all, Minda will no longer see her daughter on a daily basis and know she is safe. Minda of all people understands what can happen to a young slave girl when she is sent from the only home she has ever known to stay in a strange house with no telling what kind of men. Those exact circumstances are how Daisy came to be. Mammy and Minda have discussed their concern over Daisy's proximity to the masters Robart and Fredie, but because of the relationship Frederick knows them to be, they hope he will not allow anything inappropriate to happen. Daisy has been away from her during the summer when Mattie took her to the Middleton plantation in Virginia, but Minda remembers Mrs. Middleton puts up with no foolishness and keeps a sharp eye on the house and the quarters.

Daisy prattles on while the others pretend Minda isn't swiping tears she's trying to hide.

"Wy doan you jus shut up?" Jude shouts.

Daisy finally looks up and falls quiet. The silence is broken by Lew who stands from the table and says softly, "Minda, wese need ta be headin dat way. Mizz Stile, she be specktin you."

Minda rises and goes to the other kitchen across the breezeway, more to keep from embarrassing herself than anything else. She turns to find Daisy standing in the archway.

"Ise sorry, Mama. Bu it goan be awright. Eben Mizz Mattie stay fo a long time, her be visitin her fambly hyur, an I comes wid er. You still be seein me."

The girl wraps her arms around her mother, and Minda's shoulders relax.

"They's much you doan know, Chile, an we needs ta fine some time ta tawk, ta tawk bout mattahs yo mama shouldda tole you a long time go. Come on back down hyur fo yo suppah. I be back by den, an we tawk. You hyur me?"

"Yes, Mama, I comes if I kin. Doan be worryin bout nuthin; evahthin goan be fine."

Minda joins Lewis out back. He tries to make conversation, but Minda is in no mood to talk. Finally, Lew gives up and they make their way in silence to the Stiles' back door.

Chapter 4

Inventory

Savannah, Georgia—1844

To an onlooker, Frederick casts a handsome figure in the doorway of his warehouse as he surveys the bustle and industry around him. He loves everything about the wharves—the sound of dray animal hooves clopping on the ballast covered street in front of the loading docks as they pull their loads—the spectacle of barges and ships at anchor on the Savannah River feet from where he stands—the wafting odors of the sea, human and horse flesh, grains, and even offal. All blend—sights, sounds, odors—to create an overall impression of what has come to mean success to him. By anyone's measurement, Frederick Barret is a successful man, and he takes pride in the fact he is self-made. He is quick to take credit for his business accomplishments, yet he finds no irony in casting his personal losses and setbacks square in the lap of Providence. Even so, he is confident he can improve the behavior of those around him if he is diligent enough, control their fates as he controls his own, if he were to admit it.

Though not particularly reflective, Frederick has become aware of a sense of unease, a ruffle in the calm he deems characteristic of a man in control of his life. Since his business is going well, he decides his displeasure stems from personal matters, probably something to do with the children or the household. Though life has dealt Frederick more than one blow that might have broken a weaker man, he has moved on and upward, and it doesn't occur to him his concerns may actually be circumstances beyond his control. Throughout his adult life, only death and one desertion—that is how he views Jessie's move to Baltimore—have threatened his best-laid plans, and he has always viewed problems as nothing but bumps in the road to be smoothed out by his own indomitable will.

He drags himself away from the pleasant scene before him and makes his way up the stairs to his office. His desk faces away from the panorama of Factor Row because, gregarious as he is, he finds himself too easily distracted by the always engaging pageant of Savanah's daily business being conducted by others like himself. He sighs loudly as he sits at his desk and extracts pen and paper. He pens the words *Family and Household Inventory* across the top of a page in his minuscule, neat script. He writes in English though French is the language of his youth, and one he often prefers, but those who might someday benefit from his efforts will be more comfortable reading English. He begins his inventory by writing his eldest son's name. He thinks nothing wrong with inventorying his children as he would the wares in Barrets' Mercantile on Broughton Street.

Robart— he writes.

Why is my eldest not living up to his abilities? he wonders. Might he have inherited mental weakness from the Middleton side of the family like that exhibited in Abigail? Might latent genetic traits from my own lineage be responsible?

That he would question the weak genes of both wives is not surprising. The first died of a disease he had survived, and the second was mentally weak and took her own life. Even a reference to his own lineage is out of character, however. He dare not record what those genetic traits might be, especially in English. He decides not to commit any of those thoughts to paper. He returns to the present with which he is more comfortable.

Weaknesses—has shown poor judgment and involved in bad behavior—if his course is not righted, could lead to a life of dissolution and ruin resulting in embarrassment to himself and our family. At nineteen, has been expelled from Princeton for "intoxication" after attending classes a month.

Frederick burns with righteous indignation and shame at the memory of the letter he had received from the institution at which he would have worked himself to death to succeed had he been given such an opportunity!

Shows no real inclination toward hard work. Since returning home, stays out late with friends of a like nature. Sleeps late in the morning and can only present far-fetched dreams for the future. Lack of common sense.

Strengths—handsome, good hygiene and dress befitting a gentleman. Shows interest in military matters and drills, good horsemanship. Intelligent enough. Courteous with good manners.

Here, Frederick has to stop and reflect a while to decide what is to be done about his eldest son's future. After a few minutes, he returns to the task at hand.

Talk to Andrews about giving Robart a job at Planters' Bank.

John Andrews, Frederick's longtime friend, is the President of Planters' Bank at which he is a member of the board. Acquiring Robart a position with the respected institution should pose no difficulty. He hopes his son will be better with the bank's money than he has been with his father's. Robart's only concern for pecuniary matters in the past have been when will his father hand over his next allowance and is he willing to supplement the amount should the sum prove insufficient.

Enrollment in the Georgia Militia.

This career path would please his son more, but the accouterments of a military career will prove expensive for Frederick. Beside the entry, he writes *Last resort.* He will support the military option as a last resort if Robart cannot make at least a show of being a decent businessman.

Encourage an advantageous marriage—could provide financial resources and offset poor business sense and have stabilizing influence on his behavior.

Relieved to put the discouraging prospect of Robart behind him, Frederick moves on to his second son and his own namesake.

Fredie—

He sits quietly for a bit, unable to think of any faults, skips down a few lines and writes *Strengths:* under which he quickly lists

Accepted by Princeton at seventeen. Intelligent, handsome and of noble bearing, responsible with money, not prone to excess, courteous.

Hopes for the future: Medical doctor that he expresses he wants to be.

Frederick writes Mattie's name next but pauses a minute before returning to Fredie.

Under the title *Weaknesses*— he writes

Overly adventurous spirit. Interest in all things military.

He overlooks the contradiction in listing *interest in all things military* as a weakness for Fredie when he determines it a strength for Rob. Neither does he question listing both boys before Mattie though she is the oldest of the children.

As Frederick pens *Mattie*— he acknowledges she has suffered the most of all the children for she alone remembers Luella, her own mother who died of yellow fever, and she of the three girls is the only old enough to have grieved his second wife and her own aunt. She has suffered two tragic losses, yet she has retained her sweet, caring disposition. She has grown maternal to the younger siblings, and he thinks she will make a wonderful mother someday. Frederick has thought her a submissive and obedient daughter until recently. He had even thought he had the whole important decision as to whom she should marry finalized. He is beginning to wonder if Mattie is as malleable as he has thought and as satisfied with his choice for her as he has taken for granted.

Weaknesses—slow to make a decision—perhaps fickle in her affections?

Frederick next writes the descriptor *unwilling*, then marks the word out in favor of the gentler *hesitant* before finishing his thought.

Hesitant to listen to parental advice. Overly tender of heart when dealing with household servants but less so toward her intended.

Frederick makes no distinction at all that Thomas is actually *his* intended for Mattie even though she has declined to formally accept the young man's proposal offered several months ago.

Strengths—Lovely in feature and dress. Charming and at ease in society, wonderful hostess. Knows how to run a household when necessary.

Frederick took responsibility for many household decisions when his wives were alive, matters often left to the mistresses in the homes of his friends. As a widower, he has become more immersed. Nonetheless, he deems his daughter capable if her future husband prefers to be less involved.

Pious in faith. Maternal. Educated in all matters and subjects befitting a lady. Has the advantage of a family of means to recommend her. Has an offer of marriage from the son of one of Savannah's more prominent and respected families.

Plans for the future—Wed to Thomas Stiles. Because of his closeness to our own family in both proximity and friendship, she will remain close to the bosom of her family and be a help and an example to her younger sisters as well as an assistance and comfort to me into old age if Providence grants me a long life.

Frederick smiles as he adds the next name to his list. He thinks his second daughter a joy in all respects, so vivacious and charming he often comments he should have named her after his cousin Brigitte, so alike in nature are they. Abby had insisted on naming her after his first wife, her own sister. Luella had been lovely and charming in her own right, but he has compared, on more than one occasion, young Ella's talents for drawing people in and holding their attention to those of Brigitte. The girl may have actually inherited the dominant portion of her personality from his own French forbearers, the side of the family for which he is most proud. He conveniently forgets the father who deserted him and to whom he refuses to communicate is the closest link to those same French ancestors.

Ella—

Weaknesses—

Again, as with Fredie, Frederick is unable to think of a single character flaw. He happily moves on to her strengths.

Beautiful in appearance and spirit. Exudes confidence and energy that capture a room though she is just thirteen years old. Will be a belle in the tradition of the South. Can converse with people of all ages. Already shows an understanding of her station—exhibits appropriate deference to people of quality while refraining from familiarity with servants and lower classes (an art it would behoove her sisters to emulate). Pious enough. Sits a horse well and cuts quite the figure. Already shows an understanding of

31

how society works and gravitates toward those most worthy of admiration and in whom one can expect advantage.

Plans for future—Ella will be able to choose among suitors. She must be careful not to settle easily. I will compile a list as she ages of most desirous suitors and encourage her in association with them at functions and through invitations to our home. Encourage her to consider beaux who live and will continue to live in Savannah so she may retain the advantage of the love and support of her family.

Maxie—

She is the daughter Abby finally agreed to name after his much admired cousin Brigitte Maxwell, and she is the girl least like her. In fact, he fears she is the most like Abby. He has told her many times how much she reminds him of her mother, and though she doesn't remember Abby, the comparison pleases her. Frederick was angry for some time with Abby for leaving him and risking disgrace for the family, but now he speaks of her with deep tenderness. His own grief had surprised him. Maxie's similarities to her mother have brought him comfort, but he watches her for the signs of fragility and despondency he thinks took his second wife from him. Though he doesn't allow himself to dwell on things he should have done, or more importantly, not done, to make life easier for Abby, he has vowed to do all within his power to make sure Maxie is protected from herself if she has indeed inherited Abby's fragile spirit and mind.

Weaknesses—Shy, somewhat withdrawn in company. Prone to daydreaming and solitude. Overly attached to the servants, especially Cressa and Mammy. Probably most impacted by her mother's death. Cries easily—overly sensitive. Neat and clean in appearance but lacks interest in fashion.

Strengths: Loving, caring, sensitive to feelings of others (to a fault). Amenable and easily led. Obedient. Pious (maybe to a fault).

Plans for the future—try to provide better influences and less time with Cressa and Mammy. Expose her more to society under the tutelage of older sisters. Observe her closely for signs of despondency. Spend more time with her—encourage her to ride and interact with suitable friends. Long term—facilitate association with marital prospects kind and understanding by nature—beaux who will stay close to home so I may

*remain involved in her life and close should she need me. Encourage
Mattie and Ella to mentor and nurture her.*

Frederick exhales, pushes back from his desk, and rises. He stretches
and allows himself the reward of a few minutes at the window. He
experiences a sense of accomplishment and an easing of worry now that
he has a plan. He has organized his thoughts and has a better grasp
on what his family members need. He considers heading home for his
midday meal. Instead, he sits down at his desk with renewed energy.
He pulls another sheet of paper from a drawer, even though he still
has room below Maxie's name. He writes *Slave Property* at the top of the
page. He keeps his family and his slaves separate on paper as he would
prefer to do in life. After his experiences on the Island, he claims he
would not own a single slave had he not inherited them and were they
not necessary and expected from a man of his station. Besides, he has
too much money tied up in them, and Frederick is unwilling to suffer a
financial loss even if they weren't essential to his way of life.

*Mammy—Approximately 58-year-old house servant. Inherited from
Middleton family as part of Luella's dowry. Faithful and competent.
Good with the children. Adequate cook. Children are attached to her. Will
not sell. If something should happen to me while she is alive, bequeath her
to one of the girls—Maxie perhaps.*

*Lewis—Approximately 41-year-old house servant responsible for horseflesh
and yard as well as any other work requiring a strong male. Acts as
butler. Part of Luella's dowry. Faithful, hard-working, in good health.
Will not sell. Will bequeath to one of the boys when the time comes—
probably Fredie if Robart does not show more pecuniary responsibility.*

*Cressa—Approximately 24-year-old female purchased as a wife for Lewis
and help for the children.*

His mood darkens when he recalls the circumstances that
precipitated the purchase of Cressa. He had bought her to tend Jessie's
Diana, a child he had refused to refer to by name. He had never been
able to understand why Jessie insisted on calling the child her own. He
still becomes angry when he recalls her refusal to continue to cook full
time for the Barrets until the baby was older. His solution had been
to buy a girl to take care of the child. To solve a housing problem,

he had allowed Lewis to choose Cressa for his wife. A lot of good his machinations did him since Jessie had left anyway. Fortunately, Cressa has proved a valuable addition.

> *Good with the children. Will remain with Lewis.*
>
> *Deke—Approximately eleven–year-old male. Son of Lewis and Cressa.*
>
> *Will bequeath to Rob if Fredie receives Lewis. If sold, first option shall be given to Fredie. Vice versa if Rob receives Lewis. If neither son wants to keep Deke, my preference is one of the daughters will purchase him with her share of her inheritance.*

He remembers the Middletons' policy about keeping families intact, but he assures himself he is doing so by encouraging his children to keep him in the Barret family. He cannot imagine a future in which his offspring will not stay connected.

> *Lizzy—Approximately six-year-old female. Daughter of Lewis and Cressa. Plan to train her for service to Ella. Will bequeath to Ella.*
>
> *Dovie—Approximately 37-year-old female. Strong and capable but lazy. Caught away from the house without cause on more than one occasion. The children are fond of her, but she is probably not worth her keep. Has a son by a slave hired out by his owner to the railway—foresee her involvement with him might cause problems.*

Of all his slaves, Dovie is his least favorite. He considers her not particularly faithful or trustworthy. He had mentioned selling her when Abby was alive, but she would not consider it. He would have sold her since her death had he not feared more dismay for the children and the problems the action could cause with the rest of the help as Dovie is Mammy's daughter and the sister of Lewis and Minda. He finishes with her by writing,

> *To be sold upon my death at market value with the sum being divided among my children unless one of them wants to purchase her for market price with the sum still to be divided among my heirs.*
>
> *Ben—six-year-old male. Son of Dovie. Bequeath to Rob unless a family member buys Dovie. If so, they are to be sold as a pair.*

Frederick prides himself on making the extra effort to keep Ben with Dovie. He imagines he has gone beyond what would be expected of him.

The future dispensation of his slaves has put Frederick in a worse mood than dealing with his children. He had never wanted slaves, and unlike most owners, he has no desire for his to procreate. In his opinion, the more slaves he owns, the more likely they will be a problem, for there is power in numbers. Too, he has enough servants to run his household. Economically, the extras are drains on his resources and could become the bane of his existence.

He owns four remaining slaves not counting the five he lists as belonging to his business and accounted for in the records he keeps at his office. If he is to follow form, he will now list Minda, and being an organized, precise person, he doggedly writes,

Minda—Approximately 39-year-old female. Works as our cook. Housed in Yamacraw.

Without realizing it, he writes *Weaknesses—* as he did with his children.

Poor cook. Appears secretive at times.

Strengths—clean and comely in appearance. Obedient. Works hard. Appears trustworthy and faithful.

He pauses. How can he think her both secretive and trustworthy? *Is she trustworthy?* He wonders. *Is she faithful, for that matter?* Would he know if she were neither? *Does she harbor resentment?* He moves on.

Doesn't complain. Does whatever is expected of her.

Frederick again adheres to his family format when he writes,

Plans for the future—

He becomes agitated, and not because he has been inconsistent with his inventory.

He has refused to give thought as to what to do about Minda's future should she outlive him. He proceeds, leaving Minda unfinished.

Daisy—seventeen-year-old female mulatto. Daughter of Minda. Servant to Mattie who is quite fond of her. Will bequeath to Mattie. In all likelihood, she will remain in Savannah when Mattie weds.

Jude—twelve-year-old male mulatto. Son of Minda. My personal houseboy—performs other duties as needed.

Once again, Frederick is stumped. What to do with Jude? Should he leave him to Rob who he thinks is irresponsible and unlikely to be a good steward of the boy? Should he leave him to Fredie knowing his younger son's adventurous spirit may take him to far places, separating Jude from Minda? Will he force Minda to accept the loss? He answers none of those questions by simply writing nothing more.

Ishmael—eight-year-old male mulatto. Cripple. Son of Minda. Because of his disability, will stay with his mother when her future is decided.

Frederick decides he has done all he is willing to do today. He puts the document in a portfolio and slips it into a desk drawer. He quickly grabs his hat, locks his office door behind him, crosses the wooden bridge separating Factor Row from the sandy street, and heads home for dinner. His step is not as light as usual, and his heart sits heavily in his chest. What would Luella and Abby think of his choices for their children and the slaves they had brought to the marriage? They might judge him, but what would they do were they still among the living? He thinks Luella would probably be amenable to his decisions regarding everyone but Minda and her family. She had thought Minda sold to the Stiles, when in truth, he had set her up in a small house in Yamacraw. He fears Abby would have wanted to do something foolish like set them all free, thanks in part to the unhealthy influence of Bette Stiles. Then again, she probably would not have had the strength to go against him and her mother, a slave owner in her own right and practical in all things financial. He shudders when he thinks about Mrs. Middleton finding out about Minda's offspring. Too, she would never have separated the families. Frederick allows himself to experience a few minutes of self-sympathy knowing he will eventually have to face hard decisions.

He picks up his step, banishes all disquieting thoughts from his mind, and anticipates spending time with his family at lunch. Too bad he can no longer expect a decent meal, thanks totally to the unappreciative Jessie bailing on him when he needed her the most.

Chapter 5
Breaking the Law

Savannah, Georgia—1844

Pearl lets Minda into the kitchen of the Stiles' house. Like her master's, the mansion is one of the finest in Savannah, but the kitchen itself lacks both the size and accouterments of the room in which Minda works every day. Unlike Dovie and Mammy, she takes no pride in her owner's status. Now she glances around indifferently, taking in the details to relate to her mama and her sister because they will want a report.

Minda has been in the Stiles' home before. She had helped out for a short time after the birth of the last Stiles' child. She had come to them not because Mrs. Stiles needed her, though that was the reason the lady herself was given, but because Frederick's first wife Luella wanted her out of the house, with good reason. She had been in this kitchen only to eat as her job had been to tend the children while Bette convalesced after a hard third birth. Both Luella and Minda had thought Clarence had bought Minda, but the slave found out differently when she was moved to a house in Yamacraw, the hardscrabble section of Savannah where poor whites, free people of color, and slaves rented out in the city by their owners lived. Mr. Barret had never sold the girl. He had cunningly moved her out from under Luella's suspicious eyes and into a place to which he could come and go as he pleased. He had made his trips to Yamacraw for years before the second Mrs. Barret discovered she, not Bette, had been deceived by her husband.

Minda examines, not for the first time, Pearl's light skin and hazel eyes, characteristics Dovie would envy. In slave hierarchy, paleness often means better assignments because a light hue usually means a biological connection to the master. Instead of envy, Minda feels empathy, for she understands now what Pearl's creamed coffee complexion signifies. In all likelihood, Pearl's mother had lived a life much like the one she herself came to know shortly after Frederick had caught her alone in an upstairs bedroom while the mistress was out.

Today, as before, Pearl puts on no airs and talks to her as an equal though she speaks more like the Stiles than she does other servants. She reintroduces her to Cook, a large-boned, ebony-skinned woman who looks like she has sampled many of her own wares. Minda can see no room for her at the counter, but Cook moves good-naturedly to the side, an indication she is accepting of her new role as teacher. Her melodic voice falls gently on the ear, a contrast to her robust appearance. Like Pearl, her speech would not be mistaken for her owners', but neither would it sound natural in slave quarters.

The lesson starts with biscuits, and at first Minda thinks she is wasting time as she has been making biscuits since she stood at her mother's knee at the big house in Virginia. Soon, though, she realizes Cook has something to teach her. The ingredients each woman uses are the same, but unlike the hasty twisting of dough from the bowl and giving it a turn or two in flour as Minda has learned to do, Cook heavily dusts a wooden board and turns the whole bowl out onto it. She folds the mound from side to side, working the flour into the mixture. After balling her hands into fists and punching gently back and forth into the increasingly smooth bundle, she presses the whole into an even oval.

"If you in a hurry, or if you jus cookin fo family, you can skip the rollin, but I like my biscuits even in the pan."

Minda works her own pliable dough in and beneath her hands until Cook tells her she needs to stop or she will overwork it. Her mentor sprinkles another light dusting over the neatly confined dough, palms more flour over a rolling pin she pulls from a shelf above her head, and lightly moves the pin across the top until she produces a uniform sphere. Minda does her best to replicate the process, accepts a tin cup like the one Cook holds in her hand, and cuts perfectly round discs from the masterpiece she has worked to create. Like Cook, she places them touching in the Dutch oven to her left. The end result is pleasing to behold. Cook then stokes the fire, and they place their pans side by side in the fireplace where the older lady assures her they will benefit from the indirect heat.

"Whut nex?" Minda asks after they have cleaned up the mess they've created.

"You done fo the day in here," Pearl informs her.

"Awready?" Minda frowns. She has been enjoying herself and is in no hurry to return to the Barrets'.

"In here," Pearl repeats, "but Ms. Bette want ta see you in the parlor."

"In da pawla?" Minda repeats. Slaves are rarely called to the parlor unless it's to clean it. "Ise jus hyur ta cook. Nobidy say nuthin bout no cleanin."

Pearl laughs at the indignant scowl on Minda's face. "You not cleanin, Gul. The missus jus wannah talk with you."

This disclosure causes Minda more alarm than the thought of cleaning. "Whut in da worl da missus wannah tawk wid me fo?"

"Why doan you go find out?" Pearl asks before taking pity on her and adding, "Doan be scared. The missus ain like mos white folk you know. You see. Follow me."

Minda reluctantly obeys. They enter an entryway every bit as impressive as she remembers, but now she is daily in a house this grand. They mount the curving stairway and enter the small parlor off the bedroom where Mrs. Stiles lay throughout the entirety of her last confinement. The room is more spacious than the entire house she and her boys inhabit in Yamacraw. Before the fireplace, unlit because early spring temperatures are close to perfect, sits a diminutive plump woman whose blond hair and blue eyes put her about as far away from Minda on a racial spectrum as possible. She rises, and as if to prove this experience can become even more unreal, she approaches her and takes her hand.

"Hello, Minda. I don't know if you remembah me. I apologize I was too unavailable throughout your last visit ta propuhly make your acquaintance."

Visit? When has any black person in her acquaintance paid a visit to a white person? She looks to Pearl, her expression revealing her confusion. Pearl laughs as she did in the kitchen.

"I bring you two one of Minda's biscuits soon as they done," she tells them, then turns and leaves the room.

"Please sit down."

Bette takes her hand and leads her to one of the chairs in front of the cold fireplace. Minda sits at the edge of the seat. In Virginia and at the Barret homes, the slaves have always known they would be punished for sitting on furniture or using utensils meant for their owners. The breeze wafting through the open window is not enough to cool Minda's face which glistens with the sheen of sweat.

"Minda, I can tell you ah uncomfuhtable, and I want you not ta be. I want ta help you, ta be your friend, if you will allow me ta be."

Minda sits perched on the edge of the seat with brown eyes wide and blank as they peer directly into those of the woman across from her. Realizing what she is doing, she lowers hers immediately.

"I know this is going ta sound strange, Minda, but I would like ta teach you ta read and write."

Knocked out of her stupor by the sheer absurdity of the statement, Minda can take no more.

"Wy in da worl you wannah do dat! Whut Ise gonna read?"

Minda clamps her lips. These words could be considered insolent and cause for scolding.

Bette merely chuckles and acts like Minda's reply is the most natural thing in the world.

"I am sorry. I should have gone about this more gently. I haven't thought of how odd this offah will appear ta you undah your circumstances. And I must ask now, and hope, whatevah your answer is, I can count on your discretion. The Barrets nor my husband nor my children may evah know what I am suggestin. My husband is not of the same bent of mind as I. Both your mastah and my husband will be livid if they know I am makin you this offah. May I count on your word, Minda, that you will tell no one I have offahed ta teach you ta read? It is just not done by many of my…" Bette pauses, "friends and neighbahs, and what I am pruhposin is also illegal in ah fine state of Georgia as it is in all the South. If you ah ta accept this offah, it must be a secret. Do you undahstand?"

It takes Minda a minute to muster a nod.

"And do you agree ta keep ah secret?" Bette repeats.

"Yessum, bu wy you goan take da risk uh larnin me sumpthin Ise nevah goan use? Whut I goan read? They's no place an no time fo nobidy lack me ta read."

"It may surprise you, Minda, ta learn I know more about you than you think. I know what your circumstances ah."

Minda averts her eyes and stretches her back to ramrod straightness. Bette spans the space between them, and lifts her hand toward Minda's face but drops it when Minda flinches away from the touch.

"And I know the circumstance is not of your choosin. I know you have Daisy, Jude, and Ishmael."

Minda's eyes fly to Bette's face.

"Please trust me. I mean you and yours only good, no hahm. I want ta make your lives bettah, not worse."

"Wy, Ms. Bette? Wy you wanse ta hep my fambly. You doan eben know us."

"You helped me once, Minda. And I was a friend ta Ms. Abby, and I know had she thought she could do something ta change the way things were, she would have done it. I wish I had been strongah when Abby was alive. I would like ta in some way try ta right an injustice ta her and ta you. She wasn't strong, and you have a mastah who is. Though Abby would probably not have done what I am doin, she would have wanted things ta be different, at least in the end, faw children who have the blood of her own. She nevah told me those things, but I believe them ta be true. Abby was a kind person."

Minda's shoulders slump. She has heard nothing but positive things about her as a mistress from Mammy and Dovie, and unlike Luella, Abby had been kind when they were children living on the plantation in Virginia. Though she had never been at the big house here in Savanah with her, she remembers Abby coming to see her and trying to make things better for her and her children. Mammy, Dovie, Lew, and Cressa had all been devastated by Abby's gruesome death, and she had felt immediately responsible upon hearing the circumstances in which she died. Dovie reinforced her regret by letting her know Abby had become aware of Frederick's trips to see her. She had suspected as much the day she was out walking when she was expecting Ish. She had seen the strange way Abby looked at Daisy and Jude, had recognized the moment when truth dawned, and wanted to follow to beg forgiveness when Abby had turned and fled toward home. She could think of nothing to say, however, had she had the nerve to say it.

"I nevah wanse ta hurt Mizz Abby. Mizz L'ella, I naw care much, but Mizz Abby, her be good eben as a chile."

"Your situation is not your fault, Minda. Miss Abby would not have blamed you. Slaves have no say in their lives, and she knew her husband had a strong will, one she could not control. She would have known you could not eithah. I am not sayin she was unhurt, nor the whole revelation did not attribute ta her end, but I am sayin you cannot be faulted."

Minda's own mother had told her the same thing, but the words coming from Abby's closest friend, a white woman, ease a weight she has been carrying for years. She is unused to either sympathy or commiseration. She brushes an errant tear and sits straighter in the chair again.

"I do not think your people will always be enslaved, Minda. Many white people know the institution is wrong undah any circumstances. We hope those in powah in our country will come ta their senses and someday do away with the ungodly practice of treatin human beings as chattel, and when they do, people of cullah will benefit from havin skills only whites ah allowed right now, at least in the South. I do not know as this change will come in ah lifetimes, though I pray it will. I definitely think ah children may live in a totally different world in which slavery is not puhmitted. If I teach you ta read, you can teach your children, in turn, ta insure they ah ready if and when the time comes. Readin and writin will be a necessity for them ta prospah on their own."

Minda sits straight and silent. The slaves have overheard whispers of freedom. Her own church harbors escapees hoping to reach cities in the north where they can go unnoticed, places in which some blacks walk freely and actually own businesses, destinations that might as well be on the moon as far as she is concerned. She has heard of Jessie and Diana in Baltimore, but the thought they might live free where they are, like Jessie and Moses did before Moses died and Jessie left, is something hard to even imagine. And to read and write? Never has she thought of such a thing, not for her or her children. Truthfully, she is not interested in reading and writing. She can think of no need to write if her ability to do so has to be a secret. But her children—to equip them to survive outside the life they know is enticing indeed. Especially Jude. She has long felt a storm brewing within him, and she fears it is a matter of time before his anger surfaces and damns himself if not them all. She opens her mouth, but before she can speak, Bette continues.

"There is anuthah reason I feel the way I do. I, too, have a sistah of cullah, as Mattie does, but unlike Mattie, I assume, I have always known of her, or at least I have since I was quite small. She grew up bein my suhvant as Daisy is Mattie's, as your boys suhve their brothahs. My fathah did the right thing by freein Pearl. She works faw us, but she earns a wage, though my husband would choose othahwise. Of course, no one considahs Pearl my sistah any more than anyone would considah your children the siblins of the Barret offspring. I am convinced some people have more sensitive souls, a natural undahstandin deep within them that will not be squashed by man-made laws or powahful men. They innately puhceive some acceptable practices ah wrong, sinful even, an abomination ta the God who created us all. I am one of these people, and I hope the Barrets' Mattie and my own Reggie and Eliza ah three more. I want ta someday become closah ta Mattie and prevail upon her the responsibility she has faw at least Daisy, though I do not believe she is aware of the connection. Maybe someday she can also have some influence ovah the fate of your sons."

This elevated talk overwhelms Minda; she has been bombarded with too much at once. She came today to learn to cook, a skill she had not been overly keen to improve. Instead, she discovers Bette Stiles knows all about her life. She has brought up matters Minda could never have imagined discussing with a white woman. She feels exposed and unanchored. This lady she has shared few words with has a lofty plan, not only for her, but for her children. The whole experience is too far-fetched for her to take in. She rises from the chair slowly.

"Mizz Stile, I likes ta go now, if dat awright. I ain feelin good."

"Of course. I know this is a lot ta have sprung on you at once. Just think about what we have talked about tonight, and if you want ta take me up on my offah, we will begin tamorrah aftah your cookin lesson. You will have to take home skills you were sent here ta learn. And remembah, you must tell no one who might betray me. Your discretion is my only requirement."

Minda stares at the blond, blue-eyed mistress who is beseeching her to remain quiet.

"You needen fret, Mizz Bette. Nobidy evah goan bleve dis tale should I wanse ta tell it, an I sho cain magine dat."

Pearl appears at the door with two saucers with biscuits and a couple of cups of tea. Minda imagines telling Mammy and Dovie she has taken tea with Miss Stiles, but she cannot stay. It is all she can do to utter, "I gotta go."

Bette insists she at least take the biscuits with her. Minda docilely trails Pearl to the kitchen where Cook wraps all the biscuits Minda made earlier in a cloth and ushers her out the back door with them.

Bette stands where Minda has left her. She becomes aware of a stirring, a coldness around her. She shudders.

Pearl has returned. "You alright, Miss Bette?"

"Fine, Dear," she replies, "Someone must have walked across my grave. Is it cold in here ta you?"

"I stoke the fire. You jus worried you start somethin that might come back ta grieve you."

Instead of going straight to the Barrets', Minda turns to her place in Yamacraw. She feels like she has been hit by a cart on the way home. She lies down and is more herself by the time the boys arrive. Both are delighted with the unexpected treat their mother reveals to them before bedtime. They look better than her usual biscuits, and they are lighter, not as hard and dense as those they normally have. She chooses from her scant store of groceries a small crock of honey Frederick has gifted her and generously coats the boys' biscuits. Their happiness temporarily eases the weight of the offer Bette Stiles has put before her, but after the boys are in bed, she has nothing to distract her. She tosses and turns throughout the night. What advantages would the ability to read and write give her children? More importantly, what could they gain from having someone as powerful as Bette Stiles on their side—looking out for them? She cannot imagine the woman's will being a match for Frederick's, but, nonetheless, the protection and attention of any white person of means is not something to take lightly. And what of the prediction her children might someday be free? Minda tries to see a future in which their emancipation could be the case. Might Frederick free them all upon his death? If not, she comprehends the benefit of her children having favor with Bette Stiles. The boys already have more than most because of the house and the gifts of better food and clothing Frederick provides. If nothing else, Bette can provide more of the same if Frederick doesn't suspect Bette's motives. If Jude proves to be the handful she fears he will be, maybe Bette can intervene for him someday, if needed. But breaking the law by learning to read is no minor issue. And how will the ability affect Jude's already rebellious attitude? Minda may not have the language to articulate her troubled thoughts, but she has a sharp mind, and she recognizes this moment as a pivotal point for them. She is not as headstrong as her sister Dovie, but she has more cause to distrust white people than her siblings. She has enough spark left of her younger self to long for a better life, especially for her children, especially at this moment when the threat of losing Daisy is real.

Minda comes to a decision in the wee hours of the morning, and she finally sleeps. She is not yet confident in the promises made to her to dream of her evolving self, the one in which she speaks like Pearl and has tea with white ladies from the same cups from which they drink, but she has hope enough to put a smile on her relaxed face, something uncommon when she is fully awake.

Chapter 6
Fall from Grace

Savannah, Georgia—1844

Jude stands at his place in the corner. The dining room holds the same family members he attends on weekdays, but being a Saturday, the master is among them. The boy has already assisted Lewis in bringing the dishes up from the kitchen, and as usual, Lew has left to attend to his outside chores. Jude has little interest until the words Mattie and Baltimore catch his attention. He learns Mattie will be leaving in two weeks' time, information his mother will not want to hear. As consolation, he will offer the assurance that Master Barret expects his daughter back in early fall as he normally would when they return from their summer visit to Virginia. He will not mention Mattie herself makes no comment as to whether she plans to come back in the fall or not.

Jude fights the urge to lean back into the dining room wall. The master takes pride in this room. He has been present when Frederick made a point to bring guests in to point out the unusual curved wall, the wallpaper he picked up in New York, the egg and dart molding. Frederick calls attention to them as a means to show he can afford extravagance in a room designated for family dining. For Jude, the added elegance of the room is simply more cause for scolding should he relax his guard and support himself with the same fancy wall. Jude's body stiffens when Frederick wipes his mouth with his napkin and pushes back his chair. Before the whole family disperses to their different pursuits as usual, Frederick clears his throat and asks the boys to stay behind for a gentleman's talk. Robart and Fredie exchange looks, Robart's heavy, Fredie's expectant. First Mattie, then Maxie, and finally Ella file by Frederick to receive kisses on the way back to their rooms to prepare for their day of social visits. The man now has Jude's full attention, his presence no more conspicuous were he a cat curled in the corner.

"Sons, the time has come to talk about your futures. I know we have had similar discussions in the past, but due to unexpected developments, it may behoove the three of us to re-address your plans."

Fredie's eyes dart to his brother whose face has turned the hue of a boiled lobster. Jude can have no idea the cause of the young man's unease, but a small smile flits across his face before he has the forethought to lose it. Of all the Barrets, Robart is his least favorite, not counting the master, of course.

"Fathah, I have hoped I would be granted a chance ta explain…" Robart begins. He is immediately cut short by his father's raised hand.

"I have listened to your excuses, Rob, and I have made myself clear. I do not care to listen to more of them."

All three young men recognize the change in Frederick's inflection. His speech contains none of the rounded vowels and slurred endings theirs do, a difference he regrets. He thinks their speech indicates inclusion; whereas, his own sets him apart. When he becomes angry, his speech amplifies the difference in his upbringing, the influence of a foreign language spoken for years before the acquisition of English.

Rob and Fredie sit up straighter while Jude holds his eyes steady and wills himself to be so still no one will remember he is in the room. Frederick decides the boy should stay in case they may have some need of him, and his words may be wise for Jude to consider. Jude will not need the lesson of how a young man should behave when he reaches maturity, but a display of Frederick's authority over the lives of his sons should be a warning to Jude. If Rob and Fredie cannot thwart the master's plans, how futile would a slave boy's attempts be in comparison?

"Frederick," their father continues, and both boys know the use of the younger's full name is meant to lend weight to the message, "you are beginning your adulthood at a grave disadvantage due entirely to misconduct by one you should have been able to hold in highest regard as a role model, as an advocate, as a noble example of your family name. Instead, due to no fault of your own, you have much to overcome when you enter Princeton in the fall. You must prove to them you are not of the same ilk as your brother who graced their halls for a brief time yet managed to sully our good name. Promise me, Son, you will do all within your power to rectify the wrong done by your brother."

Fredie's own face has turned pink under his father's intense gaze. He would like to show some sign of commiseration for his brother, but he dare not.

"I promise," he says. Knowing what is expected, he sits tall in his seat and holds his father's eyes until they release him to turn their steely beam upon his brother.

The tears in Robart's eyes are those of remorse, humiliation, or anger. Robart himself would have a hard time saying which. He wants to defend himself, but his father has heard before he was not drunk as charged—he had only a drink or two with friends his father would find honorable. Nor had he helped his cause when he had tried to explain he was not alone in having imbibed—nor the unfairness of him, and only him, being the one punished. Fredie feels sorry for him and tries to think of something he can say to aid his brother. He is almost as relieved as Rob when his father's voice becomes softer, less harsh.

"Now, Robart, how do you plan to put this unfortunate incident behind you and make something of this privileged life Providence has granted you?"

Robart dares to meet his father's eyes.

"I have long thought I would make a bettah soldier than I would a student," Robart declares boldly.

"You do understand, Rob, to be a competent soldier, you must be an attentive student? No matter what path in life you choose, you must be open to learning. Do you think I have attained the life I have today without learning from many teachers? Once again you are showing an ignorance brought on, I fear, by entitlement."

Robart sighs and his shoulders sag in preparation for what he and his brother think will be the sermon they have received many times, the one about how fortunate they are to have many advantages, those he himself was not afforded. Though their father never talks about his early years in Saint Domingue, his life since moving to the United States is a different matter. His tenure as a clerk for Robart's namesake, his great uncle Robart Middleton, his learning of a foreign language, and his meteoric rise to wealth in this country are legendary among his children.

Frederick surprises them by going no further down that lane. In the end, Robart would have preferred to sit through the whole recitation of his father's past successes.

"I will not finance a military career for you at this time. You have shown no understanding of pecuniary matters and little regard for the wasted money I generously paid Princeton for what I had assumed would be a leg up in life. If you are to enter the militia, you will have to first come up with the money to do so."

"But, Fathah, how am I at just nineteen-yeahs-old ta avail myself of such a sum?"

"You will not avail yourself of such a sum at your present age. Having wasted your first opportunity, you have forfeited the chance for an easy career. You will have to earn your way and save the money you need to enlist in the militia if that is what you want to do."

Robart wants to shout he has always wanted to be a soldier, but his desires have fallen on deaf ears no matter how many times he has expressed them. He wants to blame him for the whole Princeton debacle. If his father had listened, he would never have gone to college. Further education was his father's dream, not his own. He dares not speak his mind, however, for his position is tenuous. Without his father's support, what is to become of him?

"But, if not the militia, what am I ta do? I have no prepuhration ta go into any othah line of business…"

"I wish you had given your situation more thought before you squandered an opportunity many young men would have sold their souls for. I have not totally deserted you, however. I have acquired a place for you in Planter's Bank. Through John Andrews' association, you will be given a position as a clerk from which you may work into something more desirable, or, if you are frugal, accrue the funds with which you may buy your way into the militia. My own experience as a clerk at your age can be an encouragement to you."

Robart cannot hide his dismay, but he quickly recovers.

"Thank you, Fathah," he says, "I am grateful faw your continued support."

"Please make sure neither I nor John regrets the confidence in your abilities and your moral fortitude."

"You won't, Fathah. I assure you."

Robart manages to keep his composure until his father rises, grips Fredie's shoulder in passing, tells him he is counting on him, then finally makes his way from the room. When Rob has given the man time to be out of hearing range, he throws his head down on his crossed arms and utters the oath that has been welling in his throat the entire time his father was lecturing him.

"Now come, Old Fellow. Your circumstances ah not as bad as all that!"

"Not as bad as all that!" Robart shouts, but he lowers his voice when he considers the consequences of being overheard. "I can think of little wuhse! I will be shut up in an office all day accountin faw othah people's money with John Andrews peerin ovah my shouldah informin Fathah of evah wrong move I make."

"Then don't make any wrong moves." Fredie tries to lighten the mood, but Robart refuses to be cheered.

"That is easy faw you ta say, Golden Boy. I wish I had nevah laid eyes on Princeton. Those old codgers act like they have nevah been young in their lives. One little indiscretion and they label you a miscreant and altah your future foevah. I should go inta the law and take them all ta task for the hahm they have caused me."

Fredie considers reminding Rob he had been more like falling down drunk than a little tipsy, and, if rumors are correct, he was in danger of failing had he not been expelled for misconduct. But he does not like dissension, and he is embarrassed for his brother. He cannot imagine what he would be feeling if he had suffered a tongue lashing from their father.

"Look at the bright side, Rob. You can work at the bank long enough ta save what you need ta enlist. At wuhst, this development is a small setback. You nevah wanted ta go ta Princeton in the first place."

"Do you have any idea how long I will have ta work at a clerk's wage ta save the money ta…" Rob stops in mid thought. "I wondah if Fathah intends ta continue payin my livin expenses. He will, don't you think?"

"I have no way of knowin, but how much can your livin expenses be if you plan ta stay here in the house?"

"I assume I will, but still, a man needs money ta socialize. Surely…"

"Why don't you concentrate on gettin back inta his good graces, and I am sure evahthing will sort itself out."

"Oh, Fredie, I fear I will go mad here under Fathah's eye in this house and Andrews' at work. And you won't be here ta help. You'll be exactly where you've always wanted ta be—at college."

Rob is right, and again he is tempted to tell him he has brought his present state of affairs upon himself. He is unable to imagine losing a chance to go to college, but he has always thought he and his brother to be very different people.

"I wish Fathah had allowed you ta join the Georgia Militia ta begin with, and maybe things would have been different. Surely you can undahstand how disappointed he is—when he was terribly proud of you such a short time ago. We all had ta listen ta him tell anyone he talked with about you bein accepted inta Princeton, and no soonah were you gone than you were comin home."

Fredie takes pity on his crestfallen brother and changes the subject. "Let's not waste the day worryin. There's racin on the rivah, and evahone will be out and about soon. Let's make the most of this beautiful day."

Rob's demeanor immediately brightens at the mention of a social event. They rise from the table and Rob's eyes alight on Jude still standing in the corner.

"Why ah you still here, Boy? Don't you have some work you need ta be doin? If not, I am sure I can find you some."

"Ise fine, Suh. Jus waitin ta clear da table."

Jude immediately starts stacking the dishes to transport below. Rob would be disappointed to know his harsh words have not bothered him at all. In fact, he smiles as he heads for the kitchen to tell his mother. She laughs with him until he gently breaks the news that Daisy is leaving for Baltimore in two weeks.

Chapter 7
The Island

"As I have told you, I was born on the island of Saint Domingue, a beautiful, lush place, or at least it was when I was young. I was the youngest child in the family. I had an older sister and brother, and until I was seven or eight, we lived with our parents on a small plantation."

"Your family was allowed to own a plantation?" Diana interrupts.

"Yes, the Island way of life was quite different from what we know here. The French government did not have the rules regarding race America does. Blacks were allowed to own land if they had the money, and they socialized with white people. Many white men married Creole women, and their children were educated and enjoyed most of the same privileges white children did. On the plantation—more like a farm here—we raised sugar and tobacco with the help of our slaves."

"You had slaves! I thought we were against slavery. I didn't know colored people were allowed to own slaves!"

"People of color, even other slaves in a few instances, can own slaves in America. Black owners here have many more restrictions. In San Domingue the practice was more common. Many free black people or people of mixed race were prosperous. We had five slaves—a woman and four men. The men helped with the outside work, and Nance helped with the inside chores. I hope we treated them well. I was young and accustomed to that way of life—I am not certain how my parents or siblings treated them. My father was a white man, or certainly more white than black. My mother was Creole with some white blood. The combination produced my siblings and me, and they were as light as I. We have French ancestry as did most of the white

51

people on the Island, and we all spoke French. Well, not all of us. Slaves, for the most part, spoke a combination of French and a black dialect.

"We led a rather charmed life until the year 1789 or '90. My father, whom I adored, grew ill and died with little warning. My sister Josie married soon after. I think back on that time as a turning point, though things didn't really worsen until '93. I doubt my father could have prevented all the bad things that happened to our family, for he was much too white to have been able to survive the rebellion. I would like to believe he would have gotten us away from there, but I fear he would have been like everybody else, unwilling to accept life could change quickly and drastically."

"You mean being white was bad?"

"Not until '93. Like here, being white had advantages. My own father was first married to another lady, more white than black, but she died several years after they were married. They had a daughter whom they sent to France, as did many of the Islanders, to be educated in a boarding school. I didn't meet her, but I met her daughter many years later after I came to the States.

"My father was considerably older than my mother. Because of the age difference, my half-sister was long gone before my sister Josie was born. My mother's parents were dead, so after my father died, we were relieved when Josie married well. She became the second wife to a man named Auguste, and they had a beautiful little boy we called Emile. Auguste was French. His first wife had inherited three sugar plantations left in his control after she died. He too had children being educated in France."

"Wait—" Diana pulls away and peers into her face. "I am confused. Did your father have another wife or did Auguste? And whose children went to France to be educated? And who had Emile?"

"I'm sorry. I guess I need to slow down. Both my father and my brother-in-law Auguste had previous wives. Both had children; both sent them to France to be educated. Many families there did likewise. I never met my half-sister, and Josie never met either of her stepchildren. They both later died in France. My sister Josie married Auguste, and they had Emile, my nephew. Merè, Thomas, and I lived not far from their small family. Are you clear now?"

"I think so. Thomas was your brother?"

"Yes. As the sole male, he was the head of the household even though he was young."

"Alright. I understand now."

Diana lies back against her mother's side, takes her arm and places it around her.

"One night when I was in bed, we were startled by a banging on our door. Thomas opened the door, and I will never forget how Josie looked standing there with Emile. She was disheveled and scared, as if she might drop Emile at any moment. She had walked all the way to our house in the dark through the woods because she had been told by a couple of her female servants about talk of an impending rebellion. They feared she might be at risk if she were caught alone. Auguste was not home, and she didn't trust the male slaves to drive her. Because she feared they might be a part of the rebellion, she walked."

"How far?" Diana asks.

"Two miles—maybe three. I cannot say for sure because she came through the woods, not by the road."

"In the dark? She must have been terrified. Did they have snakes and wild animals on the Island?"

"Yes, they did. I understood how frightened she must have been to set out on her own with Emile. At first Merè was angry she would put herself and the baby at risk, but she began to catch some of Josie's fear. Thomas tried to calm everyone. He said he had heard nothing of any significance. After I got older, I doubted his claim because I learned a huge rebellion had taken place in France, our mother country, and the seeds of unrest must have traveled across the sea. I guess he hadn't wanted to scare us. For whatever reason, he decided to take Josie back to her home and wait for her husband. When I touched Josie, I understood immediately she should not go back, and I tried to tell them. I begged her not to go, but Thomas said I was a mere child, and they would return if Auguste had not arrived yet. I should have tried harder to persuade them; I felt…"

Again Diana pulls away. "Mama, stop! You are crying. I would never have asked you to tell me this story if I had known how much it would upset you!"

Diana wraps her arms tighter around her mother and buries her head in her chest. Jessie recognizes a coldness she has come to associate with Moses. The chill calms her. She tugs the quilt from the back of the sofa and tucks it around both of them.

"No, I need to tell this story. Someone needs to know it, and I have told no one. I am fine. Crying is not always a bad thing—perhaps I need to cry after all these years. I was much too old for my age back then, and

I have carried guilt because I did not stop what I knew in my being was going to be a bad thing."

"But you were a little girl. What could you have done? You tried to warn them."

"I know now, Sweetheart. I had not yet come to terms with this gift—this power—this curse—whatever it is I have. I did not yet even know I was unusual. I thought if I could sense things, surely others could, too. The sensations and forebodings were disturbing, but I didn't know how to talk to anyone about what I was experiencing."

She smiles down at her daughter. "See, sharing with you does help."

"I am glad, Mama, but if it is too hard, you can stop. You can always tell me later."

Unlike Diana, Jessie knows they are not always promised a later.

"Merè had to pull me away from Josie, and she and Thomas rode away with Elb, our driver. Thank God they left little Emile with us. I never saw either of them again. Elb was gone about an hour before he came tearing into the drive and threw himself at our door. I didn't need to be told what had happened. They were dead. He told Mama slaves from all over the island were on a rampage. They were killing and burning and doing all manner of horrible things. He told us Josie and Thomas were dead—that he was afraid to try to retrieve their bodies. He had fled. He had seen fires in the distance on his way home. He told Merè to bring me and come with him—Nance and he would take us somewhere safe. Mama hadn't wanted to go, but she was not herself, and I persuaded her to listen to him. They took us to Nance's sister's house. Her husband had bought her freedom some time ago. They owned a little place with a barn. We slept in the barn that night in some hay Elb piled up in a corner. I remember being hot and hay sticking to my clammy skin. I guess my mother and I were in shock. Emile woke crying, and, thank Providence, Nance's niece Susan was nursing a child. She fed Emile and actually went back to our house with us each day. Elb would drive us home; we would bathe, eat, make sure everything was unbothered, then spend each night in the barn. We had done this for a few days—I cannot remember exactly how long—when Auguste found us one morning. He was devastated, of course, and being a member of the military, he was privy to the details of what had happened. He had found Josie and Thomas still in the kitchen. He told us he had managed to bury their bodies. Knowing they received a proper burial was a comfort to my mother.

"Auguste had long been considered a friend to free blacks, almost a liaison on their behalf. He had imagined he had some protection against the mob. My mother pointed out his connections had done nothing to save her children, and he told us his greatest regret was he had not been around to protect us all. He assured us he would never have left if he had suspected such unrest. We believed his concern for us was genuine, so his later actions were hard to understand—they were completely out of character.

Jessie is quiet until Diana squirms in her arms. "What did he do later?"

Jessie holds her tighter and returns to her story. "I am getting ahead of myself. Auguste packed us up and took us to Port au Prince to a house that had belonged to his first wife. He told us we would be safer in the city, and he left to protect us a couple of black men for whom he had done favors. He promised they would protect us at all costs, and then he left to fight with other plantation and business owners to try to regain control of the Island. He came every week, sometimes every other week, to check on us and bring us supplies. We felt somewhat safe, but we were no better than prisoners, for we dared not show our light skins in public for fear someone might recognize us as slave-owning plantation owners.

"Merè continued to care for us, but she was nothing like she had been before we lost Josie and Thomas. We still had Susan as a wet nurse. Auguste was now paying her to care for his son. She and her own baby lived with us in the city. She got news from her mother who was in touch with her sister Nance who would pass messages to us about our plantation. We learned Nance and Elb were the only servants remaining. They had moved into our house and were caring for the livestock that hadn't been taken by our slaves who had run away. We were pleased to discover our home had not been burned, but we did not know if we could ever live there again.

"We lived this way for several years with times of relative peace when we thought we might be able to go home and resume some semblance of our previous lives. Those periods did not last. Militant black and mulatto leaders vied for power, and back and forth the tide turned until the once beautiful, lush island we had enjoyed became a wasteland. Food became scarce, and we saw less and less of Auguste. Merè had never recovered from all the losses—first her husband, then her two children, her way of life—I think she simply gave up. She died the year I turned thirteen leaving me alone with my nephew and the men Auguste had left to defend us."

"Oh Mama! I cannot imagine you dying and leaving me to care for a child all by myself! Were you terribly afraid?"

"I am sure I was. I know I missed my mother every day for years, but so much had happened, I was more numb than anything else. And I had Emile. He kept me sane. He was a beautiful child with a head full of curly, light hair. He could have passed for a girl! He was a delightful little boy even under hard circumstances. He had way too much energy to be cooped up in a house all day long. I remember spending much of my time trying to keep him occupied. He was intelligent beyond his years, a little sponge. I had no difficulty teaching him to read and write. He would help me clean or read to me as I did chores. We played games..."

"Mama, you're hurting me," Diana whispers.

Jessie immediately releases her daughter. "I am sorry. I guess I forgot..."

"It is fine. I want you to hold me, just not so tightly. You and Emile were alone all day long?"

"For some time after Merè died, at least one of the two men would be with us at night, but that didn't last. They were gone longer each day, then for days at a time. Those must have been terrifying times for Emile and me. I have blocked out a lot. Sometimes the mind protects itself when life becomes too hard. I know we still had some resources, and because Susan had become devoted to Emile, she stayed with us often. She, her mother, and Nance were a lifeline for us. Nance and Elb were able to grow crops and raise a few chickens, and they were generous enough to pass part of what they had on to us.

"I forget what year it was—it was not long after my mother died—one of our defenders knocked on the door and told me Auguste was gone. He had been part of a transport of what was left of the military presence on the Island. Just like that, he vanished," Jessie snaps her fingers, "and we were alone. Emile was four or five at the time, and his father simply left him behind. Maybe he had no choice—not then, at least."

"You mean Auguste left you—with his boy? Why? What kind of a father would do such a thing?"

Jessie has no answer. She shrugs her shoulders and sadly shakes her head.

"I am not proud of what I did next, but you must remember I was a young woman with a boy to care for. Though I didn't think of myself as young, I was barely more than a child looking after a child. Imagine it, Diana. I was a year or two older than you with no means of support and no real family to turn to."

Jessie wipes the tears that have wet Diana's face and places two fingers over her mouth when she starts to speak. "I must tell you this, Dear. You are mature as I was mature. You will understand.

"Of the two men guarding our door, one of them had let me know he would be glad to become a different kind of protector for me and my nephew if I would consent to be his wife. Young as I was, girls there had married younger, and, as I said, I was mature for my age, both physically and mentally. The plan might have been an opportune one, but the man was repulsive to me. Nonetheless, I had Emile's safety to think of as well as my own. I implied I would accept his offer in the future. I told him I was still grieving for my mother and the calamity we had endured. He said he would wait—a while. The deceit bought us several months of protection.

"The war took another turn, and even the mulattos and those who claimed no white blood were at odds. The leader of the mulatto faction to the south was defeated, but not without hundreds of casualties. One day my protector did not return. We had no access to food, and I was afraid to show either of our faces in daylight. I sent a message by Susan to Elb to come for us, but to be sure to come at night. I darkened my own face and Emil's with soot from the fireplace and waited. Elb showed up shortly after dusk, and the three of us drove back to the home we had fled years before. The house was in disrepair, and little was left of our holdings, but I was comforted by surroundings that reminded me of happier times. Because the fighting was mainly confined to the cities by then, the relative seclusion allowed us some opportunity to be outside. How wonderful the fresh air was after years of being inside for hours on end! Emile and I tended the garden while Elb kept guard to warn us of visitors. Nance, Elb, Emile, and I became a makeshift family. Nance and I cooked our meals, and the four of us shared the house. I do not know what we would have done without their kindness and loyalty, and now I know what I do of slavery, I appreciate them all the more. They did not have to share with us as they did. In fact, all we had could have been theirs. They risked their own lives to help us.

"Have you heard enough, Diana? Is this all too much to take in? Shall we continue later?"

"No, Mama! Not unless the memories are too hard for you. I want to know what happened to Nance and Elb and little Emile!"

Jessie rose, stoked the fire, poured them each a glass of water from the pitcher, and rejoined Diana under the quilt.

"Life finally settled down somewhat. By the time Emile was thirteen or fourteen, the Island was calm enough for trade with other countries to reconvene. He was strong and intelligent and lucky enough to secure work at one of the shipping docks. He worked his way up to a clerk, and then, because he was the only white person around, a factor from Virginia took an interest in him and gave him a job in the States."

"Did you go with him, Mama?"

"No, not then. I wanted to go with him. Watching him sail away was almost as hard as the loss of my other family members. I remember being afraid I would never see him again. America was far away and huge; I could not imagine how I would be able to locate him if we were parted. I didn't have the money for passage, nor did I have anything waiting for me here like he did. I stayed for a couple of years. I managed to make some money sewing, selling baked goods, produce I had preserved, eggs we could spare.

"One day I heard the United States had a new president who was talking about cutting off trade relations with the Island. Emile had sent me letters, so I had the address of a boarding house where he was living. If I were to have any hope of moving to America, I must act quickly. I used the money I had saved to sail to New Orleans on a trading ship— they often sold passage to people for the return trip after they dropped their freight. The voyage was unpleasant, but I was young and healthy from living on the farm where I had decent food and fresh air. I arrived in America not much worse for the experience. I wrote to Emile, but he did not respond. I later learned he had married.

"I spent a few months in which every moment was occupied with trying to find food and a place to sleep. Fortunately, I met two free women of mixed race who helped me improve my sewing and taught me to cook. I was content enough for some time with them, but I had become involved with a man to whom I was obligated for my advancement. To escape him, I needed to make a new life somewhere else.

"At last, I found an address for the factoring house in Virginia where Emile was employed. I wrote to the factor, and he forwarded my letter to him in Savannah where he was working. You can imagine how excited I was to receive a letter from my nephew. He put me in touch with the cousin I mentioned earlier—the daughter of my half-sister whom I had never met. She was seeking a cook and housekeeper. Because the position provided an opportunity to break away from the man whose hold on me I considered unhealthy, I moved to Baltimore to work for my half-niece, though she never knew of our relationship. When her husband was posted overseas, I moved to Savannah and worked for the Barrets, and there, I was lucky enough to meet Moses and Lavinie. Through them, I received the greatest blessing of my life—you!"

"But what happened to Nance and Elb? Did Emile find his father? Where is Emile? Do you ever hear from him?"

"I signed my property over to Nance and Elb. They could neither read nor write, so we had no way to correspond. I like to think of them on our farm still, but they would be quite old by now. I pray they have been rewarded for their kindness with a long and happy life. Emile tried to reach his father who we had discovered was living with cousins in Louisiana, but his letters went unanswered. Emile has been successful because the people here do not know he is of mixed race."

"You mean his father never responded? Did he go see him? Surely he would want to help him."

"Honey, if Auguste had wanted to help his son, he could have sent for him during the intermittent times of peace. Apparently, Auguste did not want Emile in America with him. As you know, not a single drop of black blood would be welcome in a white family, and Auguste may have feared Emile's features would expose the truth—he had a mixed race family in Saint Domingue. Whatever the reason, his abandonment was an unalterable source of pain for Emile. He quit trying to contact him and vowed to forget he ever had a father."

"How sad! Do you still communicate with Emile? Have you seen him since you came to the States?"

"Yes, I used to see a lot of him, but his life and mine are too different. He passes for a white man. He cannot possibly acknowledge me as family, so we now correspond occasionally by letter. I am happy for him, and he has helped me in many ways. I like to think he still loves me and will come to our aid should we need help in the future."

"Oh, Mama, how awful for you!" Diana actually climbs into Jessie's lap and twines her arms around her neck. She kisses her cheek and lies with her head on her shoulder. "Thank Providence we don't live where they might kill you because you appear white!"

"I know, Diana, but you are old enough to know bad things happen to people here, too. You mustn't forget what happened to your father or your Papa Moses. In America, people are often mistreated, even killed because they are black. The advantages of a comfortable home, enough to eat, and nice clothes do not mean we are completely safe. We must still beware of people wishing to do us harm. You don't have to worry now because you have me, but I will not always be with you. You must understand the dangers. I have told you my story, in part, to make you cautious. We must never become complacent. Do you understand me, Diana?"

"I do, Mama. I do." Diana's face is solemn.

"One minute I am scolding you for being too serious; the next I am warning you of the horrors that can befall you. What am I thinking?"

"You are thinking about what is best for me, and I am glad. Now you've told me, you don't have to protect us by yourself. We will look out for each other."

"What did I ever do to deserve you, Sweet Girl?"

"You saved your nephew and you survived, and then you took in a child who would have been alone in the world; that's what you did to deserve me. I will make you glad you did!"

"Never has a day gone by that I would not choose you all over again. If not for Lavinie and Rube, I would not have known the joy of being a mother."

The two sit before the fire, Jessie stroking Diana's head on her shoulder until the weight of the girl numbs her legs.

"Now, it's off to bed for both of us. We have a busy day ahead."

After another round of hugs, Diana goes to her room and Jessie drags her tired frame across the room to her bed. She is exhausted from telling her story, and it is all she can do to undress before falling into bed. The minute she sleeps, Moses comes to her.

"Do you think Diana is mature enough to handle this knowledge?" she asks him.

"Jus think on whut your life like at dat age. Her strong an she got a smawt haid on dose lil shouldahs. Yo tale good fo her ta know an good fo you ta tell. You be carryin aw dat mess way too long."

"If Frederick had told Abby our story, the outcome might have been different!"

"You sholy knows wy he dint. You ain ebben tell me aw dat heartache. Her know now, an her sad he dint trust er nuff to tell da truff."

"Remind her of the consequences of his story becoming public knowledge. True, he was protecting himself, but he was also protecting her and the children."

"Her say he right. Her coudden handle da truff."

"She had more to contend with than one secret, and she imagined she had no one to confide in. I wish she had spoken to Bette or me before she did what she did, but there is no changing the past."

"Yessum, her say they's no use cryin ovah spilt milk."

Jessie sleeps in Moses' arms, and for the first time, she has a dream within a dream. She is in Savannah keeping vigil over her own. She stops by Frederick's room and sits on the bed beside him. She imagines him a young boy. She imagines his hunger, his fear. She has a hard time picturing the man before her sleeping in a pile of hay, hoeing a garden, living at the mercy of people whom he holds in such low regard today. She places a spectral hand on his cheek to stroke the stubble he never allows during the day. He twitches in his sleep. Can he feel her touch? If he does, does it bring him comfort or pain? Though he has not turned out to be the man she thought him, he has suffered enough for a lifetime. She kisses his cheek and is rewarded with a sense of peace. She goes to the window, opens it, and sits upon the sill. Morning will find her there.

When Jessie awakes, she realizes it was not she who visited Frederick in her dreams. It was Abby.

Chapter 8
A Close Call

Savannah, Georgia—1845

Minda prepares breakfast with an enthusiasm she would not have thought possible a year ago. She turns out a skillet full of golden brown biscuits onto a serving plate then checks a tub of yeasted dough rising close to the fireplace with which she will make dinner rolls and fruit pastries. The whole household has benefitted from Minda's improved cooking skills. The Barret children are now eager to dine, whereas before they dragged themselves to the table because attendance at meals was expected of them, and they had to eat. Minda's own family loves their improved meals in their kitchen across the hall.

The first month after Daisy moved with her young mistress to Baltimore, Minda revealed little interest in anything or anyone around her. Even her boys had a hard time lifting her spirits. Though she was amenable enough to making the trek to the Stiles' house each day, the girlish side of her who laughed and joked with her mother and sister, the one who good-naturedly chided her sons into doing what she wanted them to do, seemed to have left with Daisy. For a while, she put one foot in front of the other and tried to pretend she did not suffer a hole in her heart the size of a cantaloupe. Mammy was close to despairing of ever seeing her daughter whole again when one morning Minda showed up a bit less glum, with each day after showing improvement until, finally, the old Minda was back. Since then, she has become a confident, relatively content version, one as new to herself as to the others.

One downside to Minda's metamorphosis is renewed interest from Frederick. Just as he was about to give up on her as both cook and mistress, he was encouraged by the changes. His palate registered the budding transformation before his mind did. After enjoying a particularly tasty slice of coconut cake one day, he went below to discover who was responsible for the unusual offering. He caught Minda, unaware of his presence outside the doorway, humming as she flitted around the room. He was amazed at how much younger she seemed, and her renewed vigor had re-inspired his.

Though Minda is still not overly eager to meet him at her door, she exhibits some energy in bed as opposed to quiet, still acceptance. Frederick has been different with Minda than he was with his wives from the first time he took her roughly from behind on the boys' bed. Their coupling has always lacked any of the tenderness he exhibited with them. Minda has often wondered why he has kept coming back. The closest to a sign of affection from him has been a light hand placed on her shoulder or the small of her back. Now, he is staying longer in her presence, even conversing with her before or after the act. She no longer has the desire to throw up after his visits, and she can almost imagine why any woman would have wanted to marry him. He is the only man she has ever experienced, and life can be lonely with just the boys for company at night.

Mammy, like Frederick, determines the change in Minda is due to the positive influence in her association with the Stiles. They are correct, in part, but Minda has not told even Mammy the real reason for her elevated spirits. She dares not for fear she will tell Dovie and Dovie, who is becoming more daring in her exploits, will do something to jeopardize her and her sons' relationship with Bette and her servants. Only Jude and Ish know what goes on at the Stiles, and both have been sworn to secrecy. Minda has been unusually graphic with the details of what can happen to them if the master finds out they are all learning to read and write. The least of these, the termination of their lessons, is enough to keep both boys quiet, even though they want nothing more than to share the most important news of their lives with their cousins. They would like for Deke and Ben—even little Lizzy—to have the same opportunity. Someday, Minda has promised them, sharing their knowledge may be possible, but not now. Bette has admonished them as well.

Today, Minda has made plenty of biscuits. She sets a warm plate on the plank table in front of Mammy, Dovie, Cressa, Lizzy, and Ben. Lew and the other boys are finishing up their chores.

"Doze biscuit sho looks fine, an dat smell bring da boys runnin," Mammy says.

"They do smells delicious," Minda agrees.

"They do smells delicious!" Dovie mocks. "Mama, Minda turnin inta a wite gul righ hyur fo our eyes!"

Minda laughs, but she is embarrassed. Her lessons are having some effect on how she talks. She has explained to Bette that sometimes she pictures the words in her head, the way they look on the page. She is often corrected by Bette when she mispronounces them. Frederick has even commented on the change in her speech. She blamed the influence of Pearl and Cook.

This is not the first time Dovie has pointed out the difference, and Minda regrets keeping a secret from the two women she loves most, and especially Mammy.

"I mus say dat dese biscuits is delicious," Dovie persists, "an theys sho tastes good wid dese fried tatahs an matahs. You fix us some uh da massah bacon or some uh dat ham, wese be eatin bout as good as theys does upstair."

"I cain be takin meat from da sto'room. Da massah keep a shawp eye on da meat."

"Youse got da key, doan cha? He naw goan spect nuthin a piece off da side uh one uh dem ham or da side a bacon go missin."

"I takes da risk fo nuff ta season da beans, but no way Ise goan cut nuff ta feed evahbidy a piece a ham or bacon."

"Her right, Dovie. Lebe her lone," Mammy scolds. "I tells you agin, Gul, you bettah watch yosef. I doan knows whut got inta you, bu you sho goan git yosef in a worl a trouble. They's ain nobidy roun hyur ta step tween you an da massah you git sideway wid em. Wid Mizz Mattie goan, nobidy goan say nothin him take da whip ta you."

"Massah ain nevah whip nobidy," Dovie scoffs. "Sides, Minda kin git tween us. She git tween him an da mattress offen nuff."

Mammy rises and cuffs Dovie on the head. "Doan you be tawkin dat trash roun dese chilren. I be takin da whip ta you mysef you keep ackin lack a heathen in dis house."

Minda opens her mouth to say something but thinks better of it. Both Mammy and Minda worry about Dovie and wonder if her behavior has grown worse because Minda has been out of the house every day, maybe because Dovie is jealous.

Minda changes the subject. "Massah say Ise goin ta da Stiles jus three day a week now I gits good in da kitchen."

"Dat probly naw ware da massah think youse good," Dovie dares, and she receives another cuff on the side of her head for the effort. Everyone is distracted by the boys who come sailing through the door and plop down on the bench in their customary places.

"Doze biscuits look wondaful, Mama!" Jude states as he grabs one and takes a third of it in one bite.

"Hab you wursh dose hans uh yose, Boys?" Minda interjects over Dovie's mutterings about *wondaful biscuits.*

"Aw, Auntie, wese jus drawin watah an it splash aw ovah ah hans!" Deke tries.

"An Jude jus be carryin chamber pots. Da both uh you go wursh dem hans now."

Both rise and move to the basin where they quickly dip their hands and dry them on the flour sack lying beside it. Minda sighs and gives up.

Lew makes his way to the table, and the family settles into a conversation about how the day has gone and what they expect from the rest of it. Minda slips away to the kitchen. The morning meal is still hard for her, for she feels her daughter's absence most when the family is together in the morning. The missies' habit of sleeping late had provided the best opportunity for Daisy to visit with her. If Mrs. Stiles had made her offer when Daisy was young, she thinks, she might be able to communicate with her daughter still. The tidbits she receives now are from Frederick when he is in a talkative mood. One of the advantages of their improved association is she feels more comfortable asking after Mattie and Daisy. Frederick has even started inquiring about Daisy when he writes Mattie, and he offers news to Minda as he would the gift of a bag of sugar or an article of clothing for her or the boys. Minda's efforts to stay on friendly terms with him have proven more important since Mattie has broken off her relationship with Thomas Stiles and won't be returning anytime soon. The oldest Barret daughter is enamored with a young army captain with a promising future, and even better from Frederick's perspective, a family with an honorable name. Frederick had been incensed when he first received Mattie's letter, but he had soon calmed down when Bette had shown up to assure him the break was for the best, even claiming she had never deemed the two a good match. She had further stroked his ego by confiding in him her belief that Mattie's sensitive nature and lofty morals make her incompatible with her own more worldly Thomas. Frederick has not yet met the new beau but likes what he has learned about him. He has gone as far as to read portions of Mattie's letters to Minda, especially any tidbits concerning Daisy. Mattie has written she is healthy and fits in well at the Howe household. Minda hangs onto every word, seeing some of them take form in her mind, but she never learns what any mother in her position would long to know. Does Daisy miss her family? Does Mr. Howe keep his distance? Is she given enough to eat, and do the Howe servants resent her? What clothing is she provided, and what does the young girl do with her Sunday off? Daisy is eighteen years old now, older than many girls whose masters want them to marry and produce children who will add to the family wealth. Minda is glad Frederick isn't in the least interested in accumulating more slaves, but she would like her daughter to have a companion someday, and not the kind she herself has had in Frederick.

Minda's demeanor lightens as she sets off for the Stiles. She is smiling by the time Cook opens the back door.

"Well, jus look what the cat drug in!"

Minda has long given up on a response since Cook has met her with this same greeting or some variation almost every morning since she has been coming.

"What we makin taday, Cookie?" she asks.

"We not cookin atall," Cook states, and continues when the smile drops from Minda's face. "Cause Mizz Bette say you ta come dreckly ta her now you comin less."

"Oh," Minda says. She will miss the time with Cook.

"You ta come in here fo dinnah while da massah home. We ketch up then," Cook tells her.

The smile returns to Minda's face as she makes her way unattended up the stairs where she finds Bette and Pearl sitting in her bedroom parlor as usual. After greeting Minda, Pearl sets up the small wooden table for the lessons.

"You have spent enough time on the alphabet and my makeshift lists. You ah ready ta move on ta Mr. Webstah's spellin book."

Minda eagerly takes the text in her hand. She loves the feel of the book. She holds it to her nose and inhales the scent of leather.

"Da—" she begins, then corrects herself. "The boys be excited!' Minda exclaims.

"Ish will when he is ready faw it, but I have somethin else faw Jude. We ah still usin the spellah, but I have stawted givin him stories ta read. He is learnin at such a clip, I have a hawd time keepin up with his progress." Bette glances at Minda, then adds, "You, too, ah doin wondahfully. You will be readin his new book soon."

"You doan have ta tell me Jude be way smawtah dan me. That boy know things I ain nevah gonna know."

"It's not that he is smawtah, Minda. He has youth on his side. Young people tend ta learn ta read and write easiuh than adults. You have done amazingly well considerin you began as late as you did, but it is always best ta stawt eahly. Ish will be readin evahthin he can lay his hands on before long. You must not be discouraged if you take a little longah.

They do not yet have the responsibilities and worries you have ta clear your mind of in awdah ta concentrate."

"I doan know, Mizz Stiles. Jude think way too hawd on mattahs he bess naw think on atall. Sometime he a oldah soul dan me. I am scairt fo him, Missus, dat he gonna git hissef in a trouble with dat tempah of his."

"Jude does have a lot of angah, but, if we can channel his enahgy and give him hope, he may be patient faw change. I am still optimistic, because of your relationship with his fathah," Bette says, "he may be pahsuaded someday ta set him free. In the meantime, we can prepare him faw that day and try ta keep him out of trouble."

Bette has become more than a teacher to Minda—she has become a confidante. Since Minda has been unable to share the news of her learning with her mother, sister, or brother, she has begun to talk openly with Bette, something she could never have imagined a year ago.

"I been tryin ta be bettah with da massah fo a wile now. I hopin if he feel mo kinely ta me, he might be willin ta set the chilren free when he pass."

"Use your advantage where you can. In your situation, I would do about anything ta help my children, and you should nevah feel bad when you do. Now let's begin. See how much of the title of this book you can sound out."

Minda concentrates hard. Running her finger under the words she slowly enunciates, "The…" She stops and glances up at Bette. "This one too long fo me," she admits.

"It reads *elementary*," Bette provides. "It means *basic* or *easily undahstood*."

"I doan know bout dat!" Both women laugh.

"The Elementary Spelling Book," Minda sounds out.

"Very good! You…"

Both women startle when they are interrupted by a loud call from below.

"Bette, you up there?" a masculine voice Minda assumes belongs to Clarence Stiles calls up the stairs.

Bette jumps from her chair and pulls Minda from hers. "Quickly, put the book undah the cushion and help me break this table down!" Bette commands. Minda has never heard her so forceful. "He mustn't catch us at this!"

They have propped the table against the wall with the chairs when they hear Clarence mounting the stairs. Bette takes Minda by the arm, whispers, "I will handle him," and reaches the door where they face Clarence who has attained the upstairs breezeway.

"So I may assure Mr. Barret your cookin lessons ah progressin nicely, Minda?" she asks.

"Yessum, Mizz Stiles, an I mos b'holden fo da chance ta be a bettah cook fo da massah an his fambly," Minda answers.

"Commendable! Then you can tell him Cook will be glad ta continue faw as long as he wishes."

"Yessum," Minda repeats. With head bowed she moves around Mr. Stiles and cannot rush down the stairs fast enough. Bette's soft voice follows her.

"Clarence, ta whatevah do I owe this pleasant suhprise? It is unlike you ta come home this early!"

Minda does not catch his reply before she pushes through into the kitchen where she leans against the wall and attempts to calm herself. Pearl is sitting at the table and Cook is stirring a pot on the stove. Her sudden entry scares them both. Cook stops what she is doing when she notices Minda's expression, and Pearl jumps up and starts toward her.

"What happen?" Pearl asks. "You look like you see a haint."

"Mr. Stiles awmos ketch us!"

"You mean the massah home?" Pearl gasps. "He nevah git home this early. I keep an eye out from the upstair balcony but nevah this soon. Do he know what you two be doin?"

"No, we clear da table an chairs an hide da book fo he see us, bu he scare da Jesu ouddah us!"

"Come on an sit a spell, Minda. Calm yosef. I have somethin on the table fo you know it," Cook says.

"No, I bettah go. I need ta pull mysef tagathah fo I go back ta da kitchen."

"You be safe in here," Pearl tries to console her, but Minda is already on her way out.

"I see you two in a coupla days," she promises before she closes the door behind her.

Instead of going back to the mansion, she makes her way to the house in Yamacraw. She knows the danger has passed, yet she is still frightened. The walk calms her, yet she clutches her stomach as she lies on her bed in the front room. She tries to understand why she is frightened. For the first time, she acknowledges how important the trips to the Stiles' house have become to her. She would be devastated by the loss of the connection to Miss Bette, Pearl, and Cook, and the boys would be even more heartbroken to lose their lessons. Too, she would hate to face Frederick's wrath, especially since she has recently become somewhat accepting of her situation. Finally, she can pinpoint what frightens her most. Bette herself was badly shaken, and if a white woman as strong and as decent as she is afraid, there is indeed something to fear.

She lies on her bed as long as she dares before she rises. If what she is doing is dangerous, she must do what she has always done when faced with a crisis. She will talk to her mother. She goes in search of Mammy.

Chapter 9
Household Matters

Savannah, Georgia—1845

"Good morning, Fathah."

Frederick drops the pen he is holding when Rob takes the chair across the table from him.

"To what do I owe this unusual pleasure, Son?"

Robart has taken care with his appearance, his dark hair, full as is the style, combed back behind his ears, his beard a little longer than his father would like but a common length with his peers. It is neatly trimmed to leave a rounded bare shape like the letter *W* around his mouth. Fastidious always, Frederick has never worn a beard for he thinks them unsanitary, but he has admitted Robart's gives him a mature, distinguished look.

"I cannot recall the last time I've laid eyes on you this early in the day. Are you missing your sisters?"

"I do miss Ella and Maxie. The house is quiet with them away, but I do not miss a pawlah full of young swains fawnin ovah Ella."

"I know. If we could not count on Maxie's good sense to chaperone them, one of us would have to be present every evening to keep an eye on the young men. Not even Ella can charm Maxie enough to keep her from running straight to me if she thinks one of them is out of line. I wonder how Mother Middleton is managing."

Both men laugh as they imagine the rather dour Matilda Middleton dealing with the vibrant Ella. They agree Hickory Grove may be as lively as it has ever been. Even Frederick's stern and pious mother-in-law has not been able to curb Ella's enthusiasm. The widow writes she has been kept busy arranging one social gathering after another in an effort to keep the girls and their cousins entertained. Frederick almost pities her.

"I would still put my money on Grandmothah." Frederick nods in agreement.

"Some of the guys and I ah crossin ovah inta Carolina today ta hunt some field birds. Thought we would stawt eahly ta make the most of our weekend."

"Wise of you! I would enjoy a fine mess of fried quail. Who makes up your party?"

"Jeffry Daniel, Eliot Gordon, and Frenchie Willis." Knowing his father's dislike for one of his friends, he speaks the name quickly. As usual, the man is attentive to detail.

"Eliot Gordon? Robart, we have discussed before the importance of being selective in the company you keep, have we not?"

"Yes, Suh, but surely you agree the Gordon name is not one ta scoff at. His fathah is a well-respected man, not just in Savannah but all along the coast. Eliot's grandfathah was wounded in defense of the Republic in '75. How can you object ta an association with so noble a lineage?"

"I certainly have no objection to Eliot's grandfather Charles or his father James. It is with young Eliot himself I have concern. If rumors are to be believed, both his elders are displeased with his gambling, dalliances, and fisticuffs. You are quite capable of causing enough worry on your own without the unsavory influence of Eliot Gordon."

This is a topic with which Rob needs to deal carefully for he too has been accused of at least two of the three offenses.

"Surely you ah not goin ta judge a man's wuth by infuhmation attained from waggin tongues spreadin gossip on the Green. You've met Eliot. Does he not present himself a true gentleman?"

Frederick is not willing to admit he has taken a dislike to the young man, in part, because of his attentions to Ella. Though a mere fourteen, she has drawn the eye of older men, one of them being Gordon. He has already planted a seed of discouragement in his middle daughter's ear regarding the young man, and he thinks she will heed his warning, but after Mattie's decampment, he is none too sure. He has not been privy to every exchange between Ella and Eliot, and the lack of control he has over the situation makes him uncomfortable. Though courteous enough, the young man appears far too forward with his daughter, and Ella herself has been unwise in her encouragement of him.

"Wagging tongues can be heard in locations other than the Green. I've learned gentleman have a way of passing along judgments, as well, and you need to make sure you do not become any more of a topic for discussion than you already have with that Princeton debacle of yours. At least try to be an elevating force in your association with him if you insist on keeping company with the young man."

"Of course." Robart clears his throat and reveals the real reason he has arisen at this ungodly hour on a Saturday. "And do you think you can give me an advance on my allowance as we ah ta be stayin in Carolina tanight? I am in need of pocket money ta pay faw food and lodgin."

Robart jumps at the force with which Frederick's coffee cup meets the dining table.

"This, too, we have discussed, Robart. The allowance of last month was to be your last. I have supplemented your income for a year to give you a chance to progress at the bank. Have you spent everything you've earned? Have you nothing set aside for this grand plan of yours to enter the military?"

"I have been frugal, but you know as a membah of the board how penurious the wage they pay first-year clerks is. I anticipate an advancement any day, and when I receive it, I should no longah need assistance."

Frederick would appear calm if not for the flush brightening his cheeks and the ridge of his aquiline nose.

"Your brother away at school requires less assistance than you, Rob, and he has no job at all. He manages to live frugally and attend his classes and receive high marks from his professors. Why can you not learn from his example?"

Many responses come to Rob's mind, but he cannot utter them if he hopes to receive money for his venture across the river.

"I am as proud of Fredie as you ah, but what need has he of money when all he does is study? His food is provided, and he has little time faw socializin as I must do here if I am ta excel. You know the importance of bein out and about, and in awdah ta do so, one requires money ta put one's best foot fahwahd."

Frederick cannot refute his point. He has often spoken of the difficulty he faced in presenting the image he wanted when he first came to this country as a lad a year younger than Robart. He sits quietly gazing at his son. He is tempted to refuse assistance, but Rob will accompany the other young men anyway. He cannot stand the thought of him being unable to pay his own way and having to rely on the others to cover for him. He fears his son's actions will also reflect badly on him. Frederick sighs and stands to leave the table.

"Follow me. I will assist you this time, but if you cannot manage your own money, I will insist you turn your finances over to me while you live under my roof, and I will help you learn to be a better manager of what you consider your paltry salary. Too, I hope you are working hard to make a name for yourself, for I have heard nothing yet of a promotion in the works for you. Do not assume you will automatically advance because of time employed. That is not how business works, Son."

Again, Rob has much he would like to say. He has told his friends how he detests the menial job and how he longs for the day he can leave the stuffy confines behind to enter the service for which he is better suited. Unfortunately, he has not yet determined a way to save the money needed to join the military. Until an opportunity more proportionate to his ability comes along, he will bide his time and bite his tongue.

"I assure you I am doin all management expects of me and more at the bank."

Rob is relieved when his father unlocks his desk drawer to hand him several bills. If Frederick had known the truth, he would not have done so, for at work Rob has become adept at doing as little as possible, and after work and on the weekends he throws his money about as if he has plenty. He also drinks far more than is advisable.

"Remember, make this last for I will not be easily persuaded to give you more."

After Rob leaves, Frederick sits where he is at his desk for some time, his expression melancholy. After a bit, the letter lying open on the desktop catches his eye. He smiles as he dwells on the content. His cousin Brigitte is moving back to Savannah! Sad as news of her husband's death has made him, the promise of his vivacious cousin's company is delightful. Alexis Maxwell had become a dear friend, and no one had been more surprised or saddened by his sudden death from a suspected heart attack while aboard a Navy vessel. Frederick had written the grieving widow of his regrets and offered his personal assistance, and now she is taking him up on his offer.

He withdraws stationery from a drawer in his desk and writes a hasty reply, an invitation to stay with them here at Shady Manor until he can help her find suitable, permanent lodging elsewhere. Both her sons, Jeffrey and young Fred—his own namesake—are away at school leaving her no choice but to travel alone. No genteel woman should have to face the difficulties she endures without a man to help her, Frederick writes, and he assures her he relishes the role of supporter and advocate if they are roles she will allow him to play.

Please join us in November when the girls return from Virginia. I eagerly await your arrival, but due to propriety, it will be best to wait upon the girls' return. As platonic as you and I know our association to be, convention would frown upon a widow staying with a widower and his son without the requisite presence of other females. Too, I know you would find my sole company quite tame.

After finishing his letter, he picks hers up from the desk top to place in the drawer below. The envelope's removal leaves a bright rectangle on the mahogany surface. He runs his finger through the surrounding dust. Upon further inspection, he finds the whole parlor in need of a thorough cleaning, floors included. He walks from room to room calling Dovie's name, but she does not reply. He can find her nowhere. He takes the stairs to the basement. He walks up behind Minda, encircles her waist with his left hand and cups her right breast with the other. He knows she has heard his approach when she doesn't stiffen.

"Where is everyone?" he asks.

"Mama cross da way in the launry," she answers.

"Where is Dovie?"

"I ain sho," Minda replies.

"You go on back to your house. I will be along shortly," he orders.

"Yessuh," she answers simply, but she actually smiles at him before he leaves. She has not offered any physical resistance to his requests after the first few encounters, but recently he has perceived an acceptance of her role. He is glad now, though at one time that obvious resistance had been part of the attraction. There was something exciting about the secrecy and the domination. After all, If he had been seeking willingness and affection, he would have turned to his wife, first Luella then Abby. But as the years have passed and they are gone, he has missed companionship and tenderness. The change in Minda is comforting, enticing even. He wants to spend time with her, especially since both her boys are busy here at the house.

Frederick leaves Minda to cross the breezeway where he finds Mammy elbow deep in a tub of sudsy water. "Where's Dovie?" he asks again.

Mammy drops the bed sheet she has in her hand and shrieks, "Good Lawd, Massah, you done scairt da life ouddah me!"

"Sorry to frighten you, Mammy, but I have searched for Dovie all over the house, and she is nowhere to be found. Do you have any idea where she is since I have given her no permission to be off the grounds?"

"Her be roun hyur somewhar, Massah. I fine er fo you."

Mammy wipes her hands on her skirt and moves toward the door.

"I don't have time to wait around while you do. Will you please tell her I want the house dusted and floors cleaned before I return, or she is going to wish they were?"

"I tells er, Massah. Wen you thinkin ta be back?"

"She may have a couple of hours. The girl is trying my patience. I am beginning to wonder why I keep her."

"Her straighten up an do lack she spose ta, Massah. I sees ta it mysef."

"And don't be doing her work for her. Don't think I haven't seen you cleaning upstairs. Tell Dovie I want to speak with her this afternoon."

"I tells her," Mammy repeats.

He suffers a twinge of remorse for making Mammy search for her wayward daughter. She is a loyal servant. For a minute he thinks of the worry and extra work Dovie must cause her. He should have had Lewis find her.

The sultry air clears Frederick's mind of the unpleasant subject of Dovie. Unlike many of his neighbors, he loves the humid heat of the low South. If he were assured he would not be observed, he would strip down to his pants like he did as a child. The urge passes quickly, however. He is appropriately dressed in a suit like the one he wears daily to the office, for he has an image to uphold. He has always been concerned with his appearance, thinks the extra effort is a small price to pay for success, and not a day goes by that he is not grateful for the life he has here. He may miss the feel of the sun on his bare back, but that is all he misses about the Island. He is thankful, though, for the tolerance for the Savannah climate he acquired in his previous life, for many of his family and neighbors find it oppressive. They all want to flee north as soon as the temperatures begin to rise, but Frederick is quite content to stay close to home and his businesses.

Frederick decides to make a detour to his store. He picks out a bonnet in a yellow and pink flowered material and a small container of coconut to take to Minda. He has a piece of green gingham fabric cut for Mammy an apron. Before he leaves the store, he takes a stick of horehound candy from a jar on the counter for Ish as he has several times before. He never acquires anything for Jude and certainly not for the other children in the quarters. Something about the crippled boy moves him. He has studied Ish when the child was unaware, and he tells Minda he admires the way he has never sought pity or concessions because of his malformation. He tries to do as much as the other servants his age, even more. Frederick admires initiative, and if he were to allow himself to acknowledge the connection, he might have thought the trait one acquired from him. He secretly shares Minda's fear that the boy's lameness is a sign of God's displeasure with them for giving the boy life while he was a married man. Introspection is not Frederick's strong suit.

He refuses to dwell on unpleasant memories or his own shortcomings. He tells himself the candy is simply a treat for a child who has earned it, much as he rewards Minda when she pleases him.

On the way to Yamacraw, he remembers to post the letter to Brigitte Maxwell.

Chapter 10
Out Without a Pass

Savannah, Georgia—1845

Jude methodically goes room to room, floor to floor, with a bucket of coal. He returns to the basement after supplying each room, and though the work is strenuous, he's done it so often and for so long, it causes him little strain. He is finally putting on weight, and he is taller than his mother—almost as tall as Lew. Muscles bulge as he shovels coal into the fireplaces and the bins beside them. His hands are black from the coal also smearing his face, shirt front, and trousers. He is making sure each room is equipped for the fall evenings ahead. The house has been abuzz all day in preparation for the homecoming of Ella and Maxie. Even Dovie has been making beds, dusting furniture, down on hands and knees scrubbing floors and baseboards. The sight is not as unusual as it once was. Since Frederick called her to him and told her she was in jeopardy of being sold, Dovie has been working like the slave she is. Her industry has made for a cleaner house, but a more irritable Dovie. Even Ben steers clear of her as much as possible.

Jude has something on his mind besides the task at hand. He is imagining himself as Frank, the hero of the latest book Mrs. Stiles has given him. Though the text has words he cannot pronounce or understand, he has been following her instructions. Each night as he reads by lamplight, he stops occasionally to jot down a word or two. He takes his list the next morning to Bette's kitchen where they have moved their sessions. Since she and his mother were almost caught, they have started having their lessons in the kitchen, the last place Mr. Stiles would enter if he came home unexpectedly. Jude takes his turn each morning after Frederick has left for work. Cook feeds him since he is missing breakfast at the mansion. Minda has told the adults in the family what they are doing, so they no longer have to sneak around or guard their language though Minda has warned him to be careful around Aunt Dovie because the whole scheme makes her angry. Then again, everything makes Dovie angry these days, maybe because she hasn't seen Clell for months. The railroad work moved north and took Clell with it.

Jude knows his mama is about to leave for the evening, and, as usual, he goes to the kitchen to say goodbye. His timing is perfect as she is hanging her dishrag and drying cloth on a peg as she does at the end of each work day.

"You look like you been wallowin in a coal bin, Chile. Was they any coal left ta burn time you finish?"

Jude laughs. "I take a dip in the rivah, if that awright with you. Wash this dirt offah me."

"You gonna drown in that rivah, you not careful."

"I tole you I can swim now. I nevah go out so far I cain git back."

"I still doan undahstan where you be learnin ta swim. Nobidy we knows swim."

"I jus watch some uthah boys down at the rivah, an I do what they do. Ain that hawd. I not get out far nough fo the current ta catch me. We be down by the lil bay right beside the Culvuhson warf—you know the one I mean?"

"I do. But you git caught out aftah dawk, you knows whut gonna happen—an it woan be good."

"I try ta be home fo dawk, bu if I ain, doan go worryin. I can take care uh mysef."

"I knows you think you can."

Minda pulls Jude close. He squirms, but she holds him tighter.

"I doan know what I do somethin happen ta you or Ish. I awready loss Daisy. I cain lose one uh you."

"I know, Mama. I be careful. Nobidy care bout somebidy like me. I too young ta stir up much concern."

"Yo chilehood jus bout ovah, Jude. You lookin mo like a man evah day."

Jude breaks loose. "You thinks so, Mama. I lookin like a man?"

Minda laughs and tugs his short hair. "You may look like a man, but you a long way from it, an you bess membah dat."

Jude walks Minda to the gate, then returns to the well to help Deke and Ish fill the water pails they carry to their designated places throughout the house. Ish has been assigned rooms on the bottom floor because it is hard for him to maneuver the stairs with his hands full. Jude dislikes seeing the boy struggle with the load, his foot dragging along behind him. He, his mother, and Dovie have tried to talk him into swapping his afternoon chores with Ben who weeds both the house garden and Mammy's garden and sweeps out the stable for Lew, but Ish wants no special treatment. He insists he is capable of doing his part and hates any mention of his foot.

The three boys have worked out a system at the well. One draws while the others haul, timing their deliveries so no one has to wait. When Jude and Ish have finished carrying their water to the house and Deke has watered the animals, the three meet in the yard. Ben joins them, and the three younger boys lounge against the wall to chat for a while like they always do, but Jude has no time for them tonight.

"I gotta go, Boys," he tells them.

"Whar you thinks youse goin?" asks Deke.

"I goin down ta the swimmin hole ta wash this coal off me."

"Den we go wid you," Deke says.

"Not tonight. I goan meet some othah fellows from church."

"Who's you meetin dat wese cain come long?" Deke is offended.

"None yo business," Jude laughs. "We ain tied at da hip."

It is not like Jude to hurt their feelings, but Ish and Deke do not need to start going to the river. Both might try what was fine for him but could be disastrous for them. He promises himself he will teach them to swim when he doesn't have other things to do.

"Ish, you go on home—Mama be worryin where you be."

"Her worry bout you, too," Ish yells.

"I tole her what I doin. Now you go on home."

The three boys head their separate ways, all casting angry glares toward Jude.

"Youse gittin too big fo you britches!" Deke yells.

"I woudden go you ackst me," Ben adds. "Hope you freeze dat lil peckah uh yose off!"

Jude laughs until he catches sight of Ish's dejected posture as he drags his way toward home. He runs after the boy. When he catches him, he bends and speaks quietly, "When I git home, I read you some uh *Rob Roy* like I usually do, awright?"

"Awright," Ish's face brightens, "bu I doan know wy I cain go wid you."

"I explain latah. Ain somethin I can tawk bout now."

Ish doesn't reply right away, but finally he nods his head and turns for home.

"You jus be careful, Jude—an hurry"

Jude hurries to the river where he quickly jumps in, clothes and all, and scrubs away the coal dust as best he can. He then climbs out of the water, shakes himself like a dog, but instead of heading home, Jude goes to the kitchen. He is seeking food to take to the Second African Baptist Church for Clyde, the Jackson's stable boy. He's been down in hiding two days with only water, and at church on Sunday, Jude had promised he would take him what he could.

Clyde cannot seem to stay out of trouble. He has been beaten several times, twice by the sheriff himself, yet he is always in trouble with his master. Clyde hasn't tried overly hard because he hates his young owner. He went as far as to put a sharp rock under the man's saddle, and when Jackson was thrown, Clyde received the full brunt of his anger. Some of the older slaves have chastised Clyde, but Jude admires his nerve. In truth, he would love to sabotage Frederick, or better yet, Master Rob, but he might not see his family again if he did. Frederick's threat to sell Dovie has worried them all. They know their master isn't one to want a large number of slaves, and with their family growing, they have less to do than many house servants they know. Too, Jude fears the pain associated with a beating. He has seen the raw meat of Clyde's back and isn't sure he would survive it. He confides in Mrs. Stiles. She knows he loves the heroes in the stories he reads, but she has reminded him there is nothing noble in being beaten until your back favors a plowed clay cornfield. She hasn't told him not to help Clyde, but she has admonished him to be careful.

Rarely is anyone in the backyard or on the bottom floor at dusk, and Jude is glad to have the place to himself. It is still a couple of hours before Lewis makes a final sweep through the basement to close up for the night. Jude makes his way first to their kitchen, but he finds nothing. He peeks into the breezeway before entering the main kitchen. Minda has left a couple of loaves of bread and a crock of butter on the counter along with a bowl of apples, three turnips, and five tomatoes. He takes the lid off a pot to find soaking beans. He replaces the lid, then pauses in front of the bread. His mother will not be pleased if he cuts it, but how will she know someone from upstairs didn't get hungry? Surely, the children, even Frederick, come down in the night to find something to eat. Jude locates a knife, cuts the end off the loaf of bread and looks around for something to carry it in. He sees only embroidered linen towels. He darts back across the hall and grabs one made of sackcloth from beside the wash pan. He wraps the bread, an over-sized turnip, and a tomato in the cloth. He turns to go, but he realizes he has to have a way to conceal the bundle. He replaces the cumbersome turnip with a smaller one, decides against the tomato altogether, and stuffs the package down his loose fitting pants. Since a turnip and a piece of bread are a paltry offering for a starving man, he grabs an apple before making his escape. Hopefully, no one will be suspicious of a colored boy carrying an apple.

Now is when his mission grows dangerous. He has to travel away from home, and if stopped, what excuse will he have? He consoles himself with the realization that most people he might encounter won't know who he is. Maybe they will think he is on his way home or back to his master's house. Of course, he is supposed to have papers after dark, and by now the sun is going down. Still, this is an adventure, not as grand as those he has been reading in *Rob Roy*, but he is in Savannah, Georgia, not a far off land called Scotland.

Jude concocts a plausible story in case he is stopped. He can say he is taking the food to his Uncle Clell who is doing some work at the church on his off time. The excuse won't withstand scrutiny if investigated, but if he is lucky, the detainer will not want to take the time to check out the details.

He is relieved when he reaches the river. He glances around to make sure no one is watching before he pulls the package out of his pants and crawls behind the thick bushes concealing an open space half covered with a pile of dead, discarded brush. Jude places his package on the ground to free his hands for the task of pulling the brush to the side. He lifts the trap door, drops his sack on the other side, drags part of the brush after him, and lets the door fall behind him. He grabs his offering and runs bent over to keep from hitting his head on the plank and beam ceiling. Clyde has heard him coming and is standing to the side of the opening into the hidey hole beneath the church, ready to attack if he has been discovered.

Clyde is thrilled with the visitor and the food. He tears into the bread like he hasn't eaten in a week instead of the two days it has been. Jude promises to bring more, but Clyde tells him he is supposed to be smuggled out tomorrow night. Jude is both relieved and disappointed.

His mission accomplished, all that remains is to reach Yamacraw without being detected. Everyone tells the story of how Moses Tucker was captured by dogs and hung, and Jude has heard the cautionary tale more than once. He makes a point of staying close to the river and away from the houses, but at some point, he must cut across town. He is directly behind Planter's bank when someone yells, "You, Boy! Come here!"

Jude's heart leaps then lodges in his throat. He stops in his tracks. He contemplates running but cannot move.

"I said come here, Boy!"

Jude takes a deep breath. He moves toward the voice. Waiting for him is none other than Master Rob. From the frown on his face, he is not pleased.

"What are you doin out aftah dawk, Jude?"

Jude is a little surprised Rob knows his name. He ususally calls him Boy. All recollection of the story about taking food to his Uncle Clell deserts him when he opens his mouth.

"I be swimmin."

His memory lapse serves him well. The fabrication might have worked if he'd been stopped by anyone but a member of the family. Rob might know more about Clell's whereabouts than he does.

"So you often go swimmin aftah dawk, Boy? And who gave you puhmission ta go swimmin?," Robart's voice is louder than necessary and angry. "Let's see your pass."

"Ise jus duhty from da coal an I wannah clean up fo I goes home."

"You can come along with me, and we'll see what Fathah has ta say about this."

Rob grabs Jude by the arm and drags him toward the mansion on Bull Street.

Jude's clothes are still wet, so maybe his story isn't such a bad one. He could tell Rob his mother knows where he is, but he will not. He isn't about to cause her problems, too.

"You doan hafta hole me. I ain goin nowhar but wid you."

Rob clinches his arm tighter and gives him a jarring shake. The man is not much taller than the boy, and for a minute, Jude thinks of resisting, of giving him some of his own medicine. Instead, he moves limply along, trying to give his captor as little assistance as possible as he drags him across town with no more consideration than he would give a misbehaving cur.

Frederick is in the family parlor when Jude is dragged before him. A woman is sitting on the settee with her dress spread out around her; the master is in a chair not far from her. Both are holding a glass of wine, and neither appears particularly pleased by the interruption.

"Rob, what is going on here? Why have you hauled a wet darkie into the presence of a guest, and a lady at that?"

"Please fuhgive the interruption, but I thought you'd want ta be made aware of what is obviously a major presumption on the pawt of one of ah slaves, and possibly somethin gravah if the boy isn't tellin the truth."

"Please excuse us, Brigitte. I will see to this and be right back. May I replenish your glass before I go?"

"If you don't mind, Dear. The long journey has left me parched."

Frederick crosses the room, takes the decanter from the cabinet, and returns to fill her glass though his own is still half full.

"I am sorry we did not hold dinner for you. Had I expected you this evening instead of next week, I would have planned accordingly."

"Please, don't apologize," the lady assures him. "Who needs a meal when I have your company and a glass of fine wine. Is this still part of the last shipment my dear Alexis sent you?"

"It is. I hope the reminder isn't cause for dismay."

"Oh no," she sighs. "Time eases all, but as you know, nothing can ever completely vanquish the pain."

Uncomfortable as he is, Jude cannot help but notice the haste with which the lady attends to her glass. She has rid herself of most of its contents before the master has replaced the decanter in the cabinet.

"Go handle this..."—she flips her hand toward Jude—"and come back to me as soon as possible."

Rob still hasn't let go of Jude by the time they reach Frederick's office. Jude cannot tell if the master's glare is directed at him or Rob.

"It is bad enough Mrs. Maxwell has shown up early, and I am forced to entertain her without another female present. You make matters worse by dragging this disreputable looking boy in front of her without so much as a beg your pardon. What is the problem?"

"I found ah boy across town aftah dawk, and he tells me he does not have your puhmission. He certainly does not have mine. I would think you would want ta punish him accordingly!"

"Of course I need to know, but did I have to know in this manner and at this moment?"

Frederick turns his eyes and anger on Jude. "What do you have to say for yourself,

Boy?"

"I tells da young massah I be down ta da rivah ta warsh off da coal dus fo I goes home ta Mama. I doan wanse her ta haftah clean up aftah me an da mess I be."

He hopes the mention of Minda will mitigate the master's wrath. The ploy works.

"You can see the boy is wet, Rob. What do you think he's been up to, robbing the neighbors?"

"Of course not," Rob stammers. Jude watches the deep red creep up his neck and almost pities him despite his earlier actions. "Have we come ta lettin ah slaves run around town at all times of night?"

"No, we have not, but this should have waited until morning. Jude, you go straight home. As punishment, I will instruct Minda you are to be given no breakfast. I do not want to hear you have been out after dark again unless I have given you a pass."

Jude breaks away from Master Rob's grasp and is halfway out the door before the Master has stopped talking. He hears him tell his son, "Go to the quarters and have one of the girls fix a plate of something for Mrs. Maxwell—she hasn't dined. Please be quick about it. I need you back here to spend the evening with us. The widow and I should not be alone. Tongues will wag."

"Yes, Fathah. Please fuhgive me faw embarrassin you..."

Rob's last comment rings insincere to Jude. He would like to hang back to eavesdrop on the rest of the conversation, but he needs to hurry home and avoid any more difficulty. He trots happily along the path. Though he dreads his mother finding out he's been caught, he has much to be grateful for. He has received less than a slap on the wrist— he will eat his breakfast at the Stiles like he does every weekday morning. He concludes he has in some way gotten the best of Master Rob, and the victory in itself would be worth missed breakfasts for a week. He laughs aloud.

When Jude sees his mother, he decides not to tell her. She might worry all night, and why waste time he can spend enjoying his book? He finds his brother wide awake waiting. He jumps up and pulls the book from beneath the mattress, and Jude places the lamp close to his side on the floor. Before opening the book, he says to his brother, "Let me see dat foot of yours."

"I worsht it," Ish says.

"I can tell you did," Jude laughs. He picks the foot up and starts massaging it. Ish groans as his brother works his way up his calf.

"That hurt?"

"Naw. It feel good! It be achin me some tanigh, dat's all."

Jude patiently rubs the boy's leg and foot while he tells him of being caught out by Rob. He even tells him about taking food to Clyde, making sure his words cannot be overheard from the other room.

"So dat wy you dint want me ta go wid you!"

"That right. When you oldah, we have adventures tagathah. You jus need ta be a lil biggah. Mama have my hide I git you in trouble."

Ish falls asleep curled against his brother's side, and Jude lets the book fall. He is startled to see his mother in the doorway.

"Goodnight, Mama," he says before he places the book beneath the mattress and extinguishes the lamp.

"Goodnight, Son."

He can detect the smile in her voice. He waits until her shadow is gone before he throws an arm across Ish and closes his eyes.

Chapter 11
A Request from Frederick

Baltimore, Maryland—1845

The bell has not quit jingling above 208 Pratt Street before Mattie is squealing, "Oh, TaTa Jessie, I am ta be married!"

Jessie no longer thinks of the irony of Frederick's daughters calling her TaTa, the French word for auntie. White children in southern households often address the help by Auntie, Uncle, or Mammy. She notices Mattie's heavy, Southern accent. Frederick once told her he wishes he could speak like his children—that they sound like insiders in a region in which his own foreign accent sets him apart. Though he has tried, he has been unable to overcome it.

"I cannot say I am surprised, but I can say I am delighted!"

"Whit proposed last night on the back terrace at Aunt Sophie's. I was thinkin he might at Christmas, but he told me he couldn't wait anuthah two weeks ta speak his mind."

Sophia Howe appears almost as happy as the bride to be, but young Gail immediately asks, "Where is Diana? I hope she is not out—I brought her the book I promised."

"We have been slow today. She has gone upstairs to write in her journal."

"May I join her, Mama?"

"Of course, if Jessie doesn't mind. But don't be long—we have othah errands ta run."

Jessie has been astonished at the friendship that has evolved between the two girls over the past year. They have discovered they have more in common than their age. Both have sharp minds, a passion for reading, an interest in drawing, and a love for the outdoors. Jessie had been more than a little surprised when Sophia first allowed the girls to go unattended on a walk by the sea. Now they venture out together during every visit, a weekly occurrence since Mattie's return to Baltimore. Sophia's husband's Quaker heritage has influenced her. She has let Jessie know the Howes employ their servants, a fact she has not shared with her mother. Jessie can imagine what the upright Mrs. Middleton would think of the two girls being seen around town together. Perhaps she would regard the association much like any other white girl being attended by a black servant. Regardless, Jessie is grateful for the Howes' acceptance as Diana has no other friends. The girl needs someone to associate with besides a woman old enough to be her grandmother.

It isn't long before the girls are back downstairs and headed out the door. Physically, they are a picture of contrasts. Gail is thin, tall, and pale, whereas Diana is short, rounded, and dark. Both are somewhat subdued in nature except when in each other's company. Jessie has privately reminded her daughter to be circumspect in public because people will certainly resent any indication the two of them are equal in status. Once, late in the afternoon, Sophia and Mattie had allowed Gail to stay behind while they called on Mattie's fiancé's mother. The visit was after store hours, so Jessie had accompanied the girls on their outing. She had seen the looks cast their way when they were talking and laughing. The girls had been oblivious to the attention they had drawn.

When the pair has gone, Jessie goes to the kitchen to get tea she serves the ladies who sit in the only two chairs in the shop.

"Now, tell me all about your wedding plans."

"I do not have plans as yet. This mornin I posted a lettah ta Fathah. I am sure he will have opinions. He has always talked of us girls bein married at home by Pastah Acton, and if not there, at the Independent Presbyterian Church. We will have ta accommodate Whit's family and some of his friends from West Point. We need ta discuss food and my dress and my sistahs' dresses. Oh, TaTa Jessie, you have ta help us with all of this!"

"You know I will do all I can from here. And I am sure your friends and neighbors will offer to help your aunts, like Mrs. Stiles…"

"I hate ta ask Mrs. Stiles for help aftah I rejected Thomas."

"I had forgotten. You are probably right."

"We were hopin you might be willin ta return ta Savannah faw a short time…" Sophia begins but stops when she catches the shock on Jessie's face.

"I do not see how I could possibly leave with the store and all the responsibilities I have here."

"Please think about it, TaTa. It would be such fun ta have you with us, and you could ovahsee the clothes and the food. Papa would be pleased and relieved. I know Mama would want you if she were alive—it would be almost like old times!"

Jessie welcomes the chill she has come to know. She wonders if Moses is trying to comfort her or it's the thought of returning to Savannah that has brought the bumps to her skin. A visit would never be like old times, she thinks. Neither Moses nor Abby would be there, not in the flesh, at least. Instead, there would be reminders of all the bad things that have taken place, and worst of all, she would have to see Frederick again, the man she holds responsible for most of them. She tells herself she has forgiven Frederick, but the anger and hurt overwhelm her best intentions at times.

More possibilities are discussed by Mattie and Sophia, but they can tell Jessie's mind is elsewhere. The visit becomes awkward, and all three ladies are relieved when Diana and Gail come laughing through the door and the visitors move on to the errands Sophia mentioned earlier. Five o'clock arrives, and they lock up the shop and move to the kitchen where she and Diana eat cold chicken and the sweet potatoes Jessie had placed in the fireplace to bake at noon. Diana sits with her awhile and tries to recount her adventure with Gail, but her mother's lack of focus is as apparent to her as it was to Mattie and Sophia. She kisses her goodnight and goes to her bedroom to read the book Gail brought her.

Jessie paces the room after Diana goes to bed. If the mention of returning to Savannah agitates her, what would going back be like? Why would she want to revisit the place in which she was beaten and raped, and worse, lost her son Joshua before he was born? What would walking the streets she walked with Moses be like? Passing the square where they hung him from a tree for something she herself had done? Visiting graves containing their earthly remains? She has worked hard at leaving Savannah behind in distance and in thought. She has no desire to return.

After two hours of trying to read her own book, Jessie extinguishes the lamps and goes to bed though it is not yet nine o'clock. She longs for sleep and Moses, but the second cannot come without the first, so she spends a restless night.

Christmas is days away. She will be busy finishing the gifts for Diana and her customers. Mattie goes back to Savannah for the holidays, and Sophia, with her own preparations to attend to, has no time to discuss the upcoming wedding. Jessie and Diana deliver the Howe's orders to the back door and pass on holiday greetings rather than visiting as they usually do. Moses's comforting presence and reassuring words fill her dreams, and Jessie manages to dwell rarely on Mattie's request. She and Diana celebrate Christmas Day much as they have each year since coming to Baltimore. They enjoy a noontime meal prepared by the two of them; they bundle up and go for a long afternoon walk; then they return to Jessie's upstairs bedroom where they exchange gifts. This year Diana gives her the hat she has tried to keep concealed in her bedroom. It is a simple one of her own creation made from leftover materials taken from the shop and embellished with feathers she has collected on her walks with Jessie and Gail. She also gives her a story—a written account of the tale her mother finally told her of early life. She insists Jessie not read it on Christmas Day, but wait until later to make sure she has the details right. Diana's offering is a way of assuring her mother their story will not be forgotten. Tears spring to Jessie's eyes, but Diana will have none of that.

"Now, it's my turn. What do you have for me?"

"It's about time you acted excited. You have not asked once about your Christmas present."

"I love surprises! I didn't want to ruin it."

Jessie goes to the clothes press and pulls out a parcel. The contents are folded and wrapped in a square of muslin bound with a length of red ribbon. Diana takes it, gently unties the ribbon, and slowly parts the material to reveal the pale blue fabric beneath. The garment is arranged to call attention to the intricate embroidery on the bosom.

"Oh Mama! You told me this was for the oldest Cuthbert girl! I never dreamed we could afford this dress for me!"

"Do you like it, Sweetheart, now you know it is for you? I am sorry I couldn't keep it hidden, but I could find no time to work on it without you knowing."

"You know I love it—haven't I commented every step of the way? And how could I not when you let me help with the design?"

"Look closely, Darling. Can you read your name among the embroidery on the left side of the bodice? *Diana* will be worn over your heart as a reminder of your place in mine."

Now Diana is the one fighting tears.

"But before we get maudlin, let me give you these." Jessie opens her trunk and hands her daughter a set of underclothes, plain yet made from soft cotton fabric. "Those should bring you back to earth if you're getting too full of yourself. Nothing like everyday underwear to dampen your mood."

"But a woman has to have them!" Diana laughs, and the two hug before putting away their gifts. They pass the rest of the evening drinking hot apple cider and singing Christmas carols, then they fall asleep on Jessie's bed as is their tradition on Christmas, New Year's Eve, and each of their birthdays.

With the holiday behind them, Jessie knows she will have to speak again with Mattie and Sophia about their proposal. She has come up with several excuses, but before she can use them, she receives the same request from Frederick Barret in the form of a letter. Jessie is talking with a customer when Diana places the envelope on the counter beside her. She immediately recognizes the neat, tiny script as Frederick's. She pockets the letter until she and Diana are seated in the kitchen with their midday meal completed. She draws the letter from her pocket under the watchful eye of her daughter.

"Why do you think Mr. Barret is writing, Mama?"

Jessie knows exactly what the correspondence is about.

"We are about to find out," she says before she unceremoniously tears the envelope open and extracts a single sheet of stationery.

"It is quite short," Diana comments.

Without replying, her mother begins to read aloud.

"Dear Deckie."

"Deckie? Who is Deckie? What an odd name."

"I am Deckie. My father gave me the nickname when I was quite young."

"How in the world would Mr. Barret know what your papa called you as a child?" Diana asks, and not for the first time has the child proved too smart for evasiveness. Jessie hesitates a moment before admitting the truth.

"Frederick Barret is Emile."

"Emile from your story—from the Island?"

"The same."

Diana stares open-mouthed at her mother.

"Remember, I told you he had done well for himself and I had seen him often for a while."

"But if he is your nephew, why did we leave them? Shouldn't we be there? They are family—all the family we have."

"I told you no one in the States could know he has family of color. Our association became complicated; I decided staying in Savannah was unwise if not impossible."

"Oh My Goodness! This means I have cousins!"

Jessie's chest constricts. She doesn't want her to learn Frederick had considered her no kin or responsibility of his, how they had argued over Jessie claiming Diana as her own.

"Sweetheart, you must not think of them as relatives. Frederick would never admit to anyone that I am his aunt, not even his children. The disclosure would destroy all he has worked hard to achieve. You must forget you know who he is, and you must never tell anyone. Promise me now. Tell me you will keep this secret as I have."

"I promise," Diana whispers. Jessie watches her daughter's excitement disappear as the reality of the situation dawns on her. "Does anyone else know?"

"Miss Abby did." The cold pressure upon her shoulder comforts Jessie. "She overheard Frederick and me talking. She was a wonderful person, but she struggled with despondency. Learning about our connection along with some other secrets Frederick had been keeping were too much for her. She could not live with the knowledge, and because of her sickness, she ended her life. She made a horrible choice, but she was too ill to cope."

"She killed herself because she found out Mr. Barret was related to you? I thought Miss Abby and you were friends—that she cared for you."

The coldness surrounds Jessie, and Diana shudders. Jessie wonders if Moses may have company, someone who might be equally dismayed by this conversation.

"She did, Sweetheart, but neither Miss Abby nor we make the rules. She comprehended what the discovery of Frederick having Negro blood would do to him and her children."

The letter slides from her hand onto the wood surface.

"And she found out other things he had done that proved he was not the man she thought he was. The many discoveries were all too much for her at once. The illness had made her weak, and she made an extremely bad choice. I will not judge her. It is not our place to judge anyone."

"What other secrets did Mr. Barret keep from her?" Diana asks softly.

"I am not willing to discuss those with you. They do not concern us, so we have no reason to talk about them."

Diana's face reveals she doesn't understand, but before she can speak, Jessie picks up the letter and begins to read again.

Dear Deckie,

Mattie tells me you are now in possession of the wonderful news that she is to become the wife of Whitney Pierpont Hamilton. You can imagine our pleasure in an advantageous match aligning our family with both the Pierponts and the Hamiltons. With such an honor comes responsibilities, and I hope you will help me do our family proud. I am asking you to come to Savannah next year to provide the meals and the clothing needed to give Mattie every advantage upon presenting herself to her new relatives. I am willing to compensate you for the income you will sacrifice while here as well as provide housing for you and the girl, should you wish to bring her.

I am asking you to put our differences aside for Mattie's sake. If you will not do this because of the connection and memories we share, I hope you will come for our beloved Abigail, may God rest her soul. My greatest regret is she will not witness the event due to Providence taking her from her children much too soon.

I anxiously await your response.

Your devoted friend and benefactor,

Frederick

Jessie lays the paper on the table. Diana says nothing. She sits quietly waiting for her mother to speak first. Jessie rises slowly from the table, leaving the letter where it lies.

"We have work to do, Diana. I must cut the trousers for the Newton order, and you need to finish the buttonholes on the ivory shirtwaist."

"Shouldn't we talk about this, Mama?"

"Not now, Dear. Tonight, maybe."

Jessie turns and walks from the room, and neither mentions the letter for the rest of the day. It isn't until Diana says goodnight and rises to leave that Jessie realizes she is ready to talk about what has been on both their minds.

"Wait, Diana."

The girl sits beside her mother.

"Sometimes we have to do hard things despite how much we would like to avoid them. Perhaps we should consider going to Savannah for a month or so. If I tell our customers in advance, we can prepare ahead, and our absence will not be an inconvenience to them and a hardship for us. What do you think?"

"I don't know what to think? Much depends on the differences the two of you have that Mr. Barret mentions. He writes as if he is thinking of their needs alone and not ours."

Jessie is surprised at the anger in Diana's voice.

"His attitude is part of the differences to which he refers. Frederick is no longer the person I thought he was years ago—or he is still there somewhere trying to survive in a different world. Please do not be too hard on him, Diana. One has to remember the obstacles he faced growing up, the fear and the rejection he suffered."

"He would be a fine one to talk about rejection. Has he worried about the troubles you've had? I don't think he knows my name. He calls me *the girl!* He says *if* you wish to bring *her!* What would he have you do with me? Leave me here alone to carry on without you? He sounds quite selfish, Mama."

Jessie hugs her daughter. "He doesn't know you, Sweetheart, or me if he thinks our separation is a possibility. Where I go you go. You are right—he is selfish. He didn't appear to be as a boy or a young man, but a person can change. He has worked hard to build a new life for himself, and he in not willing to jeopardize it, and especially not for an aunt he lived with long ago. Likewise, I will no longer put his needs first. If we go, we go for Mattie and for the other girls, and for Abby who nursed me through some hard times, times I will tell you about when the time is right."

"What differences is he talking about, Mama? Why did you take me and leave Savannah? I have been thinking about you making such a scary move. I could understand before I learned he is your family, but now... What did he do? Did the secrets he kept from Miss Abby cause us to leave?"

"His choices regarding what to tell and what not to tell influenced my decision. The main reason I left was too much had happened. I felt he could have saved Moses if he had tried harder. He knew the truth about everything surrounding the accusation that Moses killed a man, and he was afraid of someone suspecting his own involvement and the reasons why. He let them hang an innocent man. Though I have tried to forgive him for the things he did and didn't do, I cannot forget he could have prevented the death of the best man I have ever encountered and the only one I have loved in that way."

Jessie glances over her shoulder and draws the wrap closer.

"Again, we will talk about details later, when you have your own family, but not now. If we do this, we do not do this for him. We will make sure he pays the price for our services—for both of our services."

"Seems he would prefer to do without mine."

"It is because he does not know what he is missing. By caring only for himself and his immediate family, he deprives himself of much in life. You would think he would have learned that lesson by now."

"I guess some people never learn," Diana replies.

"Aren't you the sage one!" Jessie's smile draws one from Diana.

Now the decision has been made, the two discuss how best to prepare for their time away from Baltimore and their business.

Chapter 12

Begging for Dovie

Savannah, Georgia—1846

"God will im-pawt grace ta the humble pen-i-tent," Minda reads aloud.

"God will impawt grace ta the humble penitent," Ish mimics. "What do *impawt* and *penitent* mean, Mama?"

"*Impawt* mean ta give, and we needs ta write *penitent* down ta ask Miss Bette."

Ish picks up his pencil to print the word on his tablet.

"It mean somebidy who sorry fo what he done," Jude interrupts from his pallet in front of the fire where he lies reading his own book.

"Ain you da smawt one, Mr. Jude? Ish be bettah off you the one teachin him ta read. Some uh these sentences could be French as much sense they makes ta me."

"Me, too, Mama, bu the mo I read, the easiuh it git, an it will fo you, too. We jus have ta keep workin at it."

"If not faw you boys, I not be doin this atall. I ain nevah gonna need words like *penitent* an *impawt*. Who's I gonna say or write them to?"

"We can use them with each uthah, Mama, an someday when I faw way, you gonna be glad you have a way ta read da lettahs I write. An me an Ish gonna be scholahs someday we git way from here an live up Nawth where we be free as any white foke you evah see."

Minda sighs. She has given up on trying to reason with Jude about their station in life. What she feared has come true. All this learning has made Jude more discontent with their way of life. Now she fears he will influence his brother.

"Ish, doan you pay no mine ta that brothah uh yose. He a dreamah. Someday he gonna git hissef an the rest uh us in all kines uh trouble. I glad you learnin ta read an write, bu you cain be puttin on no airs. Like Mizz Bette say, they ah tools fo us ta use the day come we needs them."

"White foke love ta make us think that day nevah come, but it will, Ish. If not here, we go someplace where nobidy know us an no one care we be own by a white man in Svanna."

Ish frowns.

"Mama jus tryin ta look ou fo us, Jude. She right an you knows it. Wese gotta be careful. I scairt ta tell Deke an Ben whut we up ta. They migh naw like us ackin like wese smawtah dan dem. You needs ta watch whut you say an whose you says it to."

Jude laughs. He pushes himself up from the floor and walks over to take the book from his mother's hand. "I take ovah here fo a while. You got things ta do."

Minda relinquishes the book and the task, but she sits and listens to the two boys interact. Jude is softer with Ish than he is with anyone else. His patience and kindness with his younger brother touch her. Minda thinks this learning worth it, if for nothing else, for strengthening the bond between her boys. She thinks about Daisy and how she wishes she could be here with them, learning what they are learning, laughing and cutting up with the boys.

All three react when three loud knocks rattle the door. Without saying a word, the boys fly into action. Jude grabs the book, tablet, and pen from Ish's hand, sweeps his own book up off his pallet, and heads for the bedroom. Ish follows. All evidence will be out of sight before she opens the door.

"What in the worl?" she exclaims when Mammy and Lew push past her. "You scairt the life outtah me knockin this time a night?"

"You think we comes a callin fo da fun uh it?" Mammy snaps. "An we ain got no time fo jawin. We hab ta git back fo da massah know wese goan. Him mad nuff awready."

"Dovie goan an done it now," Lew says. "Da massah ketch her in da sto'room wid a poke in her han. Her gathin up stuff fo God know whut. Him say him done wid er."

"Where she now?" Minda manages to get in.

"Dat da skeery pawt. Massah jus take da sack ouddah her han, tell her ta git ouddah hes sight, lock da door behine him, and go on bout hes bidness. Dovie say he naw say anuthah word. Her wanse ta come ovah hyur, bu we woan let her. I tells her ta stay in da quattah wile we comes tawk ta you bout whut we bess do."

Mammy is out of breath and Minda steers her to the chair.

"What she think I do bout this mess she git hersef inta? I been warnin her an warnin her. I wouldda hid da key in annuthah place, but I fraid the massah wondah why. I tell her he be checkin the sto'room mo, an I tell her he suspectin some stuff goan missin. She say she ain stealin, but I know bettah. We missin some meal an rice, an a ham been cut on an I dint do it. I been scairt da massah think I the one stealin."

"She be sellin it," Jude says calmly from the door. Ish tries to squeeze around him, but he pushes him back into the bedroom. "You git on inta bed, Ish. This ain nuthin fo you ta worry on."

"It my fambly too," Ish complains, but he obeys his brother.

Lewis paces back and forth across the small space. "Her goan and done it now," he repeats. "Da massah goan sell her fo sho an theys ain nuthin wese kin do!"

"That why she tryin ta git money," Jude informs them. "In case the massah go ta sell her, she have some money when she run."

"Run!" Minda almost shouts. "Jus where she think she gonna run that the massah ain gonna find her?"

"She gonna find Clell, she say. She say she follow the track, she boun ta find him soonah or latah."

"Hows you be knowin so much bout whut Dovie goan do, Jude?" Mammy asks.

Minda takes her son by the shoulders and peers into his eyes. "Jude, tell me you ain have nuthin ta do with this? You ain been heppin Dovie steal stuff from the sto'room, have you?"

"No," Jude steps away from his mother's reach, "bu I doan blame her. What she goan do the massah go ta sell her? Jus go quiet like an not make no fuss—jus be sold on the block like those po slaves down on the warf? I run in a minute I think he bout ta sell me!"

"Jus doan be doin nuthin ta gits sole fo an you doan haftah worry none!" Lew yells. "Da massah beddah dan mos wite mens. We hab it good. We hab a place ta stay in dat bettah dan mos, plenty food ta eat; wese tagethah! Dovie goan fine out whut bein a slave lack now her steal from da massah!"

"Settle down, all uh you. I needs ta think. The massah ain goan do nothin fo mornin. You git on back fo he know you gone. We doan need ta cause mo trouble than they aweady be. I sleep on it. See what I come up with. An layin wake all night worryin ain goan do none uh us no good."

Minda turns to Jude when she closes the door behind them. "I pray ta God, Jude, you not have mo ta do with this mess than you sayin. I done loss one chile—I cain stand ta lose annuthah, an if the massah sell Dovie, he migh jus sell you. You straighten up an ack right, or ah be takin a switch ta you I doan care you be fo'teen or twenty. You hearin me, Son?"

"I hear you, Mama," Jude mumbles.

"Now git yosef on ta bed."

"Aunt Dovie goan git sole off, Mama?" Ish calls from the bedroom.

"Ain nobidy gittin sold off," Jude reassures him. "Now give me yo foot an I do the rubbin tanight. Mama need ta think."

Minda paces the small area as Lew had done before. What can she do? Will the master listen if she asks him to give Dovie another chance? Talking to him about Dovie is not as unlikely as it would have been a couple of years ago. They talk now more than they ever have. Until tonight, she has not thought Mr. Barret would do what he has threatened. She has seen him angry, and he is not one to make idle threats, but he has neither beaten nor sold any slave he has owned, so drastic punishment is hard for any of them to imagine. But Frederick has never caught any of them stealing. The worst any of them has been accused of is being away from the house without permission or shirking their duties. Dovie has been the one guilty of both unless you count the time Jude was caught coming home after dark. The fact that Frederick walked away when he caught Dovie is alarming. He must be furious, and she agrees with the others—she has the best chance of intervening on her sister's behalf. The master is also fond of Mammy and Lew. Maybe if they beg him to go easy on Dovie, he'll listen. Will he want to live in the house with all of his servants angry at him?

Ish is the only one to get any sleep in the house in Yamacraw. Minda tosses and turns, and Jude lies staring off into space. Minda rises early, no real inconvenience since she is not sleeping anyway. She wakes Jude and tells him to bring his brother later. She bangs on the door at the quarters and asks the adults to meet her in the kitchen. They straggle in, all looking like they have gotten no more sleep than she has. Dovie is more subdued than any of them have ever seen her. Minda is tempted to tell her how much she resents being put in this position, but their time is limited. They talk as she prepares the master's breakfast which she must have ready in less than an hour.

"Here what we have ta do," she begins. "I take da massah his food sted uh Lew. I tell him you is awful sorry fo da way you behavin, an you promise ta change yo sorry ways."

Dovie must be terrified because she doesn't reply.

"I tells him you wanse ta say how sorry you be. You ready ta do that, Dovie?"

"I doan see how Ise got a say in da mattah, at dis point. I ain ready ta take Ben an run. Ise willin ta say whutevah you thinks hep. Da massah scairt me bad las nigh. Hes face go jus as red as yo kerchief, an I scairt he goan hit me. I cain think uh nothin ta say, sose I jus stan dare an wait fo da blow ta fall."

If Dovie is hoping for pity, she is disappointed. Minda continues as if she hasn't spoken at all.

"Mama, you try ta ketch him when he come home fo dinnah an Lew when you git a chance."

"An I says whut?" Lew asks.

"We tell him we keep a close watch on Dovie ta make sho she do what she spose ta."

"I stays ouddah trouble, I swears."

Lew glares at her; Minda ignores her completely; and Mammy grunts.

"Now git on outtah here so I can fix somethin he like ta soften him up fo I haftah go beggin fo Dovie."

Minda cannot remember the last time she has been upstairs, and she wishes she weren't climbing the treads with the master's food now. He is not yet in the dining room, but he arrives as she is arranging his food the best she can considering she has never performed the task.

"Where is Lewis?" he asks, and the stern set of his face tells her he is not going to make this easy for her.

"Mammy tell me what happen las night, an I here ta ask you not ta sell Dovie even she be deservin it."

The man's face is stoic as he places his napkin in his lap.

"Minda, I have given Dovie many warnings, and she has shown no sign of heeding any of them. I fear my leniency has misled her."

"She learn her lesson this time, Massah. I knows she have."

"If I had punished her when she didn't do her chores or was caught away from the place without my permission, her misbehavior might not have progressed to outright thievery. I knew I should have taken a firmer hand when I first became aware of her transgressions, but Abigail wanted to handle her, and I allowed her to do so. I should have sold Dovie years ago."

"Please, Massah," Minda cannot control her shaking voice for she knows for sure now the Master plans to sell Dovie. "She my sistah. You same as kill Mama you break up the fambly. Mizz Abby nevah want that ta happen."

"Miss Abby was too softhearted for her own welfare, and I have let this go too long. I fear her behavior may have already affected the younger help, especially Jude who seems capable of following in her footsteps."

Minda loses her breath. She places her hand on the back of a chair to steady herself, and tears begin to fall. "Massah, Jude be a good boy. He nuthin like Dovie. He nevah steal from you."

"That may be, but you know as well as I do he is headstrong. He certainly doesn't need any bad examples around to give him ideas."

"I only ackst you one othah thing the whole time I knows you, an that was not ta send Daisy way. Now Daisy gone. Now I acksin you one mo thing. Please doan sell Dovie or any uh da fambly. They's all I got, Massah."

"You have me and my children to care for, Minda. You have more than most servants. You have a house in which you live with your boys, and I imagine no reason for your circumstances to change."

Frederick's voice softens, and he takes Minda's hand. "But I am not an unreasonable man, and I am not without sentiment where you are concerned. I have treated you well, have I not?"

Minda nods in response as she tries to stifle her sobs.

"Your tears move me. I have never seen you cry. Making decisions like this one is never easy. I will give the matter further thought, out of compassion for you and Mammy, but I make no promises. You best tell Dovie she will be gone by morning if she so much as sneezes wrong. Tell her I will take a while to decide her fate."

"Thank you, Massah," Minda says. She raises the hand he is holding hers with and presses her lips to the back of it. He has no idea how hard the gesture is for her to make.

Dovie is waiting for her in the kitchen. "Whut he say?" she asks before Minda can set the tray on the counter. Minda turns and slaps her sister across the face.

"That is fo makin me beg fo you!" she cries. "Fo givin the man mo powah ovah me! Bu mos of all, it fo causin the massah ta be doubtin my boy!"

Dovie stands with her hand pressed against her face. "Yo boy? Jude? I mabe do some things I shouldna, bu I ain done nuthin cernin Jude."

"The massah think you causin him ta follow in yo ways, an mabe he right. Undahstan me now, Dovie. If I haftah lose you or one uh my chilren, I lets you go."

"I ain causin you ta lose nobidy!"

"An you bes stay clear uh the massah fo a wile. He thinkin on if he keep you or not. Let Mama an Lew tawk ta him, but you go on bout yo business and do the work you spose ta do the bes you kin. If not fo us, you awready gone. Mabe you still be."

Minda is too angry and afraid after talking to the master to accept Dovie's apology for the trouble she has caused.

"Action speak loudah than words," she says, and turns her back on her sister.

After Dovie is gone, she sits down and cradles her head in her arms on the table. Mammy returns and sits beside her. She puts her arm around her shoulders. After Minda tells her what happened upstairs, she asks, "Who I, Mama, ta scold Dovie? I be jus as guilty fo goin b'hine massah back an learnin ta read an write, fo teachin the boys ta do the same. I not jus defyin him; I breakin the law. What could happen ta us we git caught?" She shudders. "You think I should tell Dovie sorry fo bein hawd on her, an faw slappin her?"

"Hebben no! Her know her wrong or her hit you back!"

Minda manages to laugh, but Mammy is serious. "We needs ta do whutevah we kin ta git some sense inta dat gul's haid. An you an da boys jus needs ta be extry careful naw ta git ketcht wid enthin show you be larnin. Mizz Bette a good woman, an her thinks whut youse doin awrigh, it awrigh."

Minda sighs deeply and rises from the table. "I need ta git on with my work, Mama, but I want ta tell you one last thing. What I said bout choosin my chilren ovah Dovie—I means what I says."

"I knows you do, Gul, an I doan blame you. Less jus hope mattahs doan come ta dat."

Chapter 13
Brigitte's Reprimand

Savannah, Georgia—1846

Most evenings find Frederick in the company of the Brigitte Maxwell for she is still living under his roof. Unless one of the two is otherwise engaged outside the mansion, they are together. The lady has tried hard to take the role of mistress of the house, but she has not counted on Frederick's naturally controlling nature or the strong will of fifteen-year-old Ella. Battle lines between the widow and the girl were drawn a couple of days after Brigitte came to visit almost a year ago. On the first night of the girls' return, they found a lady strange to them, for they could not remember her well, if at all, ensconced in the place Frederick had always kept empty in honor of Abigail. Their mother had occupied the chair at the opposite end of the table from their father for the short time she lived among them in the mansion. Without consulting Frederick, Ella had immediately sent Jude to bring another place setting and instructed him to move their guest's chair to mid-table. Brigitte had done a masterful job of acting oblivious to the problem with her position. Not to be outdone, Ella had almost managed a tear or two while graciously explaining the transgression. All theatrical apologetics, Brigitte had assured Frederick the change was no inconvenience and asked all present to forgive her insensitivity. A cool reserve was established between her and Ella and persists still. Abby's spot has since been entirely squeezed out due to necessity with both Mattie and Fredie home, she to plan her wedding and he on break from school.

"Fredie, what can you tell us about life at Princeton?" Frederick asks after the food is served.

Fredie has already met with his father and spent two hours bringing him up to date, He has written a lengthy letter home every week, but Frederick never tires of hearing about what he thinks is the ideal life for the young and prosperous in America. The other children are not quite as enthusiastic about recounts of stories they have already read or had read to them. Rob is especially irritated as he suspects he is still being punished for the squandering of his own opportunity. Fredie is somewhat apologetically describing one of his typical study evenings when Brigitte interrupts.

"How wonderful you can be content to study with the other young men. My own dear Jeffrey found those evenings most trying. He had little need for the amount of time they insisted upon. Now, Frederick, he would have needed every minute had he not chosen to follow in his father's footsteps and make a name for himself in the Navy."

Seeing the scowl on her father's face, Mattie intervenes. "Frederick, Fredie, and then Frederick again! One has such a hawd time in this family knowin which one we ah discussin at any given time!"

"Yes." Ella is eager to talk about anything that takes the focus off of Brigitte. "At least we girls have diminutives or variations of our namesakes. We can hawdly be confused with one anuthah."

"Fathah, why was I not named Frederick as I was the firstborn?" Rob asks.

"Neither of my namesakes was of my instigation. Your brother was named by your mother Luella, and Frederick Maxwell was named by his mother and father. You, Son, I did name, after a man I admire above others. Robart Middleton gave me my start, not just in America, but in life. I shudder to think what might have happened to me had he not come to the Island to do business. And what a businessman he was! His combination of intelligence and compassion are unsurpassed, in my opinion. You, My Son, have a lot to live up to in order to fulfill the promise of your name."

Frederick has turned what could have been a compliment into a reprimand, and the point is not lost on Rob who becomes quite interested in his food. Compassionate Maxie comes to his aid.

"Mattie, have you completed your weddin list? Have you arrived at a numbah?"

"Since we ah havin the ceremony on the Green, no tellin how many people will attend. I do not know how we can possibly control who comes and goes."

"It isn't necessary to limit the spectators, My Dear. They won't dare take a seat if they are uninvited, and our guests will come to the house for the reception to follow."

"If it is amenable ta you, I will invite a hundred or so, countin Whit's family. Do I need ta pare that numbah down? How in the world will we be able ta accommodate a hundred people in here?"

"You leave the logistics to me. We had more than a hundred guests the night of our housewarming."

"And what a delightful evening that was! People were throughout the house and on the porches. If necessary, your guests can spill into the yard," Brigitte adds.

Frederick remembers the occasion to which she refers was the last night of Abby's life. The image of people *spilling into the yard* is too graphically accurate for Frederick to dwell on. He quickly changes the subject.

"And with the wedding being in early June, the weather should be perfect. I would like to take a look at your list. I may need to add a few of my own business acquaintances, and the like. We don't want to offend anyone."

"When will we begin the dresses?" Ella wants to know.

"Your dress would be your most pressin concern, Sistah," Maxie says, and lets out a quiet "Ouch!" when Ella sitting beside her gives her a quick pinch.

"You should be a little more concerned with your appearance, Maxie. If your skin were dawkah, you could be mistaken faw one of the help!"

"Ella!" Brigitte scolds. "You musn't pinch your sister, and you certainly shouldn't compare her to a darkie."

The quiet that falls upon the diners should be warning enough for Brigitte, but she goes on as if she has not taken grave liberties at her host's table. Perhaps her usual intake of wine has made her careless. "Mattie, I would be delighted to help in any way I can."

"Your assistance won't be necessary, Mrs. Maxwell," Frederick says coldly. "Jessie is arriving next week. Bette Stiles has graciously offered to house her and her girl as we are at capacity."

"What is this *Mrs. Maxwell*, Frederick?" Brigitte asks, still not realizing her mistake and totally ignoring the comment about his home being full. "And keep in mind, I taught Jessie much of what she knows. I insist—you must allow me to help. That is what family does."

Frederick chooses to ignore her, and the conversation continues though everyone in the room but Brigitte realizes Ella is seething and Frederick is displeased. The dinner stumbles along until they all move into the parlor where Mattie judiciously suggests they sing. Both Ella and Maxie have lovely voices, and Mattie's is fair. They coax their brothers into joining them. Brigitte, now into her fourth or fifth glass of wine, warbles along contentedly from the sofa where she seems to feel right at home. Not an hour passes before her eyes begin to close as she lists sideways on the settee.

"Dovie," Frederick calls.

She appears immediately, as is her habit since her close call over the stealing incident. "Please escort Mrs. Maxwell to her room."

Brigitte mumbles something about taking her leave, but no one can make out exactly what she is saying. She is barely out of the room when Ella turns on her father.

"Papa, how long ah we goin ta be subjected ta that woman?" she demands.

"Ella! Do not speak disparagingly of a guest in this house!"

"Guest? One would think she is a puhmanent resident. And she is an embarrassment when we have guests. She was actually flirtin with Hawvey Willis two nights ago, and he not much oldah than I!"

"Fathah," Mattie asks gently, "do you know how much longah she plans ta stay?"

Frederick is flustered. "I don't know," he says, running his fingers through his hair. "I have suggested two accommodations, and she found something wrong with both of them."

"If she is ta be here," Mattie continues, "will you make sure she doesn't have quite as much access ta the wine. I do not want Whit or his family ta think we condone drunkenness."

Mattie cunningly appeals to one of Frederick's foremost considerations always—the opinion of others who matter. She could not have said anything more persuasive. Too, she is reinforcing Frederick's own fears.

"I know. We must not allow her behavior to reflect badly on the rest of us. We have worked too hard to establish ourselves. The slightest indiscretion or rumor of one can change the tide of opinion in this town." His eyes trail around the room at his offspring. "You all need to remember that. She is not the only one who could bring disgrace upon us."

The children glance at each other, for they have not worked hard at all at establishing themselves. They were born in this city, and this is all they know. All feel nothing but at ease in their surroundings. Even Rob has suffered no ramifications for his actions other than being forced to work at a job he thinks beneath him.

"Her drinking has gotten completely out of hand. The loss of Alexis has made her intemperate. She used to exhibit such gentility."

He has come to wonder if Brigitte was somewhat of a lush when Alexis was alive, but admitting her weakness would be questioning his own judgment. It is not easy for him to let go of the idealized vision of the woman he has found enticing for years.

"Regardless, something must be done. I will find her a place and insist she be gone before the wedding." He turns to Ella. "Until she leaves, however, you are to remember your manners. You did well tonight not to respond to her reprimand."

Mattie and Maxie both regret he seems to have completely dismissed Ella's behavior before the rebuke.

"She is still a guest in this house, and we will not forget our manners no matter how overreaching her attitude. Do I make myself clear?"

"Yes, Papa." Ella puts her arms around her father's neck and kisses his cheek. "I almost fuhgot myself when she had the nerve ta act like my mothah."

"You did pinch me," Maxie reminds her. Ella makes sure her father's back is to her before she makes a face at her little sister.

"Let me see your list, Mattie." Frederick is tired of the conversation.

"May Fredie and I be excused? We ah meetin some friends out." Rob says.

"Isn't it rather late to be meeting friends?"

"It is a few of us guys gettin tagethah faw some cards. They haven't seen Fredie faw a while. I thought I would take him round."

"Make sure you don't wager more than you can afford, Son, no matter what the others may be doing."

As Rob and Fredie rise to leave, Ella takes her older brother's arm and whispers, "Tell Eliot I said hello."

Rob gives her a stern look and says, "I will do no such thing. You need ta fuhget about Eliot Gordon, and you bettah not let Fathah hear you sendin him greetins.

"Don't be such an old man, Rob. Don't make me pinch you, too."

Both boys laugh as they leave the room.

"What were you three laughing about?" Frederick asks.

"I told Rob ta place a bet faw me, and he refused. He said ladies don't gamble."

Mattie watches the interchange with a stirring of unease. Ella had been heavy on her mind before she had gotten swept up in her own romance and wedding. If the girl's mother were alive, would she be trying to alter the course Mattie fears Ella is taking? She hasn't done anything too bad of yet that she is aware of, but she does not think her father is any match for her will. She plays him and both her brothers like a harpsichord, and Mattie will not be here to guide her. Maxie will do what she can, but she will be lucky not to fall victim to Ella's manipulations. The best option might be for Frederick to send her to their grandmother who, with the help of her Aunt Anne, might be able to rein her in—or to Sophia in Baltimore. Ella would not like leaving her friends and the society of Savannah, so she will, in all likelihood, be going nowhere. She is the apple of her father's eye, and he has yet to make her do anything she hasn't wanted to do. She loves Savannah, and to date, it loves her. Mattie hopes her little sister will do nothing to fall from favor.

Chapter 14
The Wrath of Clarence Stiles

Savannah, Georgia—1846

"Goodness, Mama, this is like staying in a palace!" Diana exclaims when they awake late in the room Bette has led them to the night before.

"It is a mansion, not quite a palace," Jessie smiles.

"And this is the servants' quarters! This room is bigger than either of ours at home. Mrs. Stiles is quite gracious."

"She is—and I am grateful for her kindness. Frederick assures me she offered, that he didn't ask. He says he had planned to rent a place, but this is much better than staying in Yamacraw."

"I would still like to visit Yamacraw. May we walk by the house where we used to live with Papa Moses? I hope seeing it will bring back memories."

"Of course we can!"

When Jessie notices the time, they hurriedly unpack and trail down the stairs into the kitchen where Bette has instructed them to go for lunch. They find Cook and Pearl with Minda who has come for her usual lesson but stayed for lunch when she found Bette busy. Pearl makes introductions and apologizes to Jessie for her accommodations. Like many people, Pearl seems to forget Jessie is of color.

"The room is wonderful—more than I expected, actually," Jessie assures her.

"Miss Bette argue with the massah bout puttin you on the suhvants' floor, but he said it not right ta give you an the gul a guest room. She put

113

up a fight, but he finally wore her down. I jus want you ta know it not her doin."

"I am glad Mr. Stiles had his way. I would rather be on the same floor as you two. Diana and I will both enjoy this arrangement more."

Minda and Cook are shy around Jessie. Cook has seen her from a distance in the past, and Minda rarely. They find her as lovely and regal as they remember. The hair gathered on top of her head in a tight bun is threaded with silver, but her face is unlined. Dining in the kitchen with her is as intimidating to them as eating with a white person would be. Her carriage and language are no different than their owners other than Jessie's speech retains a hint of French influence. Something about Jessie reminds Minda of Frederick; she decides their common homeland accounts for their similar accents and the way they carry themselves. She wishes Frederick shared Jessie's warmth and compassion.

Jessie sits at the table and tries to help Minda relax by asking after the family she serves every day.

"They all in a tizzy," Minda tells her. "Evahbidy runnin roun like chickens with they heads cut off."

Diana laughs at the image. "Has Miss Gail, the Barrets' cousin arrived from Baltimore yet?"

Minda's eyes widen at the young girl who is darker than she but speaks like her mother. This is a first for Minda.

"If she here, I ain seen her. Dat doan mean she ain. I nevah upstairs at the big house." She catches the disappointment on the girl's face and adds, "But I acks Daisy if you want me to."

"Please," Diana begs. "I know she is coming, and I hope to get to visit with her some while we are here."

"Diana," Jessie reminds her, "we've talked about this. It is unlikely Miss Gail will be allowed to visit with you." She turns to Minda and Pearl who are seated across the table. "Miss Gail is Miss Sophia Howe's daughter. She is a cousin to the Barret girls."

"I membah Ms. Sophie," Minda says. "She the youngess uh the guls. She jus a young'un wen I was on da plantation."

Minda's words remind Jessie of her connection to the rest of the Barret servants.

"How is Mammy? I cannot tell you how much I have missed her and Dovie, Lewis, and Cressa."

Minda relaxes as she updates Jessie on what has happened since she left. They all eat companionably the food Cook puts before them. Minda tells her Lewis and Cressa have a little girl named Lizzy, and Dovie has Ben by a man who isn't owned by the Barrets or a close neighbor.

"I am surprised Frederick allowed Dovie to marry someone outside the family. He isn't eager to acquire new slaves, if I remember correctly."

"You membah right. Dovie do as she awways do. She jus took up with him, an fo the massah know it, she havin Ben. He dint say much, bu we all knows he be none too pleased with her."

"Sounds like Dovie hasn't changed a lot," Jessie replies, and she is surprised when Minda launches into a litany of Dovie's latest escapades and her narrow escape from being sold.

Minda turns to Pearl. "I not be tellin her bout bout Dovie if Mama ain say she almos like one uh us. An evahbidy know what Dovie be up ta enway."

"I am like one of you, Minda, and you will never have to worry about me disclosing confidences. I bet you are happy Daisy is home."

Minda's smile is wider than Cook or Pearl has seen.

"You knows my Daisy?"

"I don't really know her, but I have met her more than once. She came with Mattie to our shop in Baltimore."

"What kind a shop you works in, Mizz Jessie?"

"We have our own shop. We named it *Devereux*'s. That's our last name though I went by Davis here."

"You have yo own stoe?" Minda asks the questions, but both Pearl and Cook are interested in her answer. Jessie can imagine what they are thinking. *How can this lady be anything like us if she looks like she does, talks like she does, and actually owns her own store?*

"I do. I came to the States as a free woman. My husband Moses was a free man. We owned property here. The money from the sale of my house and his business along with my wages from for Mr. Barret gave us enough to start a small business. We make dresses and hats we sell to people like Mrs. Howe."

"We do well for ourselves," Diana, who has been listening quietly, interrupts. "Mama is the best seamstress in the city. Everybody says so."

"Everybody you know says so," Jessie corrects her. "We are fortunate enough to have all the work we can handle."

"Ah you free, too, Mizz Diana?" Cook asks. She can easily imagine Jessie living and working among white people, but Diana's skin color is more like her and Minda's than Pearl's or Jessie's.

"I am," the girl assures them. "My first mother was Moses's sister. The law says the child of a slave follows the condition of the mother. Thank

God, my mother had been freed before she had me. When she died, and my father had to run away, Mama and Papa Moses took me as their own. I am grateful every day for my good fortune."

"And I for mine," Jessie adds. Their openness encourages Minda to ask questions.

"They othah people like you, Diana, where you live?"

"Some," she tells them. "Not as many as we would like. A religious group called The Friends lives in our city. They do not believe in slavery. Mama says they are part of the reason Baltimore has more freed slaves than anywhere in America. We are lucky. The number of free colored people make moving about easier for us."

"You mean you doan have ta have papahs you go out by yoself?" Pearl joins the conversation.

"No, but Mama will not let me go anywhere by myself unless my destination is close by, and we never go anywhere at night unless we have to."

"The city has slave owners, as well, and plenty of them are not pleased with the freedom we have. Like here, they and others would prefer to keep us in bondage. Fortunately, that faction has not managed to have their way yet. And I do not think it wise for any lady, black or white, to be out on city streets after dark," Jessie tells them.

Minda remembers what happened to Jessie in the Barrets' own home. No wonder she doesn't want Diana roaming around alone.

"I sorry, Mizz Jessie, bout what happen ta Moses. I dint know him, but evahbidy say he a good man."

"The best," Jessie says shortly. "Diana, people will be wondering where we are."

They stand, compliment Cook on the breakfast, and go upstairs to gather their materials to take to the Barrets.

"You think I make her sad tawkin bout Moses?" Minda asks.

"I doan know, but if you did, he on her mind anyway. Doan go worryin on it. You need ta get on back and spend as much time as you can with your gul." Pearl tells her.

As Minda is preparing to leave, Bette enters the kitchen. All three women are surprised to see her, for she has postponed more lessons until she determines how she will manage them with guests.

"May I speak with you a moment, Minda, before you go?"

Minda is no longer shocked by Bette's polite manner, but she takes no liberties when addressing her.

"Sho, Mizz Stiles."

"I have received a note from Frederick. He has determined our cookin lessons have gone on long enough," she says. "I know we've been expectin this, but I am sad, nonetheless."

"I suhprise he let me come this long, ta tell the truth."

"He says with all ta be done with the weddin, you ah needed at his house all day. I will try ta devise a way ta come ta you, but meetin will not be easy, faw I cannot come ta Yamacraw unescorted, especially at night. And, faw some reason, Clarence is much more interested in what I am doin lately. I don't know if someone has said somethin to him or if he is simply at loose ends with Reggie and Eliza away at school and Thomas helpin him more at the office. Whatevah the cause, it hasn't been helpful faw his mood. Maybe you should ask Jude ta stay away until things settle down around here."

"I will, Mizz Stiles, an I sho doan want you takin no mo chances if they could be trouble fo you ovah us. You know Jude be helpin Ish an me. We learn mo than we evah dream we would. An we nevah foget yo kineness."

Minda cannot hide her disappointment, and Bette hugs hers.

"This is not the end, My Friend," she assures her. "Let us think of our separation as a summah break. Most students get them. Why shouldn't you?"

"A break from what?" Clarence asks as he swings through the door.

Bette shows remarkable restraint as she steps back from Minda as if hugging a slave is something routinely done. Minda is not nearly as talented an actress and her face shows sheer terror. Pearl steps in and pivots her toward the door as Cook turns her back and busies herself at the counter.

"A break from the cookin lessons," Bette replies casually. "What ah you doin in here? I cannot remembah the last time you came ta the kitchen. It is not a place faw gentlemen." Her tone implies his presence is inappropriate, and as Clarence comes from a less prosperous background, he accepts what she says for truth.

"I could find no one about, so I came searchin faw you." He sounds defensive, but he squares his shoulders and continues, "and thank Providence we will have one less dawkie ta take ah suhvants' time. You refuse ta acquire slaves, yet you use the suhvants we pay money faw ta bettah anuthah man's. A man, I might add, whose daughtah has embarrassed ah family by rejectin ah eldest as if he isn't good enough faw her."

"You may go, Minda," Bette says calmly, and she is out the door before Bette can take Clarence by the arm and lead him from the room. Their voices carry back to Pearl and Cook.

"Clarence, what in the world has come ovah you? Do you want the suhvants ta hear us bickerin like field hands? And what if Minda should tell Frederick what you said?"

"I do not think I should care," he says, but the hesitancy in his voice says otherwise. "And what if she does? What man is goin ta listen ta a dawkie spreadin rumuhs?"

"You know as well as I do Minda is not just any dawkie," Bette replies. Clarence's lack of response tells her he understands exactly what she is talking about. "And, please, Clarence, do not hawbah resentment ovah Mattie's rejection of Thomas. I told you all along they were not a compatible match."

"And, You, My Dear, have the romantic notion that any such thing as a puhfect match exists. You would do well ta stay out of such mattahs and let us with more level heads decide what is best faw ah offspring. I suspect had you done so, Frederick would have insisted Mattie come ta her senses and do what was right. They ah preparin faw an elaborate weddin evahbody who is anybody will be attendin, and we could have been sharin the advantages such an event elicits."

"Oh, Clarence," Bette says tiredly. "I wish othah's' opinions didn't mean more ta you than mine. We have been blessed with an abundance; can you not be content with ah prosperity and quit wantin more?"

"It is easy faw you ta disdain opinion, Miss Bullock, but not all of us have your fathah's name ta commend us. Some of us have ta depend on our own resources ta get by?"

"Is that why you married me, Clarence? Because my daddy was a Bullock? Was I merely a resource you used ta get a leg up in society?"

From the kitchen, Pearl hears Bette let out a quick breath, and in a second she is through the door. Clarence is clutching her mistress by the arm.

"You ah hurtin me, Clarence. Let go!" Bette tries to pull away, but he tightens his grip and shakes her. Clarence takes a sudden step or two backward, letting go of Bette as he does. She falls, and he stands gazing down at her as if he, too, is shocked by finding her on the floor.

"Is this what we've come to, Clarence?" Bette asks.

"Pearl must have pushed me," Clarence yells toward the servant still standing several feet behind where Bette lies on the floor. She glares at Clarence and bends to help Bette up. Clarence stands another moment with a dazed expression on his face, then turns and walks away.

Pearl leads Bette to the parlor and quickly runs to the kitchen for a hot cup of tea.

"Did you push him?" Bette asks.

"No, Miss Bette, I would, had I think of it in time."

"Don't evah, Pearl. I don't know if I could protect you if you did."
Bette is rattled. "It did feel as if he was pushed away from me…"

"Maybe Miss Abby shoved him away from you. I tell you befo—I feel
her here. I smell the lavendah she use ta wear, and they always cold air
come with her scent. Cook say I crazy, but I know what I smell—what I
feel."

"Don't be silly, Pearl. If Abby were goin ta be anywhere on Earth, she
would be at the Barret house."

"I doan know bout that, Miss Bette. She love you like she love her
own."

The thought of Abby's presence is a comfort to Bette, especially now
she wonders if her husband is becoming someone she doesn't know at
all.

"As much as I would like ta think Abby is here watchin out faw
me, othahs would consider such talk crazy. We mustn't give Clarence
anything ta use in claims of lunacy on my pawt."

"Even if she not here ta look out faw you, I am. An I do whatevah I
have to ta keep you safe."

Bette glances around to make sure they are alone before giving her
sister a quick hug. "And I you, Pearl." She pushes herself away. "But we
must try ta put Clarence's mind at rest. Somethin has him troubled, and
no mattah how I try ta reassure him, he remains restless and suspicious.
He is a decent man. Hopefully, when this whole Barret weddin is behind
us, he will settle down."

"If you say so, Miss Bette." The straight line of Pearl's mouth indicates
little confidence in Bette's words. "Did he hurt you?"

"No, but I must admit, he frightened me. He has nevah been violent
before. As I said, it was as if he was pushed from me. I don't think he
meant faw me ta fall."

"You end up on the flo, jus the same. Let's get you upstairs. You
bound ta need a rest."

"I'll stay here a while. You can get on with what you were doin."

What Bette doesn't say is she is afraid to go upstairs in case Clarence
is still in the house. What Pearl doesn't say is she isn't going anywhere
until she knows where Mr. Stiles is. Bette spends the rest of the afternoon
lying on the couch in the parlor while Pearl does needlework in a chair
close by.

Chapter 15
Diana and Jude

Savannah, Georgia—1846

Ella, Maxie, and Sophia's Gail stand stripped to linen shifts in the upstairs breezeway where Jessie and Diana are taking measurements for the dresses they are to make for the upcoming wedding. Mattie has left with Daisy in tow to discover if the fabric she ordered from New York has arrived, and Ella's good mood leaves with her. She has been unable to charm her sister into altering the style of her dress to one she deems less childish.

"I don't undahstand why I have ta have a dress like Maxie and Gail's when I am oldah than both," she announces to Jessie since she is the sole adult in attendance.

"They will be different in color, Miss Barret, and we can add details that will make your dress reflect your own style," Diana tries to placate the girl she considers a customer.

"I was not addressin you, Girl, now was I," Ella states rudely, "and what would you know about fashion since you ah little more than a child yourself?"

Tears well in Diana's eyes, and Jessie's lips compress; her hands stretching the measuring tape across Gail's narrow shoulders still. She is about to say something when Gail speaks.

"Diana knows what she is doin, Ella, and you ah bein unspeakably rude."

"Rude!" Ella sneers. "Since when do I have ta be polite ta a dawkie, and ta one no oldah than you?"

Maxie is about to join the argument when Ella cries, "Ouch!" and whirls toward her sister. She is surprised to find Maxie far from her reach.

"What is wrong with you?" Maxie asks.

"It felt like someone pinched me! We must have mosquitos in here. Somethin is bitin me. Look at the mawk on my arm."

A red whelp stands out on the girl's pale forearm. Jessie smiles to herself. She has sensed a presence since she arrived at the mansion, and she thinks she knows who it is.

"You deserve ta be bitten the way you ah actin. I am tellin both Papa and Mattie on you if TaTa Jessie doesn't."

"You would love to, wouldn't you? Always the snitch. Go ahead and tell Papa. I doubt he is goin ta be ovahly concerned with me reprimandin a suhvant."

"Diana is not your suhvant," Gail states hotly, "and she and Jessie don't have ta make your stupid dress at all if they don't want to. You best remembah that."

Ella appears sobered by this reminder, but she is not about to let Gail get the last word.

"Fuhgive me, Cousin, faw fuhgettin your best friend is a dawkie."

Ella squeals again and another whelp appears on her forearm. "What in the world…," Ella begins, but Jessie interrupts quietly, "That is enough, Ella. I understand you are disappointed by the style of your dress, but no one here is responsible for that decision. And if Diana and I were your servants, treating those less fortunate than yourself cruelly is unladylike and beneath you. If you would like, I will speak with your father and relate your displeasure with our services. I am sure he can find someone else locally to make your dress. Perhaps the seamstress you usually use will be more than happy to oblige."

Ella's face reddens, and all present expect her to flounce off in a huff. Conversely, she does what she often does when she is losing a battle. Her whole demeanor changes and she becomes the picture of contrition.

"I am sorry, TaTa. I have had my heart set on a lowah neckline and a widah skirt. I am fifteen years old, and Mattie is insistin I wear a dress more suitable faw a child. It is not fair she gets ta decide what I wear!"

"I do not think your sister made the decisions regarding your dress." Jessie is unmoved. "Your father had the final say. If you are displeased, you should speak with him."

"Fathah tries ta keep me a child!" Ella wails. "If my mothah were here ta make him undahstand…"

Jessie sighs and waits for the girl to make direct eye contact. "I, too, wish your mother were here. She was kind always. She treated us with genuine compassion."

The comparison is not lost on Ella, but she holds her tongue.

"It is not easy growing up without a mother." Jessie's tone softens. "But I assure you—she would not approve of you being mean to others, even those you deem your inferiors."

Ella's face turns redder, and the tears in her eyes become genuine.

"Why don't you talk to your father again? You can point out what some other young ladies your age are wearing, and I am sure he will listen. It will be best if you control your temper and speak sweetly as you usually do with him. You may not get the exact dress you want, but perhaps he'll be willing to compromise."

"Thank you, TaTa. I will. Do you think you might have a word with him, too? You ah the expert, aftah all. He might be willin ta listen ta you."

"We'll see," Jessie concedes.

"You need ta remembah whose day this is," Maxie interrupts. "No one is goin ta be lookin at us anyway!"

Gail laughs, but Diana's expression doesn't change.

"Ah we about through here," Ella asks, managing to glare at both her sister and her cousin though they are across the room from each other.

"I have what I need from you, Ella. We will cut the others' dresses first. We still have a little time before making a decision about yours."

"I will talk with Papa tonight," are Ella's lasts words before she heads for her room to dress for the evening.

"I am sorry she was rude ta you," Gail tells Diana. "She isn't always so testy. She can be pleasant when she wants ta be."

"The problem is," Maxie puts in, "she doesn't often want ta be."

Gail and Maxie laugh. Diana manages a smile.

"Miss Jessie, may Diana come with us faw a while? I would like ta go ta the Green, and Mama is more likely ta let us go if Diana is along."

"You can go for an hour, Diana, if Mrs. Howe consents. I need to work with Minda in the kitchen anyway. Find me when you come back."

Jessie puts away the sewing supplies and goes to the kitchen to help Minda prepare the meal. The two discuss what all they will have to do to prepare the food for the wedding reception. They work well together, and Diana appears before it is time to serve. She is with her mother when Jude comes rushing in to carry the meal up to the dining room.

"What we havin fo din…"

He stops dead in his tracks when he catches sight of his mother's company.

"The cat got yo tongue?" his mother teases. "This Miss Jessie an her gul Diana. You membah them from when day here b'fo?"

Jude shakes his head but says nothing.

"I remembah Jessie from Lew an Cressa's weddin, but you and Diana were jus lil tots back then," Minda adds.

"Hello," Diana smiles warmly. "We must be about the same age, then."

"Ise fo'teen, be fifteen in a coupla months," Jude says flatly.

"I am fourteen, too," Diana says excitedly. "We must have played together when we were children."

"We warn't roun da big house much in those days," Minda explains, "so you probly jus see each othah onest. An mabe at church."

The usually talkative Jude appears to be at a loss for words. When Lewis appears, Jude takes his tray and heads upstairs to deliver the food. By the time he has finished upstairs and returned to the servants' kitchen, he appears more comfortable in the presence of the newcomers. Deke, Ben, and Lizzy have none of their cousin's reservations, and Ish is downright smitten. They squeeze closer to make room for Diana at the end of the table and vie for a position next to her. Jude ends up across the table after he makes a point of washing his hands at the dishpan with more fervor than anyone has ever seen from him.

The reunion between Mammy and Jessie is entertaining for the others. Mammy actually squeals when she comes into the room, and the taller woman hugs Mammy and the two of them dance around the table. Mammy's children and grandchildren watch in amazement. When everyone is seated, Mammy says, "Ise goan come righ ou an mit I sho mist yo cookin, an we ain hab bu two new dresses sin you be goan!"

"An aftah all my hard work in da kitchen," Minda laughs, "this the thanks I git."

"Youse got plum good, Chile, but they's nobidy kin cook lack dis woman!"

Dovie and Cressa stay as long as they can, but they each have places they have to be. Minda, Mammy, and Jessie sit at one end of the table while the young people crowd around the other. Jude picks at his food which makes him fall behind the others, and his hesitance finds him still sitting with Diana after Mammy and the younger cousins, with the exception of Ish, have left.

"Ish, why doan you run long now?" Minda tells her youngest.

"I got time yet," he says, but his mother catches his eye and jerks a thumb toward the door. He leaves, but he goes with a scowl on his face. His departure and Minda and Jessie's return to the Barret kitchen leave Diana and Jude alone. Diana exhibits none of Jude's discomfort.

"What do you like to do in your spare time?" Diana asks.

"Doan have much spare time," Jude replies.

"Oh, I guess you don't."

"You foget I a slave?" he asks.

The younger children have already asked Diana a hundred questions. Jude is still trying to come to terms with the reality of the young woman across from him. She is as dark as he but owned by no one. She is dressed as well as the missies, and she wears leather shoes while his feet are bare.

"I guess so," she admits.

"That not somethin I foget offen."

Diana sits quietly, and Jude is beginning to squirm when she speaks again.

"I am aware I am lucky. I am sorry if I was inconsiderate. I don't meet many young people. I am just excited to be with all of you here."

"You say you from Baltimoe? I be a lot happiah there livin free as a bird than here where none uh us can git off this place without a pass."

"I didn't mean my life is as hard as yours. I am trying to say having an extensive family—your cousins, your brother, your grandmother, aunts and uncles—is wonderful... In Baltimore, it's only my mother and me."

"Guess that one good thing bout bein here."

Beginning to feel awkward, Diana rises.

"I like ta read at night fo I goes ta bed. Ish do, too."

"You can read? How wonderful!" Diana plops herself back on the bench. "Reading is my absolute favorite thing to do. How did you learn? I know it is illegal for slaves to read and write."

"A lady teache us—well, taught us. She cain no mo on count her man migh find out. An she give us books."

"She must be nice. This lady teaching you is a secret?"

"Yes, and you cain tell nobidy. Even my cousins. They be all kines of trouble if the massah find out."

"I won't tell. I promise. You can trust me. It is awful some people are not allowed to read and write. Depriving people of that joy is possibly the worse thing a person can do! It's downright cruel! What have you read? What is your favorite book?"

They are still discussing the different books they have read when Jessie comes for Diana.

"There you are, Sweetheart. Mattie is back with the material. We have work to do."

It is clear to Jessie neither Diana nor Jude is eager to leave. After the two part company, Jessie stands where she is as Diana goes ahead of her. A couple of creases appear between her eyebrows as she reflects on what she has witnessed. She intuits, as only she can, that she has witnessed something touching in its innocence and its potential—its raw connection. The realization brings her hope, a sentiment she cannot rationally justify.

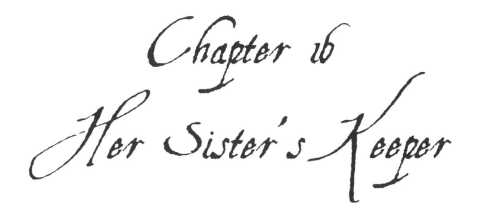

Chapter 16
Her Sister's Keeper

Savannah, Georgia—1846

It would be hard to decide who is having the harder time concentrating—Jude or Ish. Diana sits between them on the floor, book open in front of her, tablet in her lap. Minda sits in a chair behind her. All three students have tablets of their own. Bette has set tasks for each and sent them by Diana who has now become a go-between and substitute teacher. Diana has given Ish an assignment with the understanding she will check his work, but his completion of the task doesn't appear likely since he keeps listening to what she is telling the other two. She has shown him a list of words in the book, and he is supposed to be forming sentences with them. His goal is five different statements. Fifteen minutes after Diana arrives, he has yet to compose the first. Minda is writing a letter to Bette who will correct it and send it back on Diana's next visit, at which time Minda will be expected to rewrite it. Jude's assignment is to solve several arithmetic problems involving money. All assignments are practical exercises to help them should they ever be free or in need of assistance.

"If I had me twenty dollahs," Jude says, "I sho woulden be spenden it on no coal!"

"You would if you were in Baltimore," Diana tells him, "unless you could find yourself a pile of firewood. And you should say, 'I surely wouldn't spend it on coal.'"

Jude takes no offense at the correction. He stares at Diana's mouth as he mimics her words. The dimples that make an appearance when Diana smiles in approval are his reward.

"I surely wouldn't spend it on coal," Ish repeats.

Diana laughs. "Ish, could you more easily complete your assignment if you sat across the room?"

"No, I be quite. I promise."

"I *will* be *quiet*," Diana corrects automatically, and Ish parrots her words.

Minda is not at all sure it is wise to try to change the way she and the boys speak. She understands the advantage reading and writing can give them, but what will happen if Frederick or other white people detect a difference? She keeps telling the boys they must be careful around people, even other slaves. The boys are unlikely to have much conversation with white people other than the Barret children, and dialogue with them will be limited. "Yes, Massah" and "No, Missus" don't take long to say. Minda is the most likely to raise suspicion since she and Frederick converse more than they ever have during his visits.

"Diana, it gittin late. Mabe you best be gettin back ta da Stiles. Jude, doan foget the pass Mizz Stiles give you."

Diana says "Yes, Mam," collects her materials and puts them in the bag she brought with her. As usual, Ish wants to tag along, but Minda refuses as she has every time he's asked over the last two weeks. She understands Ish's desire for she herself is drawn to the young couple and the romance anyone can see blossoming between them. Though she can imagine no long-lasting relationship between the two, she decides to let them enjoy the time they have left in Savannah.

As the pair walks across town, Jude finally works up the nerve to take Diana's hand.

"It dawkah than sin out here. Doan want you fallin or nothin."

"It's kind of you to look out for me, Jude."

"You doan know the way like I do."

"I'd like holding your hand even if I did know the way," Diana says boldly.

Jude stops in the path and gazes at her. "Good, then," he says, and the two of them walk on. They have to pass the front of the Stiles mansion to get to the back servants' entrance, and because they are talking and laughing, neither notices Clarence sitting on the front verandah.

"Boy!" he shouts. "Come up here and let me see who you ah."

The two stop abruptly. "Ise da Barrets' boy," Jude calls out.

"Come on up here like I told you," Clarence yells again, "and bring whoevah that is with you."

They have no choice but to open the gate and climb the steps to stop in front of him. "It's me, Mr. Stiles. Jessie's girl."

"What ah you doin out this late? Shouldn't you be upstairs with your mothah doin whatevah you came here ta do?"

"Her mama jus send somethin ta my mama, an I dint want her wawkin alone, sose I come wid her," Jude says.

Jude falls back into speech he knows is expected of him.

"You can't be out without a pass no mattah what you think, Boy."

"I hab a pass."

"Hand it ovah, then," he says and grabs the piece of paper from Jude's hand the minute he pulls it from his pocket.

"My wife gave you a pass?" His voice indicates he is confused and displeased. "Why would she be givin someone else's dawkie a pass?"

"She just didn't want me walking home alone." Diana tries to appear calm but the quiver in her voice gives her away.

"You get on upstairs where you belong, Girl, and, Boy, you git back ta where you came from."

Jude extends his hand for the pass, but Clarence stuffs it in his pocket. "I said get on out of here!"

The young couple hurries down the steps. They stop long enough to touch fingertips before Diana heads toward the back door and Jude turns for home. Jude is barely out of sight before Clarence lets the screen door slam behind him. He finds Bette in the family parlor. He thrusts the pass toward his wife who continues to hold her needlework.

"What is it?" she asks calmly.

"Leave us," Clarence commands Pearl who is sitting in the chair opposite with needlework of her own. Pearl's face does not change expression and she makes no move to obey Clarence. His face turns a deep crimson.

"Pearl, will you please turn our bed down faw the night. I plan ta retire soon."

"Of course, Miss Bette."

Pearl calmly rises and leaves the room as if she hasn't seen Clarence standing with fists clutched at his sides.

"That girl has gone too faw, Bette," he shouts. "I've warned you about allowin her ta think she is an equal around here, and now look at what has come of your lack of discipline. I won't endure bein ignored by an uppity slave."

"You fuhget Pearl is not a slave, Clarence, and she works here undah her own volition. I will not have you treatin her badly."

"You will not have…" he growls between clinched teeth. "I am the one who will decide what will and will not be done in this house, even if it was bought with your Daddy's money. Pearl fuhgets herself, My Dear, as do you. I am your husband, and you will do as I say no mattah who you think you ah."

"Oh, Clarence," Bette sighs. "What has you riled up this time? Neithah Pearl nor I have done anything ta wahant such hostility. Please, get control of yourself and stop shoutin."

"It is not I who is out of control. It is you. You allow dawkies ta behave as whites in ah own home. You act like you ah a boardin house faw othah people's dawkies. Now you ah writin passes faw slaves that don't blong ta you! Why would Barret's boy have a pass written by you, pray tell?"

For the first time Bette reveals she is not as composed as she lets on. She has set the sewing aside, and her hands shake in the face of her husband's anger.

"I simply didn't want Diana ta be alone aftah dawk, Clarence. You are upsettin yourself and the whole household ovah nothin."

"Why would you allow Diana out aftah dawk, Bette? Have you fuhgotten there ah laws for keepin the peace, and the civilized people of this town will not appreciate your cavalier disregard faw their wishes?"

"I have broken no rules!" The color rises in Bette's cheeks. "And what possible hahm could Diana and Jude have caused? Why ah you upset about this, Clarence?"

"Because this incident is one more instance of you flauntin your abolitionist craziness in the faces of people who recognize the detriment of such foolishness! I have been patient with you, Bette, but I am at my limit. I will not let you degrade ah reputable name and jeopardize all we have built so you can play savior ta a bunch of heathens who wouldn't know what ta do with the privileges you give them if you weren't around ta show them. And if you keep this up, you may not be around ta show them."

Bette rises slowly from her chair. "What do you mean, Clarence? Why wouldn't I be around? Ah you threatenin me?"

"I have no need ta threaten you, but I have evah right ta control my own wife if she cannot control herself. Not a handful of people in this town would disagree with me. I can take measures ta git our house back in awdah, though Heaven knows I would hate to. I can banish certain influences, free or not, and I can puhchase suhvants who ah wise enough ta respect their superiors. And there ah places you can be sent ta help you regain your senses, and I am well within my rights ta send you ta such a place."

Bette's face is ashen, her compressed lips almost blue.

"And you would send me ta such a place, Clarence. You would commit the mothah of your children? The woman who gave you this powah you wield imperiously? You would cast out the woman you know ta be my sistah? Is this the man I married, that I have shackled myself to faw life?"

"Don't you dare speak of that woman bein your sistah!" Clarence shouts. "And I will do what is best faw this family! Thank God ah children ah not presently undah this roof ta witness what you have become."

"Have become? I am the same I was the day you met me. You were aware of my egocentricities, as you have called them, from day one—I made sure you were. Now you have secured what you want, you declare me a crazy person, one who must be controlled."

"Many will say you ah lucky, Bette." Clarence's voice becomes soft. He actually smiles, any trace of anger gone from his face and posture. Bette finds the quick transformation chilling. "You ah fortunate I am here ta keep you from your own undoin. We will tolerate the woman and her daughtah you have taken in until aftah the weddin. When she leaves, I suggest you send Pearl with her. I am sure you will be comfuhted by knowin she will be with someone you trust and obviously admire. Since your fathah foolishly freed the poor wretch before I had any say in the mattah, she can go nawth and live with the rest of those dawkie-lovin do-goodahs. I will spend the time between now and then procurin us some house suhvants who will know their place."

Tears stream down Bette's face though her expression doesn't change until she flinches when he reaches out to wipe them.

"Try not ta worry, Dear. Evahthing will settle down and be bettah than evah soon. I would nevah send you away unless I determined I had absolutely no othah choice."

Clarence stands as if waiting for some reply, but receiving none, he finally turns and leaves. His heels tap across the floor before the screen door slams once more. Bette goes to her bedroom where she finds Pearl standing perfectly still. Bette can think of nothing to say. She shakes her head in despair.

Jessie stands in the shadows on the upper landing. It is just as well the man of the house has not seen her, for the anger on her face might have made him rethink his decision to allow her to stay until after the wedding. She agonizes for both Bette and Pearl and wonders how long Abby's dear friend has been living with his anger. A storm is brewing, and trouble is coming to the Stiles' mansion. She would love to be far away when it arrives, but Mrs. Stiles and Pearl may need her. She sighs deeply and tries to shake off the foreboding that permeates the house.

Chapter 17
Brothers

Savannah, Georgia—1846

"You goan break that doe plum off the hinges! What the mattah with you, enway? You near scairt me ta death!" Ish has jumped from his place in front of the cold fireplace. His tablet lies on the floor where he dropped it. He glares at his brother.

"That Stiles man what wrong with me! He treat Diana an me like we criminals. He keep it up, I may be one. I wrap my hans roun that scrawny neck uh his til he remembah who he talkin to!"

"He hurt you or Diana?"

"No," Jude admits, "but he take my pass an tell me ta git on home like a cur beggin fo scraps. He make me look like a coward in front uh Diana."

"She know you no coward, Jude," Ish places a hand on Jude's shoulder, but he shrugs away and paces the small room.

"An he goan take his angah out on Mizz Stiles. I find out he do, I kill him fo sho."

"An then you hang fo sho. An what good all Mizz Stiles help do us or her then?"

The fear in Ish's voices registers with Jude.

"You cryin?"

"No!" Ish denies. He turns toward the fire to hide the tears. "I jus thinkin bout Mama. What she do she lose you aftah she lose Daisy ta Mizz Mattie? She be left with me, an what hep a cripple goan do her, tell me that?"

"Doan call yosef a cripple, Ish. That not like you."

"Why not? That what evahbidy else call me?"

Jude sighs, his anger spent. "Who call you a cripple? Nobidy we care bout. Since when you be lisnin ta people doan know nothin?"

"Since you sho ta do somethin stupid, an I haftah watch out fo Mama by mysef." Now Ish is the one who is angry.

"You doan haftah watch out fo nobidy by yoself." He wraps his forearm under his little brother's neck and gives his head a scrubbing with his knuckles.

"Quit that!" Ish yells and pulls away. "I glad Mama not hear you tawk like a crazy man!"

"Speakin uh Mama, where is she? She here when I left."

"She back at the Barrets' doin weddin stuff. I be glad when dis mess ovah an things can git back ta normal."

"Normal?" Jude repeats. He sighs and slides to the floor. "Who wanse normal? An you foget Daisy be gone an we probly nevah see her again?"

"Sho we will," Ish sits beside his brother. "Mizz Mattie come back ta visit her fokes, an Mizz Jessie tell Mammy an Mama she like bein here mo than she think she would. Mabe she come mo now an bring Dinah with her." Ish pauses long enough to get up the nerve to ask his next question. "You loves Mizz Dinah, then?"

The boys' eyes meet but skip away.

"It Di-an-a," Jude corrects. "What I know bout love? All I knows I like bein round her."

"She sho pretty," Ish says.

"She be mo than pretty. She talk ta me like I somebody. Like I ain jus some slave boy that doan know nothin. An I ain nevah see a cullad girl talk or act like her. She read an write. We talk bout things besides what da massah do now or what one of the missies up to. She undahstand things I nevah will."

"You smawt, too, Jude! You da smartess boy I knows!"

Jude laughs and grabs him around the neck again. "You doan know many boys then."

"I knows plenty," Ish pushes him away. "Da one thing youse not smawt bout is that tempah uh yose."

"Yours," Jude automatically corrects.

"Yours."

"One of these days you goan git mad at da wrong time, an you goan do somethin Mama or Mizz Stiles cain get you ouddah. Then whar you goan be? An Mama? An me?"

This time Ish doesn't try to hide his tears. Instead of trying to hug him again, Jude picks up his leg and begins to massage.

"An why you and Mama keep doin that? All the rubbin in the worl ain gonna do no good. It nevah will." Ish rises from the floor with his tablet in hand. "Ise goin ta bed."

Jude gives his brother a few minutes to get settled then follows him to their room. He lights the lamp and takes a book from under their cornshuck mattress. He can tell Ish is not asleep by his rigid back. He opens the book and begins to read aloud. Ish makes no comment, but Jude keeps glancing his way until the boy's shoulders relax. He waits until his soft snores indicate he is soundly asleep before putting the book away. He lies quietly replaying the evening in his mind. He wishes he could sleep as his brother is sleeping. Though no tears fall, it would be a relief if they would.

Chapter 18
The Ire of the Crow

Savannah, Georgia—1846

T he mansion is overflowing because mere hours remain until the eldest Barret child will wed. Normally, Frederick would be in his element entertaining family and friends, but the occasion has made him more reflective than usual, and though he would never admit it, he is already tired. He stayed up late with the boys and Mattie who was too excited to retire early.

He lay awake most of the night tossing and turning and thinking about what this occasion would be like were Abby still with him. He has missed her more in the last few days than he has in years. It is as if he can feel her presence, a fact he has shared with no one. Frederick is not one for sentimentality, and he judges this uncharacteristic sensitivity a result of the occasion.

He is glad when dawn breaks and he can see clearly enough to make out the furniture in the room. He arises before the servants are about and dresses himself. The wedding is to be held at noon, a couple of hours later than is customary in Savannah. Frederick has convinced Reverend Acton the extra time is needed for them to prepare the house and the spread for the reception to follow. By nine o'clock, Frederick manages to rouse Robart and Fredie, and the three of them help the servants set up chairs on the Green across the street from the house. A beautiful Saturday morning in June has proven to be the perfect time for a wedding. The lawn and the trees are green, and the rows of chairs march like white-clad soldiers beneath the lace of Spanish moss. It hangs from the limbs of the live oaks like they, too, are wearing veils for the occasion. Frederick smiles. Mother Nature is doing her best to give Mattie the wedding she deserves.

Upstairs, Maxie has finished with her bath, and Ella is stepping into the tub. Mattie sits at her vanity with Daisy arranging her hair. She wears a long linen undahsheath with pantaloons peeking out from under them. She and Daisy talk easily as Daisy wraps a lace band across Mattie's forehead and tucks the ends behind her ears to tie to the side where they trail past her shoulder. It takes little to create a head full of dark ringlets because, like her two sisters, her curls are natural. Her widow's peak peeks from below the bottom of the band.

"Do you think we should covah my peak or let it show?" she asks Daisy.

"I likes it, Mizz Mattie. Sides, it goan be hawd ta keep covuhed. I knows mine be."

Mattie's eyes go to Daisy's widow's peak, one every bit as pronounced as her own, one from which the girl's kerchief sits far back.

"Yours is as low as mine."

"Theys da same, you acks me. Theys a sign we blongs tuhgethah," Daisy smiles at her mistress's reflection in the mirror.

"We do, don't we, Daisy? I cannot imagine leavin home without you. Ah you as nervous as I am about runnin a household by ahselves?"

"You be da one runnin da househole. I jus dare ta look aftah you!"

"You probably know as much about runnin a home as I do. Fathah has left little faw me ta do here. Ta tell you the truth, I am scared ta death. I wish Mothah was here ta have puhpared me bettah. Or TaTa Jessie would stay with us faw a while."

"Mizz Jessie gots er own bidness ta tend to. Wese jus gonna haftah do da bess we kin."

"I hope Whit's suhvants know what they ah doin. Do you think they will accept us? You know how dawkies can be."

"I guess I does, seein as I be one!" Again, both girls laugh.

"Sometimes I fuhget, Daisy. You've become more of a companion than a suhvant."

"I be tellin you dat da nex time you acks me ta fetch fo you. Now quit yo worryin. Theys haftah do whut you says; youse da missus. Theys may eben haftah do whut I say—Ise da missus' gul."

Their banter relaxes Mattie. She is not nervous when the time comes to go downstairs. Noon finds them all on the Green. Ella is every bit the belle she hoped to be, and the yellow silk dress she is wearing shows how much influence she has over her father. The dress has few similarities to

Maxie's who stands beside her. Ella's waist is cinched to a circumference at which she cannot breathe deeply, but her skin glows beneath her own crown of dark curls, her yellow half bonnet almost disappearing in their mass. The neckline, though not as low as she wanted, shows enough cleavage to convince anyone daring to doubt, she is indeed a full-grown woman. Maxie stands beside her in blue, the dress's skirt and waistline cut like Ella's, but her youthful figure in no need of a corset. The boat cut of the neckline is suitable for her age.

Ella does her best to peer through her eyelashes at Whit's best man, and she will not be the only young lady doing so today. Both attendants and Whit in military uniforms are enough to give starry-eyed girls dreams of similar occasions of their own.

Maxie, like Whit, has her eyes on the bride on her father's arm. Guests fill the chairs. The girls' aunts Anne and Sophia are in attendance with their daughters. Mrs. Middleton didn't feel she could make the trip, and their uncle is staying with her while Anne is away. Relatives, neighbors, and the servants from many households create a spring bouquet upon the backdrop of the lawn. Bette sits beside Clarence. Both are stiff and distracted—Bette by the turmoil at her house, Clarence by fear someone may remember Mattie's rejection of their son Thomas. Pearl and Cook stand with Diana and Daisy who are sandwiched between Jude and Ish just inside the picket fence across the street in front of the mansion. They will stay long enough to witness the bride and groom say their vows. The other servants and Jessie are working feverishly to prepare for the onslaught of guests who are about to converge on the house.

Reverend Acton stands in front of Mattie who is a sight to behold in the dress Jessie made for her. The bride chose white as most young women are doing since Queen Victoria's wedding to Prince Albert. Her picture in her own white gown has inspired a new trend in England and in the States. The choice is a flattering one for Mattie with her dark hair and olive complexion. The dress is silk like Maxie and Ella's, and like theirs, it is short-sleeved with a V waist, but unlike theirs, the bodice is covered in fine pleats that meet at the waist, pleats that took Jessie hours to shape in a way to get them to taper and form a point. Instead of wearing the veil over her head, she wears it draped over her shoulders. She appears serene, revealing none of the jitters she confessed to Daisy. She appears not at all intimidated by the occasion or the throng of guests surrounding her. She is focused solely on Whit as her father hands her off to him. Whit is not as composed, and the hand he places on Mattie's forearm trembles. There are tears in Frederick's eyes as he steps away from the pair and sits in a chair between Fredie and Rob. The wedding vows remind him of his own, and the guilt he usually keeps at bay washes over him. He broke his vows long before Abby did what she did. He admits he hurt all those put in his care. Nonetheless, Mattie is radiant and his other children happy and united. He claims comfort and casts all negative thoughts aside.

The wedding party moves inside with the guests who admire the house and the furnishings and quickly consume the food it took Jessie and Minda days to prepare. Frederick wonders if any of them remember the last extravagant event in this house and the news that greeted them the next day. He wants nothing to mar his daughter's wedding.

Frederick walks among them, the picture of prosperity and hospitality. He makes sure the servants, decked out in starched white as they were for the housewarming, are behaving as instructed. He likes what he surveys and at last is able to overcome his melancholy. He becomes gayer as the evening progresses, as does Brigitte Maxwell who stays as close to his side as possible. Frederick drinks little—he never does. He likes to be in control at all times, and he thinks drunkenness poor form and an indication of inferior breeding. He removes a cup from Rob's hand without comment. The young man replaces it as soon as his father's back is turned.

Rob and Fredie converse with two young ladies, one of them Letty Henry, the daughter of a couple they have gone to church with since the Henrys moved to Savannah. Letty has grown into a lovely lady, but the visitor she brought with her has claimed Rob's attention. He is at her elbow throughout the afternoon.

As much as Frederick mingles, he cannot be everywhere, and Ella is counting on his preoccupation with the guests. She takes Eliot Gordon's hand and leads him to a pair of double, floor-length windows open to allow the cool air to flow throughout the house. She giggles as she tugs him along the side verandah, through the back courtyard, in front of the carriage house, and into the wooded lot they own next door. She leans her back against a tree and draws Eliot toward her in a way that leaves little doubt this is something they have done before.

"Ah you sure we should be out here?" Eliot is nervous. He shudders to think of what Mr. Barret would do, guests or no guests, if he caught him with his daughter. He would not blame Ella, for Eliot is eight years her elder.

"This is what ah weddin will be like some day," she whispers.

"If your fathah doesn't kill me first."

"Don't be such a scaredy cat," Ella teases. She pulls his face down and presses her lips to his, and Eliot forgets his reservations.

Both of them are startled by a shrill cry from above, and Eliot jerks backward in time to see an angry crow dive toward his head.

"Damn!" he yells and swats at the bird that ascends enough to avoid the blow but immediately dives again. Both are too distracted to register Eliot's breach of manners. Never would he have cursed in front of a lady had he been thinking clearly. Now, his sole objective is to keep the crow from taking a chunk out of his scalp which seems its mission.

"Shoo!" Ella cries, flailing her arms toward the creature as it continues its assault on the man stumbling backward in retreat. The bird finally makes contact, and Eliot cries out in pain as its beak digs into his skull. He finally falls to the ground and cowers with his head pulled between both arms. Ella is desperately searching for a stick with which to discourage the crow when it turns on her. She screeches in dismay and turns to run, but the squawking crow clinches a strand of her dark hair and flies upward. Ella, too, falls to the ground and takes shelter beneath her arms.

The attack ends as abruptly as it begins. Several moments pass before Eliot or Ella muster the courage to rise. Finally, Eliot jumps to his feet and rushes to Ella's side where he gently lifts her by the arm.

"Ah you alright, Dawlin? I am sorry I left you defenseless."

Ella is trying hard to regain her composure, and she is immediately dismayed at how she must look. One glance at Eliot makes her less self-conscious, however, as his usually immaculate hair is standing out around his head, and she can see a small thread of blood from a puncture wound on his forehead. If she were not still in shock, she might laugh.

"I don't think you had much choice!" she says.

She is busy trying to smooth her own hair when another raucous call comes from above. Both sets of eyes dart upward to the small, ebony bird, its head cocked to one side as if contemplating its next move. They are in time to see a long strand of black hair floating from the bird's beak toward them. Without comment, Eliot grabs Ella's hand and they dash toward the building. Once in the open, Ella leads him through the back courtyard into the bottom floor breezeway and into the servant's kitchen where they will not be seen by anyone who matters. She finds Dovie apparently taking a break. The servant's mouth falls open in shock, not just at their disheveled state, but by the fact Ella is in the servants' kitchen. She has never seen a member of the Barret family there.

"Quit gapin at us and pour us some clean watah!" Ella orders.

Dovie does as she is told, and the minute she has produced a pan of water and clean cloths from the laundry, Ella tells her to get back upstairs where she should have been all along.

The young lovers do their best to right the wrongs of their appearances, then decide they cannot possibly reappear from the bottom floor. They will have to go back the way they came, and to do so, they must re-enter the courtyard and make their way to the side of the house. When they get outside, both glance around to make sure the violent crow is nowhere to be seen. Ella thinks something should be done to eradicate the beast, but she can think of no way to report the bizarre attack without sharing where they had been and why.

The skies are clear when the two exit the breezeway. They quickly make their way to the side of the house and into the party still going strong. Ella gently touches the sore place on her head where the hair was yanked out and hopes no one spots the soiled places on their clothes or the red mark left on her beau's forehead. Eliot hopes his sweetheart will soon forget the ignominious way he cowered from a mere bird.

Back in the courtyard, the small crow sits high above at the attic window serenely preening her feathers.

Chapter 19
Wildflowers

Savannah, Georgia—1846

The mood is somber at the Stiles' mansion. Since Diana's encounter with Clarence on the front porch, she has spent as little time there as possible. An aura of gloom and foreboding pervades the home. Jessie is worried about Bette who has not been herself lately. Through Minda she has verified Clarence is still planning to make good on his threat to send Pearl away—possibly Cook, as well. The man has not spoken directly to Jessie on any matter, but the claim is not hard to believe. A storm is brewing, and though she hates to leave Bette alone with the man, she thinks Pearl and Cook may be safer if they are removed from the house. The darkness in Clarence frightens her, and one would have to be blind and deaf to be unaware of his disdain for all people black. Jessie had been shocked by his treatment of Diana and Jude, two young people who have little to do with him and have given no cause for grief.

Last night, when Jessie and Diana arrived late from the Barrets', they met Pearl exiting the room that belongs to Miss Eliza when she is home. Apparently, Bette has moved from her own bedroom to distance herself from her husband. Jessie finds it unfortunate neither Eliza nor her brother Reggie has come home for the summer. She wonders if Clarence is responsible for their absence. Perhaps he is keeping them away until he can make changes they might try to prevent.

Diana has risen early and is breakfasting with Minda and her crew at the Barret mansion. Finding no one stirring in the part of the house reserved for family, Jessie heads to the kitchen in search of Pearl. She can imagine the distress she must feel by the prospect of being sent away from her life-long home. Jessie quietly opens the kitchen door and finds her with Cook. Cook is working at the stove, and Pearl is seated at the table with what looks like wildflowers on a thick sackcloth in front of her. Her face shows no emotion, and the fact she and Cook are not chatting as they usually do leads her to perceive both are distraught. Instead of arranging the wildflowers, Pearl is dissecting them. She has on a pair of cotton gloves, and she picks up each flower, denudes the stem of its green and white petals, and throws the cluster away. She then picks up the stem and presses down the length in a milking fashion. The stalk releases a small amount of yellowish, oily liquid into the bowl. The fluid turns a rusty color within seconds.

"Foke say it smell like parsnip," Cook speaks without turning around.

"Let's hope it taste like them," Pearl replies.

"When you gonna do it?" Cook asks.

"I have ta wait til the time be right. Best when nobidy else aroun."

Odd, Jessie thinks. It is unusual for servants to work outside their roles unless instructed to, and she would not expect Pearl to cook.

Jessie raps lightly on the door facing. Both women gasp loudly.

"You scare us half ta death!" Cook cries.

"You took ten year off my life!" Pearl adds before sitting back down at the table to resume her task.

"I am sorry I startled you. What makes you two so jumpy today?"

"Who not jumpy round here lately. Massah been on a tear fo days."

"Is he still threatening to send Pearl away?"

"He plan for her ta go when you an da gul go. An he get rid of Pearl, I ain goan be far behind, you can count on that. The reason he not send me now, he have nobidy ta cook fo him an the fambly."

"Can Miss Bette not persuade him to be reasonable?" Jessie asks.

"They have ta be speakin fo that ta happen," Pearl says.

Jessie sits at the table beside Pearl. "May I help you with that?"

Pearl drags the pan in front of her farther down the table. "No. No use you gittin yo hands dirty. I bout finished."

"What is that?" Jessie asks. "I don't think I've seen that plant before."

"Probably not. It's a plant my Mama taught me was good ta use in the gawden ta keep bugs off the plants. You have ta thin the juice with watah or it be too strong—kill the plants."

"I guess you are wearing gloves to protect your skin?"

"Yes. Don't want the juice seepin in. Make you sick."

Jessie leans closer. The plant has small, umbrella-shaped clusters of green and white petals. Again she thinks it is some kind of wildflower.

"Good thing you have to add water because you aren't getting much out of those skinny stems."

"Surely you dint come in here fo a gardenin lesson from me, did you?"

Jessie is instantly ashamed of herself. Of course these women do not want to make idle chit chat at a time when the only way of life they've ever had is coming to an end.

"No, I didn't."

Though the atmosphere is dismal, Jessie decides to take the opportunity to talk with them while she can. She sits at the table. Cook turns long enough to tell her biscuits are in the warming shelf and jam is on the opposite end of the table from Pearl. Jessie pours herself a cup of water, takes a biscuit still warm from the cast iron skillet, slathers it with butter from the crock, then adds peach preserves from the bowl beside it. Though she doesn't feel particularly welcome, she begins a conversation she believes needs to be had.

"Pearl, I would love for you to come to Baltimore with me. Our space will be crowded, but we can make you somewhat comfortable until we can find you employment and possibly a place of your own."

Pearl keeps her eyes on her task, and her effort to laugh sounds more like a snort.

"A place uh my own! Who wouldah thought uh such a thing. I been here longah than Miss Bette—this the only home I evah had. We blong togethah, an no man no bettah than a horse tradah have the right ta come prancin in here breakin up ah family."

Tears form in Pearl's dark eyes. Cook turns from the stove, walks over and places her hand on her friend's shoulder and says, "Da Massah ain say nothin bout when he sendin me way, but when he do, Miss Jessie, it be awful good ta know I got a place ta go."

"Neither of you will have a hard time finding work in Baltimore, not with your talents and your papers proving you are free. You may find you like living in another city…" She starts to say with no one to tell you what to do, but she stops because that will never be the case for any of them. They may be called free, but as long as they are suspected of possessing a single drop of negro blood, they will answer to the white powers that be.

"I cain leave her alone, not with him."

Neither Jessie nor Cook need to ask to whom she is referring.

"An the two younguns. They like my own chilren—the only ones I got. Thomas use ta be the same. He was a sweet chile. Then he grow up ta be like his papa."

"It is not like you will never see any of them again. You can come back, and Bette and the children can visit you anytime in Baltimore. The city is not a perfect place to live, but circumstances are better for us. A significant part of the population is made up of a religious group called the Friends. They consider slavery a sin. They even help runaways. The change will be hard at first, but you can be happy there. I am."

"I cain leave Miss Bette with him," Pearl repeats, and Jessie decides to drop the subject for now. She walks to Pearl and places her hand on her shoulder. It is her turn to be startled. A shudder runs the length of her body, and she is relieved when Pearl breaks the connection between them by pulling away. She says nothing more as she leaves by the back door. She has the walk to the Barrets' place to try to make sense of the sensation contact with Pearl gave her. The touch had evoked a mixture of emotions. Jessie had felt turmoil. She had read contradictions: deep love but a matching depth of anger and determination, a sense of foreboding but feelings of hope. Jessie cannot discern what any of what she felt means, but she selfishly wishes she could be far away before the portended happens. She reflects on the plant with which Pearl was working and replays the conversation between her and the cook she had overheard. She vows to protect Diana from whatever is about to happen in the Stiles' mansion, and the only way she can think to keep her safe is to make sure she stays as far away as possible until they leave.

Chapter 20
Tribulations

Savannah, Georgia—1846

Sunday is Minda's day off. She rises early as she usually does, wakes the boys, and fixes their breakfast. Her routine ends when Mammy throws the door open without knocking, and though short of breath, exclaims, "You sistah goan an done it dis time!"

Minda settles her in a chair and plies her with a cup of water before allowing her to recount her sister's latest exploits. Though Mammy doesn't say so, Minda can tell she wants her to intervene again with Frederick. She probably thinks Minda misses church to give herself time to come up with a plan. The truth is, she is too tired to go and certainly too worn out to face Frederick about Dovie's latest shenanigans. Telling the boys she wants some time alone, she sends them off to church, admonishing them to behave as if she were sitting beside them. No sooner are they out the door than she thinks of following them, but, of late, she has been a little angry at God and is in no mood to sing praises to Him when He has allowed Miss Mattie to take Daisy all the way to Richmond for no telling how long despite her fervent and frequent prayers. She does not want to go to church, but neither does she want to be alone to dwell on what she considers the loss of her daughter and Dovie's possible fate. She decides to return to the mansion to finish some chores she was too tired to do after the wedding.

The mansion is quiet when she arrives. Mattie and Whit have left for their honeymoon in London, but they have sent Daisy back to Virginia with Whit's parents where she is to help prepare the newlyweds' home for their arrival. Minda hates she will be alone in new surroundings among people not even Mattie is well acquainted with.

Minda doesn't stay long at the Barrets. Everyone is in church, the Barrets no doubt basking in the praise for the wedding and the gala afterward, her own family likely praying hard for their troublemaker to be spared the master's wrath.

The June skies are blue and the breeze still cool enough to enjoy, but the beautiful weather is lost on Minda. She walks slowly back to Yamacraw allowing herself to focus on Dovie's predicament. Dovie was caught leaving the house after the wedding reception despite swearing to anyone who would listen she was a changed woman after being caught last time. Thinking the family members would be exhausted, she had left in the wee hours of the morning with a sack of wedding delicacies she had gathered from the kitchen. Minda isn't sure if she was taking them to someone else or was going to try to sell them, for she is not saying. Frederick, who had been keyed up from all the excitement, was standing on the upstairs balcony when she came out of the back door with her bounty. Her snow white uniform had stood out like a beacon under the light of a barely waning moon. He almost scared her to death when he yelled, "Where do you think you are going?" It didn't help matters that she was standing practically on top of the spot where Miss Abby breathed her last. Her scream brought Lew running from the quarter with Mammy close on his heels. Mammy had grabbed the incriminating sack and returned it to the house with Dovie in tow, and all Frederick had to say on the subject was a promise to address the situation later. Now, all are a bundle of nerves, especially young Ben who has been living under the threat, for some time now, that his mother may be sold. He knows he could be sold, too, or worse, separated from her.

With dawn had come hope in the quarters. Mammy said they think Frederick's elation over the success of the wedding may render him generous enough to let the infraction go. Minda understands the master better than any of them, and she is not optimistic.

Minda decides she can do nothing about Dovie at the moment. To distract herself, she tries to turn her mind to more pleasant subjects. She thinks of Jessie and Diana. They are scheduled to leave the day after tomorrow, though Frederick has offered Jessie everything he can think of to keep her in Savannah. Jessie has asked that Diana be allowed to stay at the Barret mansion as much as possible to keep her out from under Mr. Stiles' feet. Minda can certainly understand this desire, and Jude is beside himself with excitement because he will get to see more of Diana before she leaves.

Minda lies on her bed and stares at the ceiling. She is worried about Miss Bette and the change in her behavior. She has seen little of her because her husband is watching her like a hawk. She misses her lessons and her teacher as well as the camaraderie she has shared with Pearl and Cook. What will she do if she loses their friendship? With Daisy gone and Dovie's fate in question, the future looks bleak. Minda rarely allows herself to wallow in self-pity. Now she is doing what she has lectured her sons not to do—longing for life to be different and wishing she had choices other than accepting whatever it throws her way.

Her boys arrive home to the unusual sight of their mother lying quietly on the bed in the middle of the day.

"You alrigh, Mama?" Ish asks.

"Sho am," she says. "Jus restin a bit fo I put you dinnah out. You can keep me compny and tell me what the revren talk bout."

The desperate look the boys throw each other make it hard for her not to smile.

"Diana was in church today," Jude changes the subject. "It alright we take a walk."

"Sho you can, soon I git some food in yo belly."

"I goin too," Ish says.

"No, you not eithah!" his brother tells him. "You evahwhere we be, and jus this once, we want ta go alone."

"Why?" Ish is genuinely confused. "What you goan be doin that I cain do, too?"

"We ain goan be doin nothin, but we want ta do nothin with jus the two of us."

"Diana say that?"

He reads the answer on Jude's face.

"I thought so! You jus doan want me ta go!"

It is unusual for the brothers to fight, and both Minda and Jude see the hurt on Ish's face. Jude turns his pleading eyes to Minda, and she intervenes.

"Son, I was hopin ta go fishin', an I doan feel right goin by mysef. Do you mind goin with me?'

This offer is tempting, but Ish is almost as enamored with Diana as Jude. His eyes alight with a plan.

"Less all go fishin! I put da crickets on Diana's hook an evahthing."

Jude's face falls.

"I had rathah it be jus us this time, Son. I be busy with the weddin, an I ain see nothin but yo tail en goin out the doe or you humped bidy on the bed. Less pack us a bite an have a picnic on the bank, jus the two uh us."

Ish casts a glare Jude's way and finally acquiesces. "Alrigh, Jude, but you ain eatin none of our fish, you doan hep ketch em."

Minda packs two sacks of leftovers Frederick allowed for the servants from the wedding feast. She gives one to Jude who hurries off to find Diana who is hanging out with Mammy at the big house until he can get away. Ish and Minda make their way to the river. The sun on their faces and Ish's obvious enjoyment in finding crickets and catching several fish sooth Minda's frayed nerves. She vows to practice what she preaches and make the best of her situation. Daisy will come to visit with Miss Mattie, and Frederick has never sold a slave. She is almost content when she and Ish head for home.

"I guess I let Jude have some fish. They's plenty an it a shame ta let them go ta waste."

Minda laughs aloud for the first time in a long time. She hugs her youngest to her side and thinks everything may be fine in spite of Dovie's reckless behavior.

Chapter 21

Carrots

Savannah, Georgia—1846

Bette Stiles is determined to try one more time to talk some sense into her husband. She has asked Cook to prepare a meal of his liking, and noon finds the two of them sitting down to pork chops, creamed potatoes, green beans, and candied carrots. Pearl is serving as usual, and Bette wonders who will take over the task if she is unsuccessful in changing Clarence's mind.

"I am suhprised you suhve carrots the last day you ah here knowin your mistress detests them," Clarence smiles. Unlike the women, he is almost gay.

"I not the one ta choose. Cook had carrots, so she cook carrots," Pearl replies.

"It is fine, Pearl. I have plenty of othah things ta eat."

Bette smiles sadly at the woman who has always been a part of her life. Pearl smiles back, and Bette is comforted to see she does not seem as disconsolate as she herself is. There is an odd energy about her. Bette senses an excitement, one out of character with her nature, but the woman's life is about to take a path none of them can predict. It is no wonder her behavior is different.

"You may go," Clarence tells Pearl. "I am sure you have things ta do ta prepare faw your depahture in the mornin. You will be leavin early. I will be checkin your bag. You might want ta remembah that when you pack."

"Good Heavens!" Bette cries. "Can you be any cruelah? Pearl has been nothin but faithful all the years of my life, and this is the way you treat her?"

"You may go, Pearl," Clarence repeats, and without acknowledging either of them, Pearl leaves the room. Bette can hear her making her way up the front stairs, a last rebellious act on her part since Clarence has forbidden the servants their use unless they are cleaning them.

"See," Clarence sneers, "this is the reason she has ta go."

"I will nevah fuhgive you faw this," Bette says quietly, for she realizes no amount of pleading will change his mind. Though her face shows no expression, tears form two paths to wet the collar of her dress. "There is no hope faw us from this day fahward."

"You ah upset now, Dear," Clarence says, "but given time, you will admit I am right. This move on my pawt may save you from a faw gravah fate. Now, please finish your meal—it's gittin cold. Mine was delicious, though the sauce on the carrots was unusual—had an almost bittah flavah. I am not sure I like it. Will you have a word with Cook?"

"You must not have disliked it too much," Bette replies. "You ate evahthing on your plate."

Bette rises and leaves the table. Clarence calls for her to come back and finish her dinner, but she ignores him. She climbs the stairs to the servants quarters, opens the door to Pearl's room, and is surprised to see Pearl sitting calmly on the side of her bed.

"Let me help you pack," Bette offers.

"Not in the mind to yet."

"I know this is hawd, Pearl, and if I didn't think you goin was best faw you, I would be fightin hawdah ta keep you here." Bette's tears are unabated now. "You will be fine with Jessie. She has promised me she will help you. As she told you, you can stay with her until you can find somethin faw yourself. Think of the possibilities, Pearl. You can be free in Baltimore in a way you can nevah be here."

"I plenty happy here til the massah come along. An I ain evah gonna be happy knowin you here with him an me too faw away ta help you if you need me. I be fine with Miss Jessie and Diana, but you ain nevah gonna be alright here with a man like him."

Bette sits beside Pearl and sighs deeply. She wipes at her watery eyes and red nose; her shoulders slump forward, her whole demeanor one of defeat.

"I have made my bed, Pearl. I chose poorly, and I am payin faw it. Clarence can have me committed if he wants. I will bide my time, and surely God will show me a way. We can write, and I will get ta Baltimore when I can."

Pearl actually smiles. "Evahthing gonna be fine, Miss Bette. You see. God ain gonna let someone the likes of the massah git the best of someone as good as you."

"Bette!" comes a shout from below. At first Bette ignores him, but when he calls her name again, she rises.

"I guess I bettah go."

"I guess you bettah," Pearl replies.

Bette goes as far as the first landing and calls down, "What do you want, Clarence? I am retirin faw the evenin."

Her husband doesn't reply, but she hears a noise, possibly a groan. She reluctantly descends the rest of the stairs and enters the dining room. Clarence still occupies the chair in which she left him, but instead of sitting upright, he is bent double. Something is obviously wrong. He is clutching his stomach and moaning. Vomit forms a puddle on the floor in front of him. Cook is clearing the table as if everything is normal.

"The massah be feelin poorly," she says and turns to the kitchen with the last of the dishes in her hands.

"Cook, get Authah. I need help in gettin Mr. Stiles ta bed," Bette calls after her.

Cook doesn't respond, but Arthur hurries into the room. He is the Stiles' one male servant. He acts as driver and fills any other role asked of him. He is a small man, and it is all he and Bette can do to get the heavy Clarence out of the chair and headed toward the stairs. Clarence mumbles something about a doctor, and Bette promises she will send for one as soon as they get him to bed. They meet Pearl halfway up the stairs, and she grabs both of his feet. The three of them manage the task in spite of Clarence's moaning and writhing.

"Go, Authah," Bette tells him. "Get Dr. Warin. Take the carriage—it will be fastah."

Clarence isn't any more comfortable in bed than he was below. He is still retching, but nothing is coming up. Dry heaves turn into tremors, and though Bette has never witnessed spasms and twitching of the nature Clarence is having, she realizes they must be seizures. His mouth gapes open, and he jerks all over. When he grows still, his eyes focus beyond Bette's shoulder and he cries, "What is that? Git it out of here! It's gittin mud evahwhere! Git it out of here!"

No sooner has Bette gotten him to lie back than he sits upright again and yells, "There's fire! There's fire evahwhere! Git the children out!"

"He's hallucinatin," Bette says.

Pearl hands Bette a wet cloth. "Here, this may ease him some."

"Where ah we?" Clarence asks, his eyes fixed on Bette's above him.

"We ah in ah bedroom, Clarence. I have sent faw Dr. Warin. I don't have any idea what is wrong, but he will be here soon. Can you try ta lie quietly?"

Bette's words or the wet cloth she wipes his face with calm him, or he simply gives into exhaustion after the wildness of the last half hour. He falls back onto the pillows, his eyes half closed.

"Thank God!" Bette says, "What in the world could be wrong with him? He was fine at dinner."

"No tellin, Ms. Bette. He seems ta be restin peaceful now. The worse must be ovah."

"I pray so," Bette whispers. She sits down on the edge of the bed to catch her breath. "I have nevah seen anything like this!"

The worse is indeed soon over. Bette verifies he is no longer in the land of the living when a hand placed on his chest detects no movement whatsoever. Pearl realizes he is dead when she perceives a disturbance in the air around her. She will later tell Cook the temperature in the room dropped, and it was as if she were besieged on all sides by anger. In spite of her fear, she keeps her face stoic. She takes the liberty of sitting on the bed beside her mistress, an act that will further infuriate her newly departed master if it is actually his presence she is sensing. Bette turns to her for comfort, and the two women sit quietly. Finally, Bette pulls away.

"I cannot say I have loved Clarence faw a long time, but I nevah wanted him ta die."

"You too kind ta wish somethin bad on anybidy, no mattah how much he deserve it. But appears I won't be goin ta Baltimore aftah all."

Bette's eyes grow wide. She takes her sister by both arms and faces her. "Oh My God, Pearl, what have you done?"

"I have not done anything that dint need doin." Pearl says calmly.

Bette is saved from answering by the sound of Arthur leading the doctor up the stairs.

There is nothing left for Dr. Waring to do but pronounce Clarence dead. He turns his attention to Bette who appears to be in shock. The doctor tries to question her, but she is incapable of words. He gives her something to help her rest. After Pearl helps her to bed, she follows the doctor downstairs.

"Girl, is anybody here other than you?" he asks.

"Cook be here an Authah who come ta fetch you. The Stiles hire cleanin help, but the three uh us all that live in."

"I mean any other family member. I need to discover what happened."

"Then you best come back an talk ta the missus in the mawnin. She the only one here when the massah took sick."

"What did he act like when he got sick?" Dr. Waring asked.

"I wasn't there. You needs ta ask Miss Bette."

The air is so thick Pearl has difficulty breathing. She wonders if Clarence can actually kill her from the grave.

The doctor studies her, eyebrows drawn downward. "Someone needs to prepare the body. I will send the undertaker and I will be back to check on Mrs. Stiles in the morning. I will let myself out."

Pearl stands where she is until the door closes. She releases the air from her lungs and moves to the kitchen where she finds Cook elbow deep in dish water.

"I done clean up the dinin room flo an all the dishes. They ain nuthin left but the bidy."

"Good. I talk ta Miss Bette in the mawnin an see if she can't foget some of the puhticulahs."

"You sho you oughta?" Cook asks. "You sho she ain gonna tell the doctah mo than he need ta know?"

"I cain be sure, but I doan think so. We been tuhgethah a long time. I doan think she do anything ta hurt me."

"You bess be right, or both uh us gonna hang."

"Do you feel him here?"

"I feel somethin, an it ain good. Mabe it jus be our guilt talken ta us."

"It goin ta have ta talk loudah ta make me feel guilty bout doin somethin that goin ta make the world a bettah place."

Pearl sends Arthur to the Barret mansion to tell Jessie what has happened. Jessie leaves Diana to spend the night on the cot in the Barrets' laundry room with Mammy as she has since her encounter with Clarence. She enters with Arthur to find the house quiet, and she seeks out no one. She quickly makes her way to the attic rooms where she opens the windows wider than they already are. The aura of malevolence is less oppressive in her room than in the lower rooms, but still her spirit struggles. She lies on her bed with the muslin sheet pushed to the side, yet she is still warm. She dozes fitfully before finally falling into a deep sleep. The next morning she will wonder, as she sometimes does when she communes with Moses, if her relationship with him is nothing more than dreams. Tonight's contact is different. She is not with Moses as usual; she is an observer. She plays the role of eavesdropper as she listens not just to Moses, but to Abby. It reminds her of the previous dream in which she saw Abby with Frederick. She is not completely surprised because her dream Moses has told her long ago that Abby is still at the Barret mansion. The possibility has brought Jessie both comfort and regret. She is happy envisioning the children's mother looking out for them as she truly believes Moses performs constant vigil for Diana and her. Abby still wears the dress she died in but appears quite healthy and content, more so, in fact, than she did at times when she was living.

"How da man ack wen he dyin?" Moses asks Abby.

"He threw up until he could throw up no more. He twitched and jerked all ovah. Toward the end he was talkin out of his head. He died quickly—his symptoms couldn't have lasted ovah an hour."

"Sound like whut theys call watah hemlock. Only thing I knows dat kill dat fast."

"Now Clarence is in the house, and he's rantin. I couldn't stand ta be around him! We can make ourselves felt if we are agitated enough, and I don't see how any of us could be mo worked up than Clarence. He knows they killed him. I am not sure I can stand ta be ovah there anymore."

"Jess an Diana be walkin inta a powdah kaig, an theys ain nuthin I kin do bout it cep go wid em an hope Jess can git some sleep sose I kin tell her whut happen."

"They are in no dangah physically, Moses. In fact, I cannot imagine him breakin through any time soon. It took me years ta learn I could impact the livin, and you have yet ta do it at all. He frightens me because he is hostile!"

"If dat mean whut I thinks it do, him dat way fo him die, sose no wondah him still be. I guess eben a good killin cain take da meanness ouddah a bidy."

Moses smiles, and Abby laughs.

"We ah awful, Moses!" she says.

"Naw," he replies, "wese jus human."

When they realize what he has said, they laugh harder.

Jessie wakes gently, carrying with her the happiness of seeing Abby again and the friendship she and her husband have formed. Later, she will question the reality of what she has seen. She may have the most realistic dreams ever had by anyone, or the phenomenon may be another facet of the gift she was born with. Whatever the case, she cherishes the dreams. They have given her what she badly needed after Moses' death, and she thanks God for the comfort they bring her. Finally, she falls asleep again and listens to Moses tell her what she already knows.

Chapter 22

Business Matters

Savannah, Georgia—1846

Jessie arises early, but no earlier than the doctor. She finds Bette sitting in the front parlor with him and Thomas. The young man must be stunned by the recent development. Bette, gracious as usual, asks her to join them.

"No, please, I didn't mean to interrupt." Jessie turns to leave but is stopped by Dr. Waring.

"It's my understanding you are a guest here."

Jessie nods.

"I would like you to stay in case you might have something to add."

She can think of much she might add and refrains from smiling at the thought of citing her source. She stands hesitantly until Bette repeats gently, "Please stay, Jessie. Your presence is a comfort."

Jessie sits and the doctor resumes his questioning.

"He was out of town all day the day before yesterday," Bette says.

"Where had he been?" the doctor asks.

"I don't know faw sure. Business of some sort."

"Fathah rode down ta Hinesville ta the courthouse. He said he had some business ta attend to and was goin ta talk with a man about some dawkies he had faw sale while there. Said he and Mothah were goin ta puhchase some suhvants so he could quit spendin money hirin othah people's slaves."

The doctor turns to Bette as if he expects her to elaborate, but she sits still, hands folded in her lap. She gives no indication her son's information is news to her.

"Did you see him when he returned?" the doctor asks Thomas.

"No, my landlady provides meals through the week, and I dine with Mothah and Fathah on the weekends. Why is it important faw you ta know what he was doin the day before he died?"

"I am trying to discover if he may have exhibited symptoms of his malady that can give us some idea of what kill...," the doctor pauses before substituting the less offensive "took him."

"Mrs. Stiles, how did he appear when he got home day before yesterday? Was he complaining of any pain?"

Bette meets the doctor's eyes. "Now you mention it," she says, "Clarence did say he had a catch in his side. He said it made him uncomfortable on the ride home. He said he had eaten a heavy noontime meal, and he went ta bed without suppah."

Jessie decides Bette is embellishing, but if the doctor suspects, he gives no indication.

"Did he vomit or complain of diarrhea?" the doctor asks.

"Not then. Yestuhday aftahnoon, aftah dinnah, he complained again of side pain, and I asked Authah ta help him upstairs. We put him ta bed, and the pain grew worse. I sent Authah faw you immediately. It all happened so fast..."

"These things do sometimes, Mrs. Stiles. Did he eat dinner yesterday?"

"Yes, we had pork chops, creamed potatoes, and green beans."

"And did you eat the same thing he did?"

"Yes," Bette claims. "I ate less than he, but we ate the same things."

What Bette doesn't tell the doctor is Pearl had come to her this morning and told her she was worried the carrots she helped Cook prepare might have been off—that she hoped she hadn't accidentally got some poisonous greens mixed in. Bette assured her his illness couldn't have been caused by something one of them did. Now, she decides not to mention the carrots at all.

"At first I thought he might have ingested something tainted, like milk from a cow that had gotten into some poisonous weed," the doctor tells them. "But if that had been the case, he would have shown other signs—convulsions even. If the cause were some kind of food poisoning— and it could have been—the source must have been something he ate in Hinesville or along the way because he was complaining of pain as early as the day before. However, I am inclined to judge your husband's death to be a result of a ruptured appendix. Men are more likely to play down the severeness of their pain, especially to the fairer among us. He was probably hurting more than he let on. I have no way of knowing for sure without an autopsy, and I am not equipped to do one. If you want, I could try to get someone in to assist me..."

"It won't bring him back, and I cannot stand the thought of tellin Reggie and Elisa their fathah's body will be subjected ta such handlin before he can be laid ta rest," Bette says sadly.

"And what will people think if we request an autopsy?" Thomas adds. "Those aren't done unless one suspects foul play, and how in the world could that be the case here?"

"You are right, Thomas, and I do not see any reason to make a hard situation harder. I fully suspect he died of a ruptured appendix; I will list that as the cause of death. This will be the end of my involvement, and your family can be left in peace to grieve and do what is necessary."

Jessie sits mutely, glad the doctor has forgotten her presence. He is up and moving toward the door when he notices her. "Miss...."

"Devereux," Jessie offers.

He pauses as if he should recognize her but continues when he cannot place her. She would be surprised if he could. Her face had been beaten beyond recognition the one time he had attended her. Of course, he might have seen her out somewhere when she last lived here.

"Can you add anything more, Miss Devereux?"

"Not at all, Sir. I have been mostly at the Barrets' helping them with the wedding of their daughter. The Stiles were gracious enough to let me sleep here."

He stands resting his eyes on her face awhile longer as if he is trying to pull up a memory. "Ah then," he says and turns to move on. "I am sorry for your loss, Mrs. Stiles. I wish I could have done more."

Jessie stays to help with tasks a sudden death like Clarence's requires. Messengers are sent to bring the younger Stiles children home, to Reverend Acton, to people who need to be informed. At noon, as Bette is thinking she should instruct Cook to prepare more for dinner, Thomas suggests they send for their solicitor.

"Mothah, I will send faw Grayson ta see what we need ta do ta transition Fathah's affairs."

"What do you mean by transition, Thomas?" Bette asks tiredly. "Can't a meetin wait until aftah the funeral?"

"I suppose, but problems can be avoided by clarifyin mattahs immediately."

"I cannot imagine what problems could arise unless there is something pressin with the business. I assume you are prepared ta take ovah Clarence's role, ah you not?"

"Of course I am. Fathah has long told me the business would be mine someday. I wasn't expectin the transition ta be necessary so soon, but I assure you I am up ta the job."

"Sit down," Bette pats the divan beside her.

Jessie is penning messages at a small table near the door, and intent as she is on what she is doing, she doesn't at first overhear the discussion or think it might be one best held in private. Both Thomas and Bette have forgotten her.

Thomas sits beside Bette, and she wraps her arm around him. "Oh Thomas, I regret you ah havin ta step inta his shoes while so young. I am glad Reggie will be out of school before long and available ta assist you."

Thomas jerks away as if stung. "What do you mean? I am not at all sure Reggie will want ta work faw me. The two of us view many things differently. He's soft, Mothah. He is like you as I am like Fathah. I have the deepest affection faw my brothah, but I am not at all sure I want him as an employee."

Jessie's attention is drawn by the rise in Thomas's voice. She thinks to leave but fears she may cause more disruption by doing so. She sits quietly and listens in spite of herself.

"He will not be an employee, Thomas. He will be your pawtner."

"You are mistaken. Fathah and I have spoken of this, and I am sure the will specifically names me as the sole ownah and opuhratah of the business. But you needn't worry. I will always have your best interests at heart. And I am sure there is enough money in the estate ta set Reggie up in a career more suited ta his abilities."

"Please sit again, Thomas."

"I don't feel like sittin, Mothah. We best speak with Mr. Grayson immediately so you can rid yourself of these foolish notions before you can confuse Reggie with them."

"I have a copy of the will, Son, the one your fathah and I made out shawtly before our weddin with the undahstandin he would sign it once we were wed. He did as he promised. I retain ownuhship of evahthing upon his death—my fathah made sure—and the only way he could was ta insure Clarence agreed ta the provisions at the beginnin of ah marriage. Clarence could have made changes, but he saw no need. He controlled evahthing by law, and he was a fairly young man."

"But he told me the business would be mine…"

Bette knows he did—what Thomas is saying is true. Clarence also planned to change the will. She has seen a draft of the new one in his papers.

"Mothah, Fathah would nevah have trusted you with what is best faw this family, and Reggie is cut from the same cloth. He should have been a daughtah—Eliza is more capable of makin the hawd decisions that have ta be made in business than Reggie is. Like you, he'd try ta free evah slave we have and pay hawd-earned money ta keep the place runnin. Neithah of you has the sense ta comprehend that, without slaves, we cannot stay afloat—it is financially impossible. Fathah would nevah let you retain control of the family holdins. He'd told me he worried about your mental stability…"

"Beware what you say, Son."

Jessie chances a glance and witnesses the color rise in Bette's face.

"Puhhaps you should talk with Grayson. He can inform you of what you can and cannot do, but may I offah you some advice? Think hawd about what you do at this juncture of your life. Remembah whose family name carries the weight in Savannah. It is Bullock, not Stiles, and I am the closest tie ta my Bullock relatives and the old guard here. I do not think they would be pleased ta have their family name blackened by insinuations of mental illness. Though your fathah might not have agreed with my views or ways of doin things, he knew, without doubt, I am sane. Maybe not as pliable as he would have liked, but certainly in possession of my mental faculties. Anyone claimin othahwise would have ta prove my instability, and as I said, claims like those would be extremely unwise on the pawt of someone young and needin the backin of his extended family and friends."

Thomas stands, nostrils flaring, fists clinched. Bette's face softens, and she walks across to place a hand on her son's shoulder. "Don't cause a rift in our family, Thomas, especially now when we need ta cling ta each othah. We have all suffahed a grave loss, but evahthing will work out. You will see."

"Yes, we will see." Thomas's reply is terse, but he leans forward to place a kiss on her cheek. "Now I will bid you Good Aftahnoon. You must need ta rest aftah what you have been through."

"Won't you stay faw dinnah?" Bette takes his arm to keep him with her.

"I have things ta attend to at the office, even if it may not be mine."

"It will be yours, Thomas. It just will not be yours alone."

"I must go now. Please try ta rest. The next few days will be tryin."

Bette sits down again, and Jessie is trying to decide how she can best make an exit when the lady of the house addresses her.

"I am sorry you had ta witness that."

"I didn't mean to intrude. I couldn't think of a way to gracefully leave."

"There was no need. Abby trusted you, and I would be delighted if you could stay an additional few days ta help us through these unchawtahed watahs."

Jessie restrains a sigh. She would like nothing more than to take her daughter and return to Baltimore as quickly as possible, but Bette has been the most gracious of hostesses even if her husband has not.

"Of course, Mrs. Stiles. I will help in any way I can."

"Your presence is calmin. That alone is worth much. I promise not ta detain you long."

Jessie rises from the desk and walks to sit beside the desolate woman. She takes the woman's hand and holds it in her own. She is relieved to tell Bette truthfully, "I feel everything is going to be fine here. In fact, life for you and yours should be better in the future."

Jessie stops, fearful she may have spoken inappropriately considering Bette has just lost her husband. Bette, however, meets her eyes and smiles.

"Comin from you, those words ah a great comfort. Abby has told me of your…gift. See, you are calmin me already."

Chapter 23
Goodbyes

Savannah, Georgia—1846

Frederick and Bette talk of how quickly the time has passed since Mattie's wedding and Clarence's death, but the four months she has remained in Georgia have dragged for Jessie. She cannot help being unsettled in the Clarence-plagued house of her new friend Bette. Though life for all who reside there appears to be much more tranquil than when the master of the house was on this side of the realm, the presence she senses is growing angrier by the day, and she is not the only one experiencing the effects of his rantings. He has actually created movement on occasion. He has managed to rattle objects, alter flames, slam doors. Pearl and Cook like to think their indifference infuriates him. The real detriment to his refusal to leave is Bette is having a hard time keeping hired help because they are not as immune to his shenanigans as those who live there.

Pearl had Arthur paint the porch ceiling and eaves what she calls haint blue, a precaution against him, but the effort has proved futile. Pearl shrugs her shoulders when pots continue to bang, flames jump erratically or are snuffed out altogether, and doors slam as they had before the paint job. She and Cook keep the fires burning higher to offset the cold pockets they had never noticed before Clarence's abrupt death, and Cook has commented more than once on how much cooler her kitchen is to cook in since he died. Word has gotten out of the wages the free Pearl, Cook, and Arthur make, and they have become the envy of every slave in their acquaintance. There is no danger of the three of them being run off by the impotent rage of a master they had detested to begin with.

Bette's servants are not alone in their joy at Clarence's departure. Frederick has irreverently felt Clarence has done him a wonderful turn by dying expeditiously. His demise has kept Jessie in Savannah when he could not. Diana, too, has been thrilled to stay longer, but her joy has been added concern for Jessie. One would have to be blind not to notice the bond developing between Jude and her. Every spare moment Jude has away from his duties finds them together.

Minda and her boys spend more time than ever under the Stiles' roof since Bette doesn't have to worry about being caught in her own home. Thomas is still angry with her, but he visits on Saturday to keep up appearances. Bette has decided she and Eliza will summer away as usual next year. Reggie is in his last year at school. She has encouraged him to travel abroad before settling down to become part of the family business. Though summer is still months away, Jessie decides she can stay no longer. She has told Bette of her plans, and now she has to make Frederick and Diana aware of their departure. The latter she dreads more than the former because Diana has formed attachments unlike any she has made in Baltimore other than those with Gail Howe.

Today is the day, Jessie decides, but before she takes care of the unpleasant task of speaking with Frederick, Jessie picks some late-blooming flowers from the Stiles' garden and walks to the graves she has visited often. There are none among them like those from which Pearl was extracting juice.

Jessie goes to the gravesites more for her son's sake than she does for Moses', for she feels much closer to him in sleep than she ever has at his grave. Still, she takes pleasure in tending their plots, an act of love, a way of showing her devotion to both of them.

She arrives early at the gravesites. They are nothing like they were when she first came back to Savannah. Since she had small markers made and placed, she will never again have to scratch away to find the graves. She has left the rocks Moses placed on Joshua's grave when she was incapable of rising from her bed, let alone arranging for the burial of the miracle a vile slave trader had beaten from her body. Today, she tenderly places more than half of the flowers she has brought beneath the headstone carved with the name Joshua Tucker and the date of his death. She sits beside the site she has outlined with smooth rocks she gathered at the river. Seeing his and his father's graves clean and cared for brings her comfort. She thinks she will ask Jude to tend them when she is gone. She can send him some money through Bette for the task.

Before she leaves, she does what she does every time—she sings Diana's favorite song from her childhood. She places her hand on one of the rocks Moses placed there and says, "Be happy, My Son." She swivels in place, unconcerned about the damage the earth may do to her dress, and places the remaining flowers on her husband's grave. Her spirits lift.

"I will talk with you later, Sweetheart."

She would ask him to look after Joshua, but they have talked of him often, and if his manifestations are real at all, Joshua is at peace somewhere because he is nowhere to be found in Moses' dimension. They both deem his absence a blessing, for they understand those who remain cannot or will not let go. Their son must have gone on to his destination unfettered by his violent death or a connection to a mother who grieves his loss still.

After rising from the ground, Jessie decides to walk by the home she and Moses shared. This is something she has done once with Diana, but she musters her strength to go without the comforting yet distracting presence of her daughter. The walk is short, and when she arrives, she stands square in front of the small building. Her eyes take in every detail of the porch as she remembers her first physical contact with the man she loves more than she thought possible. She smiles when she remembers his response to her question, "How old are you, Moses?"

"I be old enough to accomplish anything you might want done, whatever that might be," he'd replied, only he had said it in his unique Moses' way.

The conversation had been the first of many and the beginning of the happiest period of her life, despite the horrible assault she had endured at the hands of the man who had taken their son's life. But there had been one thing Moses had not been able to accomplish. He could not survive. He had died for something she had done. She had killed the man who attacked her, and Moses had paid the price. If not for the gift of his nightly visitations, she doesn't think she could have found peace in this life.

For a moment, Jessie allows herself to blame Frederick. She quickly shakes the anger off, for holding onto animosity will hurt her alone. Still, remembering he could have done more to save her husband makes telling him she is leaving again more of a pleasure than a chore.

Jessie is snapped out of her reverie when a middle-aged white woman opens the door and steps out onto the porch.

"Can I hep you?" she asks.

Her demeanor is neither friendly nor unwelcoming; it is indifferent. The woman wears a dress so faded Jessie cannot tell what the print once was. She has her hair covered with a kerchief much like many servants wear, and in her hand is a homemade broom. Behind her appears the uncombed head of a youngster Jessie can identify as neither male nor female. Taking in her appearance, Jessie is not surprised the flowers she planted have been left to die.

"No," Jessie replies, "I was taking a minute to rest."

She decides not to tell the woman she once owned the house she lives in. Few white people would want to be reminded they are renting a home a colored person could afford. Jessie moves away, and the door closes behind the woman and child.

She and Diana have also visited the boarding house Moses built. She decides not to go again. The place has become run-down—the porch railing missing boards, a new sign obviously printed by an amateur displaying a name she didn't recognize. The deterioration had saddened her, and she purposely has not mentioned the changes to Moses in any of their nightly talks.

Deciding she has procrastinated long enough, Jessie determines to beard the lion in his den. It is a week day, so she makes her way to Frederick's office on River Street. He is standing at his window and spots her as she crosses one of the bridges connecting Bay Street with Factor Row. He opens the door, and she can tell he anticipates the reason for her call by the expression on his face. He welcomes her as he would any female white visitor and points to a chair she takes though she would prefer to state her business and leave.

"I assume you have not come to pass the time of day in pleasant conversation," he says.

Jessie smiles, determined to keep the conversation civil.

"No, though I might enjoy reminiscing about our shared past."

Without meaning to, Jessie has taken the upper hand in their conversation. Any reminder of their history frightens Frederick. He glances around to make sure no one is close by. He walks to the back door that opens to a stairway leading downward to the dock. He peers through then closes it behind him. He returns to stand in front of Jessie.

"I prefer to forget the past, if you don't mind."

Frederick's posture is rigid, and Jessie sighs. This is not the tone she has planned to set. She would like to remind him of the pleasant times they shared, but she has to admit they were few and far between.

"Of course not," she says simply. "I have come to say goodbye. I may see you when I take my leave of the girls and your servants, but I will probably be there while you are at work. I didn't want to abruptly disappear without letting you know I was going."

"I would hope not!" It is Frederick's turn to sigh. His body relaxes, and he allows himself to slide into the chair facing her. "When will you go?"

"As soon as I can book passage. I have yet to tell Diana, but I will tonight."

Frederick makes no comment at the mention of Diana, and this makes Jessie angrier than anything he could say to her.

"You could actually acknowledge my daughter. You have acted as if she is nothing but an inconvenience since I adopted her."

"Adopted? I don't remember there being a legal document drawn up saying she is your daughter."

"In our world, papers aren't necessary, but I assure you she is as much mine as your children are yours."

"If you say so. I guess there is nothing I can say to make you change your mind about staying? I have dared to hope with things going well..."

"Going well for whom?" Jessie asks. "This may come as a surprise to you, but we have a lucrative life waiting for us in Baltimore."

"You could have an equally rewarding life here if you weren't determined to be obstinate."

"Frederick, rehashing old grievances will serve no purpose," Jessie rises, "but your attitude toward my daughter is one of the many reasons I must go. If you harbored an iota of the affection for my child that I have for yours—all of yours—I could possibly have come to terms with your behavior, but your lack of concern for Diana is indicative of your disregard for me. Goodbye, Frederick."

She is to the door before Frederick is out of his chair. "Good Lord, Jessie, the girl is colored!"

"As am I," Jessie turns to meet his eyes. "As are you."

Jessie is rewarded by the shock on Frederick's face. Let him stew on her departing words, she thinks. He needs to be reminded of who is in possession of what information.

Jessie hurries to make her traveling arrangements. She wants to spend her remaining time in Savannah with people who sincerely care about Diana and her.

Chapter 24
Parting Words

Savannah, Georgia—1846

Jude is told of Diana's imminent departure by Ish who has eavesdropped on Jessie's farewells to his mother and grandmother in the kitchen. Ish is sad but Jude is in no mood to commiserate with him. He is on his way to get the details from his mother when he runs into Jessie on her way out.

"Is it true?" he asks. "You takin Diana back ta Baltimoe?"

Jessie finds his wording telling. He does not view their departure as the two of them going back to their home; he considers Diana's leave-taking as something being done to her. She isn't surprised because Diana's reaction, though more subtle, had given her the impression their departure would not be her daughter's choice.

"We must go, Jude. I have a business there—and we enjoy a life we can never have here."

Jessie immediately regrets her own choice of words. Jude already bridles at his lack of freedom, and she has reminded him of how different Diana's life is from his own. Hoping to give him something to be happy about, she says, "How would you like to make a little money in your spare time?"

Jude starts to remind her of how little spare time he has, but he remembers he is speaking with Diana's mother.

"A lil money is always hepful," he says. "How I gonna make it?"

"My husband and our child are buried here. When I arrived, I had a hard time finding their graves. I wonder if you would be willing to tend them for me since I cannot."

"I be glad to, but they no need ta pay me. They be Diana's papa an brothah. It be somethin I can do while she goan."

169

Jessie decides not to remind him that Diana will not be coming back soon, if ever. She cannot imagine agreeing to come to Savannah again, even for the other girls' weddings. She also decides not to tell him she will send the money through Bette despite his willingness to help. She hopes he will take it once it arrives for he and his family may need additional resources regardless of Frederick's support. What a difference having some money stuck back has made in her life, and with Jude's temperament, she fears there may come a day he will strike out on his own regardless of the law. She doesn't want to encourage his desire for freedom, but she certainly understands it.

"I will get permission for you to go with me so I can show you where they are."

"Ain no need. Diana show me a while back. I know where they be."

Jessie wonders how the two found the chance to get away and thinks again their departure may be for the best. Her presence may be more of a threat to Jude than to herself. She is free to go where she wants as long as she has her papers with her, but Jude could be in serious trouble if found roaming without a pass.

"When you leavin?" Jude asks.

"I booked passage for the day after tomorrow on my way here. We will leave early."

Jude's shoulders slump and he studies the ground. "Where Diana now?"

"She's home packing her things. She wants to be available to visit with you and your family tonight."

Jude's countenance brightens a little. He starts to walk away but remembers his manners.

"You have safe travels, Mizz Jessie."

She watches as he walks away. Jude is no longer a boy, as Diana is no longer a child. She fears she has been wrong in believing their attachment merely a crush. Young people have been married at their ages, though she would never condone such a thing. He turns and walks back to her.

"Will it be alright if I write ta Diana?" he whispers. "Miss Bette will mail da lettahs fo me."

Diana must have told him she has shared his secret with her.

"Of course." She is glad to be able to say something to lighten the blow of their separation. "And if you will, please send word of your family to me. You are all important to me as you are to Diana."

"Thank you, Mizz Jessie. I jus wish you dint have ta be faw away."

"I wish you could be closer, too, Jude."

"Mabe someday we kin. Mizz Bette say she think someday we all be set free. If that happen, I find you in Baltimoe. I promise Diana that."

Jessie fears Bette has given hope none of them will live to realize.

"I hope so, Jude. I sincerely hope so."

Jude returns to his chores and tries to think of the evening ahead, not the future beyond tomorrow. He finishes early and takes the pass from his mother. It enables him to go to the market which he will eventually get to after he picks up Diana along the way. Minda rarely lets him have the slip of paper she attained from the master. She must feel sorry for him. He promises Ish he will bring Diana to Yamacraw before dropping her off at the Stiles' mansion. "She will want ta say goodbye," he says.

Diana is waiting for him though he has sent no word he is coming. She is in the kitchen talking with Pearl and Cook when he arrives. He tells her he is on the way to the market. Cook gives Diana a basket in case they are stopped. They walk along side by side, neither talking much until Diana stops in the middle of the path and turns to him.

"Jude Barret, let's not waste our last day being sad. Let's make the most of it. I want to see a smile on your handsome face."

"Cain see much ta smile about. An doan call me Barret. That not my name."

"Then what is your name if it isn't Barret?"

"Jus call me Jude. I doan want nothin ta do with Barret."

"Don't all slaves go by their masters' last names?"

"I doan have ta be reminded uh who owns me, do I?"

"I am not sure I want to go with you if you are going to be cranky. I would rather go spend time with your mother and brother if we cannot enjoy ourselves."

"I am sorry," Jude says. "I try ta be happy. I mo scared than mad. What if I nevah see you again? You leavin doan seem right. I doan know how ta git ta Baltimoe I git a chance."

"You listen to me, Jude. Don't you go and do something stupid. Don't you be running off and getting yourself whipped or killed."

She takes his face in her hands and makes him look at her. "Promise me, Jude. Promise me you won't do something stupid."

"Then how we evah gonna see each othah agin?" he asks quietly.

"We are young, Jude. There is a whole lot of life ahead of us. I'll be grown someday, and maybe Mama will bring me back. Maybe we can save and buy you. I'll talk to her. She will help; I am sure she will. We have to believe everything will be alright. You have to stay out of trouble and be safe until we can find a way."

Neither Jude nor Diana fully appreciate what they are committing to, but neither can stand the thought of never seeing each other again. Jude takes her hand and they continue a few steps before Diana retrieves hers.

"There's time for that later. We can't call attention to ourselves out here where someone can find fault with us. Let's get what we need and get back to your house."

"I doan need nuthin," Jude admits. "I jus use the pass so I can come see you."

Diana smiles. "Then let's get something and go back to your house. I want to say goodbye to Ish and your mother. You can walk me home afterward, and we can go to our spot behind the smokehouse for a bit. Now Mr. Stiles is gone, no one will bother us."

The two purchase some fall apples and put them in Diana's basket. Jude carries a bag of turnips, the cheapest produce he could find to show should he be stopped. They hurry back to Minda's cabin where Jude tries his best not to rush Diana, but Ish is still unhappy when they take their leave. The evening goes as planned, and they find themselves on the bench they have pulled up behind the smokehouse at the edge of Cook's vegetable garden. They both laugh when Jude places his bag of turnips not far from those growing feet from them.

They spend much of their time with Diana telling him all she can think of about Baltimore. He wants to learn everything he can about the city he has built up in his mind as a sanctuary, a safe harbor, if he can get there someday. When Diana finally acknowledges they can be out no longer without someone searching for them, she stands and slowly draws her hands from his. Desperate to do what he has been wanting to do since he first met her, Jude gathers his nerve, reclaims her hands, and leans in to place a kiss squarely on her lips. She does not resist. He kisses her again, this time more thoroughly. They embrace for some time, experimenting with their first physical intimacy. Finally, Diana pulls away, looks him squarely in the eyes with tears in her own and whispers, "I love you, Jude."

She is gone before he can respond. He walks slowly home, head down, his bare feet scuffing the sand as they did when he was a boy. He lets himself into the cabin, lights a candle, and crawls into his bed beside the sleeping Ish. He chooses a piece of paper from the stash he keeps between the corn-shuck mattress and the ropes supporting it. He laments the sorry state the paper is in, but these scraps are all he has. He writes a declaration of his own to send by Miss Bette. If he weren't too old for such things, he would cry. He would like to kick himself for not sharing his feelings in person while he had the chance.

Chapter 25
Rude Awakenings

Savannah, Georgia—1847

Frederick is pleased overall with life at Shady Grove, partly because ignorance is bliss. Rob has spent the last two evenings in the company of Eleanor Peavy, the cousin of Letty Henry. Since the wedding, Frederick has urged Brigitte to find out all she can about the girl and her family. The girl's father owns a plantation in Southern Georgia and two in Texas. Though Frederick knows almost nothing about Texas and has no desire to own the number of slaves such a huge operation would require, their research has assured him the girl could be an asset to the family, and, hopefully, one who will mold Rob into the man he wants him to be. Rob is unaware of his father's snooping, and Frederick has chosen not to comment on the girl's prospects. Rob is interested in Eleanor for her personal virtues, and for this Frederick is glad. It will take more than money to transform Rob into a steady, responsible man. His son is happier than Frederick can remember him. He spends all his non-working hours in route to South Georgia where he stays at the Peavy summer home. He tells his father he plans to declare himself soon, and he is basking in the favor the news has brought him.

Fredie continues to live up to his father's expectations. He has graduated from Princeton and will finish his first year of medical training at the University of Pennsylvania in the spring. He is currently home during a short school break, and their talks have convinced Frederick his second son will be the one to make the Barret name even more respected in Savannah. Maxie is her usual sweet self, and then there is Ella. She comes and goes as she pleases while her father is convinced she adheres to his slightest wish. She is the apple of his eye. Frederick still wears the blinders through which he has viewed his second daughter since birth. Ella is almost as adept at sneaking around as Dovie, and Frederick will soon be forced to condone the relationship between his daughter and the dubious Eliot Gordon or do something to end it. Because Frederick is unaware of Ella's escapades, if he were to find fault with his household, it would be with the slaves he is forced to abide in order to be the successful Savannah gentlemen he is.

Nothing of too much importance, in his mind, has happened in the life of the servants other than Cressa was beginning to show with child when she tripped carrying a rug out to beat and landed hard on her stomach. Several days later she told Mammy she was showing a bloody flux, and after a day or two, she delivered a partially formed fetus that breathed not at all. Lewis had taken the child and buried it. Mammy reported the loss to Frederick who was relieved, as, unlike other slave owners, he has no desire to increase his holdings, especially since the Middleton family into which he married does not believe in selling them to outsiders. If Cressa and Lewis mourned the loss, they did their grieving out of his sight. Frederick is not observant enough to recognize the bond the couple have with their two children. If he were to give their situation much thought at all, he would assume they simply accept matters they can do nothing about, failing to remember the early years of his life when his circumstances were worse than theirs.

Dovie is sneaking out again. If he were to follow her, he would discover she has taken up with one of his own warehouse workers, an association that might be sanctioned if she could convince her master she had become acquainted with him at church and Sunday is the only time she associates with him. Dovie has not asked for permission because she will not settle for seeing the man on Sundays as she will be required to do if Frederick agrees to it.

These are the circumstances of Frederick's household on the Sunday afternoon he sits in the parlor with the girls and a couple of their friends. Chaos is about to ensue, and the unexpectedness of its arrival will make Frederick more unsettled than had he known of the possibility. When will he ever learn, he will think later, to expect the worst when times are best? He is basking in the tranquility brought about by an edifying sermon and a pleasant dinner shared with his daughters and their friends. The cadence of the soft, rounded words spoken by the females is lulling him, soothing him. His words are the only ones in the room not produced by the charming culture of the Low South, or they are until his cousin whirls into the room with more vigor than usual and at an unprecedented early hour. She often doesn't sleep off the ill effects of the previous night's libations until early afternoon.

"Frederick," she says, "I must speak with you!"

"Now?" he sighs. "As you can see, we have guests."

"It is imperative I speak with you now," she throws a disapproving glance toward Ella. "Alone, if we may!"

If she wanted privacy, Frederick thinks, they would have been better served had she entered calmly and pulled him to the side, but doing so would have deprived Brigitte of the drama he has grown to expect from her. Now, Frederick has no other choice but to rise and lead the lady to his office.

Ella is wide-eyed. The disdain Brigitte casts her way is not lost on her. Though the lady has long disapproved of her, she usually is careful to hide her opinion from Frederick.

Ella nudges her friend Cassandra Andrews. "Please excuse me," she whispers. "I best see what dire news the good dowagah is fillin my fathah's ear with now."

"Where ah you goin?" Maxie asks.

"It is not lady-like ta tell," she says, implying she is in need of relieving herself. She quietly makes her way to Frederick's office door pulled partly but not completely closed for propriety's sake. Ella has barely reached a vantage point in which she can overhear clearly when she gasps at Brigitte's news.

"Eliot Gordon has killed a man!"

Ella leans heavily against the wall and covers her face with both hands.

"Good Lord!" Frederick swears, then immediately catches himself. "Please forgive my language, Brigitte."

"It is understandable, My Dear. Who wouldn't swear under the circumstances—to think your daughter has been associating with a murderer."

If she were in a position to see as well as hear, Ella would have been gratified by her father's scowl. "He is an acquaintance of my daughter as he is with all young people of an age and class here. Please do not talk of them as if they are a couple!"

Brigitte's eyebrows lift, for she has learned far more about Ella's activities than he has. Today, she lets Frederick's error slide and continues with the story she has come to tell.

"Anyway, I have news from a reliable source he has shot and killed his own friend—Frenchie Willis—in a duel, of all things!"

Ella slides down the wall. A pocket of cold air slows her descent. She shudders and wraps her own arms around herself, trying to leech warmth from their contact.

"Good Lord!" Frederick says again, and this time he doesn't think to apologize. He walks to the cabinet and pours himself a drink before remembering his manners and asking Brigitte if she would like one.

"Do you have something a little milder, perhaps a glass of wine. The hour is early, but one can make concessions when faced with shocking news."

"No, but I have sherry."

Frederick automatically pours Brigitte a small glass of the liquid and is oblivious to the disappointment on her face.

"Whatever could bring two friends to such barbaric extremes?"

"Young Willis took offense at something Mr. Gordon said last night at the Chatham Club—something to do with billiards. Young men who witnessed the altercation say Gordon apologized—claimed his comments were in jest—but Willis was somewhat of a hothead and would not listen to reason. The two met early this morning across the river into Carolina where most of these savage confrontations take place."

"I've told the city council nothing beneficial can come from our young men frequenting Chatham or other clubs late at night. I've tried to get backing for a curfew to prevent just such idiocy as this. I seem to be the only man in town concerned with what our young men are getting up to—probably because some of my associates are right there with them."

"Young men will be young men regardless of where they are. Surely you are not too old to recall how you and my own dear Alexis frequented clubs like the Chatham until the early hours of morning."

Frederick ignores the comment completely. "Thank God Rob is not in town, or he would have surely ended up as one of their seconds, foolish as he is. Young men and their ideas of honor! They have too much time and money on their hands, if you ask me. I assure you I would never have jeopardized my future over something as silly as a comment made across the billiard table!"

Brigitte crosses the room, places her hand on Frederick's shoulder. "I fear there is more, and it grieves me to have to relate it."

In this, the lady is sincere, for it is one thing to bring news that will cast a shadow on the duplicitous Ella, but she genuinely hates to tell of young Fredie's part in this disaster for he has been nothing but a gentleman to her.

"You cannot expect the young of today to have your own wisdom, Cousin."

She strokes his arm, and he allows it. Though Frederick has finally managed to get Brigitte out of his house, he is still susceptible to her fawning.

"It was our Fredie who acted as Mr. Eliot's second since Rob was not here to do so."

Frederick jerks away so quickly Brigitte actually stumbles.

"You are wrong!" he shouts. "Fredie would never jeopardize his future and social standing in such a way. Had you said Rob I would have believed you, but not Fredie. You have gone too far!"

Brigitte is taken aback by his reaction.

"Surely you do not blame me for trying to forewarn you of what is to quickly become common knowledge. I come to you in love for you and your family. I do not deserve your censure."

Frederick's face reveals the battle within. He regains control and apologizes.

"I am sorry, Cousin, but I cannot credit what you are saying. I must investigate for myself. He turns to leave, but Brigitte has not yet said all she has come to say.

"Both Fredie and Ella are fortunate they have a father of such good repute and discernment. Your quick action may prevent any detriment to Fredie's future and to your daughter's name should someone connect the two, misinformed as the gossips may be."

"I have already told Ella how unsuitable an association with Gordon would be, and she has been wise to listen. I am much more concerned about the harm this tragedy may do to Fredie, even Rob. He is about to declare himself to Miss Peavy, and there can certainly be no whisper of scandal that could make her father think twice of the match."

Brigitte sighs and bravely pursues the subject.

"Ella may have prudently heeded your advice, Frederick, but you cannot go wrong in forbidding her any future contact whatsoever with the man, can you?" There is a smile on the woman's face, but there is steel in her voice. "I am trying to protect you and yours. With you a widower, you need the insight a woman can give in matters such as these. You do not appreciate how ruthless society can be! As wealthy and irreproachable as Bette Stiles is, her husband's untimely death has been the subject of gossip. I fear it may hurt the marriage prospects of her children, and her people were founders of this cliquish city. Imagine how much more susceptible your own children could be!"

Ella fumes because Brigitte is playing to her father's greatest fear—of being judged by society and found wanting. Ella is astute, but with her limited information, she cannot possibly comprehend Frederick's insecurities. He thinks he has avoided rumors of Abby's death with a tale of a broken banister and carelessness on her part, but part of him wonders. Too, the shadow of his upbringing casts darkly over him, and never more than at a time of crisis.

The girl can stand no more. She quietly picks herself up and sneaks back to the parlor.

"I was about ta come lookin faw you," Cassandra complains.

"You ah white as a sheet!" Maxie's young friend Julia says.

"My lunch has not settled well, I fear," Ella lies.

Julia, the daughter of Reverend Acton is a kind girl, much like Maxie. Cassandra, however, is more like her father, John Andrews. As Ella's closest friend, she is privy to much of the details of Ella's relationship with Eliot.

"Cassie," Ella says now, "let's retire ta my bedroom where we can talk while I rest."

"Ah you sure you feel like talkin? If you ah unwell, I should leave…"

"I assure you I feel like talkin," she says pointedly. Her tone and the look she sends her friend's way convey the message she intends, and both girls are arm-in-arm at the doorway when they encounter Frederick.

"Where are you going, Ladies?"

"We thought we would rest in my room faw a while, Fathah, if you can spare ah company. I am feelin a little unwell."

"Certainly, My Dear," Frederick agrees, "but before you go, I fear I have some unsettling news you will hear soon enough. I had rather you hear the account from me rather than idle gossips."

"What has happened?" Maxie calls from across the room, she and Julia practically holding their breath.

Brigitte has followed Frederick into the room. Uninvited, she makes her way to a settee from which she has a clear view of Ella's face.

"Ella is ashen," the lady smiles demurely. Perhaps the news can wait until she is well."

"Nonsense!" Frederick interrupts. "Though they are acquainted with young Willis, he is not a close associate of either."

"Ah you speakin of Frenchie Willis?" Cassandra asks.

"Yes, I am afraid so, and I can think of no other way than to simply say it. The young man has needlessly died in a duel at the hands of Mr. Eliot Gordon."

Cassandra, Maxie, and Julia all gasp. Ella shows no emotion, and her composure is not lost on Brigitte. Cassandra immediately puts her arm around her friend's shoulder.

"This is shocking as news of this nature should be. I hate to further dismay you by telling you, Ella and Maxie, your own brother Fredie has taken leave of his senses and acted as Eliot's second. That such a thing can still happen between men of genteel breeding in this modern age is inconceivable. There will be much heartbreak within their families and in our own for the part one of ours has played. All left for you young ladies to do is pray for them."

Ella in now leaning heavily into her friend. "Fathah, I fear Mrs. Maxwell is right. I am feelin quite ill, and the shock of your news has not helped mattahs. May I be excused?"

"Of course," Frederick says, and his eyes meet Brigitte's as the two girls leave the room. "Do you think I should send for the doctor?"

"Not yet," Brigitte advises. "Let's give her a little time and see how she fares."

In the concern for Ella, neither adult has noticed Maxie's quiet weeping. When her father glances her way, he is immediately contrite.

"Once again, Mrs. Maxwell, you are right. A hardened widower like me has no understanding of the sensibilities of young ladies. Maxie, Sweetheart, please don't let this news upset you so. Your brother will be fine."

Maxie goes into his arms. "It is so sad, Fathah! Both Mr. Willis and Mr. Gordon ah such kind men, and now one of them is dead, and the othah may go ta jail! Will Fredie have ta go ta jail, too? And will Ella have ta wear mournin?"

"No, Darling." Frederick smiles. Maxie was too young to remember her mother's death, but she has recently seen Mrs. Stiles in church wearing the black denoting the loss of one close to her. "One wears black if a family member or an intended dies. Neither involved fits that description."

"But what if Mr. Gordon is hung! Then he will be dead, and Ella will be a widow b'fore she evah had a chance ta get married!"

Quiet falls on the room. Frederick pushes Maxie back and peers into her face. "Maxie, you do not understand. Your sister is a mere acquaintance of Mr. Eliot, and one can only be a widow if she is married."

Maxie cries harder when she realizes she has said too much. Now she has the added fear of what her sister will do to her for telling her secrets. She pushes away and runs for the stairs. Poor Julia is left behind.

"I will leave now, Mr. Barret, if my depahture is not an imposition."

"No trouble, My Dear," Frederick manages. "Let me get someone to walk you home." He glances at Brigitte and his frown deepens—the smug expression she is wearing infuriates him.

"And Mrs. Maxwell, I have some things to clear up here. The two of you may be escorted together."

"Are you sure there is not some way I can help, Cousin. If nothing else, I can lend a sympathetic ear."

"No," his mouth is set in a firm line. She is oblivious to his anger and the effort to mask it. "I will send someone up immediately. I will be in touch later."

Frederick leaves the room. Brigitte looks at the young girl sitting across from her.

"Well!" she says.

Chapter 26

The Crushing of Grapes

Savannah, Georgia—1848

Frederick has used the month of April to plan. It took no effort to remove Fredie from the public eye after the duel debacle, for he returned to Pennsylvania as planned. Ella has not been as easy to manage. Frederick has two choices regarding his second daughter's headstrong behavior: he can admit to himself she has been obstinate and manipulative all along, or he can blame her bad behavior on the influence of Eliot Gordon. He can either give Brigitte credit for her foresight, or he can claim prescient judgment of the young man he has been suspicious of all along. To settle on the first observation, he would have to acknowledge his own poor judgment and lack of supervision. There is little question in his mind what has happened. His sweet, naïve daughter has been lead down a slippery slope that will end in her own destruction if he does not intervene. He plans to rectify matters before he can be tried in the eyes of the locals and found guilty of ineptitude in managing his own household.

In addition to the news of his children's indiscretions, he has been informed by his foreman on the dock of Dovie's loitering among the workers there—of her stepping out with Cyrus after dark. Dovie could not have picked a worse time to be caught breaking more rules, and Frederick has decided to make an example of her, not only for the slaves who might be influenced, but for the town folk who might get the impression he is both a negligent parent and a lax master. After many lone hours in his study and in his office at work, Frederick is ready to put his plan into action. He has already written Mrs. Middleton and Jessie to inform them they will be having visitors. The letter to Mrs. Middleton was much like the one she receives every year, except this summer he has notified her she can expect Mammy's help with the girls and a shipment from the warehouse by buckboard driven by Lewis and Jude. This tactical move has especially pleased him because the arrangement allows him to assist his mother-in-law while removing Dovie's brother and nephew from Shady Corner. He has thought of sending Lewis alone, but there is something about the boy Jude that makes him uneasy. He has encountered his steely gaze on more than one occasion, but each time the young man has quickly looked away leaving Frederick wondering if he is seeing hostility where none exists. Jude's growth and muscular bearing also leave him uncomfortable, or *uncomfortable* is what he would call it if he were forced to name the reaction. *Intimidated* would be the more appropriate word choice were he to be honest.

Having dispersed with Dovie's mother, brother, and nephew, he is left to consider the person who can cause him the most grief over Dovie's departure. He has not allowed himself to dwell on Minda's reaction when she finds her sister gone; he has focused on the need to get her out of the way long enough for the transaction to take place. He thinks it prudent to give them time to accept his decision before returning to Shady Corner. Jessie has provided the answer to his problems by agreeing to have Minda as an apprentice. Since Minda has become a proficient cook, both Jessie and Minda would be suspicious if he were to ask for more culinary instruction. He has claimed, truthfully, the household is in need of someone with seamstress capabilities beyond mere mending. Jessie has acquiesced readily enough, other than to remind him Minda is one person and incapable of doing all the cooking and the sewing. She has also asked him to send Ish. She claimed Minda will be much happier with the trip if she doesn't have to worry about Ish managing without her or Mammy. Having a soft spot for the boy, Frederick quickly agreed. Now, the only task left to do is inform all parties involved.

Both Ella and Maxie take the news of their May 1st departure with little comment other than to ask what is to be done about the two weeks of lessons they will be cutting short. Maxie is eager as always to go to Hickory Grove where she will be joined by her sister Mattie, her cousin Gail, and who knows how many other cousins. Ella's response is lackluster as all her communication has been since being forbidden to see Eliot Gordon. Even she has not been able to get around the restrictions laid out by her father. If she is to have no say in her own affairs, she has claimed dramatically, she is indifferent to any plans made for her.

Frederick sends Dovie to them to help them pack. Believing it has been some time since she has been caught misbehaving, she deems nothing amiss in Frederick's congenial tone with her. In fact, she prides herself on being extra careful. He actually smiles when he says, "Dovie, you are going to have to assume more responsibility with everyone away this summer. Cressa will have to prepare my breakfasts, and you and the younger ones will have to take on more of the chores. I will be away myself part of the time. With Rob here by himself, you should not be overly tasked."

Dovie has to bite her tongue to keep from asking where Minda is going. The master would not appreciate the impertinence. She is envious but brightens when she realizes she will be able to visit Cyrus every night with only Rob to avoid.

From his talk with the girls, Frederick makes his way to the kitchen to see Minda. He experiences a twinge of guilt when she turns and smiles at him. They have enjoyed a semblance of closeness for some time now. Frederick has convinced himself Minda actually welcomes his visits, and he dreads the damage Dovie's removal will do to the status quo. He casts those thoughts aside, for he cannot allow the objections of a slave, no matter how special, to determine what is best for his family and home.

"I have some news for you, Minda."

Minda is immediately apprehensive, for news often means change, and change in her world often corresponds with loss.

"I am going to be away on business for most of the summer. I see no need for all of you to remain here when Rob will be the sole occupant, and he will be visiting his lady friend when he has days off work. I have decided to send Mammy with the girls to Hickory Grove and Lewis and Jude with a wagon load of supplies for Mrs. Middleton."

"Jude?" Minda repeats. "Why Jude? You ain nevah send him b'fo."

"He is now old enough and strong enough to be of help. I am not comfortable leaving him here with just Rob for supervision. The boy has a way of getting into mischief. Once they are in Virginia, my mother-in-law may use them with the planting, but if not, they will be back soon enough."

Minda almost tells him Jude hasn't been in trouble for a long time but decides not to risk changing his mood. Jude will be overjoyed to get to see places beyond Savannah, and she thinks time away from the master may be good for him. He needs a distraction since months of separation have not diminished his infatuation with Diana.

"While he is there," Frederick continues, "he can get news to bring you of Daisy who will be there with Mattie. You will like that."

Minda raises her hand to her chest, elated at the thought of knews of her daughter.

"And as I say, Jude and Lewis will be back before you get home."

"Me git home! Where I be I be gettin home from?" Minda presses her splayed fingers across her chest to calm the thump in her chest.

"I am sending you by steamer to spend the summer with Jessie. You have made such progress in the kitchen, I thought you could use this time while I am away to learn something about sewing. In your spare time from cooking, I hope you will be able to at least make the servants clothing as Jessie used to do."

Minda's first thought is of her youngest son.

"Please doan make me go. Ish gittin old nough ta stand on his own, bu with his foot an all, he still need me."

"Those were my thoughts, as well."

Frederick gives no credit to Jessie for the plan to send Ish with her.

"I've decided he will go with you. Jessie thinks she can find someone local there to teach him a trade requiring little physical agility—shoemaking, silversmithing perhaps—something. I am sure she will find a way to make him useful."

Minda hears the words Frederick is saying, but they are hard for her to believe. Both her sons are going to be allowed to travel, and she is going to get a full summer with Jessie whom she admires. The information is too wonderful to be true. She sits on the stool she keeps by her work table and laughs aloud.

"Are you so happy to get away from here?"

Minda's straightens her face and sits upright while she tries to come up with a plausible reason for laughing. Frederick smiles at her, and her shoulders relax. She actually thinks of hugging him, but having never initiated contact before, the move is too awkward to fathom.

"When we leave?" she asks.

"You will sail with the girls next week on the First, and Lew and Jude will follow as soon as we get things situated here. I will write to Jessie with instructions regarding your return."

"Will you send news uh Daisy, an evahbidy here ta Mizz Jessie? I ain been nowhere since I come with Mizz L'ella. I gonna miss them."

"Sure I will," he says.

Frederick leaves the house and is surprised at how light-hearted he is to have pleased Minda. The optimism doesn't last long, however, when he remembers the deal he is about to finalize for Dovie's sale. Guilt is not a familiar emotion to him. He squelches it, irritated at having his mood darkened. None of these orchestrations would be necessary if Dovie were not forcing him into doing something neither Abby nor Mrs. Middleton would approve. He doesn't allow himself to consider how Maxie or Mattie will react when they are told. He will have to remind them of Dovie's transgressions and the many chances he has given her to change her ways. He simply cannot allow women to sway his own judgment which is superior in matters of this nature. They are simply too led by emotion.

"One has to crush some perfectly good grapes to make a quality wine," he mumbles to himself before entering his office to do what he has convinced himself must be done.

Chapter 27
Adventures

Savannah, Georgia—1848

Minda is glad she receives the news of their travels late in the day for two reasons. First, she would have been unable to concentrate on her work had she been told sooner, and, secondly, she is eager to see the boys' faces when they learn the news. This is by far the most exciting thing either of them has experienced, and she wants to be the one to tell them.

Minda wraps up the three leftover corn fritters and boldly picks up a small crock of sorghum molasses before leaving. She tells herself Frederick wouldn't mind since he has gifted them with foodstuffs on several occasions. Still, she makes sure to place the wrapped container at the bottom of the flour sack she carries back and forth from her cabin. She has time to warm the fritters and have them, the molasses, and three cups of water on the table before the boys show up.

"Why the pawty?" Jude asks immediately.

"Jus thinkin you might be hungry aftah a hawd day work," Minda says.

"We wlways hungry, bu this the first time we git somethin ta eat this soon aftah suppah."

"Well, if you doan want it…"

Minda acts as if she is about to clear the table, and Ish rushes to his place and hovers protectively over his plate.

"Doan pay him no mine, Mama. I doan need no reason ta eat!"

The boys sit on the crates Frederick brought long before the boys were born. Minda pulls up the lone straight back chair.

"What you boys git up ta today?" Minda asks.

"What you think we be up ta? Same thing we be up ta evah day, day on end. Carryin coal, carryin watah, carryin shit pots…"

"Stop it, Jude! Mama jus tryin ta be nice, an you ruinin it. It ain her fault you ain got no lettah."

Jude says nothing because Ish is right. Diana has been all he can think about since she left, and he has battled the hopelessness of his situation every day since.

"You ain got word from her yet, Son?" Minda asks.

"Jus those two times, an I been ta Mizz Stiles' almos evah day. She tell me she leave a lettah in the kitchen with Cook soon she git one, bu they ain been nothin fo three months now."

"That ain that long, Son."

"Long nough. She say she write an she doan."

They all sit a moment, Minda reflecting on the wonder any of them could actually be awaiting a letter. The two Jude keeps tucked beneath his mattress are the only ones any of them has ever received, and Jude has read aloud the parts he is willing to share several times.

"Well, I fraid you goan miss it when it do come, seein as you woan be roun ta go ta Mizz Stiles."

Minda has caught both boys' attention, and Ish is the one to ask the question. Jude is left to glower at her in confusion since he has crammed the last of his fritter into his mouth and cannot speak around it.

"Why woan Jude be roun, Mama?"

Ish's eyes are wide because both boys have finally picked up on Minda's excitement.

"None uh us be roun," Minda says, a smile breaking across her face. "Cause we goin travelin this summah."

Both boys are off their crates in a second. Jude chokes on his full mouth of cornbread, and Ish is irritated they have to wait for him to down his cup of water before their mother can continue.

"Whar we goin?" Ish cries the minute he decides Jude is in no danger of dying.

"Jude goin ta Hickry Grove with Lew, an you an me goin ta spend the summah with Jessie an Diana."

Ish squeals in delight. Jude's face goes blank. "You two goin ta Baltimoe, an I goin ta Vahginia?"

"Ise fraid so. Ise bein sent ta learn ta sew an Ish ta learn a trade. You spose ta hep with a load uh supplies fo the widow. I know you rathah be goin with us, an I rathah be goin back ta the plantation I live on til I oldah than you. But think on it, Jude! We all gittin outtah Svanna, you two fo the first time in yo lives! No tellin what you see travelin by wagon all the way ta Vuhginny. An Ish, we goan ride the steamah sittin in the harbah, the one with the smoke comin outtah the top. We goin as far as Mizz Jessie with the missies an Mama; then they go on ta Hickry Grove. An Jude, here the best pawt. Daisy be there when you be! I glad ta trade places with you fo the chance ta see my gul agin."

Jude's emotions war within him. For the first time in his life he will be allowed to leave Savannah and the master; he will see some of the world; and he will spend time with Daisy. But Ish and Mama are going to stay the whole summer with Diana. He thinks of complaining, but when he catches the joy on his mother's and brother's faces, he cannot spoil their happiness. He smiles, too, and the three of them join hands and actually dance around the room.

"When we go, Mama?" Ish asks.

"Nex Thuhsdy!"

"How many days that be?" Ish has little reason to keep up with the days of the week. One might as well be the other to him, except Sunday which is their one day off from chores.

"Five!"

"Wait a minute," Jude interrupts. "Who goan do ah choes we all be goan?"

"Dovie, Cressa, an the lil ones cause they ain goan be much ta do. Massah Rob be the only one home. Seem the massah goin travelin, too."

"Ooh, Dovie ain goan like that," Ish says.

"No, she ain," Minda says, "bu lease she be able ta do jus bout anythin she please."

Ish's smile fades. "I wish Ben an Deke an Lizzy could go."

All three sober as they think of those they will leave behind. Minda thinks of Cressa who will be without Lew for no telling how long, and soon after losing their baby, but she refuses to let their moment be spoiled. Occasions for celebration are few.

"They time come. Deke an Ben been ta Hickry Grove with Dovie an Cressa. You two awways stay behind. They be awright. Sides, they goan have a easy summah with evahbidy goan."

Ish is too excited to eat his treat, so Jude finishes the fritter for him. The three sit talking late into the night though they have to be up early the next day. Each tries to imagine what his trip will be like. Ish is fascinated with the ship he will sail on, begging his mother for details of her one voyage when she was not much older than Jude. The boys compare the details to those Jude has read aloud from his books. Minda wonders where they will sleep at Miss Jessie's and if the town is like Savannah. Jude estimates how many days of freedom they will have on the road before getting to their destination, and all speculate on the length of the adventure. Right before bed, Jude finally voices the question he has been wanting to know all along.

"Mama, how far Hickry Grove from Baltimoe, you think?"

Chapter 28
Amid Cotton and Grain

Savannah to Baltimore—1848

Practically the whole Barret household is at the harbor to see the travelers off. Frederick is there to take leave of the ebullient Maxie and to try one final time to coax a smile out of Ella who is still pouting. Noticing her demeanor, Minda is glad Mammy will be the one who has to contend with her on this trip. She is relieved the job is not hers. Lewis and Jude are there with the luggage, and Minda manages to whisper to her brother to look after Jude. She doesn't have to tell him why. He is aware of Jude's disregard for rules and his master's wishes. Like Mammy, he has a heavy responsibility. She is glad she has already given the letter to Jude she laboriously wrote for him to read to Daisy should he have the chance, for they are soon separated by the crowd. In her pocket is the folded note from Jude to Diana he is sending by her though he is leaving Savannah without the expected one from her.

Minda trails Mammy and their mistresses as closely as possible, desperate not to lose sight of them, for she will not be able to board until much later unless she is thought to be with her white owners.

When Minda discovers how much the harbor has changed since she arrived years before, she is glad she will be traveling with her mother and the Barret girls. Though she will not be staying with them in their private cabin on the upper deck, their close proximity will be comforting. People are everywhere, and Ish clings to her hand as he stumbles among the crowd. Travelers clamber to board; servants push carts laden with trunks and baggage. Dray animals have left deposits everywhere making it almost impossible to avoid stepping in their offal and puddles. Minda wishes she had a free hand to press a handkerchief to her nose to filter the stench created by many bodies, human and animal. After what seems like hours of waiting, she asks Ish to hold to her dress while she tugs the handkerchief from her pocket, but instead of shielding her nose, she wipes the sweat from her eyes. She is used to kitchen heat, but the pressing bodies make her feel faint.

At last they clear the boardwalk, and Miss Ella rouses herself enough to provide the documentation needed to get them all aboard at the same time. The two young ladies make their way up the gangplank and to their cabin to insure Lewis and Jude have managed to get their trunks safely on the vessel. Mammy reminds Minda she needs to stake out a spot on the freight deck among the cotton bales and grain sacks. Because she has an eleven-year-old boy slave with her, she will not be allowed to sleep on the floor with her mother in the girls' cabin. She drags her son along with her, his head swiveling back and forth in an effort to take in his surroundings.

"You goan have plenty uh time ta look, Son. Righ now we need ta find us a decent spot ta sleep fo they's all gone."

She has tried to tell Ish what to expect, but this melee little resembles the one she remembers. She had been with Miss Luella, Mammy, Dovie, and Lew. All but Lew had slept on pallets in their mistress's room, so this camping on deck experience is as new to her as it is to Ish. They follow other servants and poor people and find the deck that, at first glance, appears packed almost solid with freight. As they get closer, she is relieved to see there are narrow pathways between the cotton bales and full burlap sacks she assumes are filled with grains. She looks around for possibilities, deciding the walk way along the outer railing will be cooler than the areas away from the water. She imagines others jostling for positions at the rail and worries they will have little protection from the elements if there should be a storm. She is turning to pull Ish back the way they have come when he tugs her to a stop.

"Hows bout in there, Mama?"

She looks to where he is pointing and is relieved to see he has spotted a small area behind three stacked bags next to the beginning of rows of cotton bales.

"What if those sacks fall on us?"

"They ain that tall. Ain gonna kill us if they does."

Deciding he is right, she squeezes through the narrow opening left between the shorter stack of grain sacks and the wall of cotton to the side. She inspects what will be their home for the next several days. The deck floor left open is spacious enough for Ish to lie down, but she will have to lean up against either cotton bales or grain. She decides she can curl up if necessary. The nook is warm now but will provide protection from wind and cool night air. She deposits her bags—the one containing her and Ish's change of clothing and the one holding food—tucks her skirt high between her legs, and scales the three sacks to join Ish on top. They sit grandly gazing out over the city as they leave the harbor behind them. They both decide they have chosen well when the wind cools their faces and the fresh aroma of grain and cotton wafts around them. Their fellow servants have not all fared as well. Those boarding after them have had to settle for what they can get, and some wistfully eye their comfortable point of vantage. Minda wonders if they will have to defend their claim, but there turns out to be honor among them, and their territory remains theirs for the voyage.

Having been forewarned about the relentless sun, Minda has brought a two-ply muslin sheet to act as protection from the sun by day and a cover by night. After realizing no one is going to try to take their place, they spend many waking hours in the company of Mammy as she trails Ella and Maxie on the upper deck. The latter catches Ish's excitement and guides him around the ship, taking him into rooms and places he cannot visit alone. After his tour, he settles into their makeshift room for the night.

"Wish I membah ta bring my tablet an somethin ta write with. You thinks somebidy migh give me a piece uh papah an some ink? Sholly I kin find a quill wid all these birds roun."

"Doan you dare ask nobidy fo those things!" she says.

"Bu I fraid I ain gonna membah evahthin I sees! How I gonna tell Jude?"

"An jus what you say you be wantin those things fo? You goan say this slave boy need a tablet ta write on so his biggah slave brothah can read it latah? That what you goan say?"

"I guess I ain thinkin straight. I jus wish Jude could be here with us. Nex best thing is if I kin tell him whut I sees."

"You tell me evahthin you see, an I hep you membah. Sides, yo brothah be on the road bout now. The two uh you goan be busy a long time tellin each othah bout yo adventuahs."

About halfway through the voyage, the two of them are awakened by a strident cry, one both are familiar with. The racket sounds much like Mammy's Missy, but this crow is practically screaming in their ears. Both sit up immediately. Perched directly above their heads is a large, shiny black crow, his eyes trained on the two of them as if he's been sent to deliver a message, and he is eager to do his job. Ish laughs at the sight of the bird cocking his head from one side to the other as if to give each of them equal attention. Minda is not amused.

"Git on outtah here!" she scolds and waves her hands toward the bird. Ish grabs her arm.

"They's somethin wrong with him. He standin on one leg like somethin wrong wid the othah one."

They stand to examine their visitor more closely. The bird's left leg is bent at an unnatural angle. It's clearly broken. Ish extends his hand, and the creature hops agilely from the bale to alight on his forearm.

"Look, Mama. He a cripple like me!"

"He mus be somebidy pet ta be tame. An how you sho it a boy?"

"I sho," Ish laughs. "Bu I doan know how ta prove it one way or the othah."

Minda tells him she has no idea how to check a bird's sex either. She also warns him not to get too attached. "Somebidy come lookin fo that crow fo long."

"I doan think so, Mama. He be a pet, somebidy do somethin bout that laig. It jus a danglin there in the way. Kin I keep him?"

"Doan think him stayin or goin be upta you. Crows go where they wannah. Like Mammy's Missy. She stay cause she wanse ta."

"He like me—I kin tell. I sho he be stayin fo a wile."

By the second night, Minda decides Ish is right. Ish's new friend leaves long enough to feed but returns quickly, and Minda finds him perched on Ish's shoulder most of the time. He rides along when Ish walks about the deck. The boy proudly shows it off to Maxie and Ella, and Mammy is especially impressed with the bird's quick adoption of Ish.

"Him come alookin fo him," she tells Minda. "Dat bird show up an stays fo a reason. Crows be special creatuahs, an theys know things. You bess let da boy keep him."

The object of their attention flutters his wings and lands on Mammy's shoulder. She laughs, extends her hand and peers into the dark beady eyes when he takes her up on her offer.

"Ain no need ta thank me." She strokes his black head. "Now, you git on back ta Ish. I hab my own crow an her naw take kinely ta a new fellah."

He obediently flaps back to Ish's shoulder.

"Dat one smawt bird, Minda. Ish could do wus dan a frien lack him."

Minda's eyebrows draw down and her lips form a straight line.

"I ain keepin the boy from that bird if he wanse ta stay…" She starts to tell her mother she is growing more superstitious, but it is odd the bird has shown up from nowhere and taken a liking to Ish. No one has come to claim him, and it is quite wild with anyone but Ish—and now her mother.

Ish grows impatient with the women and asks if he can return to the freight deck. Minda later finds him atop the grain sacks with the bird sitting quietly on his upper leg while he separates a length of baling twine into thin strands.

"What you doin with that twine, Son?"

"Cotton's laig dead as a twig. It be in his way. I goan hep him git rid uh it."

"Cotton? What kind a name is Cotton fo a black bird?"

"It be the one I gives him. I ain nevah name nothin in my life, sose I think hawd on it."

Minda is less shocked Ish has named the crow Cotton than she is by the bird's perfect stillness, as if it is in agreement with the procedure.

"How you know ta do that?" she asks.

"I jus do."

Minda is quiet for a while, fascinated by what she is observing. When Ish has finished his task, the bird flies upward, then floats downward to rest on Ish's shoulder on his one healthy leg while knotted twine hangs from beneath his shiny under feathers. She climbs up beside her son and gazes out over the water as he and the bird are doing.

"Why Cotton? Coalie be bettah? What black bird wanse ta be name fo somethin white?"

"Cotton like it. Sides, Cotton be a good name. We foun him on a cotton bale, an evahbidy like cotton—an it white. Mabe his name make up fo bein black an cripple."

Moisture wells in Minda's eyes. Ish has never complained to her about his foot.

"He yo crow. I guess we calls him Cotton. You sho it a boy?"

"I tole you Ise sho," he says. "I knows from the beginnin."

Several days follow uneventfully other than the rainfalls their thin muslin sheet is no protection against. Because the cover dries quickly in the sun, as do their clothes, they are uncomfortable for short periods of time. Their backs ache from sleeping on the deck, but the freedom they enjoy makes up for it. They would dread the end of the voyage if they were returning to Savannah, but they are excited at the prospect of arriving in Baltimore.

It is the day before they are to dock, and Minda and Ish are standing at the rail trying to spot creatures in the water. Maxie and Mammy have left them to go in search of Ella. The deck is becoming crowded with white people, so Minda decides they should return to their place amidst the freight. They have turned and are crossing the open space where many passengers are taking the sun and talking among themselves when one of them confronts them.

"Well, lookie there!" a male voice says. "'It's a lil crippled Jimmy Crow with a crippled crow on his shouldah!'"

Minda comprehends exactly what the man is referring to, but Ish's faces registers confusion. He stops and turns toward the man. Minda gives him a shove and whispers, "Keep movin."

"Hold on there, Gal," the man calls out again. Minda stops, and Ish stops with her. "It's gotten mighty monotonous on this voyage. We could use some entahtainment."

Minda darts a glance at the man who has risen from a chair beside which one other man and two ladies sit. Behind them stand two negro servants. The man who has risen is middle aged and easily recognized as a member of the planter class by his white hat, white suit, and the cane he carries. He turns to his servants and says, "Appollo, go fetch your fiddle. Let's see if these two crows can dance on the two good legs between them."

Minda takes Ish by the hand and tries to lead him away, but their accoster takes her by the upper arm. "Let go of the boy," he says, and stand out of the way over there." He takes Ish by his arm and forces the two apart. "Now, You, Jimmy, you stand right there until my boy comes back with his fiddle."

"Ise Ish, not Jimmy."

"You ah Jimmy if I tell you you ah," the man says, and he gives Minda a push that almost makes her fall. His two female companions laugh, and the other man begins to clap and stomp his foot to a beat he alone can hear. Apollo returns and strikes up a tune and the man in the chair is joined by the women as they clap and tap their feet in time with the music.

"Now dance, Jimmy," the man commands and strikes Ish on the leg with the twisted foot.

Ish looks desperately at his mother, his eye with confusion and fear. Cotton screams in protest and dives for the man's hat. Ish's tourniquet has done its job, and Cotton's one good leg is no longer impeded by the damaged one. His claw is free to grasp the crown and lift it from the man's head. The suddenness of the violence leaves Minda stunned, but the fear on Ish's face spurs her into action. She rushes to him and again tries to pull him away. She ignores the blows from the cane. The man tries to fight off the attacking crow, lash out at her, and retain his grasp on Ish. Minda remains steadfast against the blows, but she cannot stand against his strength when he grabs her again and throws her to the floor. She is trying to rise when she recognizes Miss Ella's voice. Never before has she been so happy to see the young mistress.

"What in Heaven's name do you think you ah doin?" Ella asks at a level somewhat louder than usual but not quite a shout. She is standing with Maxie beside her and Mammy behind them. The young mistress's back is ramrod straight, her head held high and slightly back. She points her unopened parasol at the man mistreating her servants as if she is wielding the staff of Moses.

"How dare you!" she continues. She pulls Ish to her and hands him off to Maxie who wraps an arm around him and presses him to her side. "Mammy," Ella says, "help Minda."

Mammy needs no encouragement. Minda has already regained her feet, so she takes her hand, and the two join Maxie and Ish.

"Have you no breedin?" Ella's gaze takes in the man whose bald pate has been left to the sun's rays now his hat is nowhere to be seen. "If you wish ta make a spectacle of dawkies, use your own! I may have the law on you. Maxie, see if you can find Captain Marsh. No, wait. We shall go tagathah. We will not stand faw this."

"Now, Missy, there is no need ta get all riled. We were merely tryin ta enjoy a lil entahtainment. Your dawkies ah unhahmed. There is no use causin a ruckus…"

"Not hahmed! You have pushed my girl ta the floor, and you were hittin her and the boy with a cane! If abuse is your idea of amusement, you should have a cane taken ta you."

Ella turns to the women who have dropped their heads and found much interest in their feet. The other fellow has disappeared.

"And you call yourselves ladies, I suppose. I will discovah your names, and I assure you, neithah of you will be received in any polite society of which I am a pawt."

With those words, Ella turns on her heel and marches to her cabin. Maxie with Ish by the hand, Mammy, and Minda trail along in her wake. Maxie takes Ish into the cabin with them though they know it is against the rules. Minda pulls Ish to her as soon as they are alone. He begins to cry quietly, and Minda cannot quit shaking.

"Now, there is no need faw hysterics," Ella says, but her hands are trembling, too. "Let's give that ruffian time ta make himself scarce as he surely will have the sense ta do, and then you two can go back ta your place on the deck. Mammy, you might as well find them somethin ta eat while I have a word with the captain." She reaches the door, then turns back. "Maxie, you come with me," she adds, and Minda recalls how young she is in spite of the brave front she is exhibiting. Minda vows to never say another harsh word about her young mistress.

After they have eaten, Minda leads Ish back to their haven amidst the cotton and grain. Ish asks if they can stay there until they depart the next day. Minda assures him they will, and the two climb atop the grain sacks to catch the afternoon breeze.

"Mama, why that man call me Jimmy an try ta make me dance?"

Minda sighs and tries to calm the anger threatening to bring on another round of shaking.

"It bout a foolish song some low-life white mens make up bout cullad fokes. They paint they faces black an they talk like they say we talk an they dance roun an they think they's funny, bu they's jus mean."

"Dat man was mean," Ish says. Minda is surprised to see a smile spread across his face.

"What you findin ta smile bout, Son?"

Ish raises his hand for Cotton. He strokes the bird's feathers. Minda finds the bird easier to look out since the mangled leg has fallen off below the string Ish tied around it.

"Ise thinkin bout Cotton here. He tear inta that man like him a eagle. Snatch that hat clean offah dat bald head!"

"Wondah what happen ta his hat."

"I spy it floatin in the watah right fo Mizz Maxie drag me long aftah Mizz Ella. The white stood ou on that blue like a clean pelican."

Mother and son break into laughter. They sit where they are until long after dark. They are relatively quiet until one of them laughs again, inspiring the other to do the same. After they have crawled into their shelter and are lying side by side waiting for sleep, Minda speaks.

"Ish, when you membah what happen taday, doan think on the bad pawt. Think on how Mizz Ella look when she givin that bad man a piece uh her mind, an then think bout Cotton snatchin that big, white hat offah that bald head, an how it was jus a bobbin ou there on the watah."

They laugh one last time before both sleep well in spite of what they have been through.

The next morning, they wait until Mammy comes for them before mixing with the white passengers up front. They can see Baltimore in the distance, and it is not long before they spot Jessie and Diana waving from shore. Mammy and the two young ladies depart long enough to converse with Jessie and Diana, and Minda is relieved to see Ella's mood is much improved. Maybe the altercation of the day before was good for her. She seems genuinely glad to see Jessie, and though she is nowhere nearly as cordial to Diana, at least she is civil.

The foursome stays at the Baltimore Harbor long enough to wave the others off. Both Jessie and Diana are surprised to meet Cotton, and Ish is relieved he will be allowed to keep him. The three women, the boy, and the bird make the short trek to Jessie's home on Pratt Street. Minda marvels at the sign above her door and the well-appointed store beyond. Never has she been in a shop owned by a negro. Her responsibilities for the Barrets have allowed her to visit few businesses of any kind, even those owned by white people. Still, this one is impressive when compared to those she has walked by in Savannah and here on the way from the harbor.

Ish is shy in the presence of Diana now he has seen their prosperity. She is more like his white mistresses with the way she dresses, the way she talks, and the way Jessie and she make a living. Diana senses his withdrawal. She takes his hand and leads them through the store and into the kitchen. Minda looks around, more at ease now she is in the private part of the house. The kitchen is small, and though much better equipped than the place in which she stays in Yamacraw, she can see evidence of economy. There's everything one might need, but the furnishings are spare and simple.

She moves to the bare corner farthest from the fireplace and lowers her bag of clothes to the floor. She no longer carries the food bag that has long been empty.

"I imagine you two must be hungry," Jessie says.

She removes a cloth covering food on the table, and Ish immediately overcomes his timidity. They sit, and by the time the meal is finished, they are talking and laughing like they did when they were in the Barrets' kitchen. Ish has further reason to be excited when Jessie tells him she has arranged for him to apprentice with the man who made her front door and the sign above it.

"He is a woodworker, and he does work of all kinds. He can do almost anything involving wood, You will be able to learn many skills from him. I hope woodwork is something you can become interested in, Ish. I couldn't think of anyone else in my acquaintance who has a trade you might find useful when you return home."

"That soun fine, Mizz Jessie. I likes buildin things."

Minda wonders how Ish knows he likes building. She has never known him to have the opportunity. "He a white man?" she asks.

"No, he was once a slave but has been freed. There are a lot of them here in Baltimore. I am told he was trained by a master who allowed him to work in his free time and eventually purchase his own freedom."

Minda is glad to see Ish's interest, but she is concerned with him getting ideas about slaves purchasing their freedom when Frederick will never allow that to happen with her children.

"You both are tired." Jessie rises and crosses to put a pot of water on the hook to boil. "How about I prepare a bath and let you two refresh yourself from your long trip?"

"I'll show them their room, Mama," Diana offers.

"Room, Mizz Jessie? You got an extry room?" Minda asks.

"Diana and I used to share a room, and we will again while you are here. You two will share Diana's room."

"We cain take Mizz Diana's room!" Minda objects. "We be fine right here in the kitchen. It a sight bettah than where we stay on the boat."

"That might be, but I won't allow it. Diana, take them upstairs while I get what they need for a bath."

Minda follows Diana upstairs closely trailed by Ish whose left foot thumps along the boards. They emerge into a small hallway off which two doors open. They pass one into which a quick glimpse reveals a settee and a bed. They enter the second smaller in which the floor space is taken up by a bathtub already in place for their use. The vessel is almost up against a bed covered by a flowered spread made, no doubt, by either Jessie or Diana. There are bright, hand-drawn pictures pasted to the otherwise plain walls. Hooks for clothing dot the wall by the door. Minda cannot imagine her two changes of clothing adorning those pegs. The remaining items in the room are a washstand on which sits a matching china wash bowl and pitcher. Minda and Ish are speechless.

"Mizz Diana, it ain right we takes yo room. We be mo than fine in the kitchen…"

"Please, Miss Minda, I want you to have my room. Mama and I are excited to be sharing again. Besides, I want to do something nice for you. You and your family were good to me while I was in Savannah. Now we want to repay your hospitality."

Jessie enters and pours the hot water into the already half full tub.

"This should take the chill off. Ish, let Diana show you some of her books while your mother bathes, and then you can take your turn."

Jessie hands Minda a bar of lavender scented soap, and the three leave her alone in the room. She stands awhile wondering if she should continue to object, but the warm bath water entices her, and she strips the dirty clothing from her body and climbs in. She thinks herself selfish for staying until the water cools, but her tired muscles and dry skin are more persuasive than her conscience.

She crawls from the tub and dries on one of the two towels Minda has placed on the bed. She is dismayed when she examines the clothes they have brought from their bag, for they are as dirty as the ones she just discarded. Her mood lifts when she remembers the bath water she can put to good use after Ish is finished.

She glances at the bed and regrets there is no time now to lie on it. She is exhausted from their travels and would love to close her eyes for a little while. She reminds herself they will be allowed to go to bed soon enough. She cannot believe their luck. They will be here for the whole summer with two people who treat them like company! If Jude and Daisy could be with them, their stay would be perfect. Thinking of Jude reminds her of the letter she brings Diana. She finds the paper still deep within the dress she is wearing, crumpled yet intact. She opens the door and goes in search of Ish. She waits until he leaves for his own bath before handing the bedraggled note to Diana.

"Finally! I thought he had completely forgotten me."

"He fearin the same thing. He prickly as a rose bush cause he ain hear from you fo months."

"What! I wrote often, even after he stopped replying!"

"That a shame. I wish they was a way ta tell him. He be with Mizz Middleton soon. He gone there ta hep out."

"I will write Gail there! Surely she can get a message to him, if our postmaster is actually sending my mail on. He doesn't seem to think people like me should be writing. His wife is more accommodating. I will try to make sure I post when she is there."

"Mama!" Ish yells from down the hallway. "What I spose ta put on?"

Minda leaves to help Ish and to wash their dirty clothes. Diana closes the door behind her, presses the letter to her chest, and prepares to enjoy the long awaited communication from Jude.

Chapter 29
Hickory Grove

Hickory Grove, Virginia—1848

Jude should be relieved when they pull the buckboard up to the front of the Middleton's plantation home, the one he has heard much about from his mother, his grandmother, his aunt and uncle. He is tired and he is hungry. He and Uncle Lew have made their way along rugged roads, across rolling creeks, and through small towns where they were eyed with suspicion, searched for contraband of the human kind, and questioned at length in spite of the papers both carry to prove they have the right to travel. But Jude is not pleased to have reached his destination. For the first time in his life, he has enjoyed a sense of freedom. There have been times Lew and he have had no one telling them what to do or where to be. They have slept either under the wagon or beneath the stars; they have eaten what they can snare for themselves or buy along the way. They have washed their clothes and bathed their bodies in water belonging to no one, and Jude has loved every minute of their adventure. He has been untroubled by the searches and demeaning treatment, for there is one advantage to being owned. No one is likely to lay claim or do harm to them for fear of having to answer to an owner of means. It is possible brave traders might try to make the two of them their own cargo, but there was more danger of their wares being stolen than their lives being at risk.

Jude has had much time to think, and if Lew had guessed what direction his thoughts were taking, he would have been worried sick. Jude has contemplated trying to persuade his uncle to keep driving, to take the load somewhere they can sell the wares and slip away into crowds in which they would be two dark faces among many. Jude knows little about geography other than the globe he studied at Mrs. Stiles, but he knows three things: he has been traveling north; he is closer to Baltimore than he has ever been; and there are cities somewhere around with populations large enough to make them less conspicuous. Jude keeps his thoughts to himself, however, because there are ties in Savannah even he cannot sever. He cannot imagine leaving Mama and Ish and the rest of the family, so he knows Lew would die before he would desert Cressa, his kids, his sisters, and his mother. Jude has spent hours trying to come up with a scenario in which those he loves can be united and free. Thus far, the effort has proven futile.

Jude forgets his displeasure when he takes in the contingent gathered to greet them. When they drive up to the back porch where they will be directed as to where to unload their wares, lined along the railing are several waving, smiling black people who Lew apparently recognizes. His own excited countenance and wildly waving hands tell Jude this is a homecoming for his uncle, and he cannot be sad when Lew is obviously overjoyed to see them. Jude steps down from the wagon and arms encircle him from behind. When he whirls to confront his assailant, he is glaring down into the eyes of Daisy. He grabs her and swings her in a circle, putting her down when she pulls his ear in protest.

"Jus look at you!" she cries. "Youse grown a mile since I sees you!"

"I finally tallah than you, Sis!"

"You may be tallah, but Ise still da oldess, an you bettah membah dat!!"

The reunion is short-lived, for there is work to be done by all of them. Daisy promises to find him later, and an old man named Justice talks with them while they unload the buckboard before making their way to the barn. There, Lew leads him to a loft partially filled with hay. Jude has never been in a barn of this size, and he gazes around with interest after the two have dumped their few belongings on the loose hay on which they will sleep. He likes the building. The interior is overly warm at the moment, but the slatted windows opening on all sides will allow cool night air as the sun goes down. He likes the view through the slats on one of the windows. He looks out to the creek slithering like a long garter snake between two fields.

"Is that the creek the Howe boy drown in?"

Lew walks up beside him and follows the direction of his pointing finger.

"Dat be da one. Only one on da place."

"That ain deep nuff ta drown a chicken."

"Youse a long way off up hyur. You ain see da thing at full roar. Dat crek a sight ta behole wen it git goin. Mama skin our hide we git close wen it rainin. Come on now. Less go."

"Where we goin in such a hurry? We doan have ta go ta work already, do we?"

"No, but wese joinin da fokes in da quattah. Theys be cookin fo us, an they may eben be some singin an dancin fo dis night ovah."

"I be long in a minute. Jus gonna rest a bit. You go catch up with yo friends."

Lew studies him a minute, decides there isn't much trouble he can get into in a barn loft, then climbs down the ladder. Jude can see him from his vantage point as he leaves the barn, rounds the corner, and is gone from sight. Jude stands a while longer noticing the way the creek runs parallel to the road they came in on, then continues past the plantation and into a forest he deems northward. From here, he cannot tell which way the creek is actually flowing. Doesn't matter, he decides. No stronger than the current, one could wade the depth, even upstream. If one had a mind to, he would need to make sure there was no sign of rain, according to what Lew had said.

Jude turns back to the hay loft and surveys the space. They have passed several barns on their travels, and he has no reason to think they are not similar to this one. He crawls behind the stacked hay and opens the door positioned in the center of more slatted windows. He is surprised to find himself on level with a hillside drive situated to make unloading hay and supplies directly into the loft easy. The hill slopes gently toward the sprawling white house all his kin worked in when young. He decides he likes barns. A structure like this one provides a view in any direction.

He takes better note of the ladder as he descends. Built at a slant, the stair-like rungs are easier to use than those on a vertical ladder. The boards are broad and thick and provide for solid footing while hauling things to the loft. The bottom floor backs up to the hill. Several stalls with solid doors line the back wall. In each door is cut a small square window with four narrow slats tacked vertically from top to bottom. He peers into the dark recesses and judges the piles to be grains of some kind. Along each of the barn side walls are open stalls much like those they have in the stable at the Barret mansion. All are empty at the moment. They must be shelter for the horses he saw earlier in the field or perhaps some of the cows for milking. He walks out the door he and Lew entered earlier and realizes the ceiling above his head is the floor of the loft which forms an outdoor roof for the animals. The structure is surrounded on three sides by a corral made of planks and painted white to match the barn and the plantation house.

On his walk to the quarters, he passes several outbuildings and tries to guess their purpose. He has no trouble finding the quarters because workers are coming in from the field. He follows a young man with a hoe over his shoulder who looks to be younger than him. Unlike Jude, he is thin and wiry. He must sense Jude behind, but he trudges tiredly on with his eyes set before him as if he is dimwitted. The boy leads him to two rows of facing shacks. Jude counts five structures down each side. The ten cabins vary from one room to two, all built up off the ground with stacked rocks providing support at each corner and in the center. All have rock and mud fireplaces, and most have chickens pecking around on the bare earth in front and under them. Varying shapes and sizes of vegetable gardens back the shacks. A couple have a pig penned to the side. In front of the shacks, there are fire rings at which women are preparing to cook. The boy disappears into the second hut on the left, and Jude continues to walk. There are easily twenty black people mingling in the area between the two rows of cabins. Jude has never seen this many in one place, besides at church, for slaves are prohibited from congregating in Savannah. Some of the people recognize him as the young man who arrived with Lewis, and they smile. One lady tending a black kettle at a fire pit calls out to him, "You lookin fo Lew, him down da las house dare wid Ole Justice."

"Thank you," Jude offers. He is relieved to find his uncle sitting on an upturned stick of wood outside of a one-room cabin with the man he had learned earlier was Justice. The older man rises and drags another stick of wood from beneath the cabin. He returns to his seat in the open doorway. Jude is about to be seated when Justice yells. Startled, Jude misses the makeshift stool.

"Sarey, I tells you naw ta be puttin dat dirt in yo mouf. You does dat gin, I takes a switch ta dat hine en uh yose."

The offending Sarey is no more than three or four, and instead of dropping the clod she has in her hand, she hurls the dirt at a younger boy sitting in a circle of several young children.

Jude is glad Justice doesn't catch his tumble even if his uncle does and is laughing at him. Jude manages to be up and in place by the time the old man turns back to them.

"Dis wat I gits fo aw dose yeahs uh hawd work. I hab ta sits hyur aw day long wid dis bunch a rascal. They's thinkin I ain much good fo nuttin else sin dese hans swole up da size u mush melon."

He offers his hands for inspection, and Jude is shocked at how gnarled and swollen they are. They remind him of ginseng roots his mother has had him pick up at the market for Mammy's medicinal purposes.

"Da missus jus naw wantin ta cause you mo pain. I doan think I mine sittin hyur all day wid dese chilren. Dat choe beat da daylight ouddah bein in da fiels aw day long makin sho da othahs do whut theys spose ta."

"Me naw bein dare be tolable fo me mabe, bu it sho naw bess fo dem. Missus gabe mys job ta Gerty's Cletus, an him like nuttin mo dan layin stripes, tickerly cross da back uh da guls."

Jude has to listen hard to understand what Justice is saying. Even Lew's speech has changed.

"Da missus 'low whippin nowaday?" Lew is shocked, as is Jude. His family has told him Mrs. Middleton didn't sell her people or beat them.

"Da missus doan knows wat go on in da fiels no mo. Her lack me—gittin too ole—an her ain seein none a wat him do. Her know wat go on uppah da big house, bu Cletus do wat he wanse ou hyur."

"Wy doan you tell er, den? Her lissen ta you. Her know you ain carryin no tale dat ain da truff."

Justice examines his feet. "Ise ain brave lack I uset ta be. Cain fight off a gnat wid dese hans, an dat wat I haftah do I pays a visit ta da missus. Cletus mean as a coppah haid."

"Den I tells her!" Lew states. "Ise still young nuff ta take care uh mysef."

"Youse jus lack yo daddy! Looks lack em, tawks lack em. I sho miss Pleas aw dese year him be gone. Good ta hab youse hyur."

"It good ta see you, Justice, but I sho ain wantin ta be back hyur. Life in Svanna a sight easiuh, an I hab a wife an two chilren now. Town life jus ain hawd wen held up ginst dis. Wese eats in da big house—I gits ta stay wid my fambly. Back hyur, Mama jus see my daddy on Sundy she lucky. Now Ise grown, I wondah how theys foun da time ta make us chilren."

"Theys make da time, an naw jus on Sundy, I knows dat fo a fack. I be da ovahseah at da time, youse recklect. Him be wid yo mama an youse chilren evah time him gits da chance, an sometime wen him dint."

The wrinkled face loses its smile. "Den naw lack it be now. Yo daddy be daid from da whip dat snake naw bit him. Him too proud ta bow ta da like uh Cletus, an dat wat us hab ta do now jus ta git by."

"I tawk wid da missus, dat whut I do."

"You bess be headin South da minute you does."

"What you mean, if that snake not bit him?" Jude interrupts.

"Yo grandaddy git bit by a coppah haid in da cotton fiel. Him git hep in time, him migh still be hyur."

"You thinks Cletus…" Lew begins.

"Tell me bout my grandpa," Jude interrupts again.

"You means you doan knows nuttin bou Pleas?" Justice looks at Lew with disapproval.

"Doan be castin dat face dis ways. I knows nuttin mysef. I dint eben membah hes name be Pleas! Ise jus a youngun wen him up an die."

"I guess dat da truff. Peers I cain hang on ta a idee longah dan it take ta come inta mys haid, bu I kin membah wat happen foty year go plain it be yestidy. Seem lack no time yo ma an pa dancin righ hyur in dis quattah an Pleas be youngah dan you be now." He nods at Lew. "Make me sad ta think on it."

"I doan want ta make you sad, Justice, bu I sho would like ta hear da story. No one evah mention the man that I recall."

"Sho thinkin on da way da man pass ain sumptin Daisy wanse ta membah eithah."

Jude wonders what his sister has to do with his grandfather's story until he recalls Mammy's given name is Daisy.

"Theys be da pair! Pleas blong ta da Simmon place. Dat un nuttin lack dis un. Ole man Simmon die an dat jus leab da ole lady an Pleas. Pleas run da place ovah dare, an da ole missus naw knowin whar him be mos da time. Her naw worry on wat Pleas upta long as da choes git done an him show up evah mawnin. Yo mama," he waves a gnarled hand in Lew's direction, "hab da three ub youse by dat time, an da missus gib er a cabin ou back hine da worsh house. Her brung youse younguns down hyur ta be ten ta wile her in da big house."

"I membah bein down hyur wid da othah chilren til theys stawt trainin me fo house work," Lew says.

"Yep, da missus take a shine ta Daisy, an da whole bunch uu youse git pict fo da house. Dat make somes roun hyur green, bu evahbidy lack yo mama wen her stawt socializin wid da res uh em lack her no bettah or no wuss."

"How she meet Pleas?" Jude asks. Before Diana, the story of romance wouldn't have interested him, but now, any explanation of how two slaves got together may be of use to him.

"Cuz Pleas da one dawkie on da Simmon place, he git lonesome, an he be hyur wid us jus bout evah evenin. Peers he spot yo mama ow doin sumptin, an fo wese knows it, theys be hoppin da broom! Pleas play da fiddle at da weddin eben dough it be theys."

If not for the lanterns and the fires, the quarter would be dark. Jude discovers they have been joined by some of the other men and several children sitting cross-legged in the dirt listening.

"Tings be nigh as good as Ise evah membah," the smile slides from his face, "an theys nevah be dat good agin aftah yo po papa die da way him do."

"Hows him die, Unc Justice?" one of the children ask. "Do Cletus git em?"

"Naw, dat long fo Cletus shows is sorry backside roun hyur. Dem days, Ise be able ta deal wid dat kine. Lack I says, Pleas blong ta da Missus, him migh be libin still. Bu him git bit by da coppah haid in da Simmon cotton patch, an da Missus ovah dare dint knows nuttin bou healin. Her po some kerosene on it, an da time da po man drag hissef ovah hyur ta see hes fambly, dat laig swole up bou da size ub yo whole bidy."

He points to a young boy of about eight who has crawled within touchin distance of him.

"Daisy runs fast as er laigs ud take er ta git da missus. Her puts em righ dare in Daisy own bed an sen fo da wite foke doctah. Him comes an him jus shakes hes haid, bu him say him do wat him kin. Theys fill Pleas full uh whiskey da missus brung from da house, an Daisy hole is haid in er lap wen theys commence ta cuttin. Da pain brung im roun, an I cuddah hyur em screamin aw da way down hyur hab I naw been dare heppin hole em down. Dat da furse time theys cut. Da red line come back aw da way ta is…" Justice stops and considers the children, "is man pawts. Da doc come agin an says him too faw gone, but Daisy beg. Pleas say 'cut da res ub it off, naw doin me no good no ways,' an theys fill em full uh whiskey agin. Pleas gulp it like watah cuz him knows wat comin." Justice shakes his head and his chin puckers. "Da doc dint eben lebe nuff room ta tie da stump off, bu doan mattah no ways b' dat time. They's blood evah whar an Pleas nevah wake up."

It takes the listeners a minute to register the ringing dinner bell. Interesting as the tale has been, nothing can compete with supper, and the crowd scatters, the children the first to go.

Jude has lost his appetite. He looks to Lew who is sitting staring blankly at something only he can see.

"Come on, Boys. Youse haftah eat," Justice says, and the two rise and follow him to the closest kettle. Everyone is holding a tin plate and a cup and standing in line to be served. Justice produces a plate an cup from his cabin and hands them to Jude. "Go on, Son. Be quick bout it sose yo Unc hyur kin eats wen youse done."

"What you goin ta eat out of?" Jude asks Justice.

"I ain dat hungry dese days."

"I ain eatin while the two of you wait," Jude protests, and what ensues is a shuffling of the two utensils among them until a neighbor woman appears with two more cups and plates.

All three thank her, but she says nothing before walking away.

"Dat be Gerty," Justice states. "I doan know howse a kine woman lack er en up wid a mean, no count boy lack Cletus. I nevah knows is daddy, bu him mustah be da debil hissef."

Both Lew and Jude turn to study Gerty. She is a nondescript little woman about Lew's age or a little older.

"I doan recall knowin her. Who her blong ta?"

"Her naw one uh ours, Son. Theys comes tagathah bou five year back. Him a hawd workah an knows how ta tawk ta da missus. Her fool by dat split tongue uh hes an think him smawt nuff ta do mys job. An him doin it, awrigh. Gittin mo work ouddah da fiel hans. Dat wat da missus know. Doan know howse him goin bout it."

Jude eats his boiled cabbage with onions and carrots with a slab of skillet fried cornbread. He thinks he tastes a bit of pork in the soup. He drinks the water from the borrowed cup, washes it and the plate in one of the black kettles now filled with water and returns them to Gerty. He speaks to her. She nods her head in acknowledgment, then enters her single cabin. Cletus must live elsewhere.

As Jude is trying to decide what to do next, the singing begins. He recognizes the words from church, but the song sounds different here in the dim light between these two rows of shacks with the sky above and the dirt below. The voices hold a melancholy he has never heard in church. They moan and wail, ebb and build. As the voices rise, his companions begin to move. Soon, most are swaying and some are dancing. Jude is surprised to see Lew join in as if he has been singing and dancing every day since he left Virginia, and as if he hasn't minutes before listened to the most gruesome story Jude has ever heard about his father. Jude finds himself sitting alone, watching the others but thinking about his Mammy seeing her husband bleed to death. The tempo of the music grows even faster, and Jude can no longer dwell on his own thoughts. He is amazed when he spots the young man he followed in from the fields, the one dragging his tired carcass home, now laughing and singing with the rest of them.

Jude is worn out from the long drive and drained from Justice's story. He tells Lew he is going back to the barn where he can lie on the hay and listen to the voices from there. Lew says the party is in his honor, so he will stay. There is little daylight left as he approaches the barn, but he can still recognize Daisy as she runs toward him. She falls in behind him and follows him up the steps and into the loft. Jude was right; the night air has already cooled the room. He grabs his jacket and is in the process of rolling it into a pillow when the crackle of his mother's note catches his attention.

Daisy is already sitting cross-legged on the floor with her skirts pulled around her when he hands her the envelope.

"Somethin from Mama ta you," he says.

She takes the envelope and opens it, pulls forth the sheet of words, and turns to her brother for an explanation. Her forehead is creased, and he laughs at the expression on her face.

"What this?" she asks.

"What it look like?"

"It look like a lettah."

"That cause it a lettah."

"Quit playin wid me, Jude. Whut dis got ta do wid me?"

"Mama wrote you a lettah."

Daisy's eyebrows rise, and she glances over her shoulder as if she fears someone is listening.

"Mama cain write no lettah. Mama cain write. Sides," she whispers, "it ginst da law fo us ta write.""

"Then we all be breakin the law fo some time now."

"Who we?" she whispers again.

"You can quit bein scared. Nobidy hear us up here."

"Who we?" Daisy repeats a bit louder. She switches the letter to her left hand and uses her right to pull him down beside her. "Whar youse learnin ta write?"

"We be—Mama, Ish, an me. An we can read, too."

"Ish?" Daisy squeals. "Lil Ish?"

Jude cannot help but laugh again at the disbelief on her face. Laughing feels good. Daisy slaps him on the leg.

"Now quit teasin, Jude, an tell me whut youse tawkin bout."

"Mizz Stiles ask Mama if she can teach her ta read an write first."

"Mizz Stiles! Mizz Abby frien?"

"That the one. Then Mama start teachin Ish an me, but I git head uh her, so Mizz Bette stawt teachin me herself. I read books, Daisy. Big books!"

"Ain Mama fraid you git in trouble? Whut da massah say?"

"The massah cain know. Mr. Stiles start suspectin, but he dead now. He one white man doan mattah no mo."

"Now I knows, you sounds diffrent. You tawk mo lack wite foke."

"I can talk even mo like white people if I want to, *if I should so choose*," he demonstrates.

Daisy giggles and slaps him on the leg again.

"Read Mama's lettah ta me. Hurry."

Jude reads the short letter aloud. Her choice of words saddens him, for he can imagine the effort forming each letter cost her. He vows to help her with her writing when he returns to Savannah. The thought of going home makes him even sadder. He glances up to catch tears in Daisy's eyes.

"I miss ya'll evah day, an now, evahbidy bu me kin read an write. Ise bein leff behine!"

"You the main reason Mama want ta learn. She want ta be able ta read yo lettahs when you learn someday."

Daisy shakes her head. "I ain nevah gonna read an write. Who gonna teach me, tell me dat?"

"Mizz Bette tell Mama she thinks Mizz Mattie mo like Mizz Abby than the massah. She think someday she teach you, an mabe even set you free."

Daisy shakes her head harder than before. "Dat mightah happen fo her marry Massah Whit, bu dat nevah happen now. She a missus ersef, an her spectin a chile. Massah Whit like Massah Barret—mabe mo set in his way. Him scole Mizz Mattie fo bein too easy on da hep. Her still my Mizz Mattie an her good ta me, bu theys ain goan be no learnin an freein in dis lifetime."

"Mizz Bette think we all be free some day. She wants us ta know how ta do when the day come. I teach you ta read an write myself when we can be tagathah."

Daisy's smile does not reach her eyes. "Youse sweet, Jude, jus like you awways be. Tell Mama I love da lettah, an doan tell her I acks lack a crybaby."

Jude turns the topic to home, and Daisy is soon laughing again.

"Ise gottah go. Mizz Mattie know whar I be, but it gittin late. I come agin tamorrah night if I kin."

Jude extends the letter, but she shakes her head. "Whut I do wid dat? They be trouble fo aw uh us somebidy sees it."

Jude lies awake long after Lew comes in. He remembers what Justice said about his grandfather.

"Unc Lew, why we nevah know bout yo papa bein bit by a snake an dying?"

"Mama nevah like ta tawk bout it. I cain pull his face up in my haid. Whut I do membah, him a happy man. Like ta play an cut up. Him play da fiddle wile mama an da othahs dance. I membah Mama carryin on somethin awful wen him die. Scairt me an Minda bad. Dat bout aws I membah."

So Lew and Mama and Dovie dint have a papa most they lives eithah, Jude thinks. He cannot sleep for some time for thinking about what Lew and Justice had said, about what he's learned about Daisy's master. He guesses his life could be worse, and he is glad he doesn't live on a plantation. He wonders what kind of man this Cletus can be to mistreat his fellow slaves when he is one.

He will not have long to wait to find out.

Chapter 30
Rob's News

Savannah, Georgia—1848

The sun is up when Frederick awakens. He decides to dress and tend to his own needs because Deke is filling in for Jude. His decision has nothing to do with Deke's performance. Though he is not yet as efficient as his cousin, he has a temperament more to Frederick's liking. There is often a smile on the young man's face, and he doesn't have to tolerate the resentment practically seeping from Jude's pores. He has decided to reward the young man by giving him the job permanently when this mess is behind him. To appease Minda for what he is about to do, he will find an apprenticeship for Jude, one that will get him out from under his own roof yet keep him close enough to supervise. Though Jessie's idea of training Ish in a trade has put the plan in his mind, he gives her no credit. He thinks of how magnanimous he is being, not only to Minda, but to the boys themselves who are being afforded opportunities and advantages over many other slaves. He has already had the conversation with Minda in his head, the one in which he tells her he will allow the boys to keep a percentage of their earnings, a gesture he hopes will preclude any more foolish talk about freeing them some day.

Frederick uses the chamber pot and covers it to wait for Deke's attention. He then washes up in the water left in the pitcher from the night before, runs a cloth over both of his shoes, dresses himself with attention to detail, then leaves the room where he encounters Deke on the stairs. Deke's face first registers surprise, then fear he may have misjudged the time. Frederick puts a hand on the boy's shoulder, tells him he has no need of him, and grants him a break from his morning duties after he empties the chamber pot. Deke asks no questions and darts up the stairs before the master can change his mind. He doesn't know what has come over the man, but he decides this summer is looking up for him.

Deke had been upset when Jude and Ish had gotten to go places he hadn't, but since they left, he, his mother, and Dovie have been enjoying a freedom they are unused to in spite of the extra work. The three of them, along with his sister and his cousin Ben, are often on the place alone. Dovie has taken advantage of the lack of supervision, and this is the lone cloud in Deke's blue sky. He has worried with Ben whose mother has managed to spend both nights with Cyrus since Jude and Lew drove off in the buckboard for Virginia. The boys fear she is getting reckless. They have not forgotten the master's warnings and Mammy's admonitions even if Dovie has. After taking care of the unpleasant task, Deke runs to tell Cressa of his good luck. Had he foreseen how the day would evolve, he would have at least hugged Dovie on the way out. Instead, he finds Ben and Lizzy who assume they too are being granted time off. The three of them make themselves scarce.

Dovie herself is thrilled. If Master Barret is dismissing Deke for the morning, he must be leaving himself. Maybe he is already gone. She roams the house until she detects voices. She is disappointed to discover both Frederick and Rob are still there. She decides to dust the front hallway to put herself in a position to eavesdrop. They have come upon each other by surprise, each arising early, and this bodes well for Dovie. They must have plans, or they would still be in their rooms. She doubts either will want to linger long.

Dovie's assumptions are correct. Frederick is as surprised to see Rob as his son is to see him, both glad of the chance meeting.

"I was about ta pen you a note, Fathah."

"So I have saved you the trouble. What wakes you with the rooster, Son?"

There is a hint of apprehension in his voice that is not lost on Rob.

"News of the highest awdah. Were my haste not of the gravest import, I would have wanted ta be face ta face with you when I disclose the best news I may evah have ta impawt."

Reading the thinning of Frederick's full lips as an indication of impatience, Rob forges ahead.

"Today I ask Eleanor ta become my pawtnah in life and faw eternity!"

Being a fan of effusive language himself, Frederick is not distracted by the dramatic fashion of his son's delivery; he admires it. He clasps the prodigal by the shoulders with both hands, then overcome with the sentiment of the moment, he pulls him into an embrace, the third or fourth in Rob's memory.

"Sit, Son, and tell me how this auspicious decision has come to be without counsel from me, the one who must hold your best interest above all others."

"It has all happened quickly, and were I ta doubt eithah your approval or the success with which my entreaty will be met, I would have awakened you in the night. Upon my last visit, Eleanor and I talked of the eventuality of our union, but I was averse ta disclose the topic ta you should I be hasty and give you yet futhah cause faw disappointment in me. I have been unsure of what sentiment my proposal would evoke in Mr. Peavy."

"You should have come to me, Robart. Have I ever been loath to advise you on matters of import…"

Rob does something he doesn't often do. He interrupts his father.

"And seekin your advice was my intent, Sir, but I was suhprised with a correspondence of the most propitious nature last night upon my return from the Club. Eleanor wrote me the dearest sentiments and, with them, the assurance my tendah proposition would be met with success on the pawt of her fathah with whom she had taken upon herself ta plead my case…" Upon seeing the disapproval on Frederick's face, he hastens to add, "… with words chosen ta give evah indication I would not appreciate her speakin faw me, and that we have come ta no undahstandin and would nevah presume to without his approval."

Frederick's face relaxes, and Rob sighs in relief.

"But why would you rush off to leave me with a written explanation instead of the joy of receiving the news in person, as I am now?"

"You will undahstand as I tell you Mr. Peavy must leave tamorrah mornin faw Texas ta be delayed there faw some time. Eleanor wants both she and her fathah ta be tagethah when I ask faw her hand, and unless we come ta an undahstandin this evenin, both of us will have ta delay our hearts' desires. I knew you would comprehend the urgency upon readin my note. I will be home soon at which time we can discuss all at length. With the girls gone and Fredie away, I know we will have ta delay any formal celebration, but at least the two of us will have personal time faw long discourse as ta how I should proceed."

Mollified, Frederick grasps Rob's right hand within his own.

"You make me proud, Son. I agree you are doing the right thing by rushing to fulfill Miss Peavy's desires in regard to her parents. We must discuss, though, upon your return, what is to be asked and understood."

"I have yet more news ta impawt. Mr. Peavy intimated he has grown tired of tryin ta manage his propahty in Macon, and he desires ta set up household in Texas where he can bettah travel back and fawth between his two places there. She undahstands he intends ta gift her with the Macon plantation and the people he has workin it. I will become landed upon our union."

There are actual tears in the eyes of father and son as they share a moment both have longed for—one in which the son has his sire's complete approval, one in which the father has rare praise for how his son has conducted himself. They part with yet another hug, and Frederick decides the transaction he has been dreading must be Providential, for Rob's good news would not have come at the exact moment when he was about to implement his plan were it not the right thing to do.

As Frederick exits the parlor, he almost bumps into Dovie herself. He decides this encounter is another positive portent.

"Dovie," he says, "stay close as I want to speak with you in an hour or two. I have an errand, and then I will meet you below—let's say in the laundry. I am sure you can find something to do there until I get back."

Dovie's disappointment in the master's delayed departure is replaced by fear when the full impact of what he has said sinks in. Never has he set up a meeting with her. He has sent for her in the past, but she has been called to him at the moment, never in advance. She longs to talk to Mammy and Minda, but they are not here. She loses her breath when she is struck with the idea that their absence may not be coincidence. She remembers both Lew and Jude are gone. Could the master have sent everyone away so he could punish her without interference? Surely not. She cannot imagine him going to those lengths for anything to do with her. Then again, she cannot remember the house being this empty with him in residence. Is she to be beaten—or worse?

Dovie waits until Frederick is out of the door, then she pulls her dress between her legs and flies down the stairs to talk with Cressa, the only adult family member left on the place.

Chapter 31
Field Work

Hickory Grove, Virginia—1848

There is much Jude likes about plantation life. He likes sleeping in the barn; he likes the cool Virginia breezes; he likes bathing in the creek; he likes being far from Master Barret, and most of all, he likes the camaraderie of the quarter. He enjoys the banter, the laughter, the communal living. He is humbled by the way most find something to be glad about in the midst of hard circumstances. Jude has merely thought he has worked hard. The field hands here come dragging in about dusk after leaving at sunup. Each day he thinks they will be too tired to do anything but fall face down on their respective beds and sleep until they have to rise to repeat the day before. They seem to get a second wind, and after having something to eat and drink, the quarter becomes a small community in which they talk, laugh, gossip, and complain.

Since their arrival, Lew and Jude have put a fresh coat of white paint on the kitchen and the wash house. Today will be their first assignment in the field. Lew's obvious apprehension has filled Jude with a dread of his own. Nothing, however, could have prepared Jude for the day ahead of them.

Lew shakes Jude awake before dawn, and the two join the others in the quarter where they accept a couple of biscuits and some fatback. They eat them on the way to the field where both meet Cletus for the first time. They have seen him from a distance, but they have yet to have any reason to talk to him. Mrs. Middleton had sent instructions about the painting duties, but those tasks being completed, Cletus had wasted no time in sending a message by his mother. They were to report to him the next morning with the others. Gerty had delivered it much as she had offered them the plates and cups, with head down and as few words as possible. Jude wonders what existence is like for her among people who hate her son.

Jude would think Cletus a handsome fellow if he had not been warned about him. He sits astride the biggest bay mule Jude has ever seen. In his right hand is what Lew will later describe as a Single Tail. Lew has a whip he carries in the wagon—the master's bull whip. The one Cletus carries is shorter, four feet or so. Glancing around, Jude can see no other animal than the mule. The device must be used to inflict the human pain the others have talked about.

Cletus has a well-formed head sitting atop a short neck that tapers off into broad shoulders. His sleeveless homespun shirt reveals developed muscles. He is a stocky man, and though he is sitting on the mule, Jude judges him to be of short stature, shorter than himself, he is sure. The man catches Jude staring at him and turns a pair of steely, light eyes full upon him. Though the ebony hue of Cletus' skin speaks of no miscegenation, his eyes tell a different story.

"Lew an Jude, ain it?" the man asks.

"Yessuh," Lew answers for both of them.

"Ise goan stawt da two uh youse town boys ou slow. You kin haul da drinkin watah down ta da backy patch. I wanse one at da en uh evah othah row. You fine da buckets an da dippahs at da well house. You knows whar dat be, Ise guessin, you bein a house niggah hyur in da pass."

Lew nods. Cletus doesn't reply, just stands staring a cold hole into him until he receives the message.

"Yes, Boss, I membah."

Jude has thought he hated the master and young Master Rob, but he feels a rage foreign to him. Anger burns his eyes and numbs his face. He has grown to expect disdain and cruelty from white men, but this man is colored, even darker than he. Jude thinks he has to know how mistreatment feels, yet he harms others. *Maybe it is power and not color that creates cruelty*, he thinks.

"You needs ta fill da buckets wen needs be, den take dem on ta da nex row wen da pluckin move dat way."

Jude has no idea what he is talking about, but Lew must for he answers, "Yes, Boss," and turns toward the plantation house. Jude stays close behind him, eager to get Lew alone.

"He one mean man!" Jude says.

Lew's attempt to laugh results in a snort. "Youse doubtin dat aftah all da tales youse hyurin in da quattah? Less jus pray we doan sees a whole lot wuss ouddah him fo da day ovah. An you stays ouddah da way an keep dat mouf uh yose shut. Youse spoilt in Svanny, lock we aw be."

His uncle's acceptance of his lot in life has always frustrated Jude, as if he has never longed for more or thought he deserved better. Now he has a better understanding of why Lew may be satisfied in Savannah.

"You evah git a whip like that one use on you?"

Lew shakes his head. "I doan hawdly membah da ole massah, an da missus work us hawd, bu her doan stan fo no whip an no sellin. Back wen Ise hyur, da wuss be a day wid no dinnah or losin yo Sundy off. Da missus gittin ole or theys be none uh dis mess goin on."

"Thought you gonna tell her?"

"Ain hab da chance. Sides, I rathah waits ta righ fo we goes, cause ain no tellin whut a man lack Cletus do you crosses him."

Lew glances at his nephew. "Promise youse goan keep dat sassy mouf uh yose close so tight you hab ta suck air through yo nose."

When Jude doesn't answer immediately, Lew stops and glares at him.

"I promise. Not like I got somethin ta say ta the likes uh him anyway."

"Make sho you keeps it dat way."

If there is one thing Jude knows how to do, it is to draw water. He and Lew take turns much like he and Deke do at the big house in Savannah. They fill four of the twelve buckets at a time. The plan is to carry them to the tobacco field where the others are working, then return for the next four. The destination is at least half a mile from the wellhouse, and Jude is amazed at the size of the plot when it comes into view.

"That ain no patch!" he complains, but they laugh because they are relieved to see no sight of Cletus. Jude is glad they have to fill four more buckets. The walk up the hill and the time they have between their turns at the rope allow them some rest before hauling the full buckets down the path. The routine also kills time otherwise spent in the field. They would loiter if not for the vision of Cletus etched in their brains. By the third trip, blisters that popped up on both hands on the two previous trips break and sting. When he shows them to Lew, he laughs and calls him soft.

"Dese rope handle roughah dan da ones at home. An we ain uset ta carryin em ovah a mile at a time. Mabe youse a lil bettah ta git long wid wen we gits home."

After Lew and Jude have all their buckets in place on the pieces of wood erected at the end of the designated rows, they move with the others. Because the workers are only allowed to drink every other row, they are thirsty enough to empty the buckets often. Lew and Jude take turns making the trek to the well to fill two buckets at a time, and during the other's absence, they help the workers pluck the blooms from the tobacco plants and pull whatever weeds have shown their heads from the previous weeding. Lew has to explain to Jude why deflowering the plants is a good thing and not bad.

"You doan pull da bloom off, da growin go inta dem sted ub da leave, an nobidy be smokin dose flower. It da leave theys take an hangs ta dry. Dat whut theys sell, dose dry leave. Da biggah da leave, da beddah. Theys git rid ub dem bloom an da leave git aw da strength."

"That make sense, I guess," Jude concedes, but he dislikes casting the blossoms away with the weeds as if their beauty is not appreciated.

About noon, children from the quarters come bearing food for family members. One of Justice's charges appears with more of the fatback they had for breakfast, this time with a slab of cornbread. Though Jude and Lew are used to more and better, they wolf the fare down with the others. They have been back in the field no more than an hour when Cletus comes riding up. Jude and Lew have finished rotating their buckets and have emptied two half full ones into others. Lew is preparing to return for more water while Jude busies himself pulling blooms on the row closest to him. Out of his peripheral vision he glimpses Cletus riding down along the edge of the garden inspecting each row for signs of a job poorly done. Apparently, he finds nothing to complain about because he keeps coming. Lew looks forward along his own row to keep from casting his eyes anywhere near the man. Up ahead at some distance, he spots something resembling a bundle of rags lying on the ground. He is the only one working the row though others are finishing up behind him making their ways toward the buckets at the end. Too late, Jude realizes the mound is a young woman lying with her head resting on her outstretched arm. She is too far away for him to warn without attracting Cletus's attention. When no other options come to mind, he determines to keep his head down and hope Cletus will pass them by. The girl is not that lucky.

The mule snorts and stops at the front of the row no more than ten feet behind him. The blood rushes to his head when Cletus bellows, "Hey, You! Whut youse doin down dare?"

All the workers stop and turn their way, including Lew who stands staring at Jude.

Obviously, he thinks Jude has done something to call attention to himself. He has started their way when Cletus swings from the saddle with the whip in his hand. Lew has not made it far before the short, stocky overseer pushes past Jude down the row. Lew's shoulders slump in relief, but he keeps coming. He stops next to Jude as the whole company of workers watch the man stride down the row toward none of them knows what. The only person who is unaware of his approach is the woman lying on the ground, her body hidden from those in other rows by the tobacco plants. Cletus is right on top of her before the object of his fury rises, her eyes round with fear. Jude guesses her to be about his age.

The girl starts backing up along the row.

"Git down!" Cletus yells, and she drops immediately, her back rounded, her head already pulled tight between her shoulders, her hands protectively clasped at the crown.

"Wat youse thinks youse doin?" he shouts.

None of them, including Lew and Jude can understand her response because she is talking into the ground.

"Lookie up hyur an tawk ta me fo I cuts you in two wid dis strap!"

"I says I jus hab da chile two day go an Ise wore ou. I cain keep goin. I cide I res fo a bit, I work twicst as hawd. I shows you, Boss, soon I..."

The girl's words are cut off by the sharp crack of the whip. Jude lurches toward her, but Lew's restraining hand grips his arm.

"Ain nuthin you kin do sep bring da same down on yosef. Be still."

Jude surveys the crowd as the whip continues to descend. Many resume their work. Jude does not know if they cannot stand to bear witness or they fear calling attention to themselves. One woman stands alone staring their way. Tears run down her cheeks, her dress clinched in hands that have wrung the skirt into a knot. She is whimpering something unintelligible. Jude doesn't have to guess who she is. He wonders where the father of the child she has mentioned is. If he is among them, how can he stand by and not help this girl?

Why we allowin this? Jude wonders. *They enough of us ta ovahpowah him. We can give him some of his own medicine.*

"An den whut?" Lew asks as if he has read his mind.

"Be one less sorry dawkie on this earth."

"An probly a lot fewah gooduns."

Other than to yell, "Oh please, Boss!" and "Please, stop! No mo!" the young woman only moans even though the lashes have to be excruciating. Finally, she stops making any sound at all, and probably fearful he has killed the mistress's valuable property, Cletus stops. He looks around as if he has come out of a stupor, and motions the crying woman and one other to take her to the quarters. "Po some watah on er." In case he has appeared too soft, he adds, "An, Sal, git on back down hyur soon you does cause yo gul done cheat me outtah a day."

Lew pulls Jude back toward the buckets behind them and grabs them as if they are empty. He pushes him toward the house.

"Go fill dese up now. Ain nothin kin be done hyur. They's a bettah way."

Jude puts one foot in front of the other and walks back to the well house. When he gets there, he is shaking. His extremities feel numb. He sits on the ground to keep from falling. He is surprised when Daisy appears.

"Whut wrong wid you, Jude? I watchin you from da winda."

Jude begins to weep. Daisy drops to sit beside him.

"It Lew? Somethin happen ta Lew?"

Jude tips a bucket of its remaining water over his head and wipes the tears and grime from his face with his pant's leg. Daisy says nothing of the water he has splashed on her. Finally, he manages to tell her about the girl, the one who could have been her or Diana or his Mama or any of them. Daisy puts her arms around him, and her voice, much like his mother's, comforts him. He stands.

"I got ta git back."

"Wait." Daisy glances over her shoulder before reaching into her apron pocket and holding out her hand. "Ise goan give dis ta you tanigh, bu mabe youse needs it now. Mizz Gail come ta me dis mawnin an say ta slip it ta you. Say Diana ackst her to."

Jude reaches for the envelope with shaking hands.

"Hide it." She glances up to see if anyone is at the window from which she saw Jude.

Jude stuffs the letter down his pants and heads back to the tobacco field. By the time he places the bucket on the stump, he is in control of himself. Cletus is nowhere to be seen, and it is a good thing, for Diana's note falls out of his pants leg and onto the dirt. He quickly picks the rectangle of paper up and sticks it into the band of the old hat Justice gave him to protect his face from the sun. He wills himself to finish the day and get back to the quarter before he opens the letter. He goes to the barn loft where he savors every word he has at last received from Diana.

Back at the white house on the hill, Daisy has taken the first opportunity she has to tell Miss Mattie what has happened. She apparently does a convincing job of relating the horror of Jude's tale, for the young missus goes directly to her grandmother and aunts and tells them the story. Daisy has no idea in what danger she has put her brother and uncle.

Chapter 32

Dovie's Choice

Savannah, Georgia—1848

Talking to Cressa is not as comforting as asking the advice of her sister or mother, but her words calm Dovie some. The two sit and talk about every possibility they can come up with.

"Mabe da massah wanse you ta marry lack him do wen he tawk wid Lew back fo wese wed."

"Dat da case, wy doan him jus say, 'Dovie, time you hab a husband?'"

"Mabe he hab somethin ta do an wanse mo time ta scuss it."

"I doan thinks so. Him nevah wanse me ta marry b'fo. Him doan wanse no mo slaves, sose whut da use ub habbin me marry?"

"Mabe him hyur bout Cyrus, an him goan make you two marry or stop steppin ou."

Dovie wants to accept what Cressa is saying, but she cannot. If the master knows about Cyrus, he is going to be angry because he will have found out she has been sneaking out.

"If him know I seein Cy, he eithah goan whup me or sells me. Dat whut him says he do he ketch me misbehavin one mo time."

Cressa's eyes betray her fear.

"Sholly he ain goan sell you, not wid Minda an Lew goan."

"Mabe dat wy they's goan." Dovie cannot stop the tears from coming.

"Doan go borryin no trouble, Dovie. They's lot uh reason da massah wannah tawk ta you."

"Nevah hab b'fo."

"It mo lack him fine ow bout Cyrus, an him goan whup you. Mo lack dat dan sellin you."

"Dat ain much bettah!"

"Dat be a lot mo bettah. If him takes da strop ta you, him woan do much cause him ain nevah whupt nobidy in hes life. An you can stan a lick or two. Ain lack it kills you or nothin."

"Dat easy fo you ta say!" Dovie cries. "It ain yo back goan be raw."

"You needs ta settle down, now. Wese jus pokin roun in da dawk."

"You thinks I should run?" Dovie asks.

"Hebben no! You thinks youse got trouble now, you jus tries runnin in broad daylight. Theys hab da dogs on you fo dawk. You membah whut happen ta Jessie's Moses?"

Cressa's warning scares Dovie more. She decides to plan the best she can and see what happens. Cressa promises to be close to the laundry in case she needs help, though neither can imagine what she can do if either of Dovie's worst fears is realized.

Dovie goes to the cabin she shares with her mother. She pulls out the flour sack she has hidden under the bed. It is not heavy. It contains some off cast trinkets the missies have given her and the odd feather, a piece of ribbon, a few unusual rocks, and most importantly, a square muslin bag she has sewn herself. She opens it and counts the money she has secreted away from selling food stuff she has stolen from the kitchen. Though she cannot read like her sister, she can count. She has no idea how far her life savings of $2.85 will go. Regardless, it gives her some comfort. There is plenty of room for the Sunday dress Jessie made on her last visit along with her second work dress, both of which she yanks from a nail on the wall along with her extra kerchiefs. She takes her extra sheath from its place in the bucket in the corner, goes upstairs and takes one of Cressa's, and puts both under her dress in case she is beaten. She has heard of masters ripping the dress from their slaves' backs before whipping them, but she cannot imagine the controlled Master Barret doing any such thing. Deciding she has done all she can do there, she rushes back to the kitchen.

"You goan plum ouddah yo mine!" Cressa cries when Dovie asks for food. "Youse awready in trouble an youse goan risk stealin from da massah agin? An sho ta God you ain goan run!"

"I ain goin nowhar less da massah tell me he goan sell me. Den I hab ta run."

"An whut bout Ben?"

"Doan you go acksin me bout Ben!" Dovie yells, tears flowing full force now. "Theys ain no way I kin take my boy wid me I go. It bad nough da dogs tears me pawt; I sho ain lettin dem hab my chile."

Contrite, Cressa gathers some items, no longer caring if they will be missed. Dovie takes the items and a jug of water back to her room. She examines what she has gathered, then drops to her knees and prays more fervently than she has in her life. She wastes no time chastising herself, for, in her mind, she has done no one any real wrong.

Dovie is as ready as she can be, considering she doesn't know what the master wants to see her about. She hears him before she sees him. She sits on one of the stools beside the massive wooden tub and waits for him to come to her. He does not come directly into the room. Instead, he crosses the hallway where Cressa is waiting.

"Cressa, I want you to go find the children," he says.

"Ain theys whar theys awways be?"

Cressa must be terrified for her if she is willing to question the master.

"I don't know where they are. Would I be telling you to find them if I did? And don't worry about dinner or supper. I will be leaving."

"Does I hab ta go righ now? Can I put dis stuff way furse?"

Later, Dovie will remember the bravery of her sister-in-law as she tried her best to stay with her. Now, she is frozen in fear. Without a doubt something bad is about to happen. She wonders if she can sneak out past them. She moves quietly to the door. There she is startled by a man she has never seen before. He meets her eyes. It is not what she sees in his that terrifies her. It is what she doesn't see. The total lack of emotion in the green eyes send chills to her bones. She shudders.

"You mus be Dovie," he drawls.

He is a huge, muscular man, and though he is white, he is not a gentleman. His clothes are of a type unfamiliar to her. Soon she will learn they are what white overseers wear in the field.

Cressa meets her eyes as she leaves the kitchen. She tries once more.

"Massah, you ain goan do somethin bad ta Dovie, is you? Please think on da othahs. Youse goan hurt Mammy somethin awful, and dare Lew an Minda. Her theys own blood sistah. Please…"

"Cressa, leave now," Frederick says, his voice low and controlled, but there is no doubting the anger in his eyes.

Cressa gives Dovie one more desperate look before she runs from the hallway. She has not gone far because they can still hear her wailing. The sound is of little comfort when both men face her. She retreats into the laundry. For one of the few times in her life, she can think of nothing to say.

"Dovie, this man's name is Gus. He is going to take you to your new home. Before you go, I have a choice for you."

Thank God! Dovie thinks. *Ise goin ta git anothah chance. This all be ta skeer me, an him sho do dat.*

"Massah, no mattah whut it be, I do it. Enthin you wanse, I do it. Jus doan sen me way from mys fambly."

"I won't tolerate a scene." Frederick speaks to her but his gaze rests somewhere past her. "The decision has already been made, but I am not totally heartless. I know you must care for your son, though you've shown no evidence of it. Had you truly cared about him, you would have behaved yourself and prevented this. Now, your new owner says he will take you alone or you and the boy. Which is it to be?"

"Ben?" Dovie whispers. Her legs give way. The movement draws his gaze to her. She finds herself on the stool she had occupied earlier.

"Unless you have another child I know nothing about. That is possible, I admit."

"Youse sendin Ben wid me?"

"If you want. If not, he can stay here with Mammy and the others."

Dovie wants to cry and throw herself on the master's mercy, but the set of his jaw and the cold stare tell her begging will not help. She must think. Ben's well-being depends on it.

"Whar youse sendin me?" she manages. "Youse sellin me ta somebidy in town?"

"Hardly. You need to be far from those you have tried to corrupt. Your influence cannot be tolerated."

"I stays in a town or ou in da country?"

Now she has little to lose, she becomes braver.

"You are going to a plantation in another state." Frederick glances toward the door through which they can no longer hear Cressa. "I have told you all you need to know."

"I be a house gul lack Ise hyur?" she dares.

"Doubtful. He has all those he needs. Besides, I've told him your history, and he won't want you influencing his own house staff. Most likely you'll be in the field."

"Lawd hab mercy," Dovie mutters quietly. Her face goes rigid, and her lips tighten. "Mama an Lew ain nevah goan foget whut youse doin hyur. An Minda kill you in yo sleep!"

This last claim gains both men's attention. Frederick glances nervously at the man named Gus. "She has never been violent. You can tell Jones she is mouthy, but she is not dangerous."

He turns to Dovie, real anger on his face. "What's your answer? Do you want the boy with you or not?"

Dovie makes the most unselfish decision she's ever made. "Da boy be bettah off hyur wid da fambly."

"Take her out the front," Frederick Barret says, and those are the last words Dovie will hear from the man she has served for over twenty years. She asks if she can get a few things from her cabin. Gus answers her.

"You woan need much of nuthin whar you goin. An whut you need, they give you."

The biting grasp of Gus's hand hauls her down the passageway, through the small gate, and out onto Madison Avenue. There, he hefts her roughly up into a cart where two black men sit on the floor. Dovie catches a toe in her dress and sprawls head first into one of their feet. Her face burns from the contact, but she is glad for it. The discomfort distracts her mind from the agony that, if acknowledged, may rip her chest apart. She crawls to her knees and faces backward as the cart begins to move. Her eyes cling to the mansion for as long as it is in sight, but there is no sign of the boy she longs to see one last time.

Mammy's small crow is the only one to see her off. She flaps frantically around the top of the cart as if the driver is about to run over her nest. Her strident cries make her frantic displeasure clear to anyone who will listen. Dovie is the only one who witnesses the sendoff, and she is appreciative. A farewell from a crow beats none at all.

Chapter 33

Letters to Write

Savannah, Georgia—1848

Frederick stays away from Savannah for three days. Though he is not one to second guess himself, he is worried. He wonders now if, in trying to eliminate problems in his household, he may have created more. Rob doesn't help matters when he finds him waiting at the mansion.

"Where is Dovie?" he asks. "And what is wrong with Cressa? When I asked her where Dovie was, she stawted cryin and told me I would have ta ask you."

They are in the parlor, and Frederick pours them both a shot of whiskey though the hour is closer to noon than to one, and Rob will have to return to the bank.

"I sold her," he states bluntly. Rob chokes on the drink he has just taken.

"I had warned her several times, and what kind of message would I be sending if I didn't follow through on my word? She has stolen; she has lied; and she has been traipsing all over Savannah when she is supposed to be in her cabin at night. You know the others had to have known about her behavior and were covering for her. Her consequences will be a lesson for them all."

"But Grandmothah Middleton...and Maxie..."

Frederick realizes he has made a mistake. If Rob who is the least emotional of them is questioning the decision, he will have some explaining to do to Mattie, Fredie, and his mother-in-law. He refuses to think about how Maxie will react.

He pours himself another drink.

"Doing what is best for the family is not always easy. I fear we have let the girls get entirely too attached. It is best I have done this. You will be running your own homes someday, Providence willing, and you and they need to remember to keep an emotional distance from the help. If I could figure out an economical way to do it, I wouldn't have a slave to my name."

Rob is overwhelmed with sentiment and questions. Dovie has always been a part of his life. The girls are not the only ones who have formed attachments. Dovie was his childhood nurse in much the same way Mammy was. One of the two was always close by when he and his siblings were on the Green or at Hickory Grove. Dovie had been funny and full of life—almost a playmate. She has bathed him, dressed him, sung to him, listened to his prayers, tucked him in. He has more memories of Dovie than he does either of his mothers. He opens his mouth to express his concern, but the downing of the second shot of whiskey by the man Rob has seen drink little convinces him his father is on the defensive and now is not the time.

"Fathah, I admit I am a little shocked, but now you relate your reasonin, I know you must have done what you always do. You must have given much consideration ta the problem she presented, and you have safegawded us all against folly." Rob takes a generous gulp from his own tumbler. "Now, let's talk about somethin more pleasant. I have been waitin faw you ta git home ta give you the news. Our hopes ah not in vain! Mr. Peavy has given us his blessin along with a plantation. Howevah, Eleanor was incorrect in her undahstandin he was giftin us their ancestral home in Macon. We have now been informed Mrs. Peavy has no interest in residin in Texas. Instead of givin us the Macon propahty, he is givin us the largah of his two plantations in Texas—the one at Caney Creek—along with 123 slaves ta run it!"

Thrilled to have something else to talk about besides Dovie, Frederick clasps the hand of his oldest son and thumps him roughly on the back.

"Finally! A Barret bringing money into our coffers besides me. I wish a smaller portion of your future worth were tied up in slaves, but I guess they are a necessary evil if one is to run a plantation. Have you set the date for this fortuitous occasion? When will you be expected to take over the affairs in Texas?"

"Soon, it appears. Of course, Mr. Peavy does not want ta relinquish the reigns until we ah indeed married, but he is eagah ta be shed of the responsibility. He is not a young man, aftah all."

"I was thinking he was about my age," Frederick frowns.

"But his health is not nearly as hale as your own," Rob says, proud he thinks quickly enough to cover his blunder. "Unless some obstacle arises we cannot fosee, we plan ta marry aftah the fevah season passes and evahbody is back in Macon. Somewhere between the first and middle of Novembah, we are thinkin."

"Excellent!" Frederick says, and Rob thinks he will have no better time than the present to bring up the topic he has been dwelling on all the way from Georgia.

"I thought, with your approval, I would go ahead and submit my resignation at the bank. I want ta make sure they have plenty of time ta replace me. I would hate faw them ta be indisposed by a sudden depahture on my pawt."

"You are wise, Son," Frederick begins, and Rob immediately rejoices because there is nothing he will love more than to be shed of the tedious job, the bane of his existence, but his spirits plummet with his father's next words.

"Tell them you will be available until the last week in October. Give yourself a week to manage the last-minute details."

"But I thought I might use the summah ta git affairs in awdah here, spend some time in Texas learnin…"

"Goodness no, Rob. With the expense of our side of a wedding close on the heels of Mattie's, you'll need your income. You will not want to arrive on your father-in-law's doorstep with your hat in your hand, so to speak. You will want to go well-attired, have your own horse since the one you use now will remain here. You get what I mean. Your weekends can be spent in Georgia as Texas may be too far to travel, but your weekdays need to find you employed."

With those words, Frederick excuses his son to get back to the job he hates while he attends to letters he must write. He has decided to let Mrs. Middleton break the news to the girls and Jessie to Minda. If they are told while away, they will have time to come to terms with Dovie's absence before returning to Savannah. He even convinces himself the cowardly act of passing the dreaded chore on to someone else is for their best interest. He must craft a well-written letter to the aging Mrs. Middleton, for she had not been pleased when she thought he had sold Minda. She had been placated when he had claimed to buy her back. There was a huge fuss knowing Minda had gone no farther than another home in Savannah and was still capable of staying in touch with her mother and sisters. He can imagine what she will have to say when she learns none of them will ever see Dovie again. He decides to get the easier missive to Jessie out of the way first before putting real thought into the harder of the two.

Deckie,

I hope this letter finds you healthy and not too inconvenienced with the additions to your household. Please use the enclosed remittance to allay the cost of two additional mouths to feed. Too, I would appreciate the kindness if you would purchase something to Minda's liking that might lift her spirits after you disclose the unfortunate news with which I must further burden you. Because of her continued misbehavior and the threat she poses to our otherwise tranquil home life, I have been forced to sell Dovie to a plantation far from here. Though I have been loath to take this action and have procrastinated in my duty in hopes she would repent of her waywardness, that has not been the case. I am hopeful the time away will soften the blow for all concerned.

He can think of little else to say on the subject. He moves on to other topics he thinks she may find interesting. Knowing she is well-acquainted with Bette, he tells her, according to all accounts, Mrs. Stiles is doing well. She is traveling with her daughter but is expected back before next season. He ends the letter nonchalantly adding he is having some repairs and updates done to the house Minda and her boys live in, and she can also pass that information on to them. He is about to seal the envelope when he remembers he has said nothing of Dovie's son. In frustration, he rewrites the letter adding the sentence *Though the boy Ben is surely missing his mother, in the long run, he will be better off away from her poor example. He will soon be in the presence of Mammy and Minda, both of them being as much a mother to the poor boy as ever was the one who bore him.*

It would have been much simpler to pen the last at the end of the letter, but he feared the postscript would have been interpreted as the afterthought it was.

Frederick turns next to Mrs. Middleton. He inquires after his daughters and the health of Mattie about whom he is concerned because she is with child. Though he is excited about becoming a grandfather, he will be relieved when his daughter's time comes and she has survived what many women do not. All the Middleton women have done well, none of them lost in childbirth, and the knowledge of their good fortune consoles him.

He inquires as to whether Lew and Jude have been of help and conveys his deepest desires they be so. He asks after Anne and Sophia, both of whom are summering there, as well. Finally, when he can think of nothing else, he relates the news sure to surprise her and upset at least Mattie and Maxie, if not Ella.

My dearest mother of the heart, being the only one of which I have memory, I have news to impart I fear will be met with your censure. Please judge me not by this one act but by all those by which I have proven myself to be observant of your every wish in regard to our family. Having nothing but the gravest respect for your judgment, and coveting your approval above all others, I hope you know I would not have taken the action I have had I thought there were any other way to protect my family and my servants from one who was originally your own. I have sold Dovie whom you gave to us as part of our beloved Luella's inheritance, though I have sold one other household slave ever, and upon realizing my error, bought her back as soon as feasible. If you recall, I sold Minda to appease her mistress when she was suffering from misconceptions due to childbirth. I remind you of this so you can be consoled in the assurance I take this grave step as a last resort. Dovie was in grave danger of calling attention to herself among the citizenry here, and I feared we would soon receive a visit from the sheriff in the middle of the night due to her roamings. Unlike you with the alternatives a plantation provides, Shady Corner provides no room for dealing with a miscreant and less privacy when having to take corrective measures. I could not pass my problem on to you by sending her back to Hickory Grove, nor do I have the temperament for taking a whip to a servant no matter how incorrigible. I was left with that option or with doing what I have done. I long to remain solidly in your affections in spite of taking an action I know you find reprehensible.

From there, he implores her to break the news to his daughters as gently as only one of her devotion and judgment can. He would be grateful, he adds, if she could pass the news on to Lew should the opportunity arise. He offers the same explanation—they will benefit by the opportunity to come to terms with the change before they return to what he is convinced will be a more harmonious home.

Pleased to have both tasks behind him, he thinks momentarily of paying Minda a visit before he remembers she is not there, and if she were, he would be met with a chilly if not hostile reception. He is angry thoughts of her have ruined his optimistic mood, the one he has earned by completing a task he has dreaded. He reminds himself he will not have to contend with any of these problems for months yet, and he has the fortuitous news of Rob's betrothal to share. He is shocked to remember he failed to include mention of the engagement in either letter. The exclusion is just as well, he decides. He will send one tomorrow to tell his daughters of another wedding which members of the fairer sex seem to enjoy above all other celebrations. Now that he has remembered the betrothal, he determines to share it with Brigitte Maxwell who will be thrilled for his family, and, now he thinks of it, will be the most understanding of his decision to sell Dovie. She has always had the sound judgment not to become overly attached to one's servants. He decides this attribute is another indication of her superior breeding, one probably inherited from their common French lineage. He glances at the clock on the wall and thinks he should hurry before the day is too far gone and her too deep in her indulgence.

Chapter 34

Dalliance

Baltimore, Maryland—1848

Never has Minda enjoyed life as she has at Jessie's. In retrospect, she decides she has never comprehended the concept of contentment. She thinks this must be what life is like for white people, for she has all the freedom she can imagine. She and Ish get up when they want—which is early for she finds sleeping late impossible when one has risen at dawn her entire life. They do what they themselves decide to do, for Miss Jessie asks nothing of them. Because she does not, both guests are quick to do all they can think of to help their hostesses. Shy to cook for someone who is a legend for her abilities in the kitchen, Minda started by working alongside her mentor, the two of them cooking breakfast. From there, she became bold enough to prepare the dinner meal to spare Jessie who works hard in her shop. Now, she does all the cooking and basks in the praise lavished on her by both Jessie and Diana. After the first week, she asked Jessie for receipts she deemed simple enough for her to learn. At first, Jessie provided verbal directions, but she has progressed to writing them down for Minda. Minda reads through the instructions and asks for help with any words or details she doesn't understand. Before Ish began working with the carpenter, he sat and read the directions to her as she worked. In this way, both mother and son have been improving their reading without actually having lessons. Their evenings are often spent listening to Diana read to them. Ish sits close by her side, his eyes on the page so he can learn new words, the ever-present Cotton perched on his shoulder. At times, Diana passes the book to him and lets him read aloud. Minda proudly listens to him sound out words she does not yet know and smiles at the way he mimics Diana's cadence and manner.

They have all laughed about how jealous Jude would be if he could see what his little brother is doing.

Since becoming an apprentice to Quentin Rylee, Ish rises each morning, cleans up any mess Cotton may have created in the night, eats breakfast with his mother, Miss Jessie, and Diana, takes the sack of food Minda prepares for him, and heads to work. To his dismay, Minda still insists on walking with him though the wood shop is a short distance of four streets over.

"Mama, you acks like I six stead uh leven. You treatin me like a chile an I knows why!"

Ish scowls and Cotton cries out.

"You agree with whatevah dat boy say, you useless crow," Minda tries to lighten the mood. Ish is rarely out of sorts.

"It not cause uh yo foot," Minda continues. Ish casts her a skeptical look. "I like walkin bout like this. You goan take that pleasure way from yo Mama? How offen we git ta jus walk roun like we spose ta? Fo you knows it, we have ta go back home an this be like a dream."

"Mr. Quent goan think I ain able ta take care uh mysef. How he goan trust me with enthin mo than sweepin up an fetchin if I have ta have my Mama holdin my hand evahwhar I goes?"

She cuffs his head and smiles at him. "I think on it, Son."

What she won't tell Ish is she is coming along to see Quentin Rylee. In the beginning she was concerned about Ish walking around a strange city by himself, but he has proven himself quite adept. After meeting the man who is to teach Ish woodworking skills, she finds herself searching for ways to be around him, and, so far, all she has come up with is to drop Ish off and pick him up. Her time with Quentin will have to come to an end soon, and to visit him, she has endured Ish's displeasure rather than give up the opportunity. Rylee is the closest thing to a male friend she has ever had.

When they get to the shop with the sign denoting *Rylee's Woodworking and Repair*, the double doors are open and the object of Minda's first infatuation is already hard at work. He brightens as the two approach. Minda hopes his smile is in response to the sight of her, but he addresses Ish.

"Glad ta see you, Boy!" he says. "Grab da end uh dis saw, an less see we cain cut it inta boads fo da livry stable. Doan have ta be puhfeck, but theys need ta be straight. You thinks youse up ta da job."

Ish practically throws his lunch onto a keg of nails in the corner. He offers his bird an extended finger. "Git on offah me, Cotton. I gots work ta do,"

Cotton offers no resistance when Ish puts him gently on the floor. He hops a few steps on his single leg then takes flight. He perches on the raw wood beam supporting the length of the room. From there he peers down at Ish, cocking his head first one way, then the other, as if he is supervising what is going on below. Minda wonders who looks out for whom in their relationship.

Ish grabs the handle of the crosscut saw, but when they lift the tool into position, the table the log is sitting on places the handle shoulder high on the boy. Minda realizes there is no way he will be able to man the end of the saw while reaching upward. She is relieved when Quentin comes to his rescue.

"Dat gonna be a problem, ain it pawdna," Quentin says. He leaves for a minute and comes back rolling a tree section cut round. Without comment, he walks away again and returns with another of about the same size. He stacks the second on top of the first and gestures to the platform he has made.

"Dare you goes, Ish. Dat solve da problem."

Ish smiles gratefully and awkwardly climbs atop the stacked wood. Minda holds her breath, but Ish throws her a triumphant smirk, one that also says, *Doan you say a word!*

She ignores him and turns her attention to Quentin.

"You object ta me watchin. I cain stay long, bu I like ta see you an my boy turn that tree inta somethin useful."

Quentin smiles at her. "Gul, you can stays all day long you take a mine ta. Sight like you brighten dis place up somethin grand."

Minda has become used to his teasing. She goes to where Ish threw his lunch and lights on the top of the keg. She confronts a moment of guilt for she should be back at Miss Jessie's learning to put the dress together she helped cut out. She promises herself she won't stay long and relaxes to enjoy the show.

She tries to keep her eyes on her son, and she does long enough to judge the task is hard for him. The saw is long and bows easily, and the handle jerks completely out of his hand as Quentin pushes the saw toward him.

"Dat's whut it goan do," he encourages. "It gonna buck you fights it. Jus let da saw do da work. You gots ta pull hawd, bu you gots ta pull even, too. Da same go fo da pushin. Pull level; push level."

Soon the blade is making progress, but Minda fears Ish will be exhausted before he finishes one board. She will suffer Ish's wrath if she intervenes, so she enjoys the show Quentin's bare upper arms and back are making as he handles the saw. He is of an average size, but his muscles bulge. She assumes he has done a lot of sawing in his day, for she has never seen a man with upper arms the size of his. His flat stomach muscles flex with effort, and she wishes she could see the effects of the motion on his back from where she is sitting.

Jessie has told her Quentin bought his freedom from a man named Rylee for whom he had created doors, furniture, wagon and cart beds, anything that could be made from wood. His master had allowed him to sell work he did in the evenings and on Sunday, and when he had a tidy sum saved, he had gone to him and asked to buy his freedom. They had worked out an arrangement in which Quentin paid him what he had saved but also supplied special projects for him for the cost of the material. Too, he had trained another young man before leaving, one who could do jobs that didn't take the skill Quentin had but could handle most of the needs of the plantation.

Ish is breathing hard and drenched in sweat when Quentin calls for a break. The boy immediately heads for the water bucket, and Cotton swoops down to join him. Ish gulps from the gourd before pouring water into his palm. His bird balances on the heel of his hand while drinking daintily from the pool Ish has created. The boy creates a double basin by cupping both hands and laughs when Cotton sticks his whole head in the water, then shakes it, sending droplets flying.

"Dat feel good, Cotton? You mus be hot as I be!"

Minda eyes are on her son and the bird, so she is startled when Quentin speaks close beside her.

"You likes da show?" he asks.

"Yes! That bird is somethin else. Cotton ack like he a human haf the time."

"I ain talkin bout dem. I means you likes da show I puttin on fo you?"

Minda laughs. By now she is used to his shameless flirting.

"You sho be full uh yosef. You think you somthin I wannah see?"

"I sho hope so. I woe mysef ou fo nuthin you ain likin it."

Minda thinks of Dovie who would know how to respond to this banter. She has had a lot of experience with the opposite sex whereas the last real flirting Minda did was as a teenager in Virginia. There had been a couple of boys she might have been interested in, but she was in the house and they were in the field. Their different roles had allowed little chance for interaction. Now she tries to think about what her sister would say if she were the one joking with Quentin.

"I ain sayin I likes it, an I ain sayin I doan. All I know is I need ta git on back ta Mizz Jessie, an you needs ta git ta sawin, or that livry ain nevah goan git new boads."

The smile leaves Quentin's face making Minda think he must find her flirting skills lacking.

"I likes ta play roun an tawk silly, but, in truff, Ise a serious man. I gittin ta da age I be wantin mo dan a dalliance. An you doan seem like da dallying kine. I jus wanse you ta know dat."

Minda is speechless. She stares him square in the eye and sees something she has never seen before—an interest in her—not the kind she ignites in Frederick's eyes. She gives him a soft, sad smile.

"Why you even talkin that mess? You hawdly know me."

"I doan hab da chance ta meet many gals like you, an now I do, I ain wantin ta let you git way."

Minda's face becomes as sincere as his. "Git away?" She shakes her head in disbelief. "My massah the one ain goan let me git away. When he send fo me ta come, I be goin home. Youse free, but I am a slave now, an I be a slave fo'evah."

"Bu I gots some money. If we thinks wese good tagathah, mabe I buy you an…"

"Buy me? Mabe you need ta take a closah look at Ish. An I have two mo jus as light as he be, and da man cause dat ain nevah goan let me go til da day they put my cold bidy in da groun."

With those words, Minda turns to wave to Ish, but he is stretched out on the floor resting while he can. Cotton caws a farewell. She brushes by Quentin who makes no move to stop her. She fights tears on the way home and scolds herself for her silliness. She is also angry at herself for letting a couple of weeks away from Savannah lull her into imagining she can have a personal life that does not involve the master. This temporary freedom emphasizes how trapped she will be for the rest of her life. By the time she arrives at Jessie's, she has worked up a pout. Upon seeing Jessie's face when she enters, she decides she is not the only one having a bad day. *Misery loves company*, she thinks, but she has no idea how much worse she will soon feel.

Minda becomes suspicious something is not right when Jessie lowers the garment she is working on and says, "There you are, Minda. Let's go to the back and have a cup of tea. Diana can manage things in here for a bit."

Minda's first thought is she has taken too long to get back from Quentin's, but that cannot be true since the last thing Jessie had said to her was, "Take your time. No need to hurry back."

She turns to Diana, but Diana won't meet her eyes. Her face is splotchy, and Minda can tell she has been crying. Fear tightens her chest—it is hard to catch her breath.

"It Jude? Somethin happen ta Jude?" she manages.

"No!" Jessie and Diana say at once. "But I have had a letter from Frederick," Jessie adds, "and we should discuss the contents in the back."

At last Diana looks at her, revealing tears, before she quickly looks away. Unable to think of what might be wrong since most of her family is away, she simply stands there, waiting for the hammer to fall. Jessie takes her gently by the arm and leads her to the back where she has water boiling. She gestures for Minda to sit, and she makes them both a cup of tea. Minda knows the news is bad when Jessie pours a small amount of brown liquid into the cup meant for her.

"Jus tell me an git it ovah with!" she cries.

Jessie sighs, plops down across the table from her, and says, "Dovie has been sold."

Minda's mind goes blank. Though they have lived with the threat for years, none of them have believed the master would sell her. Minda had secretly thought Frederick would not do such a thing if for no other reason than to spare her and her mother the pain.

"Where he send her?" she manages at last. "An what bout Ben? Do he sell them tagathah?"

"No, Ben is still with him. Frederick thinks the rest of you can mother him." She doesn't relay the remainder of the message—Frederick thinks they already mother him as much as Dovie had.

"Bu why? Why now? She do somethin aftah we leave?"

"Here, let me read you what he wrote," Jessie says. She picks up the letter and reads the part starting with the news pertaining to Dovie all the way to the end.

"He think I gonna care bout a house when he jus send my sistah off somewhere I nevah see her agin?"

Jessie walks around the table and sits by Minda on the bench. She places an arm around her narrow shoulder and is jolted by the pain coursing through her body.

"Here, drink this tea. I added a little whiskey to help with the shock."

Minda automatically picks the cup up and drinks. When she sets it down, Jessie adds a little more of the whiskey she has left sitting on the end of the table. Minda says nothing, simply picks up the cup and downs it. She shudders when the strong liquid hits her throat.

"He ain goan tell us where he send her, is he?"

"Doesn't sound like it."

"How kin he sell er? He know how bad Mama gonna grieve. An Ben. He down there with none uh us bu Cressa." She stops talking a moment. Her lips tighten and her nostrils flare.

"The massah plan this. Now we knows why he send us all away. An me thinkin he tryin ta do somethin good fo my boys an me."

Tears slide down Minda's face. She makes no effort to wipe them away.

"You think Mama know by now? An Lew?"

"I don't know for sure, but they probably do. He wrote he hopes you will have time to accept his decision before you come home. I am sure he has placed the same burden on Mrs. Middleton or Mattie he has on me."

"That jus show the cold heart the man have he think time goan make any uh us git ovah what he do. I will nevah foget, an I do my bess ta make him remembah evah time he lays eyes on me." Minda rises from the table. "It be alright I go up fo a bit? I ain feelin so good."

"Of course you are not. I hope I haven't given you too much whiskey."

"No. It makin me feel kindah numb. It help."

As Minda heads for the door, Jessie drapes an arm across her shoulder.

"I regret I had to be the one to tell you this. If I could think of anything I could do to get Dovie back, I would do it. He probably knows I would since he is being secretive about where she is."

Minda lies on her bed and hopes sleep will come. Jessie brings her a plate of food and places it on the wash stand near the bed, but Minda has no appetite. The day is almost done when Ish scuffs his way up the stairs. Jessie must have told him the news because he says nothing. Even Cotton is silent. Ish crawls on the bed beside her. She opens her arms to him and lets his tears wet the front of the dress she still wears. Minda is grateful Jessie has done what she had no strength to do. She lets him cry, and soon he is asleep. She doesn't know if he has eaten, but if he has not, there is still food in their room.

Minda waits until she can see full darkness through the window. She lies still until Jessie and Diana come upstairs. She gives them time to prepare for bed. She waits longer in hopes they will be asleep. She rises, splashes water on her face, cleans her teeth, pulls her hair into a tight bun, covers it with a fresh kerchief, and leaves the room. She is glad to see no light. She quietly gropes her way along the wall and down the stairs. There is still enough light from the fire in the kitchen for her to find the front door key in its hiding place in a sugar bowl on a shelf above the water bucket. She has no trouble seeing her way through the shop for the plate glass display windows let in plenty of moonlight. She walks the familiar route she walked what seems like ages ago but is actually a few hours. Once at her destination, she is on unfamiliar ground, for she has never climbed the stairs above the business as she does tonight. Once there, she knocks lightly. She begins to lose nerve, so she knocks louder. Finally, the door jerks open, and she is face to face with Quentin. His mouth falls open, and he manages, "Whut..." before she simply walks by him into the dark room. He scrambles for a candle, but she takes his hand in hers.

"We woan be in need uh light," she says, and though she can't see his face well in the dimness, he catches on quickly. He leads her farther into the room where she makes out a curtain drawn back to reveal a bed along the back wall. She sits on the side of it and removes her shoes. He is barefooted wearing the pants he has pulled on a few minutes before. She starts to unbutton her dress. He takes her hands and says, "Let me hep you wid dat."

She registers the fresh scent of him. Underneath the soap she detects the odor she identifies as him. Arms around each other, they fall backward, and Minda gives herself to a man for the first time in her life.

Chapter 35
Cletus

Hickory Grove, Virginia—1848

Three days have passed since Lew and Jude saw the young woman beaten in the tobacco field. Last night they learned she had died in spite of the attention she received from her mother, Mrs. Middleton herself, and even a doctor the mistress had sent for when they determined how far gone she was. The girl's name was Pearl. When Jude heard it, he thought of Miss Bette's Pearl. Now her death feels personal, the unlucky girl like someone he actually knows rather than a worn-out stranger in a tobacco row.

Lew and he are up and preparing for another day, this time in the cotton field located even farther from the quarters. Today, Jude will get his first experience with cotton. Though the bowls themselves are too unformed to pick, they will spend hours hoeing the rows. Lew has experience, but Mammy jealously guards her vegetable gardens. She lets the younger children weed, but never hoe. Neither Lew nor Jude is eager to join the field workers, so Jude is glad when he and Lew are summoned to the big house. He thinks they will probably be given another task by the mistress like the ones they did when they first arrived. He would much rather paint or do repairs than be stuck in the field under a blazing sun and the eye of Cletus. Jude's pulse races every time he sees the man even though he has been more subdued since the beating took place. Jude wonders if he will be more controlled now he has killed Pearl.

The house girl who comes for them leaves them on the back porch. Jude and Lew pass time guessing what their job will be. They are shocked when Mrs. Middleton herself walks out onto the porch. This is the first time Jude has seen the woman up close. He caught sight of her from a distance when she came to the quarters to check on Pearl, but there has been no reason for him to meet her. Lew seems equally as surprised by her appearance.

"Hello, Lewis," she says. "It has been a long time since I've seen you, but I have kept up with you through Frederick. I undahstand you have a family now."

"Dat be da truff, Missus. I hab a wife an two chilren thanks ta da massah."

"You are blessed. This must be Minda's son, Daisy's brothah?"

There is a frown on the lady's face as she examines Jude. He assumes she is wondering how Minda has ended up with not just one light-skinned child, but two. The compressing of her lips indicates she has a good idea. Though the woman walks with a cane, there does not appear to be anything frail about her mind.

"Come with me. I need ta talk with you about what happened ta Sal's Pearl. Mattie tells me you witnessed the incident."

Both men follow the woman to the side porch where there are several rockers. She lowers her bulk into one of the chairs but gives no indication either of them should do likewise. They stand side by side in front of her, arms dangling awkwardly like two children about to be scolded by their mother.

"Now, tell me what you saw. Jude, Daisy told Mattie you were quite distressed. Let's stawt with you."

At least we know how she came by her information, Jude thinks. Surprisingly, he is not afraid. In fact, he relishes the idea of telling on Cletus. Obviously, the lady does not approve of what happened or she would not have sent for them. He is calm as he begins.

"I see the girl lyin in the row bout the time I see Cletus comin our way. At first I think she a pile of sacks, bu then I see it a girl bout my age." he says.

"You speak well faw a dawkie," Mrs. Middleton interrupts. "Why is that, Jude?"

Lew moves beside him. Jude says the first thing that comes to mind.

"I be tole Ise a quick study. I pays tension ta whut I hyurs in da big house, an I wid da massah all da time, me bein his boy, an aw." Jude falls back into what is expected. "Dat cain hep but rub off on a fellah."

Mrs. Middleton eyes him suspiciously. "It is best you remembah your place. No good can come from tryin ta rise above your God-given station in life, but there's nothin wrong with you bein a smawt one faw your kind. Make sure you use God's gifts faw the benefit of the family you suhve. Now continue with what you were sayin."

Jude carefully picks his way through his tale, and when he finishes, Mrs. Middleton turns to Lew and asks him if everything Jude has said is true. When he confirms the story, she says, "Very well. My son George will be arrivin today, and if he needs anything furthah, I will send faw you."

The lady stands, and they know they are dismissed. They leave the porch, and as they walk back toward the quarters, Jude glances around to see her enter the house.

"What you think that all about?"

"I thinks Cletus in a worl uh trouble, an I hopes we long goan da time him fine ou how da missus know."

"You think they do somethin bout it?" Jude asks.

"I sho do. Ise tellin you theys nevah whup theys people. Da missus doan bleive in dat. She eben make sho da preacher come by jus ta larn da hep bout Jesus. Her work her fokes hawd, bu her ain mean as some. Theys git nuff ta eat hyur an 'lowed ta grow theys own gawden. Theys kin own a pig or mo if they makes theys own money. Cletus wen an git bove hissef cause she ain bout da place nuff aftah Mizz Abby die; dat whut theys be sayin."

"What you think he do he find out we the ones who tawk ta the missus?"

"Him a mean un. Ise hopin wese back in Svanna wen him figgah dat ou. You stays ouddah da way til we lebe. An annuthah thing. You gottah stop dat fancy tawkin. Da wites ain goan like it, an da cullad foke ain goan like it. Bof ub dem think youse gittin bove yosef. Wites be sayin youse thinkin youse good as theys be, an da dawkies be sayin you think youse beddah dan dem. Sose ain no good comin uh dat book larnin you be doin, an I tole dat mothah uh yose da same Ise tellin you."

Jude frowns at his uncle. "I guess you content ta jus fetch an do fo the massah the rest uh yo life? Yes, Massah, dis, and Yes, Massah, dat!"

"You gits ta be ole as I be, den you kin stawt tellin me da way da worl be. Til den, you beddah lissen ta whut I tellin you. Youse goan fine yosef on da loop side uh a rope you goes fogittin yo place. Dat Mizz Bette a kine woman, bu her ain one uh us an her hab no idee da trouble her larnin be fo us. Her ain da one goan pay wid er life somebidy fine ou whut youse up ta."

Jude shakes his head. Some of what his uncle is saying is true, but he cannot understand why Lew is unwilling to take a risk for a better life, or even for the world his reading has opened to him. He does not intend to be a house slave forever, even if avoiding the fate means dying young. He decides to keep his thoughts to himself. Neither is going to sway the other, and he doesn't feel like receiving another lecture.

They are not called back to the plantation house which means they end up in the dreaded cotton field. Jude and Lew are a row apart and less than a fourth way down and facing a long row of weeds Jude cannot actually imagine getting through. His back already hurts and the blisters on his fingers he acquired in the tobacco patch have broken open. He hates this field work. He stops, stretches his aching spine, and glances around in sympathy at his coworkers. Lew catches him and whispers, "Doan let Cletus ketch you wool gathin!"

Jude sighs and goes back to work longing for the water bucket miles away. Lew's next words make him even angrier. "Mabe dis makes you a lil mo preciatin fo yo place in Svanna."

All eyes turn to the white man riding up on a chestnut mare followed by a black man on a mule, but no one stops working. The white man must be Master George, for he is dressed as only a landowner would be. Cletus obviously knows who he is. He has been sitting astride his own mule all morning, but now he swings down and stands to wait. Jude has not seen this subservient Cletus who acts like there is no one else in the whole world he would rather see than Master George.

"Howdy, Massah. I naw spectin you dis early in da season. We hab a wile til harvess. Ise glad youse hyur, though, sose you kin sees how fine evahthin lookin."

The white man makes no indication he has heard a word the overseer has said.

"Cletus, go clean out your cabin and go ta Gerty's and wait faw me there."

"Bu wy I be cleanin ou…"

"Now," the white man says.

Cletus starts to speak again, but George interrupts.

"Hand me the whip, Cletus. And leave your mount with Jonah. You won't be needin it."

Cletus stares at the man who must be Jonah. He looks back to his master who has his hand extended for the whip, then gazes around him at the workers in the field. Everyone has stopped what they are doing to watch the scene playing out before them. Cletus must consider his options and decide he has little choice.

"Sho, Massah. Ise be waitin up at da quattah."

"Be sure you stay put til I get there."

Cletus hands the whip to the man who is still on horseback and walks his mule to Jonah who has dismounted. They all stand in silence as Cletus walks across the adjoining pasture. No one moves a muscle until George, apparently satisfied Cletus is doing what he has been instructed to do, turns back toward the workers in the field. All bend to continue pulling weeds.

"I need faw y'all ta stop what you ah doin and gathah round."

Jude and Lew move with the others to group in front of him and Jonah, the latter still holding the reins of both mules. Jude checks the faces of the other servants to see how they are reacting. Like Lew's, their faces show interest, but no fear.

"This is Jonah," George states simply. "He is your new ovahseeah. He has been one of mine at my place, and you will find him ta be a fair man. Make sure you do what he says, and you will have nothin ta worry about."

George turns his horse and rides off in the direction of Cletus whom they can still see making his way across the meadow. Before they see him ride even with their former overseer, their present one addresses them in a deep voice.

"I goan put dis mule up. Keep weedin til da bell; den head on home. I be roun da quattah tanigh ta meet you an yo fambly."

Jonah mounts the mule he rode in on, makes a clicking sound with his tongue, and leads what had been Cletus's mule off toward the barn. Jude is stunned by the difference a few minutes can make in the lives of those around him. Jonah doesn't turn back to tell them to get back to work, but slowly they start dispersing, each heading back to where he or she had been. They are no longer quiet. Smiles break out and laughter erupts. Some go as far as to slap their legs and do a little dance in celebration. They are rid of the evil Cletus. Jude smiles at Lew, and Lew slaps him on the back.

"I tells you they's a bettah way!"

Jude is about to point out to his uncle that he has had no part in taking care of the problem when his eyes alight on Sal. She has silently gone back to pulling weeds, her face blank, her shoulders slumped.

"Too bad yo bettah way dint happen fo days go," Jude says.

Lew's eyes follow Jude's gaze and stops with Sal. He shakes his head and goes back to work. Others must remember Pearl who has been dead for a short time, for their demeanors sober as they work quietly for the next several hours. They continue to discuss what the change may mean for them, but they no longer laugh and carry on, apparently in deference to Sal.

The short celebration in the field is nothing compared to the one in the quarter when dark falls. Extra food has been sent down from the house, and the women quickly make use of it. Jonah, true to his word, is there among them going from group to group talking and learning names. He even repeats the names of the children like they are important to him. Many say the new man reminds them of Justice, a high compliment as his stint as overseer is the last peace any of them can remember.

Cletus does not make an appearance, and people wonder if he is still on the place. Justice reports he saw him enter Gerty's cabin about noon with Master George not far behind. According to the old man, the master hadn't stayed long, and though Gerty had been seen going to and from the laundry where she works, her son has not been seen at all. Quiet falls upon the group when Gerty herself emerges from the cabin, pulling the door closed behind her. She is carrying two plates and two cups, probably the same she had kindly offered to Jude on the night they arrived. Jude wishes there were something he could do or say for the woman. As awful as Cletus is, this woman is his mother, and his trouble must feel like her own. She quickly ladles food onto both plates from the nearest kettle, fills the cups with water from a nearby bucket, and returns to her cabin where she again closes the door behind her.

After everyone has had time for a first round of food, someone pulls out a fiddle, another a drum, and the music begins. A third person starts making a twanging sound with something he has cupped in his hands. The glow of one lantern after another begins to illuminate the strip of dirt in front of the cabins. Some dance while others clap. A woman at each fire pit has made a cake from flour and sugar from the mistress, and when they are done, the children line up first for a small piece on which a spoonful of molasses or honey is poured. After them come the others, and when Lew falls into line, Jude joins him.

Jude sits on the ground enjoying the treat. He looks around at the dancing figures and thinks, *If I could live among a group of colored folks, and we were allowed to live like this every day, I could be happy. Or could I?* Even if they were allowed to be carefree at times, he would still be owned. They could be sold; they could be beaten; they could be controlled. Jude wants to be like Master George. He doesn't want to be white—he wants to be treated like he's white. He wants to be able to climb on a horse to go wherever he wants. He wants to be able to choose his own wife— live with her in Baltimore. He would like to provide for himself and his family like white people do.

Jude likes back so he can gaze into the night sky. The stars are brighter here than in town, but it is not their beauty he dwells on. He wonders why God made some people colored and some people white, and who got to decide white folks were better. He does not accept what he has been told—that his people were put on this earth to serve. If God created them to be inferior, he wants no part of him for he must not love colored people as much as white people. If he gave one group of people better lives because of the way he made them, he can't be a fair God. What they need, Jude decides, is a colored God of their own—or, better yet, a God who paid no attention to color at all.

"Whut you layin dare pondahin so hawd?"

Jude is startled out of his reverie and thinks of sharing his thoughts with Lew, but he knows he will tell him to get those foolish notions out of his head. "I be thinkin how wore out this bidy uh mine is aftah a day in the cotton field."

Lew laughs. "Da same hyur. I says we goes on back ta da barn. Dese foke, theys uset ta dis kindah work, bu us town boys ain. Mawnin come early."

Jude rises. He is happy enough to turn in. For one thing, he cannot help but think about Gerty alone with her son in her cabin and Sal alone in hers with her memories and a grandchild she has to have a wet nurse to keep alive. His life in Savannah may not be as bad as he imagines. At least they aren't beaten; he doesn't have to work in the fields; and he has his family around him.

When the two of them return to the barn, without a word Lew goes to the wagon and pulls the bullwhip from its holder. Jude starts to ask why, but he doesn't want the reason given voice. Lew begins to snore within minutes of lying down. *How worried can he be if he falls asleep fo his head hits the hay?* Jude thinks he will not be that lucky, but the day's hard labor takes its toll, and he, too, falls asleep quickly.

Jude is not sure what wakes him—maybe the lack of noise. He can hear neither music nor voices from the quarter. He lets his eyes close again and is in a twilight between wakefulness and sleep when he detects a noise, a scuffing sound. Fear grips him, for he has been here for weeks now, and this is the first time he has heard a sound like this one. He reaches across to Lew to shake him awake. His hand is intercepted by Lew's. He squeezes to let him know he is aware they are not alone.

The next noise they hear is the crack of the whip he remembers all too well from the tobacco patch. The air around the motion swirls and the tip of the whip barely catches his bare ankle. He will not know until Lew tells him later that he actually screams. He finds himself on his feet without remembering how he gets there. He is glad he can feel Lew beside him. Though neither can see clearly, Lew strikes out with the bull whip and is rewarded with a cry coming from the darkness. He follows that lash with another, and yet another. Two more cries tell them he has made contact. Lew quits swinging when he meets no resistance. The quiet is broken by the sound of scuffling.

"Git da light," Lew tells him, and Jude dives for the area close to the ladder where they keep it. Out of fear of fire, they never have one close to the hay. He takes a minute to light the candle, and when he does, he can see his uncle has made his way to the doors standing open to the hillside behind the barn.

"I dint hear him open them," Jude says.

"I hyur em. Ise spectin somethin lack dis."

"I sho glad," Jude says. "An I sho glad his aim ain good as yose."

"Him gits ya?"

"Barely."

"Hole dat tapah whar I kin sees it. An doan burn da barn down wiles youse at it."

Jude raises his leg to see a stream of blood running from a spot right above his ankle, over his foot, and onto the floor of the loft.

"Mabe I shouldah sleep in my britches. I guess I bettah stawt."

"Wese seen da last uh him. I git him good, an they's sayin he be goan tamarrah."

"Yestahdy wouldna be none too soon fo me."

"Me eithah!" Lew laughs.

"Glad you kin laugh. You ain the one with blood runnin down yo leg."

Lew pushes Jude's foot away. "You ain hurt, Boy. Less thank da Lawd an git some sleep.

Before Jude falls asleep, he has a whole new appreciation for his Uncle Lew. Maybe he isn't the soft, master's man he thought he was.

Chapter 36

Upheaval

Jude and Lew sleep little, both awake when the rooster crows. There's still time before daybreak for them to rehash the events of the previous night. They both agree to keep the incident to themselves unless they are forced to do otherwise. They know there are several hours of daylight before Cletus will risk another move. They hope, by then, he will not be in any position to do so.

They gather with the field hands to eat breakfast and talk with Jonah. Unlike Cletus, he intends to take his meals with the slaves though his cabin is closer to the plantation house. They stand around waiting for the new overseer to give the order to move out, but he seems to be in no hurry. The slaves are beginning to whisper among themselves when their attention is drawn to the sound of horses' hooves. Master George rides in on the same mare on which he arrived at the plantation. Behind him he leads what they think of as Jonah's mule. He stops beside the overseer who has been talking quietly with Justice, hands the latter the reigns of the mounts, and says to Jonah, "Let's get this ovah with."

Jonah follows him to Gerty's cabin like he knows what the man is talking about. Both ignore dozens of eyes following their every move.

George raps twice on Gerty's door, and it is she who opens it. She steps out into the sunlight, her face an ebony slate of resignation. She crosses her arms, waiting with the rest of them, her eyes staring into and through whatever is before her. As much as Jude wants Cletus gone, he grieves for her in her aloneness. He wishes one of the women would move to her side. No one does.

Though the crowd can see movement inside the cabin, they cannot make out what is going on. The master's white coat and hat stand out in the dark interior, and they move little. Finally, the hat and coat turn toward the door and the wearer steps over the threshold. He turns to Gerty and places his hand on her shoulder. He says nothing and her mask doesn't waver. Behind him emerges Cletus followed closely by Jonah. Cletus's hands are tied behind his back. Lew and Jude see the angry raised stripe running from his collar bone, under his shirt, then out onto his upper arm. It matches the smaller one on his face that has swollen his right eye shut. Both have been cleaned, and from where they stand, they can see the glisten of ointment on the man's dark skin. Jude quickly glances at Lew, but his uncle stares ahead, ignoring both him and the others around him who are mumbling about how those injuries have come to be. The common consensus is the master got ahold of him after he sent him to the house the day before.

The circle around Lew and Jude may not know how Cletus came by his wounds, but there is no doubting the mood he is in. Never has Jude seen such rage on the face of a colored man. Cletus makes no move to say goodbye to his mother, and she does not look in his direction. Whatever words they have had for each other have been spoken out of sight of curious eyes.

Jonah leads Cletus to the mule George has brought for him, and with the help of Justice and a couple of field hands, they put him in the saddle and secure him with ropes. Master George is taking no chances with a man as angry and violent as Cletus. Before they turn to go, Cletus searches the crowd and finds what he is looking for in Lew and Jude. If a look could ignite fire, both would be embers. They are not the only ones who follow the direction and intensity of the glare. All eyes turn to them, even those of Master George, Justice, and Jonah. George appears more curious than concerned, but he has a journey ahead of him. He turns and leads Cletus away. They all stand where they are until the riders are out of sight, then exhale a collective sigh that opens the floodgates of discussion. Jude and Lew are immediately the centers of attention. Jude lets Lew do the talking, and he has chosen to do little. Both are relieved when Jonah rings the work bell. Still, there is a long walk to the field and a long day to get through, and by the end of the day, all, including Jonah, know Lew had defended himself and his nephew from a man callous enough to beat a woman to death. Lew has become a hero.

The day is long, hot, and tedious. Jude and Lew are exhausted when quitting time comes. They have been operating on little sleep and the added tension all the unwanted attention has brought them. They hurriedly wash up, eat their meal, and head for the barn.

The men have slipped out of their pants, shaken the field from them, and are stretched out on the sheets Cressa sent with them. They are almost asleep when a voice startles them.

"Good Heaven! Pu yo britches on! I ain nevah goan git ovah da sight uh doze bare backsides!"

Both men have been lying with their backs to the opening from below.

"What you doin sneakin up on us like a cat?" Jude asks.

"You gots some clothes on now?" Daisy asks, her back still to them.

"Gib us a bit," Lew says, and both scramble into their homespun pants.

"I yells an yells, an nobidy ansah. You mus be daid ta da worl."

"Wese plum woah out, dat fo sho. We ain uset ta dis hawd labah. Jude hyur nigh on daid fo real."

Jude shakes his head.

"An Ise da one dat pay da price, fo sho." Daisy says. "Dis ain no social call. I cain be goan long."

Daisy joins them on their makeshift bed after Jude assures her she can safely turn around. She sits with her skirts around her, all sign of humor gone.

"Mizz Ella done run off wid dat Eliot boy, an they's hell ta pay. Mizz Middleton on a tear an Mizz Mattie side ersef. Theys foun da lettah dis mawnin. Her fellah come fo er in da night, an they's in Washinton City by now. Plan ta wed furse thing dis mawnin."

Jude laughs. "That downright amusin. The massah's fit gonna make Mizz Middleton's look like chile play."

"An theys ain nothin da massah kin do bout it? He cain say Mizz Ella make a mistake an take her home?" Lew asks.

"Cordin ta da missus, they ain. She say youse legal in Washinton City youse seventeen, an Mizz Ella dat, an Mr. Eliot well ovah twenty. Mabe closah ta thirty. An sides dat, Ms. Mattie say her be ruint fo enbidy else. Da gul knows whut she doin. Theys ain gonna be no goin back now."

"You mean the massah woan evah let her go back ta Svanna?" Jude asks.

"No, Chile, Ise meanin whut done be done! If they's wed, they's husbun an wife fo life less one uh them die. An da massah migh wanse ta kill somebidy, bu he woan cause him care too much whut fokes thinks ta do dat."

Jude does not like being called a child, and he is about to tell his sister as much when she continues.

"Bu dat nough bout dat. I needs ta tell you somethin you ain gonna wannah hyur, sose you hab ta naw go off crazy or nothin."

"Hab somethin happen ta Cressa or da chilren?" Lew asks.

"No, they's fine, bess I know. It Dovie—da massah sell her like him be sayin him gonna do."

Lew's shoulders slump, and Jude jumps to his feet and starts pacing. Lew speaks quietly from behind the fingers he has spread across his face.

"We tells her an tells her ta stay in an stop traipsin roun aftah dawk. We tells her an tells her she cain be thieivin an..."

"Is that what you got ta say bout Dovie bein sold? She deserve ta be sold away from her family cause she want ta go places roun town like she a person or somethin? The massah have the right ta send her way cause she take some food her own sistah cook fo them? That what you sayin, Uncle Lew?"

"Quit yo shoutin, Jude. Yellin an carryin on ain goan bring Dovie back. Unc Lew ain thinkin Dovie shoulddah be sole. Bu dat whut happen, an theys ain nothin we kin do bout it."

"Ise jus sayin, none ub dis happen her naw so haidstrong. If her hab jus lissen ta..." Lew stops in mid-sentence. "Whut bout Ben? Da massah sell him wid his mama, or do him seprate em?"

Jude finally stands still.

"Far as I hyur, him still dare in Svanna."

"How you know all this?" Jude thinks to ask.

"Da massah write Mizz Middleton, an I be in da nex room lissnin wen her read da lettah ta Mizz Mattie, Mizz Maxie, an theys aunties. Dat wen theys foun ou Mizz Ella gone. Den Mizz Mattie tell me cuz da massah wanse evahbidy ta know fo theys come back ta Svanna."

"I bet he do!" Jude shouts. "He a coward! He send us all away so nobidy there ta try ta stop him."

"An whut we goan do we dare?" Lew asks tiredly.

"We hep her sneak away! Mama tawk him outtah it. Mammy make him lissen. There has ta be somethin we kin do!"

"I kin tell da missus dint like whut her hyur, bu she say Dovie mustah do somethin bad, an da massah hab no othah choice."

"He could do a lot uh things! He couldah lock her up fo a bit. Doan give her food fo a while. Dovie ain bad. She just wannah live like the rest uh us do, an the massah coulden stand fo a dawkie ta git the best uh him. That all it be."

Jude is crying and Daisy tries to put her arms around him. He pulls away.

"We gonna find her. We hide her somewhere safe. Mizz Bette help us. We write her, an she know whut ta do.

"I hyurs whut da massah says. Him says nobidy need ta know whar Dovie be now, dat her be faw ways whar she cain do no mo harm."

"Like she do real harm ta anybidy!" Jude shouts. "I gonna kill him, that whut I gonna do. He think we foget whut he done, he be wrong. I gonna ketch him out an kill him with my bare hands. An I gonna whispah in his ear right fo he dies, 'This be fo Dovie.'"

"Stop dat tawk righ now, Jude!" It is Lew's turn to shout. "Youse ain goan do no sech thing. Youse tawkin crazy cuz youse hurtin. Ise hurtin, too, bu you bess membah whar you be. Theys ain goan bide no yellin bout killin da massah, an theys kin hyur you cleah upta da house!"

"Git aholt uh yosef, Jude! Da bess idee you hab be ta write Mizz Bette. Mabe they's somethin her kin do. I sneaks some papah from Mizz Mattie desk. They's all in a tizzy ovah Mizz Ella, so nobidy payin much mind ta whut I do. I be back in a bit. Lew, tawk some sense intah dis boy."

"I ain no boy!" Jude shouts, but he is yelling at Daisy's back.

"Daisy, kin you gits ta Mama. Her be tore up she hyur bout dis. Bess you stop by an tell er. An bring two ub dat papah. Jude need ta write Minda. Da massah boun ta tell Mizz Jessie dis same mess. Her be needin some kine wuhds from somebidy."

Daisy does what she is told to do, and she is back before long with the paper. When asked how Mammy took the news, she shakes her head and swats at tears. After she leaves, neither man says anything. Lew rolls to his side and wraps himself in the sheet though the air is still and hot in the loft. Jude hears him weeping, but he is too angry to console him. His rage equals that he saw on Cletus's face before he was led away, and all of it is directed at Master Barret. One thing he is sure of. If he returns to Savannah, he will try to make the master pay for the grief he has caused his family. A plan is forming in his mind. He is not at all sure he will go back with the others. He may take the opportunity he has and will unlikely have again anytime soon to make an escape. His uncle Lew may be resigned to their fate, but he is not.

Chapter 37

Regrets

Savannah, Georgia—1848

F rederick has been angry many times, but he cannot remember ever experiencing such disappointment. Ella has been nothing but a source of pride and happiness for him, and for her to deceive him in the way she has is much worse for the unexpectedness of the act. A couple of weeks have passed since he received the news from Mrs. Middleton, and his rage has grown daily over the powerlessness of his position to rectify the situation. Even the letter from Ella herself asking him to forgive her has done little to brighten his mood. On top of Ella's defection is Mattie's impending childbirth and Mrs. Middleton's meddling, the latter making him second guess his decision to sell Dovie, so much so he has written a letter to Jones to ask him to send her back. The dowager has expressed a complete confidence that she can handle her on the plantation where there is less opportunity for vice. She has apologized for interfering, but she assures him he will agree when he understands the distress the action has caused not just Mammy, but both Mattie and young Maxie, as well.

Damn! The temerity of the woman to question his household management after she has allowed Ella to run off with a miscreant right beneath her nose. Still, Frederick has not been sleeping well. Every night he has spent in his own home since selling Dovie, he has dreamed of Abby, and she is not happy. He had come to know some peace since her death, and the recollection of their last troubled days had faded. He had convinced himself the good years they had and his efforts to make her nothing but content surely offset the whole Minda situation and the truth of his past Abby had inadvertently come to know. He had convinced himself Abby's despondency would have eventually brought about the same tragedy. Now, however, her memory is haunting him. Often when he awakens from one of the dreams in which the apparition is confronting him about what she claims are his misdeeds, it is as if she is there with him, either in the bed or in the room. He could swear he can feel her breath, detect her scent, sense her displeasure. His inability to rest has worn him down. The combination of Ella's elopement, Mrs. Middleton's disapproval, Dovie's absence, his worry about Mattie and the baby she is to have, and the nightmares has weakened him. For one of the few times in his life, Frederick fears he has made a grave mistake. He has grown to dread the return of his servants, for all are capable of making him pay. He especially dreads Minda's displeasure. He has missed her more than he had thought possible.

As if the women in his life were not troublesome enough, his improved opinion of Rob has been somewhat diminished by the news of the bank letting him go. Rob claimed they had told him to go ahead and take his leave as they were sure he needed time to get everything done for his new role in life, but Frederick thought the story rang false. He had not liked being outmaneuvered, so he had gone straight to his friend John Andrews to verify Rob's account. He had not liked what he had heard. In fact, he had been embarrassed. John told him Rob's work, having never been quite satisfactory, had grown completely negligent since his courtship. Management had been thrilled when he gave notice and had jumped at the opportunity to replace him without affront to one of the bank's board members. Frederick's first impulse had been to march home and tear into his son, but fortunately, he was away for the weekend, and his absence had given his father time to think. Perhaps Rob had never been cut out to be a banker as the young man had often told him. Now he can prove himself with a new start in life, and Frederick has enough problems without wanting to alienate his son and possibly his future in-laws early into the relationship. He decides to let the matter go, another behavior new to him.

On top of his worries, Frederick is lonely. He has taken one of his female warehouse workers to fulfill his needs until Minda returns. Though Delia has been willing enough, her youth is not as appealing to him as he thought it would be. She is twenty, but she acts younger, and both she and he are out of place in Minda's cabin. Thoughts of her leave him even more depressed. He thinks of paying his cousin Brigitte a visit, but at three in the afternoon, she will be heavily into her cups by now. He hasn't the patience to tolerate her heightened mood and giddiness. Still, he can think of nowhere else to go. He is headed out the door when he sees a letter either Deke or Ben must have dropped in the tray by the door. He is relieved to see the name Jackson Jones on the return address, the planter to whom he sold Dovie. He smirks when he reflects on how quickly the man has gotten back to him. He must be more than eager to get rid of the troublesome wench.

Frederick rips the envelope open and quickly peruses the contents. His legs will not support him. He is unaware of what he is doing as he slides into a nearby chair and removes the hat he has donned in preparation for going out. Dread washes over him. How will he ever tell Dovie's family she is dead? Jones claims when she ran away for the third time, her open wounds from the whippings she had received for the first two tries had frenzied the dogs, and they had finished her off before his man could get to her. He had gone on to say reimbursement would be the gentlemanly thing for Barret to do, not only for the price he had paid, but for the trouble she had caused him. Never, he claimed, had Barret told him how rebellious and unbreakable the wench was.

Frederick is not prepared for regret. An image of Dovie playing with Maxie comes to him. He remembers Dovie's ministrations to Luella as she was dying from Yellow Fever. He recalls the sound of Dovie laughing with her mother and sister when they didn't know he was close by. Unreasonably, he remembers his grandmother and visualizes her face as though he had seen her yesterday instead of decades ago in a far off land. His chest spasms. *My God*, he thinks. *I am responsible for Dovie's death.*

Frederick feels physically ill, but he cannot stand the thought of going to his bedroom to lie down. The air there has become oppressive since his dreams of Abby have taken a dark turn. Even now, he senses her, yet there is nothing of Abby's loving nature in the presence. He perceives an anger, no longer from within, but from without. To escape it, he dons his hat and hurries out into the sunlight. He starts walking with no idea where he is going. Dark finds him at Laurel Grove cemetery standing before the graves of both his wives. He turns to Abby's and sinks to his knees without concern of someone seeing him in this uncharacteristic state. Hours pass before he rises wearily and heads home in the dark. Though he has said all he can think to say to Abby, though he has waited silently for a response, he receives no absolution. He fears she will be waiting for him at home. When he is almost to Madison Square, he stops, thinks a moment, then changes direction. He walks the familiar path to Yamacraw, opens the door to Minda's cabin, and falls onto the bed on which he has spent countless hours with Minda and a more recent few with Delia. He finds peace in sleep.

Chapter 38
No Turning Back

Baltimore, Maryland—1848

Late summer in Baltimore is not as hot and humid as what Minda and Ish are accustomed to, but neither can fully enjoy the cool temperatures or the time to call their own. Both know they are days away from leaving Jessie, Diana, and Quent behind. A week ago, Jessie received a letter informing them Lew and Jude are in route to pick them up and return them to Savannah. Ish had been disappointed. He was excited about seeing his brother and uncle, but he had been looking forward to the trip by steamer, despite the traumatic experience he had endured at the hands of the man who had hit him and his mother. Enough time has passed for the boy to romanticize the voyage. He's forgotten the discomfort of being cold when rained upon, hungry when food was hard to come by, and scared when they had no one close by to stand between them and mistreatment.

Minda is disappointed, as well. She wants to be reunited with her family, but the master waits in Savannah. And Dovie does not. The home they left is not the one they will return to. Then there is Quentin. Everyone is aware she is carrying on with him. Minda doesn't care, but she does not want to talk about the relationship or bring it out into the open. What purpose can acknowledging it serve? Her time in Baltimore is almost at an end. Now, as Quentin walks her home in the wee hours of the morning, Lew and Jude must be close. Her coping strategy is to avoid speaking further with Quentin about leaving. If she doesn't talk about it, she can deny the reality—separation from Quentin, Jessie, and Diana—the end of the happiest period of her life. Here she has been able to pretend Dovie is waiting in Savannah. There, she will have to face her absence.

At the back door of Jessie's shop—the one Jessie told her makes less noise when opening and closing—Quentin holds her tightly. Neither speaks though Quentin has plenty to say. Minda has forbidden he broach the one topic he has become obsessed with, and he has no desire for trivial conversation. She has told him she refuses to mar one minute of the time they have left by discussing impossibilities. She cannot make him understand how useless any attempt on his part to buy her from the master would be. He has an answer for her every objection—he will buy the boys when he has saved enough—it may take him a long time, but he will also try to purchase her mother. Minda loves his optimism and generosity, but the one real fight they have had was over her telling him how foolish he is to assume any of his dreams were possible. Finally, she had put her foot down and said their nightly visits would come to an end if he spoke on the subject again. Now they are mere days from her departure, she feels the fight building in him again. This morning she puts her fingers over his lips to keep him from speaking, slips through the door and closes it behind her. She waits with her face pressed against the door. Detecting nothing, she turns away and slips up the stairs as quietly as she slipped out hours ago. Cotton is awake, but he graciously remains silent from his resting place on the sill at the open window.

She lies on the bed with Ish for the short time left before he stirs. She rises as soon as Ish has seen her there. If ever he wakes in the night and wonders where she is, he has not mentioned it. The day goes the way most of their days have gone. Minda is finishing up the few tasks she has to do on the impressive stack of clothes Jessie has helped her make for her family. She adds buttons to a shirt for Lew's Deke and hems a dress for little Lizzy. She picks up the shirt and overalls she has made for Ben, and tears fill her eyes. Dovie would have loved a new dress like the ones she made for Cressa and Mammy, and the thought of never seeing her again is too much to contemplate. She thinks Dovie's death might be easier to accept, for then she could suffer no more harm.

They have closed for the day and are seated around the table when they hear a rap on the door of the front room. "They's here!" Ish shouts, then runs around the table and into the store. The others follow. Through the front plate glass, they see Jude's face framed in his hands peering in at them. Minda gives a screech of delight, and Jessie runs to unlock the door. Diana hangs back, surreptitiously checking her dress and straightening her hair.

Their reunion with Lew is delayed while Jessie instructs him on how to pull the buckboard to the alley behind her house. Jude leaves him to the task and bursts through the door, met first by his little brother, then Minda who isn't far behind. Jude wraps his arms tightly around both of them, lifting them off the floor, a gesture meant to be playful and to show Diana how strong he has gotten. Diana, overwhelmed by shyness, cannot meet his eyes. Minda is going on and on about how much her boy has grown, and, in part, this is what is making Diana hang back. She left a boy in Savannah. This new Jude appears to be a man.

Jude finally pulls away and crosses the room. "An how you be, Mizz Diana?" he teases.

She smiles and goes into his arms. "I be better now you be here," she whispers.

"You mockin me now, Woman?" he whispers back.

Diana is thrilled to be called a woman by anyone, but especially by Jude. Acutely aware of their audience, she pushes him away.

"You smell like you've been on the road for days!"

"That cause I have been! But I wash in a creek last night, an here you ah callin me stinky."

Everyone laughs, and Ish pushes forward with his pet on his forearm. "Jude, this be Cotton. Cotton, this be Jude!" he says proudly.

Cotton greets Jude with a raucous Caw, and, again, everyone laughs. They all move to the kitchen toward the sound of Lew's voice. They find Jessie dishing out food for the travelers.

Jude and Lew scarf their food so hungrily Minda reminds them to have some manners.

"You ain eat nuthin but Uncle Lew's campfire cookin fo days, you be shovin a home-cooked meal in yo mouth, too."

"I dint hyur no complainin wen dat aw you hab!" Lew says, looking up from his plate. In doing so, his eyes fall on Ish's companion.

"Ish, whar you gits dat bird?"

The next few minutes are filled with stories from Minda and Ish's journey to Baltimore, the boy's training by the woodworker, then on to Jude and Lew's stay at Hickory Grove. Minda has many questions, most about Daisy, and Jude waits until they have finished the meal to pull the letter Daisy dictated to him from his pocket.

"This fo you, Mama. From Daisy."

Minda grabs the letter from his hand and clutches it to her chest. The others look at her expectantly, but she puts the letter in her pocket. "I read this lattah, y'all doan mind," she says.

Minda's happiness in seeing them makes her forget for a little bit what she is leaving. Finally, the conversation turns to Dovie's fate, and the laughter dries faster than the gravy on the men's plate.

"Him ain goan tell us whar her at, bu Jude write Mizz Bette. Daisy hab a house boy dat sweet on her sneak it inta da post on da way ouddah da doe," Lew says.

"I try ta get the massah ta git her back when we git home, bu I doan think it do much good. Mizz Jessie say she doan hold out a lottah hope any uh us change his mind."

All eyes turn to Jessie who is standing with her back to the counter so others will have a place to sit.

"I would like to say otherwise, but I know how stubborn Mr. Barret can be. Once he's set his mind, he is hard to sway. Regardless, I've already written him begging him to reconsider. He didn't mention Dovie when he wrote to tell me you two were picking up Minda and Ish on the way home. I don't think his omission bodes well."

Jessie addresses the newcomers because Minda, Diana, and Ish already know she has tried.

"I wannah tell y'all a story," Jude surprises them by saying. "One day when we in the tobacca patch, Lew an I see somethin I nevah foget."

All eyes stay riveted on him as he tells the story of Cletus beating the young Pearl to death. When he finishes, they all sit and stare at him until Lew speaks.

"Wy you go an tells dat mess? Ain we gottah nuff ta be sad bout widou you tellin dem whut nobidy evah need ta hyur?"

"I tell them fo a reason," Jude says. "I tell them cause they need ta know what can happen ta Dovie she on a plantation somewhere. An if you…" Here he stops and glances from his mother to Jessie, "be tellin me they ain no way we can save Dovie, I ain goin back ta Svanna."

Everyone but Lew is too stunned to reply.

"He be tawkin dis mess evah since he hyurs bout Dovie. I be tryin ta tawk truff ta dat thick haid from mawnin ta nigh, an him still naw hyurin a word I says."

"You tawkin crazy, Son," Minda says. "The massah come ou here or send somebidy aftah you. He do whatevah he have to ta bring you home."

"Then I woan stay here." He looks directly at Diana. "Or I woan stay here fo now. I go ways an wait til evahthing die down, then I come back."

Diana shakes her head. "Jude, I understand why you want to be free, but you have to be sensible. What your mother says is true. Mister Barret will never stop looking for you. Where are you going to go? If you don't stay here, you will have no one to help you. Can you imagine what a life lived constantly on the run will be like? My own father ran. No one has heard from him since, and we have no reason to believe we ever will. You can never settle down for fear of being caught. You would be ruining any chance of ever having a family and a home..."

"An what chance I got now?" Jude asks. "I still got the money Mizz Jessie send me fo tendin the graves. I make my own papahs an find me a job."

His calm demeanor scares Minda more than if he were raging. He has given much thought to this, and she recognizes the determination in his voice and on his face.

"An I be next. If the massah sell Dovie, he sell me." He addresses his mother. "You know he hawdly bides me. An I doan think I capable uh bein like Lew an you an Mammy. 'Yes, Massah,' dis, an 'Yes, Massah,' dat, especially now I know what he do ta Dovie. I hate the man. I best be nowhere round him evah agin."

His meaning is not lost on any of them. Jessie walks to stand behind him, purposely placing a hand on his shoulder. His anger is palpable, his purpose unwavering. All the talk in the world will not change this young man's mind.

"Let's all get some rest tonight, and we'll talk more about this tomorrow. I know you men are tired, and we've all had a full day."

Minda wants to continue to try to dissuade her son, but in spite of her friendship with Jessie, she still responds to her much as she would a white woman. Miss Jessie says it is time for them to go to bed, so Minda rises to do so. She helps Diana set up the bathtub in the kitchen along with two pallets, and she leaves Ish downstairs with the men even though she is afraid of what wild ideas Jude may put into the boy's head. She lies on her bed and tries not to worry. Her mind wanders to Quentin, and she wonders if he misses her. Surely he has figured out her son is here—his arrival has been expected at any time. Still, she hates for him to think she didn't want to come to him. She shakes her head at her silliness. What difference can her absence make now when soon that will be all either of them know?

Minda sleeps little, though she is comforted by the rumble of male voices from below. The mattress gives when Ish crawls into bed beside her, and she listens to noises the house makes as it, too, settles for the night. She is not surprised when she hears Diana creep downstairs or when her and Jude's muffled voices carry up the stairwell, probably from the store. Jessie must be aware they are down there, and if she isn't alarmed, she decides she won't be either. The level-headed Diana might persuade her rebellious son to heed reasonable advice.

Minda's hopes are dashed the next morning when there has been no improvement in Jude's attitude at the breakfast table. She sends Ish off to Quentin's, overriding his wishes to stay behind with the family. "You leavin soon. You needs ta tell Quent. Tell him we be goin in da nex day or two."

"Bu Jude say he ain goin," Ish protests.

"Jude talkin foolishness. Now go on like I tell you."

Ish leaves accompanied by Cotton who has been hopping from one of Ish's shoulders to the other, cocking his head back and forth to better cast a beady eye from one to the other of them as if trying to weigh each side of the argument. Minda sighs and plops down in the seat vacated by Ish.

"I have given this situation some thought," Jessie says, "and I have a plan. I say we delay your departure by three days giving me time to post letters to both Frederick and Bette Stiles. We won't have time to get a response, but if you, Minda and Lew, travel as slowly as possible, I should have a response from Bette or Frederick before he can get here or send someone in his place. The timing isn't ideal with Ella doing what she has done, but he will have her actions heavily on his mind and should not want another problem. He is also dealing with Robart's engagement and the birth of Mattie's child. The combination of all those matters should slow his response if not stop him entirely."

"An what you gonna say in that lettah, Mizz Jessie? You know he ain goan set Jude free jus cause you acks him to."

Jessie laughs. "No, but I can offer to buy Jude. I will tell him of Jude and Diana's attraction to each other—explain I would appreciate the opportunity to provide a better life for someone who may someday be part of my family."

Diana's eyes are huge, and she examines the table as does Jude. This talk is presuming for even them.

"Don't you two get all worked up. This is simply a plan to keep Jude in Baltimore."

"Bu, Mizz Jessie, they's no chance da massah gonna care one way or the othah bout the way the boy feel. He have a fondness fo Ish, bu he ain nevah care one way or the othah bout Jude."

"Oh, he care one way, an that way be bad. Mabe he be glad ta be rid uh me."

"You fetch a lot uh money, Son. He wannah git rid uh you, he try ta git a good price while he at it."

"That what I sayin!" Jude says, and Minda regrets her words. But Jessie is giving her hope. Though she would hate leaving her son behind, Frederick has sold Dovie robbing her of the delusion of security for any of them.

"And," Jessie continues, "I have information I cannot share with you. It may help me influence Frederick's decision. I want you to trust me in this, but you must understand, Jude, there is a strong likelihood this plan will not work. If you are determined to run, I cannot see the detriment in trying to free you in a way in which you can actually have a future, one in which you won't be constantly looking over your shoulder."

"I mean it when I say I ain goin back. I hate leavin you, Mama, an thinkin on nevah seein you or Ish an the rest uh you is tearin me up. We can read an write, Mama. I haftah run, I kin write you." He pauses and glances at Diana. "All uh you. I fraid I not be seein any uh you anyway, I haftah be the massah's boy agin. I might put somethin in his drinkin watah sides spit."

"Hush, Boy! I ain lissenin ta dat mess even you be sixteen year old!" Minda says.

"Fine, then," Jessie interrupts. "If we get a reply from Frederick refusing to sell you, he will not know you have stayed behind. I will try to find help to get you out of Baltimore. You comprehend you may never see your family again if you do this?"

Lew surprises them all by saying, "Theys ain no guarantee he be wid us long enway. Dat boy too haidstrong ta do lack he spose ta. I guess it be bess he gits ou now wile him hab a plan. Ise scairt ta death him take off up dare in Vuhginny in da middle uh da nigh."

Silence falls over the room. Once again, Minda is crying, something she has vowed to quit doing. There are tears in Jude's eyes, too.

"Mama," he says, "you remembah what Mizz Bette tell us years ago when she first stawt teachin us? She say she think someday we all be free. Mabe she right. You be young, Mama. Mabe we all be tagathah soon. If I go back, I fraid I woan live ta see the day."

"Those books you read done gone ta yo head," Minda tries valiantly to smile.

"Listen, Everyone," Jessie says, "I am going to go write those letters. You all have three days to enjoy your time together. I suggest you get to it."

Jessie leaves Diana in charge of the shop, goes to her room and takes out stationery. She sighs heavily. She thinks of writing Bette first but decides to get the worse over with first. She has written this letter in her head last night, and she refuses to be intimidated by the thought of how her nephew will take it. She presses her lips into a firm line and begins, determined to use all the weapons in her arsenal even if they cause her untold grief in the future.

Chapter 39

Inveigling

Savannah, Georgia—1848

Frederick is incredulous when he receives yet another letter containing bad news. After reading the message twice, he throws it on his desk, pushes out of his chair, and paces the room. The nerve of the woman to threaten him after all he has done for her! Where would she and the waif she insists on calling her daughter be if not for him? They would never have been able to open a shop in Baltimore had he not written letters of sponsorship. Dammit, she would never have been able to leave Savannah if he hadn't helped her sell her properties. His mind betrays him by settling on Moses and the fact she would have had no desire to leave if he hadn't been hung. Even now, Frederick refuses to acknowledge his role in the death of the freed slave. Moses had been a good man who had defied the odds and made a decent life for himself, his wife, and his orphaned niece. Too, he chooses to forget he had no real choice in Jessie's departure. She would have left despite his efforts to stop her.

Frederick weighs his choices. Acquiescing never occurs to him. He has never considered selling Jude, and Jessie's words have not changed his mind. His mind turns to damage control. What can Jessie do to harm him? And will she follow through with her not-so-subtle threats to reveal his past? Would she betray him? She had been more like a mother than the aunt she was. The two of them had prevailed against the world on a God-forsaken island, and now she claims she will forget their history for a black boy kin to her only through him? Tears burn his eyes. Her fears of him doing to Jude what he has done to Dovie are a low blow. He has no intent of freeing Minda's three children, but Jessie is implying he would sell them out of the family! He would never hurt their mother

271

that way, he thinks, forgetting the pain he has recently caused her by selling her sister.

Frederick pulls out a copy of the official looking pamphlet he keeps in a keyhole in his desk. He flips through the list of the Georgia code of law on slavery until he finds the section he wants. He then dips the nib into the inkwell and pens:

Jessie,

Your time away and the freedom you have enjoyed, in great part due to my devotion and personal assistance, have addled your reasoning. Under no circumstances will I grant the boy Jude his freedom. No amount of malicious blackmail with which you threaten me will induce me to do so. You obviously judge yourself better informed than I as to what is best for the boy after spending little time with him.

If the others have left without him, I will send a conveyance, and I expect him to be returned to me immediately upon its arrival. In case you are thinking of defying my instructions, note the following excerpt from the Georgia Code of Law.

> *Punishment of free persons of color for inveigling slaves. If any free person of color commits the offense of inveigling or enticing away any slave or slaves, for the purpose of, and with the intention to aid and assist such slave or slaves leaving the service of his or their owners, or in going to another state, such persons offending shall, for each and every offense, on conviction, be confined in the penitentiary at hard labor...*

I find it abhorrent to be put into a situation in which I must ignore my natural generous and amenable nature...

Frederick's concentration is broken by the distant knocking from the front of the house. He sits there waiting for Lewis to answer the door before remembering the man is on his way back from Baltimore with the offending Jude, along with Minda and Ish. He is going to have plenty to say to both Minda and Lewis for even allowing Jessie to appeal on the boy's behalf. After all the times Minda has begged him to keep her children close, now she appears to be willing to let the boy be sold off away from her, as if he does not know what is best for them. This is what comes of giving any of them a little freedom.

Frederick is inclined not to answer the door, but the visitor is persistent. Finally, he rises from his seat and stomps his way to the entryway. Looking out the side window, he sees Bette Stiles, and, unfortunately, she sees him. Now he is unable to pretend he isn't home.

What Now? he wonders. He tries to lose the scowl before opening the door to the woman who had been Abby's best friend but is no favorite of his own. She has always been too outspoken and independent, traits that have become more pronounced, according to local gossip, since the untimely death of her husband.

"Mrs. Stiles," Frederick smiles, opening the door wide. "To what do I owe this pleasant surprise?"

"Please fahgive me faw comin unannounced and faw puhsistin. If my mission had not been important, I would have left you in peace."

"A visit from you could never be an inconvenience," Frederick lies smoothly. "I was at the back of the house, and with Lewis gone, it took me a while to get to the door. Please pardon the delay."

Bette sweeps by him and into the entryway.

"Is there a place we may talk in private, as inappropriate as that may seem. I need ta speak ta you about somethin of grave importance, and I wish not ta be ovahheard."

"There is no danger, Dear Lady. Other than Cressa in the kitchen and a couple of boys about the place, we are alone, a state that will soon be remedied with the return of the girls and the servants. Are you sure your feel at ease under the circumstances? If you prefer to wait for their…"

"Of course not, Frederick. And will you please call me Bette as you always have? Surely ah friendship is enough ta dissuade idle gossip."

"Then follow me to the family parlor, the perfect place for a chat between two friends."

Frederick hopes his words are convincing, for he has spent no time with Bette since the death of her husband, and talk of a grave conversation is off-putting. With the way his luck has been running, he fears whatever she has to say may be of an unwelcome nature. A confrontation with Bette is the last thing he needs.

Bette stops in the entryway of the parlor and surveys the room. "Oh, Frederick, how I miss Abby. I do not make friends easily, and a relationship of such a deep and abidin nature as we shared cannot be replaced."

If she had been such a good friend, surely she could have predicted Abby's despair and done something to alter the course the condition had caused her to follow, Frederick thinks.

"I know your loss must be great, for my wife was indeed a treasure taken way too soon. Providence has spoken, and we mortals must accept the bad with the good."

Bette turns her ice blue gaze directly upon him.

"Do you not regret, Frederick, as I do, that we did not fathom the depths of her despondency and do more ta help her? If I had had any idea at the time…"

Bette stops in midsentence when Frederick's face loses all warmth. It is as if shutters have been slammed in her face.

"I have no idea what you are talking about, Mrs. Stiles. Accidents happen, even to wonderful people like Abigail. It is not our place to question divine will."

Bette remembers too late the story Frederick has put out for one and all, that Abby had leaned against a loose balcony railing and fallen to her death. He knows nothing of the conversations she has had with Jessie and the secrets to which she has been made privy. She is not yet willing to show her hand, however, so she tries to make amends.

"Please fahgive me, Frederick, but you know both Jessie and I tried ta help her when she would fall inta doldrums faw extended periods of time…"

"Those doldrums, as you call them, had nothing to do with her passing, and I certainly hope you are not spreading such a sentiment…"

It is Bette's turn to interrupt him. "Goodness, Frederick, have I sunk so low in your esteem you think me an idle gossip? I have been subjected ta false rumahs and innuendo myself. I would nevah stoop ta discussin my best friend with anyone othah than you and Jessie."

Mention of Jessie a second time puts Frederick on guard. Having just received a letter from the woman himself, there must be a connection to its content and this unexpected visit from Bette Stiles. He does not want to make an enemy of this woman, not with her familial connections. Regardless of the common opinion regarding Bette's eccentricities, her relatives will not take kindly to anyone offending her.

"I must apologize, Bette. I have overreacted. I am currently dealing with some unpleasantness—of a business nature—" he adds, "and I have not been myself. I fear my disposition is badly in need of the ladies of the house. Please, sit down. Would you like a glass of sherry…"

"Somethin a little strongah, puhhaps."

Bette fears the anger Frederick has shown thus far will pale in comparison to the rage he will display when he learns the reason for her visit. "Do you have a wine, somethin like you suhved years ago when we dined often with you and Abby?"

"Ah, those were good times. That wine came from my dear friend Alexis Maxwell, and, unfortunately, he died a few years back. His wife Brigitte lives here in town now. Perhaps you have met her."

"I have met Mrs. Maxwell on a couple of occasions," Bette says, and unable to think of anything positive to say about the woman, she changes the subject. "Then the sherry will do nicely."

"Oh, I have wine, My Dear. The memory took me back to Alexis. He was in the Navy, and he would pick local favorites while he was in exotic ports."

He walks to a cabinet and fills a wine glass half full and hands it to Bette who has seated herself in one of the chairs before the fireplace though Frederick has not invited her to do so. Hoping to further soften his mood, she takes the wine and introduces a topic she thinks will please him.

"I have been told dear Robart is gettin married! His intended sounds like a delightful woman. Ah you pleased with the union?"

"Yes!" Frederick sits opposite her with the whiskey he has poured himself. He is drinking hard liquor early in the day. She remembers Abby telling her he considered the habit a vice and the ruination of many. Obviously, either his opinion or his habit has changed.

"Robart has done quite well for himself." His face relaxes for the first time since he opened the door. "The boy has struggled, I won't deny, for several years now. Abby's death may have had more of an impact on him than any of the girls, but he is at last coming into his own."

"And how ah the girls? I used ta see Mattie often, but I haven't had the pleasure since the weddin. Is she happily settled?"

Frederick is glad there is no awkwardness over Mattie's defection on the matter of her son Thomas. Clarence had held a grudge, but his death eliminated that problem.

"Mattie is to become a mother any day now. I will be glad when the ordeal is behind her. I too have missed her terribly since she has been unable to travel. I would have gone to her had I not been kept here on business."

"Is she in Vahginia with Mrs. Middleton and the othah girls, then?" Bette asks.

"She is," Frederick says slowly, trying to discern whether Bette has heard of Ella's elopement. Her expression appears open and warm, so he decides there is no need to mention it. He is still at a loss as to how to introduce the newly wedded couple to Savannah society. He has not yet written the name Ella Gordon even when he responded to her letter. He must attend to the problem soon, but he has enough on his plate at the moment. He wonders how long Bette will take to get to the point of her call. He needs to get back to the Jude issue. He wonders if she is stalling, but he can think of no polite way to ask her to get to the purpose of her call. He politely asks after her children.

"Thomas has gone inta business faw himself. The prospect of workin with his brothah did not appeal ta him. I have given him a stawt in his own factorin entahprise. I was pleased he chose a livelihood that didn't compete directly with Reggie."

Frederick is reminded of how open Bette has always been, in his opinion, to a fault.

"So Reggie has undertaken Clarence's role in the business?" he asks. It is a question to which he knows the answer, for the freeing of his father's slaves was an outrage much talked about for some time. He, like everyone else, knows Bette's abolitionist influence has rubbed off on Reggie, and also like everyone else, he fears the boy has created problems for all slave owners by actually paying darkies wages. He suspects neither Bette nor Reggie has suffered the last consequences of their foolishness.

"Reggie is suhprised at how much he likes his new role. He tried ta talk Thomas inta remainin as a pawtner, but they couldn't come ta agreement on…certain aspects of the way the business was ta be run."

Frederick nods though he would love to have a say on that subject. Perhaps another time.

"And Eliza?" he asks. "Are there wedding bells for her in the offing?"

"No, and, though I know mine is not the normal sentiment of most mothahs of young ladies of marriageable age, I am glad. She is such a comfort ta me, and I plan faw the two of us ta leave faw a grand tour in a few months—let her see some of the world before she settles down."

"I have never been one to want our girls to marry too soon, either. They have a lifetime ahead for those responsibilities." He thinks of Ella. "I will have Fredie here with me even if the girls do get married and move away. He plans to open his own practice here in the house in a few months. We plan to set him up a space on the bottom floor in a room off the kitchen where patients can enter through the front side gate."

"How wonderful ta have a doctah right here in your home!"

"Yes, Fredie has always been my most steadfast child."

This is not a statement he would have made before Mattie left home and Ella fell from grace.

"Of course, they have all been blessings. I wish their mother could have lived to see how wonderfully they have all done," he adds.

He hopes Bette remembers this statement when word of Ella's marriage reaches her.

"I believe she does know, Frederick. I know this may sound silly, but I feel her here with us. Maybe bein where she was often, where we were tagethah, gives me flights of fancy."

"I know exactly what you mean. I feel her presence daily."

They both sit in silence for a moment. "Would you like another glass of wine?" Frederick asks.

Bette has delayed as long as she can.

"No, thank you."

Bette has never been adept at leading into a matter. She is considered blunt to a fault. She can think of no way to ease into the discussion, so she simply states the reason for her visit. "I need ta talk ta you about Jude, and I beseech you ta hear me out and not get angry."

So blunt is Bette's statement, Frederick is caught completely off guard and simply stares at her. His mouth actually gapes.

"I have received a lettah from Jessie, as I know you have." She purposely doesn't mention the one she got from Jude himself.

Frederick rises abruptly from his chair, downs the remaining whiskey in his glass, and walks back to the cabinet for a refill. Bette waits until he has filled the glass, and when he still does not turn to look at her, she, too, rises.

"Jessie has asked me ta use what influence I have with you ta puhsuade you ta allow Jude his freedom. She tells me she is willin ta puhchase him, and if she cannot afford ta pay your price, I…"

"Why would you choose to interfere in my household, Bette, when you obviously have much responsibility of your own?"

"I know I am presumin much…"

"You are." Frederick turns to face her. She wishes he had stayed where he was when she meets eyes colder now than they were when she mentioned Abby's fate.

"And why would you strain our relationship, Bette, over the matter of a slave boy? Has your widowhood misled you to ascertain it a woman's place to interfere in a man's management of his own domestic affairs?"

Bette's color rises. She tilts her head and stretches to gain as much height as her diminutive frame will allow. "I feel, Frederick, you ah at a disadvantage without the softenin influence of a wife. Abby would have…"

"Please do not presume to tell me what my wife might have thought or done."

Frederick and Bette shudder simultaneously as a chill sweeps the room.

"Please, Frederick, heed my advice in this. Faw old friendship's sake, let me have my say."

"Very well, but I can assure you, you are wasting your breath."

"I have grown ta know Jude ovah the years. He is an intelligent young man, and Baltimore would afford him a chance ta develop skills that would suhve him well in life. I am simply askin you ta give him a chance. I would think you would want him and Ish both ta learn skills that would elevate them ta a position beyond what slaves of more ordinary parentage…"

Frederick's head snaps up. "Whatever are you implying?"

Bette sighs and walks back to her chair. She forces herself to sit though the position puts her at a disadvantage. "May we please dispense with the subtahfuge? I have been aware faw some time who Minda's children ah. I knew before Abby knew. Bless her heart, she thought they b'longed ta Clarence, and I had ta endure her struggle with not tellin me faw years knowin the whole time you were their fathah."

"How dare you!" Frederick's face is as flushed as the rust cravat he wears around his neck. He is not overly surprised Bette knows of what she speaks, but voicing the connection goes against social etiquette—a code, of sorts, one all Southern genteel live by.

"How dare you, Frederick?" Bette asks quietly. "We both know Abby knew in the end, and we both know what a toll the knowledge took on her mental state."

"I am going to have to ask you to leave now."

He turns his back on her once again, pours himself another whiskey, and downs it. He picks up the decanter to pour himself his third drink within an hour, but the decanter flies out of his hand and shatters on the floor. Bette gasps and jumps to her feet, but she is not as surprised as Frederick. She has become accustomed to such displays in her own home. It is as if the container has been ripped from his hand by an outside force. The temperature in the room is so cold he can no longer ignore it. He whirls and stares at Bette who is clutching her shawl to her and shaking. He doesn't know if she is reacting to the chill, fear, or both. Frederick himself is trembling.

"I cannot do what you ask," he almost whispers.

"You must." Bette's voice is strong, and he decides the woman is not afraid in the least. She appears determined.

"Tell whom you like, Bette. I will not be blackmailed, regardless of your and Jessie's efforts to harm me. Even if what you say is true, no one in this town will care. Half the slave owners I know have bastard offspring by their darkies. No one cares."

"How well I know. I grew up with my own sistah, though heaven fuhbid I evah mention her. I know without a doubt the treatment of your own children as chattel is reprehensible. At least my fathah manumitted my sistah. He had some decency."

"Your temerity knows no bounds, Mrs. Stiles. Even if I wanted to free one of my slaves, I could not. Surely you know manumittance takes the permission of the legislature in Georgia. Even if they thought the children were mine, the offspring always follow the condition of the mother. Manumittance is a dangerous practice. Our laws prevent it for a reason. I have no intention of seeking their approval."

"You know as well as I do the law is often not enforced. If Jude were stayin in Savannah, he might face obstacles. They will nevah go aftah him in Maryland if you have given him puhmission and freedom. And he is in Maryland. The othahs are on their way back, but he refused ta come. He fears you will do ta him what you did ta Dovie. He will run if you try ta bring him back.

"Now I will go, Frederick, but not before I say somethin I hoped I would not have ta say—somethin Jessie has implied she will disclose if necessary. Puhhaps you think there is no one she can tell who will make a difference. I assure you a lettah from her would certainly catch the attention of your mothah-in-law. She and I fear what the disclosure would do ta Mrs. Middleton's relationship with her acknowledged granddaughtahs, but we also agree the lives of *all* your children ah important, regardless of their color. I would think you of all people would agree."

Bette pulls her shawl even closer around her shoulders. "I will let myself out."

She attains the front entryway before Frederick stops her. "Wait," he says. "I don't know what you think you know, but any story you might concoct would not be deemed credible. People are already talking about your state of mind, and I could easily apprise my mother-in-law of your mental frailty since your husband's death."

"Ah those the tactics you used with Abby? Was the threat of institutionalizing her one more nail you drove inta her coffin? Clarence tried ta make me and othahs doubt my sanity. True, you might get your mothah-in-law ta say she believes you, but there will always be a grain of doubt. Don't you imagine she wondahs about the light shade of Daisy and Jude now that she has met them. And my word, whethah in written form or straight from my lips, will not be as easily dismissed as Jessie's might. I still have relatives and acquaintances who value my association. An effaht ta disparage me or my name would be a slight on theirs. They would not appreciate your slandah though it would bothah me little. You, on the othah hand, care a great deal about what your associates think. You ah like Clarence in that, but in this circumstance, even I think you should be concerned. Make no mistake, right or wrong, you will be destroyed in this town. If you plan ta continue ta do business and be held in the high regawd you have become accustomed to, and if you want your children, those you acknowledge, ta be unaffected by your actions or your past, you will do the right thing."

Seeing the raw fear on Frederick's face, Bette's tone softens. "I wish you no hahm, and I certainly wish your children none, but right is right. Jude has stayed behind. I ask you ta free him, and if not now, I ask you ta do the same faw Ish when he reaches adulthood. I hope Mattie will someday do right by Daisy. Since she owns the girl now, I know of no way ta force your hand without tellin Mattie. So, if you will let Jude go now and agree ta do the same faw Ish when he is grown, if you will promise not ta mistreat your othah slaves because of this, we will pretend we nevah had this convahsation. You have until tamorrah aftahnoon ta make a decision."

Bette opens the door and is gone before Frederick can respond. Her quick departure is for the best since he can think of nothing to say. Though the time is barely past noon, he climbs the stairs and enters his bedroom. He takes off his shoes, lies on the bed, and pulls the covers over him. He closes his eyes, but his mind will not still. After tossing for well over an hour, he rises, puts his shoes back on, and goes back to his office. The piece of stationery lies waiting for him, but he has a much different letter to write than the one he has started. He tears the sheet of paper into small pieces and takes them to the fireplace where he delays until the last word is ash. He returns to his desk where he starts anew.

Freeing Jude and refusing payment for him take a mere ten minutes, most of the time spent admonishing Jessie to save every cent she can for he will no longer offer her help of any kind. He tells her he will reject any future communication, and he hopes she is pleased with the decisions she has made. He instructs her to send Minda, Lew, and Ish home immediately if she has not already done so. After not signing the letter at all, he creates two documents of manumittance, one effective immediately, one effective six years from the date. He encloses the first with the letter and addresses the envelope to Jessie. The second, he appends with a sheet of paper on which he has written, "As you wish. I have sent paperwork to Baltimore." He stuffs the document giving Ish his freedom at age eighteen with the note into an envelope. He thinks of posting the letter and delivering the other to Bette himself, but he cannot stand the thought of having to make conversation with anyone he might meet. He finds Deke and instructs him to do his errands. After ridding himself of the offending missives, he goes back to the parlor where he walks around the mess the broken decanter and sticky liquid make on the floor. He finds another bottle of whiskey, drops into one of the chairs, and proceeds to get sloppy drunk for the first time in his life.

Chapter 40

A Complication

Baltimore to Savannah—1848

Minda realizes she is carrying Quent's child before she leaves Baltimore. Because she would be away from the master, she had seen no reason to bring the Queen Anne's Lace seeds from the plants Mammy grows for her to prevent more children. In Savannah, she chewed them faithfully every morning. Once she had started slipping out to be with Quentin, she could think of no way to attain the seeds. She had taken her chances, and now she would have to face the consequences.

Minda considers not seeing Quentin the last three days of her stay. She fears he will understand what the widening of her waistline means. Unwilling to squander the little time they have left, she has not been strong enough to stay away, but she need not have worried. Because Quentin has never been married and never had personal contact with an expectant woman, he hasn't made the connection. She is glad he is spared the knowledge, for the thought of having his own child would have put foolish ideas into his head—given him hopes that could never be fulfilled. If there were a way to remain in Baltimore long enough to give birth, she tells herself she would leave the child behind with Quent. There is no doubt in her mind he would welcome the child. As a free man, his offspring would be considered free if no one could prove the mother a slave. But she must return soon or Frederick will come after her. Delaying will not endanger her alone; it would bring Frederick's wrath down on all of them. Jude would have to leave, and there would be no chance of Jessie's plan working. Minda does what she deems best. She leaves him determined he should never know of his son or daughter. She considers keeping the information from him both a cruelty and a gift.

On the morning of the fourth day after Jude's declaration of independence, Minda, Lew, and Ish rise early to get on the road. They have said farewell to Quentin the night before, and now Minda wishes she hadn't insisted he stay away. She longs to kiss again the only real lover she has ever had. Jude, Jessie, and Diana are there to see them off. She hugs her son long and hard. When she makes contact with Jessie, she stands back, startled, then quietly places her hand on Minda's stomach. Minda smiles sadly and shakes her head to let Jessie know her discovery is not to be mentioned.

The travelers are one week into the six-week wagon ride home when Minda begins to spend the first hour of daylight throwing up. After four more days of the same, Lew, a father, recognizes the signs though Quentin had not.

"Whut youse gonna tell da massah?" he asks one morning while the two of them sit on the wagon seat. Ish is in the back trying to teach his bird to say "Call me Cotton."

"I doan plan ta tell him nothin?"

"Youse think he ain gonna notice?"

"I hope not. Sides, ain much I can do bout it now."

Though Ish, thinking his mother ill, asks if they shouldn't try to get her some help, Lew doesn't mention her condition again. Neither does he avoid rough spots in the road or relieve her of any of her chores. Minda decides he thinks she would be better off to arrive in Savannah no longer expecting. He may be right, but Minda wants this child in a way she never wanted the others. She cannot love another more than the three children she has, but this is the first who will come from a union she desired. He or she will give her something of the man she had to leave behind. She hopes she can persuade the master the baby was conceived after her return, though this child is bound to be darker than his or her siblings.

By the fourth week on the road, the morning sickness stops, but she can no longer pretend she can keep her condition from Frederick. Even if he cannot tell by looking at her fully clothed, he will certainly know if he comes to her. And if he does not lie with her, he can have no doubt she has been with someone else. Already afraid of what their reception will be once they arrive without Jude, she is terrified when she thinks of him discovering she has been carrying on with someone besides him. Though he has never stated she was to have no other relationships, she is his slave, his property, in all ways. She cannot imagine him not being angry about her showing up swollen with child when she had been sent to Baltimore to improve her skills. The fact they were all sent away to make it easier to sell Dovie will make no difference. He will not be expecting this development.

"Lew," she tells her brother, "You an Mammy best try ta talk da massah inta bringing Dovie home. I doan think he be too pleased with me."

"Dat probly da truff. You best stay ouddah da way til aftah we tawk ta him."

If I can…, Minda thinks.

Minda is granted a reprieve when they arrive late one afternoon to find Cressa,

Deke, Lizzy, and Ben. Frederick is not there. Lizzy runs to the kitchen to get her mother, and soon Lew is attacked from all sides. He grabs Cressa by the waist and swings her in a circle. When he comes to a stop, both his children grab him from behind. Only Ben stands apart.

"Whar Jude?" he asks.

"He ain comin home, Ben. He stayin in Baltimoe, God willin, or he off somewhere we hope the massah nevah find him."

Minda takes him in her arms, and in spite of his ten years, he sobs loudly. The noise stops the reunion Lew and his family are having and brings Ish to their side. Minda lets him cry while Ish pats him awkwardly on the shoulder.

"It goan be awright, Ben. Jude doin whut he wanse. An Mammy an Lew an Mama goan try ta tawk the massah inta bringin yo mama home," Ish tells him.

Minda shakes her head at her son, but the warning is too late. Ben pushes out of her arms. "You thinks da massah lissen ta you? You thinks he buys Mama back?"

It hurts Minda to see the hope in his eyes. She wants to promise him Dovie will come home, but a failure will be even harder on him.

"I doan think so, Ben. We gonna try, bu the massah kin be a hawd man. Once he make up his mind, he hawdly evah change it."

Ben's face crumples again, and Ish thrusts his bird in the boy's face to distract him.

"Ben, meet Cotton. I find him on the boat goin ou ta Baltimoe. I tryin' ta teach him ta talk."

Ben's face straightens. "Kin I hole him?"

"If he let you. Hold out yo ahm."

Cotton caws, causing Ben to smile. The bird hops from Ish's arm to Ben's, and Minda sighs. He cannot be distracted every minute of the day.

Whut happen ta hes laig?" Deke asks.

"Why doan you hep Lew unload an Cressa an me go see bout gittin some food on the table. Aftah you eat, Ish kin tell you bout Cotton, an you kin play with him long you wants ta."

"I hep you an Mama in da kitchen," Lizzy says.

"No," Minda tells her, "they needs yo help with the unloadin."

She turns to Cressa and the two women hug. Cressa's eyes reveal shock when they break away from each other.

"Youse wid…" Cressa begins, but she stops when Minda glares at her. "Come on in da kitchen an less ketch up a bit fo da othahs comes in."

Minda follows her into the kitchen that has been her workplace since Miss Abby died. She enjoys no happiness at being home. The child in her womb and the ache in her chest are all that remains of the happiest months of her life. She is relieved to see Cressa has food prepared. At least she won't have to cook, bone tired as she is.

"Set yosef down a bit. How faw long you thinks you be?"

"Bout three month, I guess."

"Whut da massah goan say?"

"That the first thing your man acks, an I tell you what I tell him. I doan know what he say or do, an it too late ta be worryin on it."

Cressa takes both of Minda's hands in hers. "Oh, Gul, whut dis worl comin to?

Dovie goan; Jude goan; an youse wid chile. Da massah be sour as bile. Seem lack nothin goan be da same roun hyur evah agin."

"No, nothin ain gonna be the same, bu I ain much carin bout what the massah think othah than I pray he done with the sellin. Sholly he is cause he have ta have some uh us left ta do fo him an the missies. He mabe want ta git rid uh me when he find ou da shape I in, bu I doan think he sell me aftah all the trouble ta teach me ta cook an sew. I plans ta stay ouddah his sight as much as I kin."

"You ain worryin on him sellin da chile youse carryin?"

Cressa has spoken what she hasn't allowed herself to think.

"If he try, he have real trouble on his hands." She changes the subject. "How Ben doin since Dovie been goan?"

"You sees how he be. Cryin one minute, smilin da nex. Him still a chile, an dat hep, bu him lost as kin be. I hyur em cryin at night. I hopin him be bettah now Ish back."

"Mabe he should stay with us fo awhile. Mabe the bird an Ish be good fo him."

The others join them, and the meal is a celebration in spite of those not there.

Cressa relates the news of Rob's departure and eventual marriage, then tells them the master has gone to Virginia to meet his new grandchild. Mattie has had a boy. He will be home soon with the girls and Mammy.

"Da massah woan be bringin Mizz Ella home," Lew says. Minda and he tell them of Ella's nighttime escape and marriage to Eliot Gordon.

"Good Lawd, no wondah da massah in a tizzy!" Cressa says. "I sho hope Mizz Ella be stayin wharevah she gits off ta, cause wid er an Massah Rob goan, dat be less work fo me an da boys. Dovie be dancin a jig!"

Mention of Dovie is like a cold bucket of water thrown over the group. Bile rises in Minda's throat though she hasn't vomited for weeks now. Ben begins to cry again and stops only after Minda invites him home with Ish and her for the night. Deke asks if he can come too, and since there is no one upstairs to attend to, Minda allows it. She invites Lizzy, as well, to give Lew and Cressa a night in their cabin alone. Lizzy whines she wants to stay with her papa, but Cressa reminds her there will be plenty of time with her Papa now he is home. Cressa gathers up a bag of food in case they get hungry later and includes some eggs for breakfast. Cressa hugs Minda and whispers a thank you in her ear.

Minda has mixed emotions when she walks into the cabin. The small house has been her home for many years. Though she has many pleasant memories of her time there with the boys, they are reminders of Jude's absence. He will never call the place home again.

"Look, Mama," Ish says, "The walls been painted, an look like you got a new bed!

An they's new chairs!"

"An look at dis flo," Deke adds. The floor has been re-planked. "You kin hawdly see da cracks."

They are right. The floors have been replaced with better wood that has been sanded and varnished. The children rush to Ish's room to see if there are changes there. They are soon back in mass, Ish reporting a freshly stuffed mattress and the same resurfaced floors and painted walls.

Minda puts aside the supplies for breakfast but places the food for later out on the table. She first sits on the side of the bed, then lies down to stretch out. The cover is made of a yellow, blue, and red blossom print woven with a bright green vine with leaves. Though new, the spread neither looks nor smells fresh. She wonders what the realization would have made her feel months ago. Now she considers evidence of Frederick's own dalliances inconvenient and cause for additional laundry.

"Ish, you need ta draw us a fresh bucket uh water, then the bunch uh you ah on yo own. You woan haftah be too quiet cause I goin ta sleep in yo room tonight. Eat what you want on the table, bu stay out uh breakfast."

"I go fo da watah," Deke says. "Ish boun ta be wore ou from da trip."

Minda takes the top spread off the bed and replaces it with one she made while at Jessie's.

"Lizzy, climb in with me when you git sleepy," she says, then she crawls under the quilt in the boys' room. It is clean but smells dusty. She arises, opens the window, holds the quilt out the opening and shakes it a couple of times, then crawls back under it. This room has been painted, too, the odor present but not overpowering.

Minda places her hand upon her stomach and tries to draw comfort from the child who has not yet begun to move. Tears form in spite of her efforts to rid herself of sad thoughts. Dovie is gone; Jude is gone; and she is with child. Daisy is far away, and the master will be home soon. The changes are too much for her. She hopes Lizzy does not come to bed soon and catch her crying like a child. She must be strong for her family now. She has no idea how Frederick is going to react to Jude staying behind because she has had no way to communicate with Jessie or Bette. She decides she will go to Bette's first thing in the morning to find out if she has received any news.

The journey home had been hard and uncomfortable, the one benefit being she had fallen into a deep sleep from exhaustion each night beneath the wagon. Now, though her body hurts from weeks on the road and she has a pounding headache, she is unable to control her thoughts. The mound beneath her hand is a reminder Quentin will never know of his child's existence. If not for Mammy and Ish, she might have done what Jude did. She could have convinced Quent to run away somewhere far from the Barrets to make a life like the one they enjoyed in Baltimore. She allows herself to dream of him and a place of their own where all of them are there: Ish, Jude, Daisy, Mammy, even Dovie and Ben, Lew and his family. She lets the vision play out until she pictures Quent with a baby on his arm, smiling the smile that had first drawn her to him. She has gone too far. She covers her head with her arms and hums a hymn. She fears she will lose her sanity if she cannot block the thoughts trying to split her forehead open. She wonders if a head can actually explode from within. If so, she wishes hers would hurry up and put her out of her misery.

Chapter 41

Comeuppance

Savannah, Georgia—1848

It is the end of November before Frederick arrives with Mammy and Maxie. Though Ella is not with him, he is happier, for he had the opportunity to see her before she and the man she has married departed for an extended honeymoon abroad. Though he will never like Eliot Gordon, he must admit she has married well in regards to pecuniary matters. The knave has a father with plenty of money, one willing to share with his son and new bride. Unlike Frederick, he is pleased with the union. Frederick did not risk angering the man by airing his own views.

From seeing Ella off, his next stop was Hickory Grove where he had found Mattie still convalescing after the birth of his namesake, a handsome little man with a strong constitution. Her confinement provided opportunity alone with her to discuss Ella, among other topics, and Mattie's calm demeanor and positive outlook have helped him regain much of his optimistic perspective. He is still angry about being coerced into setting Jude free, but he has even come to see the benefit of his absence. With both Rob and Ella gone, he will need less help. He allows himself to admit he has not been comfortable in Jude's presence for some time. Something in the boy's demeanor reminds him of the Island and all the hostility he left behind. There was always the chance his influence could prove detrimental to his brother and the other two boys. Now, if he can get this ugly business about Dovie behind him, he can settle down into the pleasant routine he has enjoyed for the last several years.

Frederick has decided not to tell any of them about Dovie's death, even Rob. He could not believe his eyes when he read the letter from his son conveying the desire to buy Dovie back and take her with him to Texas. He claimed he had given the situation much thought and he was sure he and Eleanor could find a role for her in the new household considering they would be far from town and distractions. He had gone as far as to plan to wed her to someone there who might make her less restless. He had also offered to buy Ben if his father thought he could do without him.

If the least sentimental member of the family was shaken by Dovie's fate, he knew he could not possibly tell any of them the truth. He wrote Rob what he has told Mrs. Middleton and the girls—he is in communication with her buyer and has hopes of getting her back. He will wait a couple of weeks before alleging she has contracted some illness in her new environment and died. Though this will not please them, he decides the explanation is better than them blaming him for putting her in a place where she was killed in such a gruesome manner. The story will also put an end to the nagging to have her returned to them.

The voyage back from Virginia is tedious but otherwise uneventful. Though Mammy has appeared sullen, he has spent little time with her. His peace has been relatively uninterrupted. When he arrives at the harbor, instead of sending for Lew, he goes to the warehouse and instructs one of his workers to bring a buckboard to take them home. The conveyance is not the manner in which he wants himself or his daughter to be seen riding through town, but he decides the convenience outweighs the risk of being observed and found lacking.

The minute they pull into the courtyard, Lew, along with his children, are there to greet them. He takes the reins while Frederick steps down and offers his hand to Maxie who is delighted to be home. Mammy is about to jump to the ground when Deke intervenes and lifts her easily from the wagon. Frederick is glad to see how much the boy has grown. He will have no problem taking over Jude's previous responsibilities.

After giving instructions to Deke and Ben, he starts for the house. He is startled to feel something drop upon his head to be followed by several things hitting him. Being close to the balcony, he thinks someone is throwing something from there. He glances up. The sound of the raucous crowing causes him to look higher. Alighting at the attic window is what he would swear is the same irritating crow that has become a nuisance at his bedroom window. The bird stares straight at him as if trying to convey some message with its incessant squawking. He looks down and finds pebbles on otherwise bare earth. He turns in a circle, but there is no one else around. He shakes his head. Next thing he knows, he'll be imagining the crow is dropping rocks on his head!

From there, he goes directly to the kitchen. He has missed Minda's company, and not just the service she performs for him. Before she left, he had actually gotten used to talking with her about matters with which he was uncomfortable speaking to anyone else. He knows she listened closely, in part, for any mention of Daisy. He hopes the news he has to impart—Daisy has chosen a young man in his daughter's household and has married—will help her get beyond Dovie's departure. Daisy's is a fortunate situation with the boy living on site. She will have an arrangement similar to that of Lew and his family, and he imagines the information will bring Minda peace of mind. He plans to look in on her long enough to tell her she needs to get away for a couple of hours this afternoon to meet him at her place, the one he hopes she was pleased to find newly refurbished.

Minda is working at the counter with her back to him when he enters. She doesn't turn. He is surprised she has not learned of their arrival and rushed out to see her mother, if not the rest of them. She must be truly angry about Dovie.

"Minda," he calls from the doorway, "have you not heard us arrive?"

She glances over her shoulder and smiles. "Yes, Massah, I jus tryin ta finish up da meal cause I knows you probly not eat since breakfast."

Minda is more attractive than he remembers, her face fuller, her eyes brighter.

He crosses the room and takes her by the shoulders and turns her toward him. Her eyes register surprise, and if he didn't know better, fear. It is true he has rarely touched her anywhere other than Yamacraw, at least not since the early days when he had first taken her upstairs in the house he shared with Luella. Thoughts of those first encounters stoke the fire already building, and he draws her forward and runs both hands down her hips, pulling her into his groin. Face to face, the full length of his torso meets hers. She registers the change of expression the same moment he recognizes the change in her body. He pushes her slowly from him and looks down.

"Are you with child, Minda?"

If there could be any chance the child was gotten by him, Minda's expression dispels it. She is not merely uneasy, she is terrified.

"How could you!" he says, pushing away from her hard enough to send her backward into the counter. "And here I was worried about how you would feel about Dovie. You are as bad as she is!"

"Please, Massah, it not like I doin somethin wrong. I jus a slave, an I doan think I mean mo than…"

"You don't," Frederick says, "but you had a job where I am concerned, and you have sullied yourself with no telling what other vileness. Now I will have the inconvenience of finding something else for you to do or selling you to someone who won't care what damaged goods he is getting."

"I kin still cook, Massah, an I kin sew…"

"But I do not know if I can stand to look at you," he says.

Minda is surprised at what appears to be hurt in the man's eyes. For a second she experiences something like regret, but then she remembers Dovie.

"Mabe I do wrong," she says, "but I dint til I find ou you sold Dovie. I know then you doan care bout a one uh us you sell her ta some plantation like a mule or a cow or somethin."

Frederick has walked as far as the door, but he turns back to her. With eyes as cold and as lifeless as an alligator's, his voice even and hard, he says, "Dovie is dead. She ran one too many times, and the dogs tore her apart."

Without waiting for a reaction, he leaves the house and starts walking. He walks to his office, unlocks the door, and sits at his desk. He has no intention of doing any work. He simply wants a place to be alone. Some time later, his hunger registers. He leaves the office and goes back to his house. He finds Mammy in the courtyard having what sounds like a conversation with the same damn crow. In her hand she holds something shiny, and to his disbelief, she appears to be thanking the crow for it. He asks her to send Deke to him, and though she doesn't acknowledge him in any way, Deke finds him within a few minutes. He asks him to carry a meal up to him. When he brings it, he says, "Take Ish and Ben to Ish's cabin. You are to clean out all their personal belongings. Ask Lew to help you decide how to best accommodate them in the quarters."

He cannot yet say Minda's name. He thinks of Ish and remembers the change this means for him, but it cannot be helped. Sadly, the boy will have to suffer for the sins of his mother.

Frederick leaves for the rest of the afternoon. He does not want to be in the house with his own servants since they all surely now know of Dovie's death. He goes straight to bed when he returns. Mammy's crow is sitting on the window sill. He shoos it away, but the bird comes back. He prepares for bed alone, and though he would like to take advantage of the cool night, he slams the window shut. He can see the bird still there, looking for all the world like it is monitoring his every move. He goes to his bureau and takes his pistol from a drawer. He would like to kill the bird, but he has become superstitious about it. He sleeps with the gun close to hand as he will continue to do for the rest of his time lived among his slaves.

Chapter 42
Crinolines and Wagon Wheels

Savannah, Georgia—1852

What Frederick meant to be a punishment turns out to be Minda's family's salvation. She has spent the last four years in the cabin with her mother, Lew, Cressa, and little Rylee. Mammy, Minda, and Rylee sleep downstairs while Lew and Cressa have the upstairs. Lizzy has moved into the mansion where she has become Maxie's constant companion, and all three boys sleep above the stable. Ish and Deke's company are as much comfort to Ben as Mammy's has been to Minda. The other boys have helped fill the void Jude's absence has left in Ish's life. Despite the losses, the family has settled into a reasonably content existence of labor six days a week with Sunday free to enjoy one another's company.

Though Ish sleeps with the boys, he spends at least an hour every evening with his little sister as he has since she came squalling into the world assisted by Mammy and Cressa. He thinks her the cutest, brightest child he has ever seen. Minda has not reminded him he has been around few babies. She agrees Rylee is special. She already has her father's contagious smile and cheerful demeanor. She is with either Minda in the kitchen or Mammy in the garden throughout the day. Rylee has even found favor with Mammy's crow, the only human besides Mammy she seems to like. The child has a stash of buttons, light colored pebbles, and bits of shiny objects with which Missy has gifted her. Mammy jokes she has been replaced by a pint-sized piece of work, and she is not sure how she likes it. Cotton has not been easily won over. Rylee uses Missy's offerings to entice Cotton to her and cannot understand why Ish's bird favors him over her.

Because Frederick no longer has anything to do with Minda personally, the child has also avoided his attention except in regard to her name. Unlike many owners, Frederick has always allowed the slaves to name their children. When he found out Minda had called her Jessa, he had sent word the child's name was to be changed immediately. In defiance, she had chosen Rylee, a name he would have forbidden as well had he known its origin.

The child's hugs and uninhibited laughter have been a balm to the whole family. Minda knows all too well life can change her soon enough. She would do anything possible to protect her last born from the hardships her condition will bring her.

Minda remembers Daisy was once much like Rylee. Her first born had managed to retain an optimism up until the time she left with Miss Mattie, so maybe Rylee can. She hopes Daisy hasn't lost her happiness. She hasn't seen her for a little over a year, and then it had been for a brief time as she, Mattie, and her two children had stopped in on their way to visit Rob's family in Texas. At the time, Daisy had not been herself as she had had to leave her own two children back in Virginia. She still claimed Mattie was a good mistress, but she was not enamored with her master. She blamed him for the separation from her own two girls, one of them named Mindy for her. Minda had cried when she heard the baby's name. Daisy had been shocked to find out she had a baby sister. Minda found no need to explain how her existence had come about.

It has been so long since Daisy and Jude left, the ache has dulled. She hears often of Jude who writes her. Pearl or Cook brings his letters to church because she is no longer allowed to associate with Bette. At least Minda has the peace of knowing one of her children has a happy life. He includes news of Quentin, and she sends messages to him. Though Jude has tried to teach his boss enough reading and writing to better conduct his business, Quentin's interest has been more with the numbers and ledgers Jude has helped him with. Jude has graduated from an apprentice to a partner, and it is a comfort to her to picture them working side by side every day. Jude returns to Jessie's home nightly since he and Diana wed four months ago. Now Minda has the pleasure of imagining the young couple in the comparative luxury of Jessie's home, the place she had been happiest.

Jude's life has become more than she could have dreamed for him. Bette told her Jessie and she had persuaded Frederick to free Jude.

They had never shared exactly how. Too, Bette has promised her Ish's prospects are also favorable, and Minda has kept the knowledge tucked close. She has not shared it with Ish.

Like the longing for her children, hers for Quentin has dulled, but the attraction remains. Their reunion is as possible in her mind as one with Dovie in this life would be. She sends messages to Quentin of a benign nature, but she has told Jude he is to say nothing of Rylee, and she has explained why. Though Jude disagrees with her logic, he has kept her secret.

Ish has grown into a strapping young man, one taller and leaner than his brother or his father. Minda informs Jude of the changes, both physical and mental, though she assumes he has figured out the latter on his own. Ish reads everything he can get his hands on, and includes a letter to his brother with hers. He practices his writing as often as their supplies allow. They have saved every scrap of paper that comes into the house, either through the kitchen or other deliveries. They cut the findings into some facsimile of stationery, and pen their words with the ink Lizzy has managed to siphon out of the master's inkwell or homemade ink they have squeezed from various berries. Those with a goose, duck, or chicken feather as a quill have served them well. Since Ish has taken the teaching of Deke and Ben upon himself, supplies have become more treasured than ever.

Though Frederick gives every indication he remembers nothing of the relationship he shared with Minda, he has increasingly shown more interest in Ish. He has even had special shoes made to accommodate Ish's backward-facing foot, and Ish has worked hard to make the affliction as unnoticeable as possible. Like Daisy and Rylee, Ish has somehow retained a positive outlook. Jude's success in freeing himself must have given him encouragement, for he gives every indication of preparing himself for a future beyond slavery though Minda has told him nothing of the hints of such from Bette. In fact, she has even resorted to lying to keep Ish from knowing what she said, for she thinks his circumstances as they are will be easier to accept if the promise proves to be empty.

One evening he had come into the cabin and said, "Mama, Massah said somethin strange today. He said, 'If not fo the meddlin uh Bette Stiles, I put you ta work down at the warehouse. I think you could run the place someday.' What you think he mean, Mama?"

"I doan know, Son," she'd lied. "He the massah. He want you ta work at the warehouse, he the one ta say so."

"Sometimes I think you keepin things from me," he'd said. "An you foget I ain no chile no mo."

"You still a chile ta me," she'd answered, and after looking at her for a couple of moments longer, he had shaken his head and given up.

On a beautiful first Sunday in June in the year 1852, Minda and her family do what they do every Sunday unless one of them is sick. They rise early, eat breakfast in the servant's kitchen, and then walk to the Second African Baptist Church where they stay until about one o'clock, depending on how long-winded Reverend Bryan is. Today, he is unusually brief, and they are all thrilled to be back at the house earlier than usual and enjoying the lunch Minda had prepared on Saturday. All are looking forward to a full afternoon ahead of them.

"I considerin takin Rylee fo a walk along the river," Ish says. "Anybidy feel like joinin us?"

"I promise Louisa I go with her fo a walk," Deke says.

"You promise me you go oyster diggin," Ben says, his brows forming a dark line of disapproval above his eyes.

"I did, but tween you an Louisa, I goan have ta choose Louisa. She be a sight bettah ta look at an much softah ta hold."

"Youse bettah go wid Ben an foget bout Louisa. Ise tole you they's sayin er massah gonna marry her ta his boy Samuel," Lew says.

"Ole Sam ain got her yet, an she wantin ta go walkin with me. It be mo than mean uh me ta keep her waitin."

Deke pushes back from the table and leaves both Lewis and Cressa frowning at him.

"Dat boy think he grown," Cressa says.

"He jus bout be," Mammy says. "I hab bof Lew an Minda da time Ise hes age."

"Ben, you want ta walk with Rylee an me?" Ish asks.

"Come wid us, Ben!" Rylee cries from her favorite spot in Ish's lap. "Wese have fun!"

"Guess I might as well, seein I ain got nothin else ta do."

"Chilren, wy doan you wawk ovah in da square. They's sayin we needs ta stay off da walk cause some uh us be crowdin da wite foke on theys wawk," Mammy says.

"We stay out of their way, I promise," Ish says. "Mamma, you want ta go?"

Minda is torn. She would love to have some time to catch up on tasks she needs to do, like the bag of mending beside her bed. But an outing with Ish and Rylee is much more enticing, so she decides the chores can wait.

"Sho, I go with you. Let me wash Rylee face an git a wrap."

"Mys face ain duhty, Mama," Rylee objects, but she smiles when Ish says he'll clean her pretty face. She trails along behind him when he takes Cotton to a corner of the corn crib where he has constructed a cage of young willow oak branches. Neither Rylee nor Cotton like him being left behind, but it is almost impossible for Ish to enjoy a walk while being stopped every little bit to answer questions from other servants about his pet crow. Cotton is especially indignant today, for he has already spent several hours in his cage as he is not allowed to attend church. Sunday is Cotton's least favorite day of the week.

The waterfront is almost deserted when they first arrive. They meet mostly servants like themselves out enjoying the one day they have off. All are dressed in their Sunday best, and they exchange pleasantries with those they know and nod and say howdy to those they don't. Ish and Minda each have one of Rylee's hands, and she swings between them, her bare feet bouncing off the boardwalk to gain maximum height. Ben walks behind them, pleased to be there in spite of Deke's defection. The foursome walks for over an hour until Rylee becomes tired and asks Ish to carry her.

"Let me carry you," Ben says. "Ish an yo mama be woah ou from swingin you."

"No, I wanse Ish," Rylee whines.

"Then come on up here." Ish swings her up into his arms.

"She gettin too big ta be carried," Minda says.

"She still jus a little mite of a thing. I be carryin this gal til some man come an take her away from me."

"No day woan!" Rylee says. "You woan lets em."

They all laugh. "You right bout that!" Ish says.

The traffic of buggies and wagons have picked up since they have arrived. Minda enjoys seeing the finely dressed people out for their afternoon rides. Some are alighting and strolling in the same direction they are going. Far down the walk a group of white people she doesn't recognize walks toward them.

"We best git off ta the side. Look at the skirts on those women. One of them take up nigh on the whole walkway."

"We have a bit," Ben says. "We git off fo they git here."

Before coming even with the group, Minda, Ben, and Ish holding Rylee step off the walkway on the side closest to the river. Two ladies in bright spring dresses over voluminous crinolines hold the arms of young escorts dressed equally as stylishly. As soon as they have passed, Ish, holding Rylee, steps back onto the sidewalk.

"Look!" Rylee cries and points at a phaeton passing on the street. It holds a man and a young white girl about her age. Rylee waves wildly at the little girl. Meantime, the last young lady in the crinoline skirt has stopped abruptly to see what Rylee has called out about. Ish is unprepared for the sudden stop, and that, coupled with Rylee twisting in his arms, throws him off balance. He accidently steps on the lady's skirt, and she lets out a shriek that prompts her escort to turn and grab the floundering Ish by the shoulder.

"We've told you dawkies ta stay off the boardwalks!" he yells. "Now look what you've done!"

In his anger, he throws Ish from him. Unfortunately, he propels Ish, still holding Rylee, toward the street. Both Minda and Rylee scream, and Ben rushes forward to help. Ish's head is turned at an angle at which he can see an oncoming farm wagon filled with a white family. Still flailing, he manages to toss the crying Rylee toward Ben who breaks her fall. Ish is not so lucky. He manages to twist his upper body back toward the walkway, but his troublesome foot will not cooperate. He falls exposing both legs to the oncoming conveyance. He manages to pull his good foot out of the way, but the front wheel catches his left and drags him under the wagon. There is no way the wagon can stop, and the witnesses on the sidewalk scream in horror as Ish's body is twisted and mangled beneath the metal wheels.

Minda falls to her knees, but she cannot stay there. She weakly rises and takes the sobbing Rylee from Ben who then rushes into the street. All traffic has stopped, and people are hurrying to the wagon to see what has happened. Minda places Rylee on the river side of the sidewalk and tells her not to move. Rylee tries to cling to her, but she pushes her from her and scolds, "I'm tellin you not to move!"

Unused to her mother's harsh tone, Rylee obeys and sits crying in the sand while Minda runs back across the sidewalk. The young man who pushed Ish is loudly telling everyone who will listen the accident is not his fault. Their female companions are being consoled by the other gentleman who has both their faces pressed to his chest to shield them from the grisly scene. Minda finds Ben holding Ish, his upper body cradled in his arms, his lower body dangling awkwardly in the roadway.

"He breathin?" she manages to ask.

"He breathin," Ben whispers, "bu he coughin blood."

"Oh My Sweet Boy," Minda cries and sinks onto the bloody sand. "Give him ta me."

Ish opens his eyes and tries to say something, but the words cannot get past the blood. The left side of his head is an open wound. Minda wipes the blood away, but she stops when her fingers encounter gray matter. She screams as it spills into her hand as she tries to press it back into the cavity.

The man from the wagon asks who they belong to, and as soon as he is told, he casts around among the group for anyone who knows a Frederick Barret. Apparently, he finds someone, for Frederick appears. He has to push through a crowd to get to Minda who is still sitting in the middle of the street, rocking Ish, crooning. He knows immediately the boy is no longer alive. When Frederick tries to take him from her, she yells, "No! Jus leave us be!"

"Minda," he says, "You can't stay here like this. He's gone. We have to take care of him now."

Minda looks into his face ready to do battle, but she is undone by the tears in his eyes. It isn't that it is Frederick; he could have been anyone sharing a fraction of her pain. Slowly she gazes around her. There are several white people looking at what to them is a Sunday afternoon distraction. She focuses on Ben who stands a bit away, pressing the back of Rylee's head into his chest to keep her from seeing the fate of her beloved Ish, tears running down his face. Slowly she relinquishes her child into the arms of the father who has never acknowledged him. It dawns on her that Ish will never know he was to be set free. Or maybe he will. Regardless, Ish is no longer bound. Sadly, she is left behind to cope with the hell of his loss. She does not think she can bear it. She is lifted from the street and taken back to the cabin behind the mansion. She will not remember how she got there or who cleaned her up. She is not aware when Frederick comes to the cabin to check on her or that he tells them to let her rest. She sleeps through several days of laudanum before she awakes to the knowledge she must go on for the child left with her. Ish would not be happy with her if both he and she deserted his sister on the same day. Minda has no choice but to rejoin the living.

On the day Ish dies, Ben goes to the corn crib to check on Cotton. The bird's cries reach him long before he is close. When Ben opens the cage, he flies out and past before Ben can stop him. He races out after him, but the bird has gone mad. He flies circles around the courtyard, his cries joined by those of Dovie's crow. The two carry on until dark, and Ben, at last, gives up. He returns to the cabin to comfort Mammy and explain once again to Deke how Ish's death happened. Finally, he falls into bed to try to acknowledge his own grief, hoping Cotton will wear himself out and fly back to them. He falls asleep to the sound of the mourning crows, but he awakes to silence and no Cotton. Mammy has left the door open for him, but he never returns. Mammy says they should take comfort in his absence. She says his disappearance means he went wherever Ish is, but Ben doesn't believe her. He decides Cotton simply cannot stay in a place where Ish no longer is. Ben knows how he feels.

Chapter 43
Pleasant

Savannah, Georgia—1852

It has been four months since Ish's death, and Minda has refused to go to church every Sunday since. For that reason, Mammy delivers the letter to her. She finds Minda sitting outside of the cabin shelling the black-eyed peas for which Lew traded eggs from Mammy's two hens. A slave rented out to a neighbor brought them from the plantation of his owner. Because the white folks feed them to their livestock, it was easy for him to abscond with a peck. Mammy already has those they shelled yesterday boiling in a kettle in the fireplace. Seasoned with bacon grease taken from the Barrets' kitchen and onions from Mammy's garden, they, along with cornmeal cakes fried in the remaining bacon fat, will make a tasty meal.

"Dose peas sho smells good," Mammy comments.

"They do," Minda agrees, but her words reveal little enthusiasm.

"Ise hopin somethin tastes good ta you, or youse gonna dry up an blows way."

Minda has eaten little since she forced herself out of the stupor she walked around in for weeks after the accident.

Minda doesn't look up from her task until Mammy thrusts the letter under her nose.

"Pearl tells me ta gib dis ta you. Say it from Mizz Jessie."

This is only the second letter she has gotten from Jessie though she has had several from Jude. Mammy is relieved to see a spark of interest in her daughter's eyes.

"Hyur, gib me dose peas. You goes somewhar an reads it, an mabe you feel lack readin it ta da rest uh us at dinnah."

Minda smiles. "Doan I awways read the lettahs ta y'all?"

She rises, takes the letter, and walks into the woods in the extra lot owned by the Barrets. She finds a clear spot under the limb of a live oak tree. The limbs hang so low, the draping Spanish moss curtains the enclosure. The leaves are beginning to turn, and, if Minda could enjoy anything these days, she would appreciate the beauty of her surroundings and the solitude of the moment. Any interest she can generate is for the letter. She hopes to discover how Diana is fairing now she is carrying their first child. She experiences a moment of panic. What if Jessie is writing bad news? Once the unthinkable has happened, one cannot help but expect the worst.

Though both Jessie and Diana try hard to write simply, their letters are difficult for Minda. She has never acquired the joy Jude and Ish derived from reading. Being older, the lessons had been a struggle, and for the same reason, she had less energy and time to read late into the night as they had done. Now that both boys are gone, she has no one to tell her of the books they've read, no one to discuss the correct use of words. Ish had taught Ben and Deke to read and write as time allowed in their shared room before he had died, but neither boy has had access to materials as Jude, Minda, and Ish had. Still, she is thankful she took Bette up on her offer. If she had not, the boys would not have had the opportunity. They would not have been able to communicate with each other, nor would she have had a way to know what is going on in Baltimore.

Today, she sits cross-legged with her skirts tucked around her and spreads the pages flat on the ground. The letter is rather lengthy and printed in neat letters. Minda has not attempted to read script.

Dear Minda,

I pray this note finds you and yours well. All here are healthy and well as they can be while missing Ish and knowing how hard the loss is for you and the family. Diana is doing well. She is carrying high, so we will likely be having a girl. I feel she will be born with no problems to her or her mother.

Minda sighs in relief to find this is not a message of illness or loss. Jessie's prediction of a healthy outcome is a comfort, too, for Jessie has a way of foretelling impending misfortune for those close to her.

After reading the rest of this, I hope you will not think me stranger than you already do. As you may have heard, I am prone to dreams, as I call them, and they appear to be different from those of others. I want to share a dream I am having. When I first had it, I decided it would be silly for me to share the details with you, but the dream comes nightly, and in the past, when I have repeat dreams, I have had to acknowledge there is a reason for them. I feel like I am supposed to take some action. Because the dream is about Ish, I suspect I am meant to share the particulars with you and Jude. Jude claims Ish may be trying to let you know he is in a good place and content. I agree with him, but his companion in the dream has us confused.

Minda struggles with the word *companion*. If Ish were with them, he would have already come to her aid by pronouncing it and offering a definition for Rylee. She sighs when she remembers this letter would not exist if Ish were alive.

In the dream Ish is arm-in-arm with a man I know to be called Pleasant. Actually, the man named Pleasant is leaning on Ish, maybe using him as a crutch, of sorts. The man is a black man, and he is missing one of his legs. I cannot make out what they are saying, and I cannot tell you how I know his name is Pleasant. I just know. They are laughing, and the man moves easily enough though he has a single leg. Ish is about the age he was when he left us.

This is all I can tell you of the dream. Please take comfort by picturing Ish happy where he is. If there is anything real about the dream, it is telling us he is content.

The letter ends with Minda sharing the latest project Jude and Quent are working on, news of Sophia and Gail Howe, but she has nothing about Daisy to impart. Minda sits for a minute and ponders what she has read. She wants to believe Ish is doing well somewhere, but the whole thing about the legless man makes the dream difficult to accept as little more than an oddity. If she didn't know of Jessie's ability to know things others don't, she would certainly dismiss it as silliness.

Unsettled, Minda leaves her hideout and returns to where Mammy is ladling out peas to the family crowded into the cabin. Since Ish's death, they have continued to eat the Sunday meal there as they had when Minda refused to eat at all. Normally, they would take their plates and move out into the yard, but knowing Minda has received a letter from Baltimore, everyone stays inside. Ben and Deke sit with their plates in their hands on the floor; Mammy has the one chair; Cressa, Lizzy, and Rylee sit along the edge of the bed, while Lew takes one of the sticks of wood they sit on and leaves the other for Minda.

"What Mizz Jessie say, Mama?" Rylee asks. She has never met Jessie, but she has learned much about her over the years from those who know her and from the letters her mother reads to them.

"Gib yo Mama da time ta eat fo you go acksin questions."

"I read it now. I ain hungry."

"Youse ain nevah hungry," Mammy grumbles, but she doesn't argue when Minda unfolds the letter and begins to read. When Minda finishes, all are quiet. Finally, Ben breaks the silence.

"Do you think it mean Ish in Heaven?"

All have been listening so attentively, no one notices Mammy has pulled her handkerchief out of her sleeve and is wiping her eyes.

"It mean much mo dan dat," she says, and all eyes turn to her.

"Mammy, you alrigh?" Lizzy asks and moves to sit close to her on the floor.

"I be mo dan alrigh. Ise happiuh dan any uh you can undahstan. Lissen ta me. Ise goan tells you somethin none uh youse knows, less it be Lew. Lew, you membah yo Papa?"

"A lil. I membah him a laughin man. I membah you dancin wile him play da fiddle."

"You recall his name?"

"I fogits til Justice say it back in Vahginny. It Pleas."

"Shawt fo Pleasant," Mammy says. "Him missus an his mama call him Pleasant cuz him awways a smilin wen he jus a chile. Evahbidy jus call him Pleas him git oldah."

No one says a word as they try to comprehend what she is saying.

"An theys anothah thing bout dat dream. Wen Lew be somewhar bout six yeah ole an, Minda, youse bout foe an Dovie naw much mo dan a babe, yo papa choppin cotton an he step on a snake."

"A coppah haid," Lew remembers. "Justice say da snake a coppah haid."

"He kilt it wid da hoe fo he wen on up ta da house an tell da missus. Theys spread nothin lack da Middleton place. It jus a fahm, an da missus git by han ta mouf, an her hab nobidy on da place dat know nuthin bout healin. She po kerosene on da bite, wrap da laig up in a rag, an pray fo da bess. Dat happen da furse pawt uh da week, an da time him comes ta me on Sundy, da whole bottom uh hes laig swole up somethin lack I ain nevah see b'fo or agin."

Mammy is wiping tears. Her own children have rarely seen her cry, and the grandchildren have witnessed her tears once, on the day Ish died.

"I runs ta Mizz Middleton an tells er da shape him in, an her come ta look fo ersef. Wese do mos ub da healin wid herbs an sech, bu her see his laig an sen fo da one wite doctah in dose pawts dat willin ta hep cullad foke.

"Pleas fire hot an ouddah hes haid—tawkin wild. Da missus sen somebidy ta tell Mizz Simmon how bad off her Pleas be an tells her she goin ta try ta save him. Missus tells us ta put him ta bed in da cabin wese stay in, an dat whar da doctah come. Dat wite man git one look at Pleas laig an jus shake hes haid. Him say it probly too late cause they's pison blood runnin up his laig. Dat da only hope be ta cut it clean off."

Deke gasps aloud at the thought, but Mammy continues as if she hasn't heard him.

"Da doc fill him full uh corn whiskey til he ain knowin da worl him in. He singin an mumblin bout aw kine uh mess til the doc commence ta sawin. I doan know whut happen aftah dat cause I took ouddah dare an jus run. I git far nuff way I cain hyur hes screamin, an dat only work wen I covah my haid wid my hans. Wen da screamin stop, I hab a hawd time findin my ways back in da dawk. Pleas sleep on an off faw a day or two wid us pouin da whiskey down him wen da pain git bad. Dint take much cause Pleas nevah a drinkin man.

"Justice take dat laig an bury it in da cullad graveyahd. Pleas git up an git roun an theys sen word ta Mizz Simmon him kin come home somebidy come git him. Her sen back her hab no way ta care faw him an kin Mizz Middleton keep him til him heal up. Ise glad ta hyur it—dat I kin keep him wid me an look aftah him. I scairt theys cain look aftah Pleas lack theys oughtah ovah dare."

Mammy stops talking and stares off into space as if she has forgotten they are there.

"Mama..." Minda finally says.

Mammy's face collapses in on itself. Lizzy puts her hand on her knee. No one speaks.

"In da en, it doan mattah. Da pison move up hes laig an da doc come back an cut agin. Trouble be, he dint lebe nuff room ta tie da stump off an Pleas jus bleed an bleed. We haftah scrape foevah ta git da blood ouddah dat duht flo. So much blood it ovahflow da bucket. Dis time, Pleas jus scream a lil wile. I done make up my mine I wudden goan lebe him agin. Aftah he quit screamin, Ise glad him dint wake up less him kin wake up fo good, an dat dint happen."

All are still sitting with their plates of peas in their laps when Mammy finishes. There is a reverent stillness in the cabin.

"Sose you sees?" Mammy asks.

"What, Mama?"

"Ish be wid yo Papa."

Again, no one talks until Ben stands up and says, "Cotton."

The others blink and look at one another.

"Cotton!" Minda says.

"I tells you dat crows ain no reglar bird," Mammy says. "An Missy ain eithah."

The story Mammy tells them gladdens the hearts of everyone in the room, none more than Minda. She now wholeheartedly believes Jessie is correct. The dream is a message to them, and if Ish and her father have sent the vision night after night, it is wrong for her not to accept it as a gift.

Every Sunday after Minda receives the letter, she takes Rylee and they visit the little graveyard containing the remains of Moses, Jessie's son, Lewis and Cressa's stillborn, and now Ish. Frederick has provided a small stone with the simple engraving *Ishmael, Son of Minda.* If Minda had the means, she would erect something for Dovie though her remains are buried somewhere far away. She badly wants to think of Dovie here with Ish. She finds a large smooth rock, not an easy task in the sandy terrain, and prints Dovie on the surface in the ink she and Ish had scavenged. She repeats the act when the rain and the weather begin to erase the name. She and Rylee will do this for as long as they remain in Savannah.

Chapter 44
A Name of Their Own

Baltimore, Maryland—1852

Jude has worked hard on the day he finds out Ish has died. He is unsuspecting when he finds a letter waiting for him, not from his mother but from Mrs. Stiles. No matter how gently written, no matter how many times he rereads it, the message is the same. His little brother, sweet Ish, whom he still has a hard time picturing as older than the twelve-year-old gangly boy he last saw in Baltimore, is dead. He has died in a grisly manner he will play over and over in his head for years to come while he, the brother who has promised to look after him, is far away and unable to protect him.

Jude is inconsolable. He cannot accept the words of comfort Diana and Jessie ply him with. He cannot leave his bed the next day or for two days after, though Quent appears to tell him grieving himself to death will help no one. He refuses to eat. He is devastated—not only by the news of his death, but by the realization his little brother had been gone for days without him knowing. How can the person whom he had heard come into this world, who had slept beside him for the majority of his life, who understood him better than anyone—even Diana—just be gone? He cannot accept the fact nor can he refute it. When he had learned Dovie had died, he was able to pretend she was still creating havoc in Savannah. He cannot do that with Ish. Once he knows Ish is gone, he can feel the void. He lies in a hump of misery on the bed he shares with Diana until she comes to him late one evening with a plate of food and a mug of water.

"Jude, this has gone on long enough. You have to eat. If you do not get up right now, Mama is going to go for the doctor. Is that what you want?"

Jude doesn't respond to her voice. The sound of shattering glass finally breaks his stupor. He sits up in the bed to see Diana glaring at him from the center of a floor full of broken dishes. The sight alone is not enough to get through to him, but her tears and fury are.

"Darn you, Jude, you get out of that bed and come downstairs this instant and eat your dinner! If you don't care about yourself or me, you better care about this baby I am carrying. Ish would grab you by the ear, haul you out of there, and drag your sorry carcass down those stairs if he could see you acting like this!"

Her rage spent, Diana throws herself on the bed and sobs. Having never seen Diana do more than weep quietly, this display is too much for Jude. He wraps his arms around her and joins her. The two cry until they have no tears left. The emotional tumult leaves Diana exhausted, but release is cathartic for Jude. He rises from the bed, takes his wife by the hand, and leads her downstairs where he fixes himself a new plate of food from the stove and devours it. After eating, he finds Jessie and apologizes to both her and Diana. The next day he returns to work and Quent.

"No need ta tell me youse sorry. Ish a good boy, lack you in mos ways. I lucky nough ta have a son, I be proud him lack eithah uh you." He places a hand on Jude's arm. "Ise jus glad ta have you back."

Work fills Jude's days, and Diana fills his evenings. After Jessie tells him of her dreams, he is able to take out Ish's many letters and read them one by one again. It is like he is listening to Ish grow up over the last four years. Now he believes Ish is not alone, that he is happy, he can smile at Ish's stories and descriptions. Since he received his mother's last letter recounting Mammy's extraordinary story, he is not as bereft. He remembers Justice's tale of his grandfather Pleas and is a little disappointed in himself for not making the connection. He wishes he had paid closer attention to Cotton.

By the time Diana has their baby, he has found some peace. He doesn't tell Diana, but he hopes the child will be a boy he can name after Ish. By the time the child fights her way into the world, he is simply thankful both she and Diana are alive and healthy.

Ish's death and the connection to Pleas have caused Jude to reflect on the lives of his people who have gone before him. His stay at Hickory Grove has made him appreciate the sorrow and separation they have all endured—Mammy, Lew, Dovie, and his own mother. His intimate relationship with Diana has given him a fresh anger toward Frederick Barret. He cannot imagine what day-to-day living must have been like for his mother—to be taken by a man she didn't love—one she feared too much to resist. Jude thinks of all their family members when the time comes to name their girl, a soft, bright-eyed little handful about the color of wet sand. The child is a week old when he sits on the bed beside Diana and broaches the subject.

"You give any thought ta what this sweet chile's name gonna be?"

"I thought we could decide now she is here and healthy. Mama has mentioned paying respect to my mother Laviney who she says carried me miles to be close to my father and Uncle Moses. But Mama is the mother I remember, so I would like to honor her. Then there is your mother…"

"I been thinkin hawd on it. I like fo Dovie ta live on among us in some way, but I afraid ta name this lil one aftah someone who came ta such a bad end. I feel the same bout Laviney. Of late, I been realizin how important the people who sacrifice fo us ah, an that a whole bunch a people. My sistah already name a chile aftah Mama. I doan think she mind if we choose someone else. I dint even remembah Mammy's name bein Daisy til the summah at Hickry Grove. Lookin back, I feel bad. Mabe we all jus took Mammy fo granted. She been there lookin out faw us all as long as I remembah. Mammy been through a lot. If you doan mind, I like ta name this one Daisy aftah both Mammy an my sistah. I may nevah see them agin, an I think they be pleased ta know I thinkin uh them. If this chile grow up ta be good as they be, we have nothin ta complain about."

"White people give their children more than one name. We are free. We can give ours as many names as we like. And we need to decide on a last name. Others should be able to refer to you by more than Jude, and you have made it clear you won't be a Barret."

"I ain been thinkin on a last name. You think we should all become Devereux?"

"I don't know, Jude. Devereux has been beneficial for Mama and me in our line of business, but you are a woodworker. We should choose a name that will appeal to your customers. You may someday have your own sign above a business. You want something they will accept. I cannot imagine white men here wanting to buy buckboards and feeding troughs from a man named Devereux."

"Ta tell you the truth, I doan think I leave Quent long as he livin. He already tell me the place be mine I stick with him. That the case, I leave the sign like it is."

"Then perhaps we should be Rylees. All of us. Mama would understand, and we all love Quent. Your mother should be pleased considering she has her own little Rylee. We would be honoring both your sister and Quent, and in a way, your mother."

"I like the idea. *Jude Rylee. Diana Rylee. Daisy Rylee.* I like it."

"What about Daisy Lynn Rylee so we can include part of Mama's name?"

"You be Daisy Lynn Rylee," Jude says to the sleeping baby in his arms. "You have a lot ta live up to. Three names fo such a lil girl."

They share the name with Jessie but decide to wait to tell Quent until Diana is up and around. Quent has met young Daisy several times before he is invited to a special dinner prepared by Jessie. They have finished eating and are sitting around the table talking when Diana asks Quent if he wants to hold the baby.

"You knows I do!" he says. "Less see if I kin git her ta smile like I do last time. When you goan name dis chile. You doan hurry, Ise goan name er fo you."

"We been wantin ta tell you," Jude says. "We've named her Daisy Lynn aftah Mammy and Jessalyn."

"I like it. Doan know wy you take so long ta come up with it."

"We been callin her that fo a while. We waited ta tell you so we could ask you somethin."

Quent is confused. "I doan see how you needs my say in namin da chile. I just glad you lets me be a pawt uh yo fambly."

"I would like ta take yo last name, Quent. You doan object, we become Rylees. Her full name be Daisy Lynn Rylee. What you think?"

It is rare for Quent to have a hard time finding words. He sits silent, finally looking down at the child in his arms.

"That be a lottah name fo sech a little piece uh fluff," he says. His chin crumples.

Diana laughs. "That is exactly what Jude said!"

"She is going to grow into her name," Jessie adds.

The banter has given Quent time to regain his composure.

"I be proud y'all take my name. I ain got nobidy else, an you be fambly ta me. Da only way dis be bettah, be if yo Mama hyur tonight. Dat be bout da bess thing in da worl, ta be hyur wid you an Minda. Dat be a dream come true."

"It would," Jessie says.

"There's talk uh freein slaves. We see it mo an mo in the papahs. I beginnin ta think Mizz Bette right. The day may come when we all be free, an that happen, I know Mama woan waste a minute longah than she have to gittin way from Svanna if it means we all be tagethah."

"Until that day!" Jessie raises her glass of lemonade.

"To that day!" The others raise theirs.

Savannah, Georgia to Baltimore, Maryland—1864-1865

L ong after the family would usually be asleep, they are crowded into the bottom floor of the quarters behind the mansion. They have talked several times about what they should do, but now is time to make some decisions.

"You knows whut Ise goan do," Lew says.

"An I tole you what I ain doin, Papa. I ain stayin here a day longah than I haftah," Deke says.

"An I ain acksin you to, Son. It bess fo you an Ben ta go on wid Minda, bu they's too many uh us ta make a livin in Baltimoe."

"Bu Mizz Jessie an Jude say they hep us til we all fine somethin ta do. Quent send word he give us work. We kin make do til we find othah jobs fo some uh us."

"Dat too much ta spect," Lew argues. "Daisy an her fambly migh come ta Baltimoe wen theys hyur aw uh you there. Dat be mo mouff ta feed. It bess me an Cressa stays hyur—fo now enway. They's goan be plenty uh wite foke lookin fo dawkies ta do they work wen theys all come back. An haf da dawkies goan be ouddah hyur soons Sherman show up."

They have been hearing for days General Sherman is on the way and has been laying waste to the land as he comes. There have been many visitors to the mansion to talk with the master, and one of them has tried to be close each time to catch what is being said. Rumor is General Sherman has promised to "make Georgia howl," and apparently he has. Even General Hardee who was their last line of defense left two days ago taking what troops he had left and moving into South Carolina. Minda and her family do not know whether to be jubilant or terrified. The time is near for them to make a move if they are going to, and Minda has already told them she is taking Rylee and making her way to Baltimore even if they have to go alone. Now, Mammy speaks up.

"I ain say nothin wen Minda cide she goin ta Baltimoe cuz I spectin her nevah git da chance, bu now we knows dis war bout ovah, Ise goan speak mys mine. I be suhvin dis massah fo nigh on twenty five year, bu

I ain suhvin him one day mo dat man Sherman set us free. I migh feel diffrent Mizz Abby live or even Mizz L'ella, bu day boff daid an in da groun. They's da massah, Mizz Ella, an doze two chilren dat blong ta her, an far as Ise cernt, theys kin take care uh theysef. Da massah as good as kill Dovie, an a day doan go by I doan membah dat."

All eyes are turned on Mammy, most of them shocked, for, though Mammy has grown progressively quieter over the years, she has never complained about having to continue to serve the man who sold her daughter. If asked, she would have told them talking wouldn't have changed a thing. Now, Minda throws her arms around her.

"Thank God!" she says. "Thinkin on goin all that way with jus dis scrap uh a gal be weighin hawd on me."

"I thuhteen, Mama! I almos a woman if I ain one!"

Rylee's protests lighten the mood a little, but the subject is too grave for them not to take seriously. All but Rylee understand the dangers of them traveling alone without a white person to keep other angry white people from both the South and the North from doing them harm.

"You woulden uh had ta go by yosef even Mammy stay here," Deke says. "I goin with you."

"Me, too," Ben says. "The only reason I stays behin be ta make the massah pay fo what he do ta my mama, an that sho ta git me hung."

"I doan wanse ta hyur dat fool tawk!" Lew says. Ben glowers at him but doesn't respond.

"Lizzy, whut you wanse ta do?" Cressa asks.

"Whut you thinks I should do, Mama?"

"Youse twenty six year ole, Chile. You go wid dem, you migh fine yosef a husban ou dare in Baltimoe."

"I fine one hyur I be 'lowed off dis place," Lizzy says. "An if you an Papa ain goin, I ain goin."

"Day be needin boff uh youse hyur in da big house. An me. Da massah kin pay us da same he hab ta pay new hep, or wese go somewhar theys needs us an willin ta pay. Mabe Mizz Bette take us on."

"Da massah sho ta keep you. Wid Massah Gordon daid an Mizz Ella an er younguns hyur, him needs all da hep him kin git. Bu you may wanse ta fine some othah place—Mizz Ella an doze chilren ain easy ta handle," Mammy says.

"Wese handle dem fo years now, an mabe theys bettah theys knows we kin up an take off wen we a mine ta," Cressa says.

"Mama, youse sho you kin wawk all dat way you needs ta?" Lew asks.

"Ise ain dat ole! Sides, we doan hab ta run. We kin take all da time we needs, cain we? Wese free den."

There is something about Mammy, their matriarch, saying she is going that makes the possibility real. Having made their decisions, they dare to laugh and plan. Minda asks Lew to tend the little cemetery. Mammy wonders if Missy will follow her. They make plans for Lew's family to come if staying with the Barrets doesn't work out, and if the master keeps them, they hope he and his can someday visit. By the time they go to bed, they are solemn again. None of them sleep, most out of excitement, anxiety, or fear, but for Minda, she cannot rest for thinking of seeing Jude again—and Quinten. What will he think of her almost sixty-year-old-self? Their age difference didn't seem like much when she was nearer forty, but now... And how will he react when he finds out he has a daughter? Will he understand why she kept her existence from him, or will he be angry? She decides no good can come from worrying, yet she still doesn't sleep.

The next day, their faith is shaken. Word comes to them through the servant network that hundreds of freed slaves had been following the Union army. When they came to Ebenezer Creek, not far from Savannah, the army had crossed the bridge, then cut it loose from its bank stranding their followers on the other side. Many of them drowned or were left to suffer at the hands of Southern sympathizers. The few who survived told a horrifying tale. When news of the tragedy reaches Deke's ears, the family gathers again to discuss their options. Though it makes them doubt their decision to follow the army north, they feel they have little choice other than to stay behind, and no one is frightened enough to change the plan.

They have little time to worry, for early the next morning, even before they are up, the Union Army rides into Savannah, and everyone who remains in town, including slaves, line the streets to see them come. For hours the rows of men march forward, the combination of thousands of hooves creating a din even on packed sand. They appear to be everywhere. The Barret servants have a bird's eye view of Sherman and his officers as they arrive, for they are to be quartered at the home of Charles Green across the street from the Barret mansion. Their own master has been part of the plan to cooperate in an effort to keep the Union from burning the town to cinders as others have been. The strategy must work, for the occupation is peaceful other than the upheaval the influx of thousands of men and animals cause as they all seek housing, food, and eventually entertainment.

All pretense of normalcy disappears in the Barret mansion. Though Mr. Barret has remained in the mansion, he has sent Ella and her children north until he deems travel and Savannah safe enough for their return. He had planned to send Cressa and Lizzy with them, but in an unusual act of defiance, Lew had taken his family away until they were gone. Mr. Barret had been furious but impotent to do anything about the disobedience. Both sons are still in the Confederate Army, and Maxie has long been in Germany with the husband she met in Savannah years ago. She had fulfilled her father's worst fears by marrying an outsider and moving overseas with him. Frederick alone remains in the mansion. He had been afraid to punish Lew's family for fear they would leave as many of his friends' slaves have done. He would need help to control his servants, and all owners are struggling with their own. Now, with Sherman's forces in town, the slaves can do as they like. Because Lew, Cressa, and Lizzy plan to stay behind, they continue to do their jobs, but Minda and Rylee make themselves scarce while Deke and Ben long for a confrontation with the master. Out of respect to Lew, they satisfy their rebelliousness by lolling around in plain sight. Frederick says nothing to either of them, seeming to avoid them as much as possible.

Minda and Mammy make use of their time packing what few belongings they have and accumulating as much food stuff as they can. Mammy digs her fall vegetables and Minda steals meat, flour, and corn meal from the kitchen. They hurry for they know hungry soldiers will soon come for it. She hopes the master is too busy to discover what is missing, for she could be whipped or worse for what she is doing. The temperatures will be colder where they are going. In preparation, she quickly stitches warmer garments and cloth bags in which to carry them. They wish they had at least one horse or mule to haul their belongings and Mammy, if necessary, but they know horse theft, if discovered, would end in hanging. Besides, the war has made horseflesh scarce.

After doing all she can do, Minda decides to say her goodbyes. There are few people she will miss besides Lew and his family, and most live under Miss Bette's roof. She makes her way to the Stiles' mansion early one morning. Both Pearl and Cook are glad to see her, and Minda notes how circumstances have changed when both ladies lead her into the parlor and yell up the stairs for Miss Bette. Though the lady is older than Minda, she comes tripping down the stairs like a schoolgirl.

"Minda! I am thrilled ta see you. I have been wantin ta come ta you, but, as you know, I have been fuhbidden. Even with the current hubbub,

I dared not defy him. I was soon goin ta send eithah Cook or Pearl ta bring you ta me. Tell me how y'all ah and if y'all have thought about your future."

"We be goin to Baltimoe, Mizz Bette, soon as the ahmy move out. We be followin on they heels."

Bette asks them all to sit.

"How do you plan ta travel? Do you have transpuhtation?"

"We cain think of no way ta git a horse," Minda tells her, "so we be walkin."

"That's a long way ta walk, and I am not sure even Lew and the boys will be enough protection."

"Lew ain goin," Minda admits. "He an Cressa an Lizzy goin ta stay behind. If the massah doan keep them an pay them a wage, they may come ta you fo hep, jus ta try ta find them anothah place."

"I will be glad ta help," Bette says, "but I doubt they will need me. I have been informed by my uncle that Frederick sold all his dock workahs and hired othahs' not long aftah South Carolina succeeded. The gossip is he converted little of his money ta confederate dollahs. My uncle was tellin me this because neithah did I, and he was usin him as a cautionary example. He claims many of his colleagues ah not pleased with his lack of loyalty ta the confederate cause. Howevah, he has two sons fightin faw the Confederacy, and he will land on his feet as he always has. I am sure Lew and his family will have a safe place with him, and he may be one of the few who will still have money ta pay them."

"Anuthah thing, Mizz Bette. I tole Lew ta come ta you if my Daisy come back ta the Barrets' with Miss Mattie. If he do, kin you try ta git ta her an tell her if she kin make it ta Baltimoe, they be a place fo her an her famly. I doan know if she evah leave Miss Mattie, bu if nothin else, try ta git her ta learn ta read an write nough fo us ta hear from her."

"I will do more than that. I will contact Mattie herself when some time has passed."

"I gonna tawk with Diana when we git ta Baltimoe, too. She close ta Miss Gail, an mabe she can git word ta Daisy if we cain."

Bette rises to pace as she thinks. "Yes, we will find a way, though it may take time. And Lew, Cressa, and Lizzie should be fine othah than they will be separated from the rest of you. But I am concerned about your plan ta walk all the way. No tellin who you may encountah."

"I cain think uh any othah way, Mizz Bette. I worry most bout Mama, but she say she as strong as the rest uh us, an she may be. She spry ta be almos eighty."

"Oh Goodness. I need ta think about this, Minda. Can you give me a couple of days ta come up with a plan?"

"We ain goin nowhere til the ahmy do, so you have mo than a day or two."

Bette sits again, and the women catch up on one another's lives and share tea and biscuits Cook fetches from the kitchen. Minda comments on how different the atmosphere is since Mr. Clarence is gone. Cook laughs and says, "Oh, the massah still roun. He jus cain cause us no hahm no mo."

"Now, Cook, don't be speakin ill of the dead," Bette says, but there is no real censure in her voice.

When Minda takes her leave, they agree she will return in two days. When she does, Bette indeed has a plan.

"I have decided I will transport you. We will be breakin the law unless the wah is declared officially ovah by the time we leave. I will ask Reggie ta drive us, and we will take Eliza. We will take the buggy and a wagon from the business. If we ah met with any interference by the union forces, we will tell the truth—we ah takin you ta family in Baltimore. If we ah met with Southuhnahs, we will say we ah movin you out of the way of Nawthen influence."

"But what if Reggie an Eliza doan want ta come?"

"I assure you they will. Both have been helpin me with The Movement faw years. We ah like-minded. Thomas, now, he is anuthah story. He is fightin faw the Confederacy. My gravest fear has been he and Reggie would meet on the battlefield. Reggie is here now. He was wounded but is recovuhed enough ta manage a buggy. Deke and Ben can drive the wagon."

"I doan know how I can thank you, Mizz Bette. You done so much fo me an my boys."

"Don't go on now," Bette intervenes. "We have plans ta make. Reggie thinks it is vital we leave before the ahmy, as soon as the weathah turns a bit warmah. He is in a position ta know as soon as Sherman decides ta move out. He thinks we will draw more trouble if we ah behind with all the othah freed slaves."

When Minda rises to leave, Bette follows her through the kitchen to the back door as if seeing her colored visitors off is something she does often. When Minda steps out into the yard, Bette places her hand on her arm. "Minda, I regret I did not take action ta help Ish soonah. If I had, he wouldn't have been..."

She stops, her eyes wet.

"That be in the past, an they ain nothin we kin do bout it." Minda smiles sadly. "An Ish sho woulden want you ta be feelin bad. You the only white puhson evah give two beans bout us."

Time passes slowly, and food is growing sparse. The family fears they may have to use some of their hidden supplies if they do not make a move soon. Finally, in late March, Cook appears in the courtyard at the mansion. Mammy has been out talking with Missy, and she leads her into the cabin where Minda is finishing a rug she thinks will make the wagon bed more comfortable for them on the ride. Bette sends a short message. *The time has come.* She asks if they can be ready in two days.

Mammy, Minda, Rylee, Deke, and Ben leave behind Lew, Cressa, and Lizzy two hours before dawn with tears and dreams of seeing each other again. Each of the travelers carries burdensome loads of clothing, bedding, and food. Mammy keeps glancing back, but Missy does not follow. The crow makes no sound at all as they leave.

"Missy doan want ta wake da house wid her goodbyes. I tell you her a smawt bird." They walk a few more steps before Mammy adds, "Her mus know theys need her mo than us do."

No one replies, but Rylee slips her hand into her grandmother's, and Minda briefly places her own on her shoulder. It frightens Minda to feel her mother's frail shoulders. She says a quick prayer for all of them, but especially for Mammy to have the strength to endure the journey.

The group makes their way unmolested to Bette's house where the lighted kitchen windows greet them. Bette's man Arthur emerges from the carriage house and helps them load the wagon under cover of the building. When they are done, Mammy, Minda, and Rylee sit upon the rag rug and huddle under a quilt. Deke holds the reins while Ben sits beside him. Bette and Eliza walk quietly from the kitchen door, climb into the back of the buggy while a limping Reggie takes the driver's seat and urges the horses forward. They are surrounded by quiet except for the clop of hooves on stone as the two conveyances leave the courtyard. When they pull onto the packed sand, even those are muffled. They leave Savannah in the chill dampness of predawn and silence.

The weeks on the road are long and arduous, but they are much more comfortable than the wagon trip Minda remembers taking with Lew and Ish. She tries not to think of Ish and how excited he would have been to be on this adventure. Of course, he would be a grown man of twenty-eight now—he might even be married. Regardless, he would be going with her and Rylee were he alive. Nothing would have kept him from seeking his fortune and joining his brother Jude. She tries to pretend he is with them.

When possible, the Stiles find an inn in which to stay and make what arrangements they can for the others whom they refer to as their servants. On two occasions, they stay with sympathetic friends whose names they do not learn because there would still be repercussions for members of the underground railroad regardless of the negroes imminent independent state. On other nights, Reggie, Deke, and Ben erect two spacious canvas tents Reggie has gotten from the army. Each family has a tent, but they sit around the same fire and share the meals Minda and Mammy prepare from supplies each family has brought. The road is rugged and at times muddy and cratered, but the farther they get from Savannah, the brighter their spirits in spite of the hardship of the journey. Minda is amazed at the stamina both Mammy and Bette exhibit, and her admiration for both grows daily. Rylee is the most subdued of all of them, sleeping close to her mother each night. The pre-trip talks about all the risks must have frightened her. Minda tries to cheer her and wishes again Ish were with them. Most of Rylee's carefree exuberance died with her brother.

On the third day of the ninth week, the two conveyances pull into Baltimore and make their way to Jessie's shop. They go directly to the alley, and Minda jumps down and knocks on the door she has slipped out of many times on her way to meet Quentin. No one is in the kitchen. She crosses the room and sticks her head into the shop. There, behind the counter is a girl of about ten or eleven and a much more mature Diana than the one she left years before. They are finishing up with a customer, and when the door jingles behind them, the girl Minda knows to be her granddaughter Daisy turns and spots her. She squeals in surprise, and Diana whirls.

"Howdy," Minda says, and Diana rushes to embrace her mother-in-law. Young Daisy hangs back, waiting to be introduced, then all go to the back to invite the others in.

Alerted by the noise from below, Jessie descends the stairs to join them. She goes to Minda and hugs her, then to Mammy. She more formally greets Bette, but Bette's easy manner soon has them all laughing and claiming how much better the others have aged. Mammy insists she looks the oldest seeing as her hair is completely white. Jessie claims she is a close second since hers is more gray than dark. Minda admits she is willing to give them both the honor as she hopes she is still young enough to catch the eye of the man across town.

Deke, Ben, and Reggie hover in the corners of the room while the women talk and laugh. Against the protests of Bette and Eliza, Jessie and Diana insist on preparing a meal for them.

"Come ovah hyur, Daisy. I wanse ta git a good look at you," Mammy says.

Daisy shyly crosses the room to take her great grandmother's gnarled hands.

"Youse a pretty thing!" Mammy says. "I be righ proud youse name fo me. I prays life easiuh fo you dan it be fo me, an I thinks it be now wese gonna be free."

Diana is concerned by how much more fragile Mammy looks than when she last saw her. Her upright posture and spunk have made the rest of them forget she is elderly. Her hands shake as she pulls young Daisy to her, and Diana marvels she has made the long, difficult journey and is still upright. Diana sends her daughter to the front and asks her to let them know if a customer needs more assistance than she can supply. She then puts her arm around the older woman. "Mammy, why don't you have a lie down while we fix something to eat?"

It takes little coaxing for her to go upstairs. She claims to be far too dirty to sully any bed. Diana fills two pans with water from the kettle on the fire, then leads the women up the stairs for a wash-up. Minda takes her mother's arm but releases it when she says, "Ise still capeble ub climbin da stair at the big house. I knows Ise upta dese!"

When Bette, Minda, and Eliza finish, Deke and Ben throw the water into the back alley and return them to Jessie and Diana to refill. The three men then take their turn out back to do what they can to remove the dirt of the road. By the time all feel somewhat refreshed, the meal is ready and the ladies sit to eat while the men stand awkwardly but ravenously devouring the first well-prepared meal they have had in weeks. Only Mammy doesn't eat. Diana finds her sound asleep when she goes to tell her the meal is ready. They decide she probably needs the rest more than she needs the food. Jessie prepares her a plate for later.

After the meal, Bette claims they have intruded long enough and promises to visit before they leave. She plans to pay to have the wagon and buggy returned to Savannah while she, Eliza, and Reggie travel by steamer if one is available anytime soon. With the war, travel of any kind has almost come to a standstill. She plans to stay several days to recuperate and visit friends, including Sophia Howe and her husband James. She plans to make no mention of transporting their brother-in-law's slaves across the country. Again she promises Minda she will try to get word to her daughter Daisy that she is in Baltimore with Jude.

After they are gone, talk turns to Jude. Because the travelers arrived after he had gone back to work, the group decides someone needs to go get him. Minda suggests she go and reluctantly agrees to take Deke and Ben with her. Rylee wants to join them, but Minda insists she join Mammy for a rest upstairs.

"I need ta talk ta yo papa, Rylee. I doan know if his heart can take his full-grown gul showin up on his do'step with no warnin. He ain a young man no mo."

Minda has no trouble finding Quentin's workshop though much along the way has changed. Deke and Ben are fascinated by the bustling city and amazed at the number of colored folks walking around in clothing much like that of their white counterparts. Minda stops when she comes in sight of the building that still has the same sign, or one like the old one, hanging above the open double doors. Inside she sees Jude but there is no sign of Quent. The building has been enlarged—the room above now spans the length of the building. Before, there had been the one room in which Quent slept.

Now she is this close, the magnitude of their accomplishment is hard to comprehend.

"What we waitin on, Aunt Minda?" Ben asks.

She doesn't know if Jude hears Ben's voice or senses their presence, but he glances up from his work and their eyes meet. A frown of concentration becomes a huge smile, and he throws down the tool in his hand and runs toward them. Passersby stop to witness the reunion, one made almost too precious to believe for the time it has taken. After numerous hugs, Jude notices Minda's wandering eye and says, "He upstairs. Why doan you go on up an suhprise him?"

Minda smiles gratefully at her son and moves toward the building. On the way, she wishes she had had time to bathe properly and launder a dress, but he would not have waited once he was told of their arrival—not if he still has any interest at all. The Quent she remembered was not a patient man.

When she reaches the top of the stairs, she thinks about knocking but decides against it. She quietly opens the door. A man heavier than she remembers with a sprinkling of gray on his closely shorn head is sitting at a table writing in what appears to be a ledger.

"Quent," she says.

The man turns and rises. The smile she has seen on their daughter's face for the last thirteen years reaches his eyes, and Minda knows she is—at last—where she wants to be.

Acknowledgments

The Dark Side of Civil is a sequel to *A Single Drop of Ink (ASDOI)*. The first book was inspired by the Francis Sorrel family of Savannah, Georgia. Readers will find the same white characters from the first novel in the second, and most of them were modeled after the Sorrels though I took liberal license with their personalities and actions. *The Dark Side of Civil (TDSOC)* focuses on the illegitimate children of Frederick Barret by the slave girl Minda. Since everything about Minda except her name is of my imagination, her children and the plot involving them are complete fiction. Any similarities to real people are coincidental since the relationship itself is pure speculation on my part. For an understanding of the connection to the Sorrel family, you may read a short history, *The Sorrels of Savannah, Life on Madison Square and Beyond*, I wrote from notes compiled from my research. The Sorrels did have a young slave named Minda. Her name is the only one listed other than the nickname Mammy. I took the number of slaves from census records, and their mixed race influenced my thinking. As miscegenation through coercion of female slaves by a master is the leading cause for mixed race children in slaveholding households, I believed it reasonable to assume Francis Sorrel's *mulatto* slaves were actually his offspring. Because I have no proof of Francis Sorrel's blood relationship to his young slaves, I created the fictional ASDOI and TDSOC, tales of a family similar to the Sorrels in which the master, Frederick Barret, proudly acknowledges children by white mothers while keeping those by his black servant in slavery. There is no proof (that I know of) that Francis Sorrel fathered children by his slaves.

I also want to comment on the dialect I use in these books. The characters speak a language created from words and patterns taken from slave journals, post-civil war interviews with freed slaves, and examples taken from white diarists. It is important to note there is little written by actual slaves or freed slaves to be found, for they were forbidden to read or write until after the Civil War. Because almost everything we have depicting the speech of uneducated slaves has been filtered through a white writer, we cannot know how accurate these accounts are to what they spoke to each other in the absence of whites. In addition to those variables, slaves' dialects varied greatly according to their original homelands, the areas in which they were enslaved, and how much contact they had with whites or other blacks whether in urban settings or rural. I do not claim what I have written is authentic to any group of slaves. What I do believe is their speech would have been quite different from that of whites unless they were tutored by whites or some person of color who had been taught to speak as whites spoke. Too, the language of owners themselves would have varied by the levels of their own education, the areas in which they lived, and the people with whom they socialized.

One must keep in mind that holders wanted to keep their slaves as dependent and helpless as possible. Laws forbidding slaves to read or write on their own or for whites to teach them were enacted early. Because slaves were originally ripped from homelands and communities, they were often thrown into groups in which they could not understand each other or their owners. What developed was a cacophony of several languages mixed in with what English they could glean in order to communicate with their enslavers and each other. It is reasonable to believe they would have preferred to speak in a manner unlike those who held them hostage if for no other reason than to keep some identity apart from them. English is not an easy language to learn, so the absence of formal explanations of syntax, word choice, and grammatical rules would have to result in a varied and often hard to understand vernacular, as is also evidenced in uneducated whites of the same time period. Communication with a diverse group of people with little help and no education would have required tenacity, creativity, and quick intellect. What we call black dialects are testaments to all three. The words they brought with them, created, and adapted have influenced the English spoken in the United States today, especially in the South. I wish we had a better, more accurate record of black dialect during slavery and the early years after the Civil War.

I am grateful to my readers and supporters: Gina Young Becker, Sheila and Steve Jumper, as well as to my sisters and brother, Jan Larson, Pat Adams, Judy Schenk, Kathy Lord, Lisa Anderson, Mike Ramsey, and my sister-in-law Carol Ramsey. The hours they spent reading, critiquing, advising, and commiserating every step along the way were invaluable. And thank you to the flesh and blood Quentin Rylee for loaning me his name.

Made in the USA
Columbia, SC
06 December 2017